THE
FINAL
GIRL
SUPPORT
GROUP

ALSO BY GRADY HENDRIX

Horrorstör

My Best Friend's Exorcism

Paperbacks from Hell

We Sold Our Souls

*The Southern Book Club's Guide
to Slaying Vampires*

THE
FINAL
GIRL
SUPPORT
GROUP

GRADY HENDRIX

BERKLEY
NEW YORK

BERKLEY
An imprint of Penguin Random House LLC
penguinrandomhouse.com

Copyright © 2021 by Grady Hendrix

Library of Congress Cataloging-in-Publication Data

Names: Hendrix, Grady, author.
Title: The final girl support group / Grady Hendrix.
Description: New York: Berkley, [2021]
Identifiers: LCCN 2021002704 (print) |
LCCN 2021002705 (ebook) | ISBN 9780593201237 (hardcover) |
ISBN 9780593201251 (ebook)
Classification: LCC PS3608.E543 F56 2021 (print) |
LCC PS3608.E543 (ebook) | DDC 813/.6—dc23
LC record available at https://lccn.loc.gov/2021002704
LC ebook record available at https://lccn.loc.gov/2021002705

International edition ISBN: 9780593437049

Printed in the United States of America
7th Printing

Book design by Laura K. Corless
Interior art credits: Bloody handprint © Ultrashock / shutterstock.com;
Manila file folder © Ambient Ideas / shutterstock.com; Pepper plant ©
Danny Smythe / shutterstock.com; Aging worn paper © Mark Carrel /
shutterstock.com; Open file with papers © Ralko / shutterstock.com;
Ripped paper collection © ESB Professional / shutterstock.com;
Grunge background © argus / shutterstock.com; Worn paper stained
© Mark Carrel / shutterstock.com; Bullet holes © Macrovector /
shutterstock.com; Vintage paper background © Vladimir Borozenets /
shutterstock.com; Hand against glass © Morumotto / shutterstock
.com; Zombie gnome © Dragon Days Photography / shutterstock.com;
Windowsill urban background © aapsky / shutterstock.com

Amanda,
True love is putting someone else,
Before yourself.
Which is why I thought,
You should walk across that ice,
Before me.

final girl (n.)—the last and sole survivor of a horror movie

r/lastladies Posted by u/fu(bar)gate 17 months ago

LAST WORD ON FINAL GIRLS doc on youtube has 2.1 million views. WTF? Who cares about a bunch of grandmas with saggy necks. If one of them was hot okay I can understand but I'm so sick of hearing about them

Share   Save   Hide   Report

r/lastladies Posted by u/orchomenus 17 months ago

time wont be kind their 15 minutes were up 15 years ago

Share   Save   Hide   Report

r/lastladies Posted by u/fu(bar)gate 17 months ago

I wish they would all disappear

Share   Save   Hide   Report

r/lastladies Posted by u/orchomenus 17 months ago

be patient remember viper hansen, ricky walker, and walter
scroggs are in prison not dead
people say dream king still out there
one day people will totally forget about FGs
then they will get what they deserve

Share   Save   Hide   Report

—thread from r/lastladies, the Final Girls subreddit

THE FINAL GIRL SUPPORT GROUP

I wake up, get out of bed, say good morning to my plant, unwrap a protein bar, and drink a liter of bottled water. I'm awake for five full minutes before remembering I might die today. When you get old, you get soft.

In the living room I stretch and do forty knee strikes, forty palm heel strikes, and side mountain climbers until sweat drips onto the concrete floor. I do elbow strikes until my shoulders burn, then I get on the treadmill, put the speed up to seven, and run until my thighs are on fire and my chest rasps, and then I run for five more minutes. I have to punish myself for forgetting exactly what the stakes are, especially today.

The bathroom door gets padlocked from the inside while I shower. I make up my bed to eliminate the temptation to crawl back in. I make tea, and it's not until the electric kettle clicks that I have my first panic attack of the day.

It's not a bad one, just a cramp in my chest that feels like a giant hand squeezing my lungs shut. I close my eyes and concentrate on relaxing the muscles lining my throat, on taking deep breaths, on pulling oxygen into the bottom of my lungs. After two and a half minutes I can breathe normally again and I open my eyes.

This apartment is the only place in the world where that's possible. A bedroom, a living room, a kitchen, and a bathroom where, as long as I take reasonable precautions, I can close my eyes for two minutes. Out there in the world it's a nonstop murder party, and if I make the slightest mistake I'll wind up dead.

I go into the living room and turn on CNN to see what the body count is today, and from the very first image I know that the next twenty-four hours will be bad.

A live drone shot of a summer camp is buried beneath all the other junk CNN puts onscreen. It shows sedans and emergency vehicles clustered outside the cabins, men in white hazmat suits walking between the trees, yellow police tape blocking the road. They cut to recorded footage of the night before, blue lights flashing in the dark, and the slugline hits me in the gut: *Real Life Red Lake Tragedy Repeats.*

I turn on the sound and the story is exactly what I feared. Someone murdered six Camp Red Lake counselors who were shutting the place down for the season. They used a variety of weapons—hand scythe, power drill, bow and arrows, machete—and would have had a seventh victim except the last one, a sixteen-year-old girl the CNN chyron tells me is named Stephanie Fugate, shoved them out of the hayloft.

The killer hasn't been identified yet, but there's Stephanie onscreen in a class photo with her round face and clear skin, smiling through her braces with a grin that breaks my heart. After last night, she'll never be that happy again. She's a final girl now.

You're watching a horror movie and the silent killer knocks off the stoner, the slut, the geek, the jock, and the deputy, and now he's chasing the virgin babysitter through the woods. She's the one who said they shouldn't party at this deserted summer camp, break into this abandoned lunatic asylum, skinny-dip in this isolated lake—especially since it's Halloween, or Thanksgiving, or Arbor Day, or whatever the anniversary is of those unsolved murders from way back. The killer's got a chainsaw/boat hook/butcher's knife and this girl's got zip: no upper body strength, no mass, no shotgun. All she's got is good cardio and an all-American face. Yet somehow she kills the killer, then stares numbly off into the middle distance, or collapses into the arms of the arriving police, or runs crying to her boyfriend, makes one last quip, lights one last cigarette, asks a final haunting question, gets taken off in an ambulance screaming and screaming like she's never going to stop.

Ever wonder what happens to those final girls? After the cops eliminate them as suspects, after the press releases their brace-faced, pizza-cheeked, bad-hair-day class photos that inevitably get included on the cover of the true crime book? After the candlelight vigils and the moments of silence, after someone plants the memorial shrub?

I know what happens to those girls. After the movie deals get signed, after the film franchise fails, after you realize that while everyone else was filling out college applications you were locked in a residential treatment program pretending you weren't scared of the dark. After the talk show circuit, after your third therapist just accepts that he's your Zoloft-dispensing machine and you won't be making any breakthroughs on his watch, after you realize that the only interesting thing that'll ever happen to you happened when you were sixteen, after you stop going outside, after you start browsing locksmiths the way other women browse the windows of Tiffany's, after you've left town because you couldn't deal with the "Why not you?" looks from the parents of all your dead friends, after you've lost everything, been through the fire, started knowing your stalkers by their first names, after all that happens you wind up where I'm going today: in a church basement in Burbank, seated with your back to the wall, trying to hold the pieces of your life together.

We're an endangered species, for which I'm grateful. There are only six of us still around. It used to make me sad there weren't more of us out there, but we were creatures of the eighties and the world has moved on. They used to dust off the clip packages for our anniversaries or the occasional franchise reboot, but these days it's all oil spills and Wikileaks, the Tea Party and the Taliban. The six of us belong to another era. We're media invisible. We might as well not even exist.

As I turn off CNN I realize I miscounted. There are actually seven of us; I just don't like to think about Chrissy. No one does. Even mentioning her name can mess with your head because she's a traitor. So I take a minute, even though I only have three hours to get to group, and I take a deep breath and try to get my focus back.

Adrienne's going to be a mess. Camp Red Lake was where it happened to her, but she bought the place later and turned it into a retreat for victims of violence, mostly survivors of school shootings and kids who got away from their kidnappers. This hits her where she lives. At least it'll give us something new to talk about besides whatever old business we're still arguing over today.

When I can't put it off any longer, I get ready to head out. Group is the only time I leave this apartment except to go to the mailbox place across the street once a week, to check my escape routes once a month, and my biweekly trips to the corner store for supplies. I don't like risk. My hair is short because long hair can get grabbed. I wear running shoes in case I have to move. I don't wear loose clothing.

I inventory my pockets: keys, money, phone, weapons. I stopped carrying a firearm on public transport after an incident a couple of years back, but I have pepper spray, a box cutter in my right front pocket, and a razor blade taped to my left ankle. I don't wear headphones, I don't wear sunglasses, I make sure my jacket is tight so there's nothing to snag, and then I say good-bye to my plant, take a deep breath, step out of my apartment, and face a world that wants me dead.

FINAL GIRL SUPPORT GROUP
Notes by Dr. Carol Elliott
Session No. 188
September 2010

ATTENDING

Marilyn Torres
Adrienne Butler
Dani Shipman
Lynnette Tarkington
Heather DeLuca
Julia Campbell

Presession notes: Surprised to see that this month marks
the 16th anniversary of regular group sessions. Facilitating
this group falls outside my normal workload, but these women
have been my patients in one way or another longer than my
children have been alive.

Sad to note that years of strong rapport and good group
cohesion has fallen off over the past twelve months. Recent
sessions marked by crosstalk, incessant argumentation over
minor matters, and relentless interpersonal criticism.
Adrienne remains practically a co-facilitator, constantly
modeling effective behavior, but Marilyn and Dani seem
restless and irritable. Heather's attention-seeking and
improvisational approach to recovery cause constant
conflict. Lynnette's hyperarousal seems unimproved.

What remaining purpose does group serve after all this
time? Who will be the first to terminate? Should I take
steps to bring this to an end myself?

—Dr. Carol Elliott, private notes on group session, September 2010

THE FINAL GIRL SUPPORT GROUP II

A cotton ball sheep says, *Jesus Loves Ewe!*

A trio of very skinny ghosts rising from the grave proclaim, *Ghosts are scary . . . but not the Holy Ghost!*

He is Risen! shouts a multicolored tangle of Magic Marker scribbles.

That one gives me pause. All of us in group have a complicated relationship with the idea of resurrection.

We should be sitting in a circle, but the five of us sit in a ragged C because none of us will ever put her back to a door again. Dani has her arms crossed, legs spread, sitting cowboy stoic in front of a wall of orange-and-black construction paper jack-o'-lanterns and hissing cats. She's the last person on earth who needs a reminder that Halloween is coming.

Marilyn has her legs crossed, Starbucks in one hand, new purse in her lap because she won't let it touch the floor. She told Julia it cost $1,135, but I don't believe her. You can't charge that much for a faux purse, and Marilyn would never let leather touch her skin.

"It's hard for me to focus if I haven't eaten," Heather is saying in her never-ending, I-haven't-slept-since-1988 monologue, leaning forward, hands flapping around. "Because of my low blood sugar."

Apparently, today's argument will be about snacks.

Julia sits in her wheelchair, clearly bored, drumming her fingers on her wheels, wearing an ironic *World's Greatest Dad* T-shirt, staring at a large, wrinkled drawing of a flying man with his arms held straight out at his sides that reads, "Jeshus is sad dead alive."

I used to think it was weird that we met surrounded by Sunday school art, but now it's become the first thing I look at every month after checking my sightlines and my exits. Not because the artistic self-expression of a bunch of potential murder victims interests me in the slightest. I'm looking for warning signs: pictures of exploding guns and bloody knives, boys drawing themselves as neckless monsters with triangle fangs tearing their parents in half. I'm looking for signs that one of these kids will grow up to be my enemy, to be another one of the monsters that tried to kill us all.

"If you ate before group," Dr. Carol suggests, "maybe that would help?"

Dr. Carol, the only one in the room who can bring herself to put her back to the door, sits in the mouth of the C, like she has for the past sixteen years, posture perfect, pen poised, notepad resting on one knee, treating Heather's snack obsession with the same care and concern she applies to everything we say.

"That's off my schedule," Heather says. "As a recovering addict, maintaining a schedule is important to my sobriety and I have to leave the home early because, you know, the cops took my license and I haven't gotten it back yet, so it takes me longer to get here because I think it's important not to be late. Adrienne doesn't have that same level of consideration, apparently."

"I'm sure Adrienne has a good reason for why she's running behind," Dr. Carol says.

"I'll be surprised if Adrienne shows up at all," Julia says. Clearly she saw CNN, too. "Has anyone talked to her? I tried to call but it went to voicemail."

"I imagine she's turned her phone off," Marilyn says, then makes a face like she smells shit. "The press."

Marilyn refused to do any press conferences or give anyone an exclusive after her crisis, arousing the wrath of every reporter in America, and then she married into a mega-rich politically active Republican family, so she's gotten it the worst over the years, but we all know the feeling. The phone that never stops ringing until you finally pull it out of the wall; the reporter you've never seen who calls you by your first name and pretends to have gone to high school with you so convincingly you start to believe them; a distant cousin showing up at the hospital, all full of concern, with a tape recorder spinning inside her bag next to a check from the *National Enquirer*.

"I don't think it's appropriate to discuss Adrienne's situation with anyone but Adrienne," Dr. Carol says. "I'm sure we'll talk about it when she gets here. In the meantime: How do people feel about Heather's concerns?"

There's an awkward moment as we all wait to see if anyone's going to take the bait, but no one does. We're final girls. We're good at escaping traps.

"I'm just saying," Heather says, filling the awkward silence. "I have certain needs, and since I don't have the advantages all of you do, then I would really like us to have some coffee, some cookies, something, because this big bare room is depressing."

She's really not going to let this go, but that doesn't surprise me. We're the women who kept fighting back no matter how much it hurt, who jumped out that third-story window, who dragged ourselves up onto that roof when our bodies were screaming for us to roll over and die. Once we start something, it's hard for us to stop.

"I don't mind what Heather brings," Marilyn says, her bracelets dancing as she waves her Starbucks cup with its dark red lipstick print on the lid. "Bring a pizza. But can we please change the topic?"

"That's interesting," Dr. Carol says, although she's the only one who thinks so. "Does anyone else feel the way Marilyn does?"

When you've been in a room with the same six people for sixteen years, you know what they're going to do before it happens. Like a chemical reaction, if certain conditions are met, certain outcomes will take place. Right on cue, here comes Julia.

"I think people eating and drinking in group is a form of deflection," Julia says, because she can't pass up a chance to argue with Marilyn. "Marilyn's Chai Soy Big Gulp is a prop that shows us she's distancing herself from group."

"I declare," Marilyn fake-marvels in her flat Texas accent. "How do you come up with these things?"

"Two sessions ago you complained we were trapped in the past," Julia says.

Marilyn looks at each of us.

"Well, does anyone think this is as necessary as it used to be?" she asks. "The way we snipe and peck, I feel like we could all use a vacation. Isn't the point of therapy that one day you don't need it anymore?"

I feel my lungs cramp and I count breaths—seven in, seven out, keep it slow, keep it steady. She doesn't mean that. Group is the center for all of us, even Dr. Carol. Her self-help empire is built on the work she did with us back in the nineties, but the reason we're in this church basement and not one of her swank, camera-ready clinics is that this is our shared secret, our one safe place free from the stalkers and the superfans, the reporters and the profile writers. How can Marilyn talk so casually about giving it up?

"Some of us can't afford a vacation," Julia slings back. "Not everyone married for money."

"Bless your heart," Marilyn says. "Isn't that exactly what your ex did?"

That's low, even for Marilyn. Julia was still learning how to live with her wheelchair when she married her physiotherapist. I understand the urge all too well. Someone comes along saying they'll save you and you throw yourself into their arms and let them make all the decisions. You can only hope that by the time you come to your senses they haven't done too much damage. In Julia's case, by the time she woke up he'd sold her franchise rights, cleaned out her bank accounts, and left her with nothing.

"Is this how group's going to be today?" Julia appeals to us. "Slinging insults? Picking at old wounds? There's no reason we should act this petty. We're powerful, strong women. Dani's resourceful and self-sufficient, Marilyn's got more money than all of us put together, Adrienne's practically a Nobel Peace Prize candidate . . ."

"What award are you accepting, Meryl Streep?" Heather asks. "Because I am going to suffer a serious relapse if you start reciting your bio again."

"I wasn't going to say anything about myself," Julia says, wounded.

"You were building to it," Heather says.

"Think what you want," Julia says, crossing her arms, leaning back in her wheelchair.

Heather throws herself forward so her chest is on her knees, one hand raised like she's swearing on a Bible.

"I will pay you twenty dollars if you can look me in the eye and swear that you were not about to start listing your degrees."

"This is what I'm talking about," Julia says, appealing to Dr. Carol. "Instead of using our energy productively, we undermine each other. Group has gotten hijacked by personal conflict. It's counterproductive."

"Twenty dollars," Heather repeats.

"You don't have twenty dollars to bet," Julia replies.

"I'll borrow it from Marilyn," Heather says.

"'Borrow' isn't the word I'd use for what you do," Marilyn says.

"Don't you dismiss me!" Heather explodes. "I've handled crap you can't even dream about! I've dealt with some higher-level astral bullshit that would make you drop a log in your satin panties."

"Cool it," Julia says to Heather.

"I don't need you, of all people, defending me," Marilyn tells Julia.

"Yeah, Julia," Heather says.

"You watch your step," Marilyn tells Heather.

"Okay, let's step back and assess," Dr. Carol interrupts. I wonder if she prescribes herself something to take the edge off these sessions. At least no one's talking about snacks anymore. "Did anyone else notice how quickly the conversation between Marilyn and Heather about snacks turned personal? Does anyone have any thoughts about why that happened?"

If Adrienne were here we'd actually be getting along. When she's in the room, we all feel like we have to live up to our reputations.

"It was a joke," Heather mumbles.

"Stop being dramatic and buy yourself a Starbucks before you come," Marilyn says. "Caffeine is an appetite suppressant."

"Some of us can't afford rich-people coffee," Heather says. "AA always has free coffee *and* cookies. Why don't you buy me a Starbucks card? You owe me, anyway."

"Ladies—" Dr. Carol begins.

"What, exactly, do I owe you?" Marilyn asks.

"You screwed me on that All-Stars of Horror deal," Heather says. "I had everything set up and you came in and wrecked it. How'm I ever going to pay you back if you keep screwing up my business deals?"

"Who're you kidding?" Marilyn asks, rolling her eyes. "We both know you're never going to pay me back."

Heather goes ballistic, and I tune her out. We all do. We've heard every single one of her monologues before. How dare Marilyn slight her honor? How can she possibly suggest that the solemn word of a junkie who has smoked, snorted, and shot up every chemical on the planet is not legally binding? How dare Marilyn imply that Heather's word is not the verbal equivalent of an ironclad contract drawn up by a team of lawyers?

Heather's always on the hustle. She doesn't bother me and Julia because she knows we don't have any money, and she's given up on Dani because there is no way to make Dani do anything Dani doesn't want to do, but she's constantly coming at Adrienne and Marilyn with projects, licensing deals, collaborations, appearance opportunities. The bottom-feeders of this world long ago learned that Heather is our weakest link.

"I know that money is a stressor for several of you," Dr. Carol says. "Can you help me drill down on this, Marilyn? Or what about you, Lynnette?"

"Um," I say, caught off guard. "Adrienne's twenty-six minutes late."

"How is that making you feel?" Dr. Carol asks.

"Anxious?" I try.

"Look," Julia says. "Why are we talking about money? Marilyn thinks group doesn't serve a purpose anymore, and when we spend half the session deflecting over snacks I can't disagree. What's wrong with us? When did we get so petty?"

"I just want," Heather says, taking a deep breath, "someone to bring coffee and cookies. Period."

Dr. Carol is preparing to address the Great Snack Crisis of 2010 when Dani interrupts. She's usually cowboy-silent, so whenever she talks we listen.

"I have something to say," Dani says. "Then you can go back to snacks."

"Or not," Julia says.

"This is my last session," Dani says. "I'm terminating."

There's a long, horrible pause.

Dani is one of the original final girls, along with Adrienne and Marilyn. Losing her would change the group, and the group hasn't changed in forever. We did Clinton's impeachment and 9/11 together. We were here for each other after Columbine and Virginia Tech. When gay marriage got legalized in Massachusetts we all chipped in and bought a nice little Beretta Nano for Dani, and even had it engraved with her and Michelle's names. When they rebooted Marilyn's franchise and she went into hiding, she still flew into L.A. once a month to come to group.

But over the last couple of years Dr. Carol has started ending a few minutes early, Marilyn has started having less patience for people, Julia has become pushier about her politics, and I get the feeling that if it wasn't for Heather some of us would have terminated a long time ago. But there's always been an unspoken agreement that we have to keep coming, no matter what, because this is the only consistent, dependable thing in Heather's life.

Surprisingly, it's not Heather who takes it the hardest.

"I knew it was a sign when Adrienne was late," I say, and then I cover my face to get some kind of privacy because I can't go to the bathroom alone.

"Oh my God," Heather says. "She's totally crying."

"I'm just surprised," I say, wiping my shirtsleeve across my eyes. "These are tears of surprise."

"I'm sorry," Dani says softly to me.

I shrug, but I want to scream. I want to scream, *You've ruined it! You've ruined everything for everybody!* Marilyn's phone starts buzzing deep inside her purse. We used to have a strict "phones off" policy, but that's another thing we've let slide over the last few years.

"It's fine," I say. "It's fine. Let's change the subject."

Marilyn's phone keeps buzzing and I want to yell, *Answer your phone! Just answer it because if you don't you'll be wondering who called for the rest of group! If you're going to leave it on, you might as well answer it!*

"You look like you have something to share?" Dr. Carol says to me.

"No," I say. "I don't have anything to share. I just . . . I just don't think Dani understands the consequences of what she's doing."

"It's a two-hour drive each way," Dani says.

A digital xylophone plays and I shoot Julia a look and hold it until she silences her phone. Am I the only one who pays attention to the no-phones rule anymore?

"What do you think the consequences are?" Dr. Carol asks.

How can they not see it? Julia sits in her wheelchair with her grad student politics, her hipster bangs, and her ironic T-shirts, right next to Marilyn, who looks like a big, brunette, camera-ready Texas housewife on some reality show. Heather is all stick limbs, knobby elbows, scabby knees, barely held together with the clothes she's scrounged out of a dona-tion bin, and Dani looks like Bruce Springsteen if he were a woman. None of us belong in the same room together.

"It's pretty obvious," I say. "I don't think I need to spell it out. I mean, it's pretty clear to me. Dani's going to leave, and eventually Adrienne's going to stop showing up. Marilyn and Julia hate each other, and one of them will stop next, and that'll be all the excuse Heather needs to go back on drugs. Then who's left? Me? If one of us leaves we'll all fall apart. Maybe not in one session, or two sessions, or even three, but eventually this will just be a big empty room full of folding chairs and wall art. I mean, that's pretty clear. It's no big deal, it's not like it's a problem, I mean, I get that everything ends, and we all have to move on, and sixteen years is a long time, but I just feel like someone should spell it out. Someone should explain to Dani exactly what it is she's doing."

Marilyn's phone buzzes again, an irritating punctuation mark at the end of my big speech.

"I need to be around Michelle right now," Dani says. "I came to tell you in person out of respect."

I think about staying home the first Thursday of next month. I think about my life shrinking to the size of my block, to the size of my apartment, to the size of my four rooms. I think about never seeing another human being who really knows me ever again.

"But after Michelle dies you're going to be alone," I say, knowing it's the wrong thing to say. "You'll need us then. You'll come crawling back."

"Okay," Dani says, standing up. "I'm done here. You all know my email address."

"Please stay," Dr. Carol says. "There's still half an hour. Can you at least tell us what led to your decision?"

Dani sighs and runs her hand through her gray buzz cut.

"When I turned fifty I started thinking that I'm closer to the end than I am to the beginning. I don't want to dwell on my past anymore. I want to move on."

"And you don't feel like group is helping you move on?" Dr. Carol asks.

"This isn't just about the past," I burst out.

"Talk-back," Dr. Carol warns.

I ignore her.

"What about us?" I ask. "We're about the present, too. We're friends, aren't we? We're all part of each other's lives. This is about all of us. It's about . . . about friendship."

Dani looks around the circle, pausing at each of us, and Marilyn's phone starts buzzing, buzzing, buzzing like it's laughing at me, and I can tell Marilyn isn't even focused on what's happening, she's just thinking about her goddamn phone. Then Julia's hand jerks as her phone starts vibrating, too.

"All I see," Dani says, "is a bunch of women I barely know who are obsessed with what happened to them in high school."

"Who you barely know?" I ask. I can't even believe she said that. "We've known each other for years."

"What do we know?" Dani asks. "You won't even tell us your home address. When's the last time any of you asked me about Michelle? I'm tired of pretending this is something it's not."

"What about Heather?" I shout, and my voice bounces off the walls. Dani studies me, then turns to Heather.

"Heather?" she asks. "What about you?"

"I don't know what that fruitcake is yapping about," Heather says.

"She's going to relapse," I say. "You know this is why we all keep coming. Don't you know how much she needs this in her life? Don't you get that this is the one thing she can depend on? If you're not going to stay for yourself, stay for Heather."

Dani looks embarrassed. Marilyn plays with her purse. Heather pinches the skin on the inside of her wrists in a classic Heather pose, and none of them are looking at me except Julia, and she looks confused.

"I thought we all kept coming for you?" Julia finally says.

It's a joke, it's another one of Julia's stupid jokes.

"For me?" I laugh, but it's a strangled seal bark. "We don't come here for me. Why would I need this? I don't need this. I'm fine."

No one's saying anything, not even Heather, as if I'm the embarrassing one, and Marilyn's cell phone starts buzzing again, and then Julia's, and someone has to say something, so I turn to them and say what I've been dying to say for the last five minutes.

"Will you please answer your fucking phones?"

"I think we all need to take a pause and regroup," Dr. Carol says. "What do you say, Lynnette?"

"I don't need a break," I say. "Dani's the one who needs a break. This is how she pushes people away."

"*I* push people away?" Dani asks.

"What do you call this?" I say. "You live in the middle of nowhere. Your nearest neighbor is ten miles down the road. You're leaving group."

"I'm married," Dani says. "Are you?"

Julia tries to get involved because Julia likes to think she's the most reasonable person in the room.

"You guys are talking past each other," she says. "Dr. Carol's right, let's take a break."

"Oh, stick it up your ass, Rollerderby," I say, turning on her. "We only let you into group because we all felt sorry for you."

Julia wants to say something, but Heather smells blood and climbs in the ring.

"Why don't you take your own advice, Rain Man?" she says to me. "You're not even a real final girl."

I realize this has gone too far. I open my mouth to try to put everything back together when Marilyn stops me. When Marilyn stops everybody.

"My word," she says, so slowly and softly that we all turn to stare at her staring at her phone. We all know in our hearts something bad is coming.

"Adrienne's dead," Marilyn says.

ACTH dumps into my bloodstream and activates my adrenal gland, my veins constrict like a net being pulled tight, my hands and feet go cold, my pupils pop wide and the room brightens, and my muscles tense, making the hair on my forearms stand up.

The monster got her. The monster finally got Adrienne. Any one of us could be next.

If murder has celebrities, three of them share this table in Manhattan's chic Balthazar bistro. Jerry Seinfeld tucks into fries in a back booth, and Spike Lee just stopped by to greet Calvin Klein, but all eyes are on Adrienne Butler, her dark brown skin aglow, Julia Campbell, bright and animated in her wheelchair, and their soft-spoken, watchful therapist, Dr. Carol Elliott. It's hard to remember that two of the three of them are only here because they won a life-or-death struggle to survive.

"It's not how I want to be defined," Campbell says. "I did what anyone would do. My killer and I had a disagreement."

"The toughest kind of disagreement," Butler says.

"He wanted my life to end," Campbell says. "And I disagreed."

The three of them chuckle wryly.

Welcome to the Final Girl revival. These women became famous in the eighties for surviving multiple onslaughts by masked killers, launching film franchises that provided the backdrop for a decade's worth of make-out sessions and slumber parties. By the end of the eighties, however, teenie kill cinema had fallen out of fashion, replaced by high-concept blockbusters like *Ghost* and the suave sexiness of Kevin Costner. Now, thanks to Campbell, they're back, and this time they might even be good for you.

"I met many of these women in a therapeutic capacity," Elliott says, careful not to reveal too much about her patients. "And they have taught me so much. I've been lucky to learn from their lives."

The lessons she learned make up the core of her latest book, *Interrupted by Silence: Six Survivors Speak*, which uses the experiences of her final girl patients (several of whom remain anonymous) to show how our culture treats women at a moment when the commander in chief is being accused of sexual harassment and many are saying feminism is dead.

THE FINAL GIRL SUPPORT GROUP 3-D

We don't stick around, we scatter. We're final girls; taking care of ourselves is what we do. Upstairs it's one of those bright, autumn Los Angeles days where nothing bad seems possible. We could be a bunch of soccer moms leaving church after planning a really terrific carnival with face painting and pony rides. Marilyn is on the phone all the way to her E-Class Mercedes. Julia takes the elevator to the parking lot, puts her chair in the back of her minivan, and swings her way to the driver's seat on crutches. Heather cuts across front yards and driveways, wandering off down Alameda. Most people wouldn't spot the only detail that makes us different: Dani standing by her truck, a matte-black Beretta Nano in one hand, holding it behind her leg, watching over everyone to make sure we all get out safe.

I'm fragile and plastic and full of static, but I have my system and after all these years it takes over and keeps me safe. I walk to the bus stop, my suburban ESP on high. I stick to the street, staying on the outside of parked cars, avoiding the sidewalks, keeping my head on a swivel, checking my corners, assessing threats.

My focus keeps getting broken by what Julia said. I'm watching out for people following me, for cars with out-of-state plates, for men in sunglasses with their hats pulled low, but my mind keeps arguing with Julia.

I'm not the problem. Is the man sitting in that parked car only pretending to be on his cell phone? Why did he slide lower when I spotted him? I'm not the crazy one. I'm not the reason we all keep coming to group. Heather is the one we have to watch out for. She's the one who needs us. I'm the sane one. I'm the safe one. That Honda making a right turn has Utah plates. I memorize the number in case it comes back around the block. I'm watching for tinted windows. I'm watching for motorcycles. I'm not thinking about what Julia said. I'm not thinking about how no one argued with her. I'm watching for vans. Don't get me started on vans.

I don't relax until I'm on a city bus. On the street, anyone can come at you from any direction. On the bus, there are limited angles of attack. They're advertising a horror movie overhead and the red signs makes me think of Adrienne, but I need to stay focused. Some boys with instrument cases sit at the back, heads bowed, engrossed in something on one of their phones. Men don't have to pay attention the way we do. Men die because they make mistakes. Women? We die because we're female. Look at Adrienne. No, look at their shoes. Memorize their faces, their clothing, their shoes. Especially their shoes.

I take the bus all the way downtown, get off at Olive and take major streets to a nearby multiplex. Outside, I put my back to the wall and pretend to check my phone. Anyone following me is going to have to either stop short or pass me by. Bright white Nikes go through my field of vision, shined-up black Rockports, fat-laced Timberlands; if someone's following they can change their jacket or their hat, but it's a whole lot harder to change their shoes.

I don't need to look at the roofline or check windows. It's shoes I have to worry about because the monsters in our lives prefer to get up close and personal. A sniper attack would be like mailing me their penis. They need to touch me.

After I buy my ticket I stand in the lobby, back against the wall, and watch shoes again. Betsey Johnson ballet flats, beige Uggs, confetti-colored children's sneakers, Sperry Top-Siders.

My movie is on previews. I sit in the front row, then turn back around like I'm looking for my date. It's a computer-animated children's movie, so it should be easy to spot an unaccompanied adult male. It's not impossible, but chances are low that anyone following me would bring a child for camouflage. I keep my eyes on the redheaded muscle shirt with brunette twins and the blond male with the beard and the little boy. Both of them scanned the theater when they came in, like they were looking for someone.

When the movie finally begins I break for the emergency exit to the left of the screen, dash down the stairs, and come out on the street. I don't see the redhead or Mr. Beard. I do see another Honda with Utah plates but it's a different number. I memorize this plate, too, noting its dusty windows and mud-spattered bumper, the Triple A sticker on its back windshield. I catch a bus to the Beverly Center.

Riding the bus, I sit as close to the driver as possible. At every stop I watch shoes. I try to stay focused—Doc Martens, Caterpillar steel tips, scuffed Nikes, white nursing shoes—but Adrienne keeps hijacking my train of thought. She and Julia have thrown me off my game.

Adrienne was the first and best of us. She's the reason most of us joined group. Her crisis set the template. Plenty of women survive violence, but what makes those of us in group our own toxic little category of final girl is that we killed our monsters, or we thought we did, and then it happened to us again. We all thought Adrienne was the only one who never got a sequel, but we were wrong, because thirty-three years later, here came her monster one more time, back to finish the job. Adrienne thought she was safe, but she was wrong. What else were we wrong about?

Adrienne's crisis happened the same summer as Marilyn's, and they were similar enough that the press got interested, but she got really famous because of what happened later, with the movies. She was a counselor at Camp Red Lake, and staff had shown up early to get the place ready for campers. Cabins had to be aired out, hornets' nests had to be sprayed, canoes had to come out of storage. On that first night, nine of her friends were murdered. Four of them were first-year counselors she didn't know very well; five were people she'd known since they'd been Red Lake campers together as kids. It was twelve long, dark hours that changed the rest of Adrienne's life.

The killer turned out to be the former camp cook, a single dad named Bruce Volker, who claimed that twenty years ago, two counselors had let his son, Teddy, drown while they were having sex. He said that Teddy had come back from the grave to kill all the counselors for revenge, although he never really explained why Teddy had waited so long to start. Anyhow, the killings stopped when Adrienne decapitated Mr. Volker with his own machete.

Things got worse when they found out that Bruce Volker never had a son who'd drowned at Red Lake. In fact, he didn't have a son at all. Bruce Volker was just a lonely old man with a fixation on kids and a good swing, but he made Adrienne the first final girl, and Adrienne used that to make all her dreams come true.

Air brakes spit and I look around and I don't recognize a single pair of shoes. How many people have gotten on and off while I was daydreaming? A leathery grandma sits behind me with her identical spouse, both wearing identical busted Reeboks and dirty red baseball caps. I didn't see them get on.

I slap the emergency stop and can barely wait for the doors to open before I slide off. Three blocks to the Beverly Center and I can't run, because no one runs in L.A. I speed walk and get on the number 14 bus. This last leg takes me back to the Red Line the wrong way around, and when I get to the Vermont/Beverly stop the train is already at the platform, and I slip on board as the doors close. There are fifteen people in the car, and I find a seat equidistant from the doors at either end. I scan the shoes and none of them look familiar. Five stops later I transfer to the Antelope Valley line.

I need to get home, but I can't rush my routine. I need to find out what happened to Adrienne. Marilyn had read the rest of the article off her phone, but details were thin: a man killed her in her home, but that was it and I need to know more because outside of group Adrienne was the one I talked to the most, the one who brought me in after my crisis, the one I called every month to check in. Well, every other month. Sometimes every third month, maybe not even that so far this year, but it felt like a lot. The point is, Adrienne always made time for me.

When I finally get back to Burbank, I get off at the airport stop and ride the rental car shuttles for a while. When I'm convinced that only new shoes are getting on each time the shuttle stops I catch the city bus, transfer twice and, almost three hours after I started, I reach my building.

My route varies every time, but the essentials are the same: go slow, lots of small loops within bigger loops, stay alert, stay aware, watch the shoes, don't get stupid, don't get dead. The line between being too careful and not being careful enough is a line you only get to cross once.

I couldn't even tell you what the inside of the elevator looks like in my building; I always take the stairs. An elevator is a box with one door. Any man can take you in an elevator, even a big fat guy because you've got no place to run. On the stairs I've got options, plus it's good cardio. It took me a while to settle on the third floor, but it's the perfect height: too high for someone to reach my windows, low enough that I can survive a jump. I make sure no one else is in the hall, and then I unlock the double dead-bolts and step into my cage.

When I moved into this apartment sixteen years ago the building was a dump and the landlord didn't care what kind of renovations I made so long as no one complained. I still had a little money left over back then, and as a result my apartment is the one place I've been able to make truly safe.

Each of us responded to our trauma differently. Dani became self-sufficient, Adrienne got into self-help, Marilyn married up and buried her head in the sand, Heather got high, Julia went activist. Me? I learned how to protect myself.

My cage is an expanded steel mesh box the size of a phone booth bolted to the wall around my front door. The mesh is tough and the cage is so small that no one can work up enough momentum to break through. The door of the cage is sealed by four electromagnetic bolts. There is no way to open them without punching in the code on the keypad, and if there's a power cut the bolts lock down. If the code is entered wrong, the bolts lock down. It's a way of stopping anyone who comes into my apartment from penetrating further unless they have my permission. I'd have preferred a steel front door and a couple of security cameras in the hall, but that would call attention to my door, so I settled for the cage.

With the front door deadbolted behind me I punch in the code and the cage's four bolts slap open, and then I enter my apartment, shut the cage behind me, and enter the code again. The bolts shoot home with the satisfying metal snap that lets me know I'm safe. I breathe in and my apartment smells reassuringly like bleach.

"Hi, Fine," I say to my plant. "Things aren't good. I'll tell you about it after I secure the perimeter."

I'm only alive because I have willpower and self-control. I open my gun safe and take out my .38 Special. If diamonds are a girl's best friend, then reliable handguns with a lot of stopping power are a final girl's. I don't have any illusions: this kind of gun didn't stop Ricky Walker the first time, and it didn't stop his brother either, but two rounds in the center of someone's mass will slow him down long enough for me get to my panic room. Well, panic closet.

Gun in hand, I sweep my apartment. It takes fifteen minutes. It's only after making sure that it's completely empty, that my panic room door is prepped, that my cell phone is charging, that my curtains are drawn, that the interior doors are locked, it's only then that I sit down and pick up Fine and put him in my lap.

"Adrienne," I tell him, and then I realize that I can't say what happened to her without crying, but I say it anyway. "She's dead."

I sit like that for a while, my tears dripping onto Fine's leaves. I wonder if salt water is bad for him, but he's not complaining. He's a good listener. He's my best friend.

Fine is the only living thing besides myself who I'm responsible for. It took me a long time to get up the nerve to make that commitment, and then the first three plants I bought didn't make it. Number four was Fine, which is short for Final Plant. I'm a final girl, he's a final plant. We make a good team.

We've been together for nine years, and when he got spider mites two years ago I couldn't handle the thought of putting him out with the trash, so I stayed up for three days straight, rubbing his leaves with water, then a soap solution, then rubbing alcohol, then water again, over and over, nodding off over his leaves, making sure every single spider mite was dead. I wasn't going to lose another friend. He made it through, and the leaves he kept were the shiniest, cleanest leaves a pepper plant ever had. He's back at full strength now but I can still see some scarring on his stalks from the leaves I couldn't save.

I'm crying less now, and I want to tell Fine all the details, but I realize that I don't know any. Was Adrienne at Red Lake this morning? Was that footage I saw shots of her murder site? Were the two incidents even related? I take Fine over to the desk and we turn on CNN. Adrienne's face is all over the news. It's been a long time since anyone cared about a living final girl, but I guess a dead one really brings the circus into town.

Most of us stay out of each other's pasts, but lately I've been looking at Adrienne's old info for personal reasons, and the pictures they're showing on CNN are familiar. The only new shot is of the interior of her refrigerator with the mummified head of Mr. Volker digitally tiled out, which is too bad. That's the only picture I want to see.

A very concerned CNN anchor who has never been in the same room as Adrienne is speaking sincerely to the camera as if her sister has died. At least CNN has taken the time to make sure a Black anchor is delivering this story.

". . . the shocking death of Adrienne Butler, the survivor of what's known as the Camp Red Lake Killings, and best known as America's first final girl. A leader in the recovery community, Butler devoted her life to ending . . ."

If you're fifteen years old and you only watch horror movies, this is probably the first time you're realizing Adrienne is Black. They made her a white girl in the *Summer Slaughter* movies, which was their mistake. I'm convinced that's why Adrienne got the idea of going after them in the first place. She was proud of her ethnicity and the fact that they were making movies based on her life and erasing something so important flipped her switch.

The first *Summer Slaughter* movie was already a hit and the sequel was about to be released by the time Adrienne's lawyer filed his injunction. He had to file a lot more, and by the time the judge finally granted one, *Summer Slaughter Part III in 3-D* was in theaters. Adrienne had family money and a settlement from the camp owners, so she hired a real shark to batter the movie producers into submission. When the studio finally forced those fly-by-night exploitation hacks to come to the table, Adrienne told me what they said.

"What do you want from us?" they'd asked, thinking she'd take a check, an onscreen credit, something that meant things wouldn't change too much for them.

She'd smiled and told them:

"I want everything."

And she got it. By the time the case was over she owned the rights to the entire franchise: the first three films and any future installments. They even had to give her the script they'd already commissioned for *Part IV.* Adrienne's case set the precedent that the rights to the story belonged to the sole survivor, not the families of the victims, not whatever studio got their movie onscreen first, but to the final girl. Right or wrong, it changed everything. It gave us power.

Once Adrienne got her rights she burned that franchise to the ground. Everyone got fired. It took her two months to clean house while the studio squealed like a stuck pig and their lawyers tried to explain that she didn't understand how these things worked, how there were unintended consequences, how grips and gaffers would starve in the streets. Then she did the last thing they expected: she flipped the switch back on.

There was a line producer who'd been on all three *Summer Slaughter* movies, and Adrienne set her up as the executive producer with the understanding that there was only one person she needed to keep happy: Adrienne. Her lawyer negotiated an amended contract with the studio and the following summer, *Summer Slaughter Part III in 3-D* was re-released in theaters, which was what you did back in those days, and two months later, *Summer Slaughter IV* hit screens.

Before *Part IV* came out, Adrienne went on all the talk shows and made sure everyone knew the proceeds from these movies weren't going to her, they were going to her nonprofit, the Adrienne Butler Fund for the Prevention of Violence against Women. While other slashers were getting slammed as misogynistic, the press hung a halo on Adrienne's *Summer Slaughter* movies. No one felt guilty about buying a ticket because all the profits went to a good cause. By the middle of the nineties, Adrienne was the Oprah Winfrey of violence against women. Some people didn't even know about her connection to the films.

She wrote books, she gave lectures, she shot TV specials, she held seminars, she led workshops. She used her movie money to buy Camp Red Lake and turn it into a retreat for victims of violence. She was tireless, she was devoted, she was positive and upbeat. She was America's favorite final girl.

She made the rest of us feel like frauds, like we weren't living up to our fullest potential, like we should be asking what we could do for our country rather than putting security bars over our windows and learning how to shoot. But Adrienne never judged our choices, and she definitely didn't think I was the crazy one.

She was never as rich as Marilyn, but she was always more generous. She paid for Julia to make the house she loved wheelchair accessible. When Dani moved to her land, Adrienne paid for a panic line to be put in.

"It's not for you," she said. "It's so I can sleep at night, knowing the odds are a little bit more in your favor."

The *Summer Slaughter* movies were the dark engine throbbing away down in the boiler room of Adrienne's empire, turning her pain into cash. There were nine original movies in the series, more than any of us ever got. There was a science fiction version set in the future where an implacable Teddy awakens from cryo-sleep and starts to kill people on a space station. There was a crossover with Heather's Dream King that she set up to try to send some money Heather's way, but that ended badly because, well, Heather. There were action figures. Plush dolls. Strangely enough, she never insisted they cast a Black actress as the lead. Adrienne always had a realistic mind-set when it came to who Middle America thought of as sympathetic victims.

Julia asked Adrienne once if it bothered her that the man who tried to murder her, the man who murdered her friends, that this man was memorialized on lunch boxes and T-shirts. That this man was probably more famous than Adrienne.

"It wasn't Teddy who killed my friends," Adrienne said, smiling. "Teddy never existed. If Bruce Volker knew that the lie he told is helping me end violence against women he would spin in his grave, and that makes me very happy."

As Fine and I watch CNN, we learn that while Bruce Volker didn't have a son named Teddy, he did have a nephew named Christophe, and he was three when his uncle died. Now he's thirty-five and pissed that his family tragedy has become a global entertainment empire and no one thought to cut him in for a percentage.

I'm familiar with the name. Christophe was one of a dozen crazies filing nuisance lawsuits against Adrienne, but she always had more lawyers and more money, and most judges take a dim view of a killer's nephew trying to take money from one of his dead uncle's intended victims. Christophe's lawsuits became a game of Whac-A-Mole, and finally, totally broke and more than a little deranged, he decided to take a cue from Hollywood.

A few years ago, he'd started stalking Adrienne's Camp Red Lake property until they'd gotten a court order to keep him one thousand feet away. He'd respected that until last night when he'd suddenly stopped, dug up his uncle's grave, gone to the camp, killed the skeleton staff who were shutting it down for the season, got pushed out of a hayloft, limped away from the cops, then drove three hours to Adrienne's house and placed his uncle's decapitated, mummified head in her refrigerator. When she came downstairs to make her morning coffee he stepped out of the pantry and stabbed her in the back of the skull twenty-two times with an ice pick.

Like the rest of us, relationships were not Adrienne's strong suit, so no one found her body until the police came by to tell her about the murders at her camp.

Just then my cell phone rings. I check it, and know that I do not want to talk to that particular individual right now. I need to decompress. I need to settle down with something comfortable. I'm switching to Netflix and clicking through for *Love Actually* when I hear a sound that still scares me, even after all this time.

Something thumps against my front door.

I turn to Fine. He's as scared as I am. I click over to my security screen. There was no way I was going to let my door become a blind spot, so after I moved in I put a pinhole camera in my peephole.

No one's at my door.

There's another thump.

I put Fine on my desk, out of the way where he won't get hurt, and then I have my .38 in my hand and the safety off. There's a second concealed camera outside my door, this one lower down. When I switch to it I realize why I didn't see them before. The other camera was too high to see Julia in her wheelchair, knocking on my door.

I close my eyes and wish her away. She knocks louder.

"I know you're in there, Lynnette," she says, and I can hear her through the door, through my cage, across the empty room, penetrating my one safe place.

"She'll go away," I whisper to Fine. "If we just hold still and don't make a sound, she'll go away."

No one knows where I live. I don't drive because I don't trust the DMV to keep my address safe. I don't have a library card. I don't vote. I do everything in my power to stay off state databases. Federal I can't do anything about, so I can only pray they're more secure. The downside of no one knowing where I live is how would they know if I went missing? How long before someone noticed? What would he be doing to me in the meantime?

So eight years ago I took a gamble. Julia was the newest member of group, and I guess I picked her because she's the youngest. I thought that meant she'd be more likely to do what I said. I check in with her twice a day via text, at nine a.m. and at nine p.m., so she knows I'm alive. If I miss a check-in I've left her a sealed envelope. I made her promise never to open it otherwise. It contains directions to my apartment.

On the screen, Julia stops knocking and rolls herself back a foot. She's giving up. She's going away. She plays with something in her lap and then my cell phone rings. I desperately search my phone for the mute switch and silence it, but it's too late. She knows I'm home.

Pixilated Julia yells at me through my door.

"Lynnette, stop being a freak, it's important!"

Fine and I don't move, we don't make a sound, we don't breathe. Alerts bloom on my screen as this traitor calls my phone again and again. After the eighth time, she goes away.

I let out my breath and Fine lets out his and we look at each other. Now what? Our location is compromised. Do we stay in place or run? If Julia came here I have to assume that someone might have followed her and now they're watching my apartment. But I can't leave. This is my only safe space.

I've got enough food to last three weeks. I don't have to open my curtains. I'll turn off my phone and hunker down. No one can get inside. It'll be safe enough. Let the other ones handle Julia's "emergency." I need to stay alive.

Halfway through *Love Actually*, there's another knock on my door. I cut the volume, switch on my screen, and call up the lower camera, wishing Julia would just leave me alone. My skin goes tight and my muscles lock. The hand holding my gun goes numb. It's Julia, and crouched by her side is the Ghost in his black robe and white mask, pressing a knife to her throat.

It's not real, it's a movie, I must still be on Netflix and I accidentally clicked on one of Julia's *Stab* flicks. This girl onscreen playing Julia is doing a great job with fear, her eyes wide, her mouth open, chest hitching, and I'm mirroring her hyperventilation.

It's a movie. That's all. I'm watching a movie, because this can't be real because I take precautions. I'm careful. I don't take risks.

Then the Ghost turns its black eye holes to the camera and pulls out a sheet of printer paper.

"Open the door or she dies, Lynnette," the paper says in Magic Marker.

We all have a deal. We've never spoken about it, but I know it exists the same way I knew that my parents loved me and that my apartment is safe and that Fine's my best friend: when the monsters come, we help each other. No matter whose monster it is. No matter what needs doing. This is what happens when you're a final girl, and group is a monthly reminder of our bargain.

I just didn't think Julia would be the first one to call in her chips.

I tighten the grip on my .38 Special. I make sure the safety is off. Then I press the button that opens my front door and I wait for the monster to come inside.

The so-called slasher or Final Girl movie is a meat grinder with producers and studio chiefs on one end, turning the crank, and slavering male fans on the other end, lapping up their output of violent sexual fantasies. What's lost on the porno-gore crowd is the fact that these franchises are based on real-life murders in which real, actual women were brutalized by men, were assaulted by men, watched their friends be murdered by men. But the fantasies have become so vivid and mainstream that no one points out the stinking female corpse at the root of this poisonous tree, and anyone who attempts to do so is called a killjoy, as I have been many times.

The women themselves remain largely silent, leaving their participation in their own exploitation unaddressed. If any of the fans become unruly they are anesthetized with more T-shirts, more albums, more posters, and action figures featuring their favorite murderers, now elevated to celebrity status.

The word *problematic* does not even begin to address the Final Girl film.

—"Women Are Our Meat, and the Eating's Good" by Deborah Ballin, published in the *Last Word on the Final Girls* anthology, 1989

THE FINAL GIRL SUPPORT GROUP IV:
Return of the Final Girls

*B*ZZT goes the buzzer that releases the latch on my apartment door. I take the shooter's stance that I practice every night, the one that means everything has gone wrong if I'm taking it inside my apartment. I aim the barrel well above Julia's head, exactly where I think the center of the Ghost's torso will be, and my arms are shaking, my wrists are weak, my fingers are numb. I can't tell if my forefinger is on the trigger or outside the trigger guard but I'm too scared to take my eyes off the door to check. The cage will be my kill zone. I can't worry about my backstop now. I can't think about what happens to the bullets that punch through the front walls of the apartment across the hall.

I feel embarrassed.

I'm overcommitted. I'm overreacting. I've made a mistake. I've never pointed a gun at a human being in my life. You don't do things like this, not in a city, not in my house, but I'm too scared to put my stiff arms back down so I stand there like an asshole, holding my gun like I think I'm some kind of badass, like my world isn't falling apart.

The feet of Julia's wheelchair push the door open as she enters the cage, and my muscles make a microscopic snap-contraction but I don't shoot. I need to take some deep breaths before I pass out. The mesh is too thick for me to see Julia's face, but I know exactly how she feels. I've felt it before. Until you've been through what we've been through you have no idea how scared a human being can get.

There's a high-pitched ringing in my ears. I see the cage in the center of my vision and everything around it is covered in gray haze.

I'll protect you, I reassure Fine in my mind. *He can't get through the cage.*

I don't know if I'm talking to Fine or to myself.

The Ghost enters behind Julia. I don't think, I pull the trigger, and that's when I learn the answer to my question: my finger was outside the trigger guard. Sweat-slicked, my finger slips off the gun and my ice-cold hands lose their grip and I fumble. I squat fast and catch my slippery gun with my fingertips right before it hits the floor and I don't even bother to stand up or get a firm grip; my finger finds the trigger.

"Lynnette! Lynnette!" Julia's shouting.

I'll save us, Fine.

The Ghost tears at its mask, and it's weird behavior, but I'm not stopping until I'm safe.

"Lynnette! Stop!" Julia shouts.

I squeeze the trigger.

The sound stabs me in both eardrums. The room fills with smoke. My wrists snap backward and I punch myself in the face, I taste metal on my teeth. Suddenly I'm sitting on the floor.

"I pissed," a muffled male voice shouts. "I pissed myself."

"Lynnette! It's Russ. It's Russell Thorn!"

I'm climbing to my feet again, gun in my left hand. I switch it to my right.

"Lynnette," Julia shouts again. "Jesus Christ. Don't shoot. Don't shoot. What's your safe word? Jesus Christ."

I raise my gun again. The Ghost is tangled up in its black robes, trying to open the door back out into the hall, but it's stuck between the door and Julia's chair.

"Help me!" it screams. "Helpmehelpmehelpme!"

I find the center of its torso with the barrel of my gun.

"Lynnette," Julia shouts. "This is Russell Thorn. He interviewed you."

I know that name.

"Russell Thorn," I repeat, but mostly I'm wondering what stopped my bullet. Why isn't the Ghost dead? Why is the Ghost Russell Thorn?

I pull the trigger again.

The cage shakes but this time I keep my stance. This time it only feels like I broke my wrists.

"Stop shooting at us!" Russell Thorn screams.

His mask is off and I see his ginger beard and he's climbing over Julia in her wheelchair, and inside the cage it's a writhing mess of arms and legs.

"It wasn't my idea!" Julia shouts. "But you wouldn't open the door for me."

I am very, very tired. My tongue is thick. My eyelids are made of lead. The room is dim from gunsmoke, and it burns my eyes, makes me sleepy.

"I opened your envelope," Julia says. "Because we have to talk."

I have lived here quietly for so long, and now I have fired a gun twice, and in five minutes the police will come, and more people will enter this apartment in the next half hour than have come through that door in sixteen years.

My face goes numb. I punch the code into the keypad and the locks slap open. Julia wheels inside.

"You need to get a towel for Russ," she says, voice shaking. "I can't believe you shot at me. Holy crap, I'm having a heart attack."

"That doesn't come in," I say, pointing at the Ghost mask and robe.

I'm still holding the gun. Russell drops the robe like it's on fire.

"In the hall," I tell him.

He falls all over himself throwing it outside, and then he slams the door. Fine doesn't like this. He prefers when it's just us. He doesn't want strangers in here.

"It's too late," I tell him.

"What?" Julia asks, one hand pressed to her chest.

Russell is looking at me the way you look at a crazy person. He's measuring the distance to the door. I walk over, slam the cage door shut, and the bolts bang home. Russell jumps. When I turn back from the cage he's sitting in my chair.

"Sit on the treadmill," I say. "Your pants are wet."

His face turns red beneath his beard but he moves. He's taking in everything at once, and his sticky eyes crawl all over my walls, my computer, my screens, taking notes inside his head, composing sentences about me ("A spartan one-bedroom with industrial-yellow walls"), writing paragraphs that judge me ("Curtains tightly closed as if she fears the sunlight almost as much as she fears the man who hurt her all those years ago . . ."), coming up with pat thesis statements ("A woman trapped inside her apartment, serving a sentence much like the man who . . .").

He pretends we weren't speaking just last week.

I study my cage. There're two scorched dents. The guy who built it assured me that a round from a .38 would have no problem penetrating it, but he either lied or was stupid. How many other plans have I made based on wrong information?

"Wow," Julia says, trying to sound brave, fingering the dents with one shaking finger. "You really shot at us."

"It was supposed to penetrate the mesh," I say.

"Well I, for one, am really fucking glad that it didn't," Russell says from down by the floor where he sits on the treadmill.

"You're not supposed to open my letter unless I miss a check-in," I say to Julia.

"It's urgent," she says.

"This is a violation," I say. "A total violation."

"Someone in group is writing a book," Julia says. "Mr. Volker's nephew knew about it."

Suddenly, I have the flu.

"Why'd you come here?" I mumble.

Someone starts banging on my door.

"Go away!" I shout.

"I'm calling the police," a woman's voice shouts back.

I check my camera. It's the actress who lives down the hall, wearing sweatpants and unlaced running shoes.

"We're rehearsing a scene," I shout at her.

We all watch on the screen as she walks back down the hall and goes into her apartment.

"Why did you come?" I repeat.

"Because I know it's Heather," Julia says. "I need you to help find her."

Russell glares at me from down by the floor, getting his confidence back. Julia wants answers. The man who killed Adrienne knows that someone in our group is writing a book. Julia thinks Heather is writing a book?

"I need a minute," I say. "I need you both to shut up for a minute."

Julia's killer was the Ghost. He wore black robes and a Halloween mask and he turned out to be her boyfriend, a horror buff who wanted to transform her into his very own final girl their senior year of high school. He shared his Ghost costume with his best friend and together they carved their way through the student body of their graduating class. To them, all those dead girls were one big meta-joke.

They were clever kids with good SAT scores and college in their future, kids who didn't take anything seriously because they assumed they were smarter than everyone else. The one thing they didn't think through was that if Julia was going to be their final girl she had to kill them. Turned out Julia didn't have a problem with that. She said the worst thing was their quips. No matter how many times she shot her boyfriend he kept making stupid quips.

America had lost its taste for final girls by the nineties, but when Julia went to college her sequel happened and suddenly America perked up. We call it a sequel because they almost always come back. One of her classmates, hungry for his fifteen minutes of fame, took on the Ghost disguise. He killed five people, got arrested, got his capital sentence commuted to life, and made Julia a star in the process. Everyone loves a comeback queen.

The way she stopped the second Ghost was by tackling him out a window to save her roommate's life. She received an incomplete fracture of her L1 vertebra for her trouble. Ever since, she's been in a wheelchair with only partial mobility of her upper legs. They left that part out of the movie when they cast a doe-eyed, able-bodied ballerina in her place. And it turns out she broke her back for nothing. Her roommate died on the way to the hospital. That's life: always kicking you when you're down.

Julia's physiotherapist got promoted to husband and convinced her to hit the talk show circuit. I know what it's like. You don't want someone angry at you, especially a man, so you say yes to things you don't want to do because there's no road map for where you are, nothing to guide you except a neon sign in your head that says *Do not make men angry*.

The talk show circuit didn't count on how pissed Julia was. She says she didn't realize it either. Her first appearance was with Sally Jessy Raphaël. Sally called her an inspiration. Julia looked her dead in the eye and said, "Then why don't you get inspired to put in some goddamn wheelchair ramps around here." The producer for her next booking called halfway through the show and left a voicemail saying they were so sorry but she was being bumped for Ed Begley Jr. and his biodiesel car. They never rescheduled.

Adrienne was the one who brought Julia into group. We almost didn't take her because all she did was pick fights. Julia even fought with Heather, and within ten minutes of meeting her you know that fighting with Heather is a waste of time. Then, after a session in which Julia spent fifteen minutes lecturing Marilyn about American imperialism, Adrienne invited her out to Camp Red Lake for the weekend. Julia stayed for a week. She won't say what happened, but whatever it was worked. When she came back she buried herself in books and earned her paralegal degree, got a master's in sports medicine, took self-defense classes, learned to shoot from her chair. She started shutting up, as much as Julia is capable of shutting up.

She also figured out that her former physiotherapist, and current husband, had "misappropriated" all her money. A divorce kept things from getting worse, but it took a while to put her life back together. Once a year, Ray Carlton, the second Ghost, files an appeal and once a year, the judge swats it down. Julia does the paralegal work on her own case. The prosecutor's office is happy to get the free set of hands, and it gives Julia a sense of satisfaction.

"You've endangered my life," I say to her.

"It's a plastic knife," Russell says.

"That's not the issue."

"We've got bigger problems than your paranoia," Julia says.

"You endangered my safety," I repeat.

"Ladies," Russell says. "Before the catfight commences, maybe we can have a more substantive discussion."

His tougher-than-leather attitude is undermined by his whiny voice and wet crotch.

"How do you know someone's writing a book?" I ask Julia.

"I told her," Russell says.

I am at a loss for words. Whatever script I was given, he just took it in a direction I don't understand. My go bag hangs from a hook by the cage. I can grab it and be out of here in seconds.

"Christophe Volker," Julia says. "You've seen the news? You heard what he did to Adrienne?"

I don't trust myself to speak, so I nod.

"That Stephanie Fugate, the survivor in yesterday's Camp Red Lake killings," Julia says. "She told the police that Christophe was a Chatty Cathy. The entire time he was coming after her he would not shut up about women this, single mothers that, the homosexual agenda, Obama's birth certificate, FEMA death camps. One of the things she remembers him saying is that he'd talked to someone in our group. That they were writing a book and asked him for details about his lawsuits with Adrienne."

"Essentially," Russell says, "you ladies have a leak. And this lunatic knew about it."

"It's Heather," Julia says.

Julia doesn't use the words most people use like *I think* or *in my opinion*. She just states her opinion like it's a fact.

"Heather wouldn't do that," I say.

"She doesn't feel the same loyalty we do," Julia says. "She tried to write a book before, so we know she's not opposed to the idea, and she always needs money."

"It can't be Heather," I say.

"Of course it's Heather," Julia says. "I tried her halfway house, but she hadn't come back from group. It's likely she heard about Volker and took off because she knew we'd kick her ass."

"But you think I'm crazy," I say.

"What?" Julia asks.

"At group. You said that I was the reason group stuck together, not Heather. That I was the crazy one. You made a big thing out of it."

"Well . . ." Julia looks around my apartment. "This doesn't exactly look like the product of a healthy mind."

"Not to be rude," Russell says, "but I had no idea you were a total lunatic."

"Shut up," Julia tells him. "Lynnette, I'm sorry if I hurt your feelings and violated your trust. But right now, Heather is writing a book and that puts us all in danger. Any book about group is practically a how-to manual for every unstable fan with an urge to take a shot at the castrating mommy figure who killed their psycho supergod."

"Heather doesn't have the patience to write a book," I say. "And she's too selfish to split the money with a ghostwriter. The book's not important. How'd Volker get Adrienne's home address?"

"He's a stalker," Julia says. "They stalk. You're missing the point. Do

I really need to explain what will happen if some *Final Girl Support Group* tell-all comes out courtesy of Heather DeLuca?"

We've all spent a lot of time in the public eye, but the public doesn't know about group. I think of our monsters rotting in prison and on death row and their fans on the outside; I think about the press who suddenly seem to have a taste for our blood again now that one of us has been murdered. I think of what would happen if they knew we met once a month in a church basement in Burbank.

"I still don't get why he's here," I say, pointing at Russell with my chin.

"He called me about what that kid said about Volker," Julia says. "He also asked if I knew where you live. I didn't know he was going to follow me here."

"I did manage to get your door open," Russell brags, as if his pants aren't stained with his own piss. "Proving that I am not unresourceful. You'll find that cooperating with me will only be of benefit."

"He told you what Volker said?" I ask. This obnoxious bottom-feeder has been a mosquito in all our ears for years. Maybe I can still turn this around. "How do you know he's not lying to you?"

Russell lets out a frustrated sigh, probably wishing we were men because then he could communicate with us like adults, and he strides to the window, pausing dramatically by my blackout curtains, striking a pose known as Counselor Addressing the Jury.

"You ladies have always underestimated me," he says. "I suggest, however, we enter into a new spirit of cooperation."

He has my curtains parted, looking down at the street. I never open my curtains. It presents a target. The windowsill is thick with dust and dead spiders.

"Close them," I say.

"Someone called the police," he says, looking out at the street. He yanks my curtains back. The flood of light drives me deeper into the room. "This block is positively crawling with law enforcement."

"California has castle doctrine," I say. "I am perfectly justified in firing my weapon inside my home."

Glass breaks with a metallic snap and the street noise gets louder as something slaps the opposite wall. Plaster dust puffs up. Thunder rolls down the street outside.

slap-pow boooom

There's another one. The curtains in Russell's hand twitch and something shoves Julia backward in her chair, her head making a hollow-coconut *thonk* on the floor. Fresh air blows through two holes in my window. I stare at a shard of glass that hangs for a second, then separates and tinkles off the windowsill. Then my windows explode.

slap-pow slap-pow slap-pow slap-pow slap-pow slap-pow slap-pow boooom

My castle becomes a shooting gallery. Lead teeth shred the curtains into tatters, blast glass across the floor, chew the plaster walls into chips. White dust chokes the air and coats my throat. A sniper. I see pale muzzle flashes from the roof across the street. It's higher. They have perfect sight-lines. I never thought of a sniper. I never thought they'd try to kill me from so far away.

The noise sounds like my world ripping itself in half and it's never going to stop.

Russell cowers on the floor, shoulders hunched, holding his hands over his head.

Everything goes silent.

"They're shooting!" Russell shouts in the sudden silence. "They're shooting at us!"

Electricity races down my spine and I drop my gun, rising to a crouch, sprinting across the room, making for Fine.

Got you, I think at him, as I scoop him up. *I'm not leaving you behind.*

Then I turn to where Julia lies tangled up in her chair. She doesn't move. I take one long step toward her and the world explodes again.

slap-pow slap-pow slap-pow slap-pow slap-pow slap-pow slap-pow boooom

"No! No! No!" Russell shrieks. "Help me!"

I try for Julia but the wall divots in front of me, plaster dust covers my eyes. I reverse, digging my feet into the floor, overbalance backward, and go down hard on one hip. Fine spins across the floor, trailing dirt.

"Fine!" I shout as he comes to a rest in the far corner. Russell launches himself off the floor and runs for the front door, stepping down hard on one of my hands.

slap-pow slap-pow slap-pow slap-pow slap-pow slap-pow slap-pow boooom

He flies sideways and hits the wall limp, then drops to the floor. I am on my feet, trying again for Julia, but the gunfire drives me back, makes my brain go red, and before I can think I'm changing direction, grabbing my go bag, slapping in the code on the keypad and the bolts smack open. I prepare for a bullet to tear through my back. Everything I've spent years being terrified of is happening all at once. My old scars ache like fresh wounds. My entire field of vision is the door to the hall. I'm not looking so paranoid right this minute.

slap-pow slap-pow slap-pow slap-pow slap-pow slap-pow slap-pow

The cage vibrates all around me.

slap-pow slap-pow slap-pow

I owe that guy a thank-you for selling me defective mesh. I throw the hall door wide, and I run.

I'm sorry, I think over my shoulder at Julia and at Fine.

Lynnette! Fine shouts after me, or maybe it's Julia. *Don't leave me!*

Then I'm in the hall, leaving my home behind, leaving my best friend behind, leaving Julia behind. It turns out that when push came to shove, I only saved myself.

Audiences were sick of Satan in the late seventies, but no one was quite prepared for *Panhandle Meat Hook*. A big blunt title for a big blunt film, the genre tropes hadn't yet calcified into camp and so they hit viewers in the head like a sledgehammer. A massive word-of-mouth hit in a season when the other big blockbusters were *Rocky II* and *Moonraker*, *Panhandle Meat Hook* and then *Alien* were the one-two punch that changed cinema for good in the summer of '79. The only difference is that *Alien* cost $10.7 million dollars to make and *Panhandle Meat Hook* cost $140,000.

Using the name of the real-life Final Girl, Marilyn Torres, the producers also employed the actual names of the killers, adding an unsettling verité vibe to the explosive outbursts of violence. *Panhandle Meat Hook* disoriented and dislocated the American heartland, remapping it as a landscape of endless cruelty, implicating viewers in its industrial death farm logic. As Daddy Hansen claims while feeding a young woman into a meat grinder, "This is food fit for a man—feeds his stomach *AND* his soul."

American Screams: Mapping Horror's Heartland, second e

THE FINAL GIRL SUPPORT GROUP'S NEW NIGHTMARE

I make a left and run past one cracked-open apartment door after another, each one featuring a stacked totem pole of faces too scared to help but too curious to stay inside. I crash through the door at the end of the hall and bang down the stairwell, praying the police are coming up the elevator, securing my go bag straps over my shoulders, running too fast to feel guilty about Fine, too fast to think about Julia, taking the concrete stairs five at a time, pulling my plastic paint scraper out of the side pocket of my backpack.

I will come back for Fine.

I promise.

I didn't have a choice.

Julia will understand.

At the bottom of the stairs is the emergency door leading out back with a Detex pushbar and a red sign that says *Push to Open, Alarm Will Sound*. The bolt is exposed and, just like I've practiced a hundred times, I slide the paint scraper between the pushbar and the doorframe and pop the bolt without activating the alarm. The door casually clicks open like it's no big deal and I slip outside.

The air is gray, the sky filled with orange clouds as the sun sets over the hills. The back of the building faces a chain-link fence and beyond that is the back of an identical set of shitbox apartments. I toss the paint scraper and sprint across cigarette butts and crushed beer cans to the low hole in the fence that I snipped a long time ago and check once a month.

I slither on my belly into the next parking lot. As I trot across the old asphalt I strap on the fanny pack that was duct-taped to my go bag, comforted by the weight of the M&P Shield inside. It doesn't have a lot of stopping power, but beggars can't be choosers.

I don't think. I let the program take over. I trot onto the street, slowing to a fast walk, heading away from my apartment, not looking back. Behind me, I can hear Fine's cries fading away inside my head. I left him. I'm sorry.

I left Julia.

I stay with the program.

Turning away from my building, I make my way to the parking garage. A siren rips through the twilight as my house turns into a cop magnet sucking all available emergency vehicles to itself. Another one dopplers past. This city is a trap. I can't breathe.

It takes exactly fifteen minutes to reach the parking garage. I go up stairwell A with my car key in my hand, heading for my escape vehicle on the third level.

I decided long ago that I couldn't risk having my home address in the DMV system, but I have a couple of fake IDs that're good enough to use in an emergency, and for the past five years I've rented a space in this garage for a Chevy Lumina I bought for eight hundred dollars. Once a month I make sure she still runs. I keep camping gear in her trunk, and the plan is to drive toward El Paso, then disappear off the grid along the way. It's a big country and I can move fast.

The first thing I see when I come off the stairs is my car sitting too low at the other end of the deck. Hand on my Smith & Wesson inside the fanny pack, it takes until I'm halfway there to see the problem: someone slashed all four tires. My mind goes white but I trust the program and without hesitating I turn and trot down stairwell B. I feel eyes crawling all over me.

I don't believe in coincidence. Somehow someone knew about my vehicle and they compromised its integrity. Closed this escape route.

I don't scream because they might still be watching. I don't have a panic attack because I force my lungs to fill with air, even as they try to cramp closed. I don't run down the center of the street shooting anyone who looks suspicious because I planned for this. I have a backup plan for my backup plan because one is none, and two is one. Dani taught me that.

I find L.A. City Cab in my contacts and press call. I meet the black-and-yellow by the doughnut place on the corner and take a picture of his hack license. The driver monologues about his T-shirt business while I sit against the door, go bag in my lap, barrel of my Smith & Wesson pointed at the back of his seat. How did someone find my car? They must have followed me one night. They must have planned this far in advance and now I'm playing catch-up, which means everything's on their terms. But Van Nuys Self-Storage is my ace card.

I get out on the corner and pay cash, then duck around the block, walking against traffic to the massive beige storage bunker. The lockers are on the first floor and I enter my door code to get into the facility and head for A132. It holds a duffel bag containing three thousand dollars in cash, three changes of clothes, another gun and ammunition, a credit card, and more fake IDs. The plan is to head for Union Station and go anywhere domestic, chosen at random. I've got enough money to lay low for a while, and when things settle I can consider my next move.

My only excuse is that the inside of my skull is a swarm of bees. That's my only excuse for why it takes until I'm halfway to my locker to realize the lock isn't mine. I put on a gold Yale combination lock. This is a silver weatherproofed Master Lock. I freeze. I am so scared my knees won't bend. My feet root themselves to the concrete. I feel the CCTV camera boring into the back of my neck. I feel someone watching me from the dark halls.

They knew. They knew about both my escape routes. I can't trust anything that's inside my locker now. My IDs are compromised, the emergency credit card, they maybe marked my paper money and tampered with my ammo. They could be watching me right now.

I tear my feet away from the floor and force my heavy legs to turn around *now* because if they knew about this route they might still be here, waiting for me to show up. I walk as fast as I can on numb feet because I can feel someone in a hoodie coming up behind me, pressing me to the lockers, butcher knife moving like a sewing machine needle in and out of my kidneys, but the room is empty.

I am a turtle without its shell, no protection, just raw flesh exposed to the world. I am roadkill. That's what Heather called me once. Not even a real final girl, just someone who stumbled into a monster's path.

No plan survives contact with the enemy, but I didn't expect all my plans to fail so quickly, so completely. Both my escape routes out of town have failed. I trusted Julia with my address, and she failed. I thought I could use Russell, and that failed. I thought my cage would work, and it failed. I thought I would protect my friends but I ran away and left Julia to die, and I failed, I failed, I failed.

I'm sorry, Fine.

The next thing I know I'm on a Burbank bus. Time has been spliced out of my life and I drop back into my surroundings with a jerk. I examine everyone's shoes but realize that I have no idea where I am. Just when I needed it the most, my focus, my concentration, my own brain has betrayed me.

I hit the emergency stop and get off and trot down the street against traffic, trying not to run, dissolving into the crowd, slipping onto an Orange Line bus just as it's about to pull out.

I sit behind a transit cop, windows on my left, hand resting on my fanny pack, and I force my brain to slow down and think about facts.

Someone was shooting at me.

They knew both my exit routes.

Julia is dead.

Scratch that last one. Never count a final girl out until you see the body. We've all taken damage before and kept on ticking. She's alive. I didn't leave her behind to die. She's alive. She has to be. Then I add another one to the list:

People are in my home.

Right now, tactical boots and duty shoes are stomping across my floors, kicking Fine, shattering his pot, crushing his roots, looking through my rooms. Getting on my computer. Searching for me. Four gun safes and Russell's corpse are enough to get them interested in who I am. I need help.

I hit the request stop button, get off, and immediately see the empty streets and realize I made a mistake. I'm too exposed out here. I dump my phone in a garbage can, find an open Starbucks, and go inside. I take a table in back by the bathrooms.

Inside my go bag is a disposable cell phone, fully charged, loaded with my contacts. I crack it open and make my call.

"Hello." She answers on the second ring.

"Dr. Carol," I say. "It's Lynnette. Someone just attacked me. I need help."

She takes it cooler than I thought she would.

"Where are you?" she asks. "I'll come pick you up."

"Tell me your address," I say. "I'd rather come to you."

"I'd rather not have you in my home right this minute," she says. "Not if you're in danger. Please understand."

"Someone tried to shoot me," I say. "They shot all of us. Me, Julia, a reporter."

"Lynnette," she says. "Where are the police in all this?"

"I don't know," I tell her. "I ran. It was . . . they were shooting at me. Through my window."

"And you're sure it wasn't just kids? Or fireworks?"

"Julia got hit," I say.

"Oh, God," Dr. Carol says, and it's the first time she sounds less like a professional and more like a person. "Is she hurt?"

"I don't know," I say. "I ran."

"You ran?" There's judgment in her voice.

"After I called 911," I lie, then lie more. "I made sure Julia was okay first. I wouldn't just leave her bleeding on my floor."

Except I did leave her bleeding on my floor.

"What hospital did they take her to?" Dr. Carol asks.

"They were shooting at me," I say. "I didn't stick around to make small talk with the paramedics. I did the right thing."

"You did the right thing," she agrees. "Meet me at my office. Give me half an hour to get there."

"No way," I say, looking at my bus map. "Nowhere that's part of your pattern."

I give her an address and tell her to meet me there in fifty minutes. We hang up and I take a minute to check my bag. I'm so caught up in making sure there's a round in the chamber of my M&P, checking the box cutter in my pocket, taking out my TAP card for the bus, that I don't notice the shape loom up beside my table.

"We're closing in five minutes," the manager says. I almost cut him.

Instead, I duck my head and nod and apologize, acting in a way that is totally forgettable, and I head out the door and begin my system, switching buses, doubling back, knowing that now, without a doubt, someone is trying to follow me. That makes it easier.

I'm at the Starbucks on the corner of Montana and 7th in Santa Monica, drinking my second bottle of water (panic is dehydrating), and it's full dark when I see Dr. Carol's black Audi S5 roll past. She's taking the corner slow, looking for me on the other side of the street, when I pull open the front door and drop into the passenger seat.

"Drive," I say.

"Jesus, you scared me," she says.

Thankfully, she picks up speed and we cruise into a maze of suburban houses.

"Are you all right?" she asks. I don't answer. "Lynnette?"

I'm checking to make sure there are no nasty surprises in the back seat.

"Lock the doors," I say.

The power locks clunk shut, and I click on my seat belt.

"The freeway is better," I say. "Stick to big streets without traffic lights. Don't slow down at stop signs if you can avoid it."

"Where do you want to go?"

"I want to go *home*," I say, and it sticks in my throat, so I swallow it again. "But I can't, so just keep moving."

"What happened?" she asks.

While we get on the 10, I tell her everything. When I finish she's quiet for a minute.

"I'll call the hospitals, see if I can find out what happened to Julia," she says. "Could it be Billy Walker? Do you know where he is?"

Hearing his name is like licking an ashtray.

"Uintas, solitary confinement," I say. "I check every week."

"What about a fan?"

I shake my head.

"It's not just one of mine," I say. "Adrienne this morning, then me and Julia this afternoon. Someone's coming for final girls."

"Let's not jump to conclusions," Dr. Carol says.

"I told you all earlier," I say. "We don't need meetings anymore because it's over? Someone always wants to kill us. It's never over."

"We need to go to the police," Dr. Carol says.

"No way," I say. "Garrett P. Cannon didn't do squat for me before, and his buddies won't do squat for me now except lock me in a cell and make me a sitting target."

"I know trusting law enforcement is a scary step for you," Dr. Carol says. "But they are the right people to deal with this. Someone tried to kill you, Lynnette. Someone shot Julia. This is serious."

"I own a lot of guns," I say through clenched teeth. "I have a dead person in my home. Someone sprayed automatic gunfire all over my building. A cop's going to think three things: terrorist, terrorist, and terrorist."

"I'll talk to them," Dr. Carol says.

"By the time they stop overreacting and start listening it will be too late," I say. "Don't you get it? I only get to make one mistake and then I'm dead. They've been watching me for months. They knew where I was going to go. The only reason I'm not dead is because I was too fast."

I pull my legs up onto the seat and hug my knees. I grip the hair at my temples so hard it feels like I'm going to tear it out.

"Dead, dead, dead, dead, dead," I say.

Dr. Carol puts a hand on my arm. I flinch and she takes it away.

"They're in my house," I say, and I hate how my voice rises to a whine. I press my forehead to the window and start to slowly bounce it off the glass.

"Do you have someplace to go, Lynnette?" Dr. Carol asks.

I think about a hotel, or a motel, or a bar, or a church shelter. I can't go to Marilyn or Dani. Not now. Someone's out there waiting for us to bunch up again and make their job easier.

"Can't we just drive around for a while?" I ask.

I've always thought better in cars.

"Lynnette," Dr. Carol says. "Let's go home, okay? You can come to my house and rest for the night. We'll call the other girls and make sure they're informed if you feel that's important, and in the morning we'll sit down and talk this through."

"Who's in your house?"

"It's just Skye and Pax," she says.

"Men," I say.

"Pax is eight years old," she says. "And we're lucky if Skye comes out of his room once a day. He's always on his computer. I've got an alarm system, a gate, and a guest room. Come home."

The only people I trust are the other final girls. We'll always have each other's backs.

Except for Julia. Who had Julia's back?

But Dr. Carol understands us. She's been there for us for sixteen years. If I'm going to trust someone who's not one of us, it's her.

"Is there a room with no windows?" I ask.

"I have a gym in the basement," Dr. Carol says.

It's not like I have a lot of choices.

D r. Carol lives in a white two-story hacienda in Sherman Oaks that's designed to soothe and comfort your spirit, but it's still got the full complement of rich-person security accessories: motion-activated flood-lights, an automatic gate, an indoor two-car garage, ADT stickers tucked discreetly in the corners of its windows, tastefully concealed cameras. Even so, I'm glad I'll be sleeping in the basement.

Inside, a blond kid missing a tooth hops from foot to foot in the kitchen while sucking on a Go-Gurt.

"Mom!" he says. "Mom! Mom! Mom!"

"Pax," she says. "This is Lynnette. She's a patient and she'll be sleeping here tonight."

He stops hopping and narrows his eyes at me.

"Are you crazy?" he asks.

"Pax!"

"Fuck off," I say.

"Lynnette!"

"Mom! She said a bad word!"

"Pax, hush!" Dr. Carol says. "Lynnette, this is my home and my family. You need to be respectful while you're here."

The windows over the sink look out into the backyard and I see a wall around it, which is good. Still, I put myself out of the window's direct line of sight.

"I'm sorry," I say, trying to make peace with the kid. After all, I need his house at least for the night. "But I'm not crazy and I don't appreciate being called that."

The kid ignores me and hands Dr. Carol a Post-it note.

"Mom!" he says. "The police called! You're supposed to call this guy back!"

Dr. Carol does her best not to look at me, but kids have ESP.

"Are they looking for her?" he shouts. "Is she a criminal? Is she a terrorist?"

"Pax, go to the activity room," Dr. Carol says.

"No!" he says. "I'm not leaving you alone with a suicide bomber!"

He's giving me a headache.

"Why don't you show Lynnette your comic book while I call these people back?" Dr. Carol says.

Not taking his eyes off his mom as she dials the number on the Post-it note, Pax grubs in his backpack and pulls out a sheaf of paper that's been stapled together.

"Here," he says, shoving them at me. "It's *War Ghost*. Pay me five dollars."

I ignore him and listen to Dr. Carol.

"Hello, this is Dr. Carol Elliott," she says on the phone. The comic hangs limp in my hand. "I got a call from this number, from Officer Fuller. Mm-hmm . . . mm-hmm . . . that's awful. No, I don't know. Have you found her?" She listens for a while, then: "Please, if you hear anything at all, please call me back at this number at any hour. I go to bed late and get up early. Actually, let me give you my mobile phone number. You can call there twenty-four hours a day. That's right."

She gets off the phone.

"Pax, go in the other room," she says.

"Mom," he whines.

"Now!" she snaps.

He yanks *War Ghost* out of my hand. I'm staring at Dr. Carol, waiting for the bad news, but she's waiting for Pax to be totally gone. When she's convinced he can't hear, she turns to me.

"Heather's halfway house burned down," she says.

"I told you!" I say, but she's shaking her head.

"They found drug paraphernalia in the basement where the fire started," she said. "No one died, but a few people are hurt. Heather's missing. They think she started it."

I would think that, too, if I wasn't a final girl.

"They're coming for us," I say. "One by one, they're coming for us. We need to call Uintas and double-check that Billy is still there. We need to find out where all of them are, all the monsters. This is the sequel or a crossover, or I don't know what."

"Lynnette, you need to calm down," Dr. Carol says. "We don't know anything right now."

"I know everything!" I shout. "I know what's happening! Why won't anyone listen to me?"

"Don't yell at my mom!" Something sharp hits my leg.

I look down and Pax is baring his teeth at me, gripping a sharpened pencil in one hand. It didn't break the denim but I'll have a bruise.

"Leave her alone!" he snarls.

I shove him hard, and he goes down on his butt, his mouth forming a comical O. I look at Dr. Carol and her mouth is making an identical shape.

"I need to be alone," I say, and leave the room.

Dr. Carol gives me some bedding and an air mattress, and the gym locks from the inside. There are no windows, and once I drag the elliptical over to block the door I make a nest in the corner and plug in my phone, turn the ringer up loud, and slide my Smith & Wesson under my pillow. Then I try to figure this out.

Who's coming for us? A fan? That has to be it. The monsters in our lives are as particular about their final girls as people are about their Starbucks order. Black nonfat camp counselor with high threshold for pain and an extra shot. A double soy lesbian babysitter who's not afraid to stab someone in the eye, hold the foam.

But how are they this organized? Final girl fans are lonely and loony. The kind of people who relocate to be near a serial killer and who dream of having a maniac's baby. The kind of people who dressed up as Ricky Walker and marched around outside my house, who followed my foster mom to malls and tried to steal her used Kleenex for voodoo rituals. These are not logical thinkers.

Right before I fall asleep I realize I know who it is: all of them. In the darkness of the house around me I can feel all the monsters creeping through the shadows. Ricky and Billy Walker, sneaking down the stairs and shushing each other. Nick Shipman standing at the front door with an absent grin on his big round moon face. The Hansens fumbling around in the garbage by the back of the house. The Ghost coming in through the garage door. Teddy Volker standing in the light of the refrigerator. The pale Dream King lurking in the shadows of the mirror on the other side of the room.

There's a sound in the hall, and my heart rate spikes. I take eight deep breaths and tell myself it's probably that creepy little kid. I'll have to remember to look at his comic book in the morning, check it for signs of aggression, see if one day I'll have to worry about him, too. Even an eight-year-old can be dangerous if he gets the drop on you.

I feel naked. They knew my plans. They knew my exits. They were inside my computer. They're inside my house. I feel so violated I don't think I'll ever feel clean again.

I left Julia behind. It was the right thing to do. She'd have done the same thing. I didn't have time to worry about her. I only had time to save myself.

I put two five-pound barbells next to my bed, just in case. I don't want to have to shoot Dr. Carol's kid. I'd rather just stun him.

When I first came to L.A., I thought I was going to die. Men followed me wherever I went. I stopped leaving the house. I stopped going to group. Then they started ringing my doorbell and I realized staying home wasn't safe either.

Dani told me I should learn how to shoot, it'd make me feel safer, but I'd never held a gun before and how could I go to a range? I couldn't bear to have my back to all those people, facing an empty field, my total concentration focused on a tiny paper target seventy-five feet away. Adrienne told me Red Lake was renovating and it still had its rifle range. She drove me there.

We were the only two people on the property and we stayed for three days, and every day I unloaded rounds until my wrists went numb while Adrienne sat beside me in her white sweater and jeans, wearing red ear protectors, watching my back. She didn't believe in guns but she believed in me.

Adrienne is dead. Julia might be dead. Heather might be dead. In the blink of an eye, half my life is gone.

The hard thing about sleeping on an air mattress is that when you cry, the water pools. It's got nowhere else to go.

#7—*Gnomecoming* (1 movie, 1989)

There's a bar in Seattle that's been screening *Gnomecoming* every Friday night for fourteen years, but that's not a sign of the movie's cult following, it's just one more reason to hate Seattle. Not even so bad it's good, it wasn't even worthy of a sequel. Canada's first Final Girl was also its last Final Girl for one very good reason: she sucked.

#6—*Slay Bells* (4 movies, 1993–1997)

Izzy Gallagher's effects work is truly face-melting, and with enough beer it can be fun, but *SB* was direct-to-video and it shows: none of the installments clock in over ninety minutes, the quantity of Yuletide puns could be considered a war crime, and the "Menorah Mutilator" in *Slay Bells 4: Festival of Frights* is like something my racist uncle Larry would come up with after a few too many eggnogs.

#5—*Panhandle Meat Hook* (5 movies, 1979–2003)

The 2003 remake isn't bad in a midriff-baring, CW-cheekbones kind of way, and the first film savagely decapitated American family values and still induces nightmares today. But *Part II* took a nose dive into camp, the less said about *Part III* the better, and even though *Part IV* will always be one of the most subversive horror movies ever, it was shot on a shoestring as a Hail Mary by desperate producers, and it shows.

#4—*Deadly Dreams* (4 movies, 1989–2003)

Is Heather DeLuca a real Final Girl or is she a studio-created publicity stunt? Did *Deadly Dreams* kick the slasher genre into overdrive with mainstream budgets and slick special effects, or did it lobotomize the genre with its emo killer and PG-13 aspirations? Either way, we can all agree that the tragic murder of his family by producer Avi Poolos on opening weekend of *Deadly Dreams IV: The Final Frightmare* ended this series on a sour note.

#3—*The Babysitter Murders* (3 movies, 1981–1986)

The deeply weird *Babysitter Murders III: Samhain* drove this franchise right into a ditch, but it doesn't take away from just how relentless, tension-inducing, and downright terrifying *Parts I* and *II* remain to this day. Crafted from nothing more than a Steadicam, a drum loop, and a cheap Halloween mask, *The Babysitter Murders* did for $7-an-hour sitting jobs what *Jaws* did for the water.

#2—*Summer Slaughter* (10 movies, 1980–2003)

We'll give the original points for kicking off the biggest, longest-lasting franchise of them all, and *Parts II, IV,* and *VI* are genuine classics. But in the case against Teddy Volker you've got *Part VIII (Teddy Goes to Washington), Part IX (Teddy: Zero G),* and let's pretend *Part X* was only a bad dream. Still, Teddy's an icon, and three perfect films, plus two that provide serious fan service, more than earns it the silver medal.

#1—*Stab* (2 movies, 1 TV series, 1996–2003)

Quality over quantity makes the *Stab* movies near-perfect examples of how to do it right. After the snake-devouring-its-own-tail, super-smart, meta-thrills of the first *Stab*, no one expected much from the sequel. How wrong we were. An exercise in suspense, it was the slasher Hitchcock would have made if he'd been able to lure Tom Savini onto his payroll, and it had an ending that actually made you cry. The TV series only lasted a season, but even it was smarter than it needed to be. If this list can get one more person to check it out (recently released on DVD), then our work here is done.

—"The Slasher Franchises Ranked" by Russell Thorn,
Rue Morgue magazine, August 2010

THE FINAL GIRL SUPPORT GROUP VI:
The Next Generation

I don't sleep, I don't close my eyes, but somehow I go into a trance where time seems to be taken out in chunks. I don't see the sun come up. I don't hear birds start chirping. But then it's morning and someone is trying to open the door, banging it into the elliptical machine over and over like a confused robot.

donk . . . donk . . . donk . . .

I'm awake, on my feet, gun in my hand, when Dr. Carol sticks her head around the door.

"Lynnette—oh, Jesus!" She ducks back around the door, leaving it open.

"Are you alone?" I ask.

"Did you bring a handgun into my home?" she calls from behind the door.

". . . Yes?"

"Lynnette, are you still pointing that handgun at me?" she asks.

"No," I lie.

"I appreciate that you feel threatened," she says. "But my children are in this house. You need to let me lock that weapon in my safe while you're here."

"I'll put the safety on and keep it in my bag," I say. "But I'm not locking it up."

I put it in my fanny pack but don't put the safety on. That extra half second might be the difference between living and dying. Then I drag the elliptical away from the doorway. It feels heavier than the night before.

Dr. Carol stands in the hall wearing a soft charcoal sweater and light gray slacks. She's already done her hair and makeup.

"Show me," she says.

I unzip my fanny pack and show her the gun. She's one of those people who has never held a gun before, so being this close to one makes her nervous. She doesn't even check whether the safety is actually on before I zip my bag back up.

"I came to see if you want breakfast," she says.

Upstairs in the kitchen, there's a man with blond stubble and bed head standing at the sink in sweat pants, dirty white socks, and a lacrosse T-shirt, trying to open a package of bacon with the tip of a foot-long carving knife.

"Let me do that, honey," Dr. Carol says, going over and taking the knife from him.

He watches her do his work for him and I realize that he's her other son, Skye. Seeing how old he is makes me feel old. He's stringy, not much body fat. He probably runs. He's taller than I am, longer reach, good stamina; I could take him but I'd need to get in my first hits fast and make them count. These are the things I notice, not that he's attractive for his age, not that he's got a good chin.

"Why are you still here?" Pax asks, materializing on the other side of the counter, lipping a piece of toast.

"Because she is our guest," Dr. Carol says. "Elbows."

He takes his elbows off the counter and goes back to sucking his toast.

"Not my guest," he says.

"Not mine, either," Skye says from the sink. "I didn't know you let patients into the house."

"You both need to be respectful, Skye," Dr. Carol says, finally getting the bacon open and taking it to the stove.

"Make sure you cook it long enough," Pax says. "Extra crispy."

It's degrading to watch the woman who hauled us back from the brink reduced to the status of waitress for her children. Eventually they won't have their mother to be their short-order cook and laundress and maid. They'll have to trick some poor woman into marrying them to get all that for free again.

Dr. Carol makes scrambled eggs, bacon, whole wheat toast, and mango smoothies. I stick with fruit. I prefer my food prepackaged and when I'm in an unsafe environment the closest I can get is fruit.

Everyone sits at the table except Pax, who stays on his stool, spinning lazily from side to side, smacking his toast with his mouth open so I can see gummy brown gobs of bread. He's looking at his brother when he starts to smirk. Skye smiles.

"What is it?" Dr. Carol asks, wanting to be let in on the joke.

"Pax has something to say," Skye says.

"No," Pax says, shaking his head, clapping one hand over his mouth.

"Don't be shy, Pax," Dr. Carol encourages him.

Pax looks over at me and tries to keep a straight face.

"Nice rack," he says, then falls off his chair giggling.

Something inside my chest tightens.

"Pax!" Dr. Carol says, genuinely shocked. "That is not nice."

I haven't seen one of those T-shirts in a long time, but clearly someone's been googling me. I refuse to let this useless little boy get under my skin.

"It's all right," I say to Dr. Carol. Then I level my gaze on Pax. "You want to see the scars? You want to see how funny they look?"

Dr. Carol doesn't know how to navigate this situation. Pax senses his mom's discomfort and stops laughing.

I cross my arms at the wrist and grab the hem of my T-shirt. "I don't mind showing you if you're that interested."

"Go upstairs and get ready for school, Pax," Dr. Carol says.

We all watch him go. At the bottom of the stairs he looks back, sees us all watching him, then turns and runs upstairs.

"I do," a soft voice says.

Skye is looking at me.

"I'm sorry," he says. "When Mom told me who you were I googled you and Pax saw."

"You cannot tell any of your friends that she is here," Dr. Carol says.

"Duh," Skye says.

I stand.

"Lynnette, I don't want you to do this," Dr. Carol says.

I turn around and lift my T-shirt to just below my breasts.

The scars on my lower back are the worst. They're the ones I show Skye. I feel his eyes on me. He lets out a puff of air.

"Why is it so messy?" he asks.

"The brow tine and the bay antler were what took my weight," I say, facing away from him, speaking to the window. "The royal antler dug out pieces of me while I swung there."

"What did it feel like?" he asks.

I drop my shirt and turn around. My scars usually shut people right up. I'm impressed he's still talking. His mom's face is pale.

"It hurt," I say. "And it was humiliating. But after the first five hours, the pain started to seem normal."

"That's enough of this kind of talk," Dr. Carol says.

The three of us go back to eating, but I catch Skye sneaking glances at me. After we're done, he disappears upstairs to his room. Both he and Pax left their plates for Dr. Carol to rinse and put in the dishwasher. Without my computer, without my guns to clean, without my systems and my schedule, I don't know who I am. I stand in the corner, trying not to look awkward. It's a relief when Dr. Carol finishes cleaning up after her sons and says, "Let's go to my office."

It's a sunny extension with too many windows built onto the back of the house, looking out onto their walled garden filled with a bunch of bamboo. The giant windows and French doors make me very nervous.

I perch on an ottoman, putting my back against the one small scrap of wall, trying to see all around me. Dr. Carol sinks into an armchair and lays down the law.

"I apologize for Pax's behavior," she says. "He's eight years old and doesn't understand empathy. But I do not want you interacting with my boys the way you did."

"He asked," I say.

"And you lifted your shirt," she says. "I know this is a challenging time, but this is my house, my family, and my rules. If you can't respect that, I'm going to have to ask you to leave."

I think about my options. There aren't many.

"I'll stay," I say.

"And?" she says.

"I'll respect your boundaries."

"Thank you."

She's only a few years older, but she's been treating me for so many years that I let her talk to me like a mom. I want her to be happy with me. I don't ever want to lose group.

We're interrupted by soothing digital wind chimes.

"Excuse me," Dr. Carol says.

She picks up her phone and has a muttered conversation. I know it's not good because she looks at me three times.

"Is it Heather?" I ask when she hangs up.

She stares at the hard straw carpet between us for a minute, then raises her eyes and studies my face. It's clear she doesn't like what she sees. Then her expression shifts back and she's good old Dr. Carol again, public mask strapped on tight.

"Dani shot a police officer," she says. "She's in custody."

"What?" I say.

I feel slow, I feel stupid, I feel like prey.

"I'm going to have to ask you to let me hold on to your firearm."

"Don't you see how much danger we're in?" I ask. "First Adrienne, then Julia and Heather, now Dani?"

73

"Whether or not these events are connected," Dr. Carol says, "I won't have a weapon in my home."

"No," I say.

She sits up straight, meeting my eyes, going into her professional mode.

"Let me lock it up or I'll have to ask you to leave," she says.

I'm hyperventilating. I put my head between my knees. I try to relax my throat. I try to take deep breaths. I'll be exposed. I'll be defenseless. But I can't leave this house. It'll be worse out there. What happened to Dani?

I make my throat muscles relax, I pull oxygen into my lungs, and finally, I take my gun out of my fanny pack and hand it over, and then I excuse myself to the bathroom and go downstairs, where I unzip the bottom compartment in my go bag and take out my little .22 and hide it in my fanny pack. One is none.

When I come back upstairs she brings me up to speed.

A couple of weeks ago, the New Jersey State Police reopened their files on Dani's case for some reason. They must have found something because they contacted the FBI, who contacted Dani's local sheriff's department, who assured them they had a good relationship with Dani. This morning at the crack of dawn the sheriff took the FBI out to Dani's ranch and asked her to come with them for questioning. They didn't count on Michelle.

Michelle's cancer is killing her. The way Dani tells it, things took a turn two months ago and now every day is a deathwatch. She's lucky if they can squeeze out a good half hour here, a tolerable twenty minutes there, and that's how Dani spends her days, trying to patch together as much lucid time as she can while the woman she loves dies. They've been together for nineteen years, and there is no way Dani is going to let herself be moved from Michelle's bedside for anything other than group.

The sheriff suggested they interview her in the living room. The FBI wasn't having it. She was coming back to the station, period. Dani had just gotten back from L.A. She told them to get off her property. When they didn't, she went back inside and got her gun. She started shooting.

I don't believe Dani shot a cop. She's a law-and-order values voter who lets the local sheriff's department use a corner of her property for their annual barbecue. She sets up a shooting range out there for them and they run and gun on timed courses, plinking sheet metal targets she cuts for them while Michelle roasts a pig. Cops are her heroes, and I remember how hard she took 9/11. So I have a hard time believing she shot anyone in law enforcement.

Dr. Carol doesn't quite believe it either, so she works the phone until she gets the real story.

"She didn't shoot anyone," she finally says with a sigh of relief. "There was confusion. She shot into the air. They Tasered her. I knew she wouldn't point a weapon at police officers."

It turns out that isn't the only good news.

"And Julia is alive," she says. "She was shot three times and she's in the ICU, but she's not awake yet."

"I knew she was alive," I say, and feel my shoulders relax. I hadn't realized how scared I was.

Dr. Carol moves on.

"I have to tell you some more bad news about Dani. The reason they reopened her case. Someone else confessed to the crime."

I meet her eyes.

"They need to put her on suicide watch," I say.

Dr. Carol nods.

"I'll make a call."

K illing is hard. Killing your brother is even harder. Finding out you killed your brother for no reason is the most impossible thing of all. Dr. Carol is able to get through to someone and they move Dani to an observation cell. She fights them all the way, screaming for Michelle. The cops sent an ambulance and moved Michelle to hospice. In her condition, I can't imagine that added much to her life expectancy. They love that ranch, and Dani promised Michelle she'd die there. There's nothing Dani hates more than breaking her promises. She must be in Hell.

It's a familiar place for her.

Back in the eighties, Dani's older brother, Nick, liked to kill animals. He was big and hard to control and he thought it was funny to hurt things that were smaller than him. When Dani was seven, Nick hurt their baby-sitter one night. He hurt her so badly he got sent to an institution. Her parents took Dani to visit on his eighteenth birthday when she was ten. She says he was so doped up on Thorazine he couldn't even swallow and the front of his shirt was soaked transparent with drool. She never went back.

"I was a kid, but that was no excuse," she said in group. "I should have gone back."

She didn't see Nick again until she was seventeen. A storm knocked out the power at the institution and a bunch of inmates escaped. Nick stole some overalls and made his way back to their pretty little suburb, wondering why his little sister never came to see him. He had a mask. He had a knife. It was Halloween.

Dani was babysitting that night, saving money for her get-out-of-town fund. By then she already knew she was gay and wanted the hell out of New Jersey, the hell off the entire East Coast. She wanted to head for the Wild West where the air was clear, the horses ran free, and maybe she could find a rodeo romance.

Wearing his mask, Nick worked his way through their neighborhood, looking for Dani. Along the way he killed four people and two dogs. Some-one told me he tried to eat one of the dogs. He finally found Dani. She put up a fight, trashed the house, stabbed him with his own knife. Cops showed up at the last minute and shot him so many times he went out the second-story window. They couldn't find his body.

We get subjected to sequels. That's what makes our guys different, that's what makes them monsters—they keep coming back. Dani's brother came back that same night.

The cops took her to the hospital, doped her up, and left her in a room with a cop at the door. Nick went through them like the wrath of God. Eleven people died. That's what always upset Dani the most. They were doctors, nurses, cops, EMTs. These were people who ran toward natural disasters and car accidents, not away. According to Dani, some of them threw themselves in front of Nick to buy her time to escape. She says they never hesitated.

Out in the hospital's parking garage, Dani found Nick. He was walking down one of the ramps, coming right at her, no mask, just plodding forward, smiling like an angel. She beat his brains out with a tire iron. She had no choice.

Nick's fans formed a posthumous death cult around their fallen god. Over the years, they've spread the rumor that the masked man who committed the murders and Dani's brother were two different people.

"Do you think it's true?" I once asked Dr. Carol.

"It's not my place to speculate," she'd said.

That was Dani's nightmare: she'd killed the wrong person. One of the inmates who got out of the institution that night was never found. Harry Peter Warden, a big guy, about Nick's size, with a history of violence, bed-wetting, hurting neighborhood pets. What if this guy and Nick traveled to her suburb together? Nick telling this guy about his sister, about how he wanted to see her, talking about her all the way home. There's no way to be sure. The killer never took off his mask.

What stuck in Dani's head is what if that was just Nick coming to her in the parking garage? What if that was just Nick, veins still full of Thorazine, stumbling forward, wanting his sister to take him someplace warm and give him a chicken noodle Cup-a-Soup like their mom used to? What if that was her brother, come home at last, wanting to ask why she never came to visit, and she beat him to death with a tire iron?

When she told us that, it was the only time I ever saw Dani cry.

How did anyone know about this? How could someone know this was Dani's worst fear?

They knew because she talked about it in group.

They knew because they read it in a book.

Music rattles Skye's door in its frame. After a lot of irritating conversation, Dr. Carol has convinced herself that she's convinced me that the best thing is to go to the police. With Adrienne dead, Dani in lockup, Julia in the hospital, and Heather missing (also: suspected of arson), the sooner we start sorting things out with law enforcement the better. The police will have questions and I should cooperate. I agreed.

"I'm fried," I said. "Let me get my head together today and we'll go first thing tomorrow morning."

Dr. Carol hugged me.

"I won't do anything to create a situation where you might get hurt, Lynnette," she said. "I'm going to make sure you're safe."

I have no intention of being here come sunup.

Skye's door isn't locked and it swings open and his music runs over me like a truck. I'm lost on a freeway of bass beats and Auto-Tune. The noise bruises the air. I step inside and close the door behind me.

It smells like cleaning products in here: Febreze and carpet shampoo. No unwashed-boy funk despite the dirty clothes tossed all over the floor, piled high in one corner, spilling from an open duffel bag, jumbled into drifts on his bed. His carpet is some neutral color—Sisal? Seashore? Sandstone?—and Skye is at his desk, shirt off, back to me, worshipping his computer. The room is dark except for his halogen desk lamp. I shout his name but my voice gets lost in the music. How can people let themselves be so vulnerable? I've got a mirror taped to my computer so I can always see what's behind me.

It looks like he's rubbing his stomach, and when I get closer I realize his shorts are pulled down to his knees. Violence I can handle, but this makes my mouth go dry and my palms prickle. I think it's a natural reaction when you see your therapist's twenty-six-year-old son whacking off.

I'm suddenly extremely conscious of my body beneath my dirty clothes. I don't know whether to tap him on the shoulder or turn around and walk out of the room. While I'm considering my options he catches me out of the corner of his eye and jumps out of his chair, electrified, scrambling to cover himself, backpedaling away from me, legs tangled up in his shorts, hands over his groin, losing his balance, arms windmilling, and he lands hard on his ass, penis flopping all over the place.

"It's okay!" I shout, holding my palms out to show I'm unarmed.

I can't hear what he's saying over the music but I can see his lips making the shapes for "Jesus Christ!" and "Get the fuck out of my room!"

He wriggles his shorts up over his hips and throws on a dirty T-shirt that says *Pablo Hunting & Bait*. He picks up the remote and magic-wands the music down until it's barely rattling my teeth.

"I'm telling my mom," he says.

I notice he's not throwing me out, though. That's a twenty-six-year-old for you: strange woman catches you choking the chicken, but you don't want to go all-in on outrage because maybe you'll get lucky.

"Does she know you're into this kind of thing?" I ask.

He furrows his brow like he doesn't know what I'm talking about until I nod at his computer and his cheeks turn red and he lunges across his room and slaps his laptop closed. I'll never stop being surprised at what the average American male finds arousing.

"What do you want?" he says, pissed off because he's embarrassed.

I can't have that. I need him helping me of his own free will.

"Trust me," I say. "I've seen things that make your porn look like Dora the Explorer."

"Will you please not say"—his voice drops quieter—"'your porn'?"

I've been thinking all morning. I don't like asking anyone, but I figure if he's Dr. Carol's son and he's right here in the house, I'd be a fool not to try. And I need to get him back on my side.

"Are you actually good with computers?" I ask.

"I set up the website and all the email servers for my mom's business," he says.

"I need you to drive me to my apartment, help me sneak inside, and tell me who's gotten into mine," I say.

"Why?"

"I need you to drive because I don't have a car, I need you to help me sneak inside because police are going to be watching my building, and I need you to tell me who's gotten into my computer because I need to know who's trying to kill my friends. I don't expect you to do it for free."

"How much?" he asks.

"Five hundred dollars."

"Fine," he says. "Meet you downstairs at ten. Get out."

And he turns the volume back up until the jelly inside my eyeballs shakes.

I trust Dr. Carol as much as I trust anyone, and that extends to her kids. I wait until she takes a call in her kitchen, then I go back to that sunny extension and pop the lock on her office door with an old library card I hang on to for this kind of thing. If she can't set up her own email I'm assuming she still keeps paper files, and sure enough there are filing cabinets under her wraparound desk.

I go through the top drawer immediately to the right of her chair first, assuming it's where she keeps her family papers, and it's nice to be right. Elliott, Pax, followed by Elliott, Skye. If I'm going to be cooped up in Skye's car tonight, I want to know what kind of threat I'm facing.

Skye's got a college transcript to UC Berkeley, no disciplinary actions, no arrests. No prescription medications except Patanase for hay fever. No psychiatric treatment except some time working with a speech therapist as a kid because he couldn't say his Rs. He's clean, or as clean as men get. He'll do.

I take a minute to look through her other drawers. Patient names, last name first, one after the other: Dier, Sandra; Klein, Deborah; Mason,

Tamara; Moraine, Violet; Sanchez, Vera. They're all women, which isn't so strange since Dr. Carol specializes in victims of violence and that's the only thing women ever seem to get too much of. I flip through a few and see that they're all women who encountered a monster but didn't kill him. Fetal final girls.

I slide the drawer closed and check out the desk. Over it hang framed diplomas, citations, pictures of her shaking Arnold Schwarzenegger's hand, the cover of *Time* magazine featuring her and Adrienne and Julia. I didn't do press the way the three of them did back in the day. The thought of being exposed to everyone's eyes like that makes my skin crawl.

Next to her PC sits a file rack holding a single manila folder. I flick it open and see a familiar face paper-clipped to the inside cover: Fugate, Stephanie, grinning the way she'll never grin again. Something about that smile, so dorky and unguarded, flips a switch and I'm seeing Gillian's smile, and I try not to think about Gillian anymore, I try to keep her out of my mind at all costs, because then I think about what happened to her, and then I have everything back exactly the way it was and I'm out of her office, locking the door, before I start crying again.

I sit in the gym looking at the wall across from me, trying not to think about Gillian and how I couldn't save her, definitely not thinking about running away and leaving Julia behind on my floor. I think about this for a long, long time. I can't make a move until tonight, and the time just evaporates when I start thinking about all the ways I've failed the people I know. When Pax bangs on my door and asks if I'm coming to dinner I ask him to tell his mom I'm going to bed early. Big day with the cops to-morrow.

I know we're Dr. Carol's business, but seeing those files makes me feel like I'm a collector's item, a limited-edition action figure, a butterfly pinned to a board. I skimmed Fugate, Stephanie's file before I put it back. She was at Red Lake because three years ago, when she was thirteen, her school tennis coach started poisoning his players, obsessed with his champion racquet slinger, and Fugate, Stephanie figured it out during a meeting in his office before he could give her a fatal dose. Red Lake wasn't her first crisis, it was her sequel. She's like us now. Poor kid. Another doll in Dr. Carol's collection.

When my watch says 9:57 p.m., I creep out into the hall, go bag over my shoulders, fanny pack around my waist. I can hear Dr. Carol in the back of the house on her phone, talking to someone in clear, confident tones. Her voice fades as I make my way to the side door where Skye waits.

"Ready?" he whispers.

I look down. He's wearing heavy black tactical boots, way too clunky and noisy for sneaking out of the house.

"Change shoes," I whisper.

"They're my Under Armours," he whispers back. "They're badass."

I roll my eyes. Boys and their toys. He pops the side door and we both listen, but Dr. Carol's voice keeps echoing through the kitchen uninterrupted. That's a good sign. We slip into the garage. His boots make exactly as much noise as I expected.

"Hey!" a shrill voice says before I can close the kitchen door behind me. "Where're you going?"

It's Pax. I start closing the door in his face, but he grabs it.

"Are you sneaking out? Are you guys going on a date?"

"Zip it," I whisper.

But I don't know what to do after that. Hit him? Tie him up and gag him? I turn to his brother.

"Do not tell Mom," Skye whispers at Pax.

The little creep's eyes sharpen into two black pinpricks.

"What's it worth to you?" he whispers.

At least he's whispering now.

"You'd better give him something," Skye tells me.

"What do you want?" I ask.

Pax bounces from toe to toe, turning his head around to check out the interior of his house, and then he turns back to me with a jack-o'-lantern grin.

"Buy my book," he says, waving the comic book he tried to push on me earlier in the day.

"How's five dollars?" I whisper, reaching into my wallet.

"How's a hundred?" he says.

I give him a look but he's serious. I look at Skye, who shrugs. Helpful. Held ransom by a little brother, I count out five twenty-dollar bills and remember what it felt like to have a little sister. It hurts deep inside my chest and that makes me hate this ankle-biter even more. He shoves the comic at me; I take it out of his hand and cram it into my bag.

"Sayonara, suckers!" He laughs.

"Let's go before he changes his mind," Skye says, and we walk out of Dr. Carol's garage into the night.

Despite going straight to video, the *Panhandle Meat Hook* franchise delivered one of its smartest installments in 1988 (*PMH IV: The New Generation*), and that same year saw *Summer Slaughter VI: Endless Evil*, the most popular movie in the franchise. But the following year, two movies almost destroyed the genre: *Deadly Dreams* and *Gnomecoming*. For general audiences, *Deadly Dreams* was a high point, serving up a franchise-friendly, slick, Hollywood horror movie with a goth dreamboat killer uttering pretentious platitudes, but this bid for mainstream success sent slashers down an artistic cul-de-sac. And the less said about the pitiable Canadian addition to the canon, *Gnomecoming*, the better. In less than four years, *Slay Bells* would make its direct-to-video Blockbuster debut and seemingly throw the final shovelful of dirt onto the genre's coffin.

—*Screaming Virgins and Machete Monsters: The Making of the Slashers*
by Johnathan Stokes, 2008

THE FINAL GIRL SUPPORT GROUP VII:
Son of the Final Girls

I'd really prefer it if you didn't sit on the floor," Skye says, shifting gears.

I'm folded into the leg well of the passenger seat, knees at my chin, back pressed against the door, the glove compartment shoving my head forward. There are eyes outside, looking for me. I'm not taking any chances.

"It's not up for debate," I say.

Skye sighs and keeps driving, headlights from oncoming cars stroking his long face from right to left. Right to left. Riding in cars always makes me sleepy, bouncing my head, making my eyelids heavy, filling my chest with sleep-smell.

He makes a right-hand turn and the door handle digs into my back. My go bag is on the seat, partially unzipped, and my hand rests inside holding my .22. The rough grip feels sweaty.

"What kind of stuff?" Skye asks.

"What?" I say.

"In my room you said you'd seen stuff that makes the stuff I was looking at look like Dora the Explorer," he says. "Like what?"

That's one of the warning signs, abnormal sexual interests. I'm not sleepy anymore. I make sure my grip is secure on my weapon.

"Sorry," he says. "That sounded pervy."

He flicks his eyes down to me and gives an embarrassed half smile. I remember how ashamed I felt of every single thing that came out of my mouth when I was only a little younger than he is now. I cut him a break.

"There's a guy named Kenneth Hampson," I say. "He worked Boy Scout camps outside Laredo under the name the Desert Reaper. He's got a scam going in prison where he sells vials of his semen under the name Reaper Seed."

"No!" Skye says. "Get out!"

"A guard sneaks it out in his thermos," I say. "Then sells it online."

"How do you know?" he asks.

"There's a whole world out there," I say. "Everyone wants a piece of these psychos. They call it *murderabilia*. Dirt from the graves of their victims. The prom dress Colleen van Deusen was wearing when the Knight in White Satin chopped off her head. That sold for eight thousand dollars."

"How do people get away with it?" he asks.

"Her parents are the ones who sold the prom dress," I say. "Sometimes you need the money more than you need to live with yourself."

"Have you ever done that?" he asks.

It's a fair question, but I'm angry. He's stuck his finger in a wound. I count to five to calm down.

"No," I lie.

"You like this stuff," he says. It's a statement, not a question, and there's judgment in his voice, just like his mom.

The car's taking a curve and then he's twisting his shoulders around to watch traffic before he merges. Now we're moving so fast that I have to shout to be heard over the engine.

"Tell me how I chose this," I say. "Tell me how I picked this life. I was minding my own business and a monster came through my door. Not because I ignored the *Keep Out* signs and snuck into the old asylum, not because I built my house on top of an Indian burial mound. I didn't 'ask for it,' this was done to me."

"Yeah," he says, loudly. "But you keep dwelling on it. I mean, Mom says this happened, like, a hundred years ago. You could move on."

My back is killing me. The way I'm sitting crushes my left kidney, which hasn't been in great shape ever since Ricky Walker stopped by. I fight the urge to haul myself up into the passenger seat.

"You're right," I say. "None of us have to be defined by the worst thing that ever happened to her. Unfortunately, those things have a bad habit of coming back and trying to kill us again. After a while, you start to realize that your life isn't the thing that happens between the monsters, your life *is* the monsters."

"But you don't have to look at a guy selling his jizz online," he says, making a left. It takes some pressure off my poor kidney. I'm holding my pistol with my left arm and my shoulder burns.

"Do you read the newspaper?" I ask.

"No," he says with contempt.

"Online news?" I ask.

"Yeah," he says.

"Why?" I say. "None of that stuff is going to happen to you. If you didn't know about Deepwater Horizon you'd get through your day just fine. Why bother?"

"Because I want to know what's going on in the world," he says.

"Exactly," I say.

He thinks about it, then shakes his head.

"It's not the same thing," he says. Before I can point out to him that it's exactly the same thing, he says, "We're coming to your street."

He takes a right. Kidney pinch.

"Cruise by slow," I say. "Look for any vans with TV station logos on the side or big antennas."

He's driving too slow, twisting his head from side to side too conspicuously, but he's the only partner I've got. I just hope he doesn't get spotted and blow it for both of us. I don't want to die, and I don't want Dr. Carol to find out I've dragged her kid into this mess.

"Three vans," he says. "KTTV, KTLA, and one unmarked, but they're all parked together."

"Okay," I say. "Now keep looking for any late-model four-door sedans with two men sitting inside doing nothing."

We're almost at the end of the block.

"There it is!" he whisper-shouts. "Gray Pontiac Bonneville. Two guys, one black, one white, drinking Red Bull."

"Keep driving," I say. "Take a right at the end of the block. Don't speed up, don't slow down. Just cruise through."

He does what I tell him and I guide him to the parking lot of the apartments behind my building. I reach up and unlatch the door, then haul my aching bones out. The first thing I do is scan the lot to make sure we're alone. Like I expected, no one thought to put anyone out back where the sole door can only be opened from the inside. I transfer my pistol to my fanny pack so it's easier to reach.

"You had a gun in my car?" he asks in disbelief.

"In my bag," I say.

"Was it pointed at me?"

"No," I lie.

"You totally had it pointed at me!" he says.

The orange sodium streetlights turn his face into a pumpkin and his eyes into panda circles of shadow. I grab a Trader Joe's bag out of his back seat.

"Man up," I say. "Here's what I need you to do. Take some crap from your car and fill this bag. Walk around the building and go in my front door. Here's the keys. Don't rubberneck, don't pause, don't look around. Walk like you belong there, sort of bored, sort of bossy. Take the elevator to two, then come down the back stairs and use this to open the fire door."

I hunt around and find the paint scraper where I tossed it behind the building yesterday.

"You were going to shoot me," he says.

"You want the rest of your money?" I ask.

I've only paid him two hundred dollars so far. He nods. I peel off the bills.

"Make sure you don't press the alarm bar when you open the back door," I say. "Repeat it back to me."

He does, and then, bag crackling by his side, he walks around the building. His back is orange, then silhouetted, and then it's gone. If his shorts were high and tight instead of low and baggy, if his hair were shaggy and long instead of styled and close, he'd be a ringer for Tommy.

Julia had a theory.

"We're just the high school quarterback, talking about the touchdown pass he threw in '72," she said. "High school was everyone's glory days. For us, high school is all tangled up in memories of our trauma. We have the same normal nostalgic inclinations as other people, but when we walk back in our minds to this supposedly wonderful time we have people trying to kill us. For us, nostalgia and violence are inextricably linked."

I think about her in the ICU, face bruised, a machine breathing for her, spine probably shattered again. I try not to feel like it's my fault.

Something fumbles at the other side of the door, metal scrapes across metal, and then the door clicks open and light spills into the parking lot. Moths hurl their bodies through the crack in the doorway as I slip through.

"Did they see you?" I ask.

"I totally strolled right past them," Tommy says. I mean, Skye. That's what Skye says.

"Let's go," I say, hitting the stairs.

"We're not going to take the elevator?" he asks from behind me, still standing on the first floor of the stairwell, looking up at my ass.

"Are you kidding?" I say. "It's only three floors."

He grumbles but after a second I hear his sneakers scuffing up the stairs behind me. I wait for him to catch up with me on three, then carefully crack the fire door. My hall is clear, and I move down it fast. I don't want someone peering out their peephole and spotting me. Skye ambles along like he doesn't care.

Three strips of yellow police tape cover my door and there's a paper

Burbank PD seal over my lock. There's also a padlock hanging from a newly installed hasp.

"Shit," Skye says. "I guess that's that."

I dig into my go bag and pull out a small Velcro pouch. From it, I pull an Allen wrench I ground down, and I insert it in the padlock's keyhole, put some downward pressure on it, then use a hacksaw I filed into a lock-pick and in about twenty seconds I pop the lock.

"Wow." Skye whistles.

"Hush," I say proudly.

I slice the seal and push inside. My cage hangs open. They must have taken sledgehammers to it. The hinges are torqued and the door is almost bent in two. The room is flooded with orange from the streetlights. My curtains lie in tatters on the floor. Through the broken windows I can hear a couple walking by talking about where they parked and the girl laughs. Everything in my apartment is gone. It's empty.

"You got ripped off," Skye says, crowding in behind me. "That sucks."

"It's evidence," I say.

I do a walkthrough, making sure Skye stays by the front door. A book lies open in the middle of the living room floor with a boot print stamped across the pages right next to brown drag marks—Julia's blood. In the bathroom, a lonely bra hangs over the shower rod. All four of my safes have been drilled, and they all gape open, empty.

In the living room, Skye crouches in the corner looking at something.

"They trashed your plant," he says.

I shove him aside.

Fine! I think at him, relieved he's safe.

I get nothing from him but icy silence. He's lying on his side in the corner, a forlorn little twist of garbage. His roots cling to a ball of dirt. I find a soup pot in the kitchen and scoop up as much of his soil as I can and put him in. It's too big. I water him in the sink.

"Is that what you came back for?" Skye asks from the kitchen door.

"No," I say. "But there's no point in killing my plant."

Or running away and leaving him behind to die, Fine adds in my mind.

I'm sorry, I tell him, but he's gone back to the silent treatment.

I carry Fine into the living room. The treadmill is still there and so is my desk. I put Fine on the treadmill, then squat in front of my desk.

It's clear of monitors; there's no keyboard, no mouse, even my printer is gone. They took the CPU that sat on the floor beneath my desk, but I press a panel I chopped in the drywall behind a tangle of wires, and it pops open to reveal my actual CPU. The one they took is a dummy. One is none, and two is one.

"I want to get into that," I tell Skye, hauling it out.

"Sure, we can bring it back to my mom's," he says.

"Can you do it here?"

"I've got a busted-out laptop in my trunk," he says. "It can double for your monitor and keyboard."

"Go get it," I say. "Go out the back way and leave the door propped open."

While he's gone I head into the kitchen and open the cabinet under the sink. A board on the bottom of the cabinet comes up, and I brush aside bottles of cleaner until I can stick my arm into the space between the cabinet and the floor. My fingers snag slick plastic.

I drag out the big Ziploc freezer bag. Inside is three thousand dollars in twenties wrapped in three fat, heavy rolls. I slip them into my go bag.

Twenty minutes pass before Skye comes sauntering back, whistling, a laptop and cables under one arm. The younger generation really needs to learn what "hustle" means.

"What?" he asks as I give him a look. "You said to act natural."

It's another few minutes before he has his laptop hooked up to my CPU. We sit on the floor next to each other. It takes all my willpower to hold still. Three news vans downstairs, one unmarked cop car, it's only a matter of time before someone comes upstairs to check out the crime scene. All my senses are on high alert for the sound of the elevator doors opening or footsteps in the hall. I'm worried they'll see the missing padlock and come inside. Or someone on the street will see the laptop light on the ceiling. Or our knees might touch. I tell Skye to work fast.

"It would help if I knew what I was looking for," he says.

"Something I may have downloaded, or that would have installed itself," I say. "Some way that someone could have taken a file off my computer without me knowing."

Skye taps around in the unadorned code for less than a minute, briskly sifting the punctuation mark soup that actually powers my computer.

"There you go," he says. "Someone installed TeamViewer."

"What's that?" I ask.

"It's a program that allows them to remotely operate your system," he says. "It's been on there a while. You got hosed."

I'm embarrassed my security was breached and even more embarrassed that it took him approximately five seconds to find out. I've gotten sloppy.

"How'd it get on there?" I ask, feeling defensive. "I didn't do it."

"Probably something you downloaded," he says.

"I've got a good firewall," I say. "I've got antivirus software."

"Yeah, but once this was in they could install permissions, so your system ignored it," he says.

"How did it get there in the first place?" I ask. I feel my skin tighten. "Did someone come in here?"

"They could have," he says. "But it doesn't have to be so dramatic. It could have been hidden in an attachment you downloaded."

"I don't download attachments," I say. But I do.

I've downloaded them from the Utah Department of Corrections. I've downloaded them from Amazon. I've downloaded them from the other final girls in the group. I've downloaded them from Dr. Carol.

My mouth tastes like garbage. I was so arrogant to think I was safe. Arrogant and stupid, the way I was before I met the Walkers. The world has gotten more sophisticated and I haven't kept up. While I was guarding my door they snuck in through my computer windows.

"Get unplugged," I say, taking out my multitool, angry and curt.

He puts his laptop to sleep and disconnects the cables. I unscrew the back of my CPU and take out the hard drive, my screwdriver constantly slipping out of the tiny screw slots. By the time I'm done, the knuckles on my right hand are shredded and sore. I grab Fine, tuck the hard drive into my bag, then close up the CPU and take it with us.

"Leave it," Skye says. "It's useless."

I don't answer. I close the padlock behind us, my pupils dilating painfully in the bright hall, and I replace the crime scene tape, trying to make it look like no one was ever inside. There's nothing I can do about the Burbank police seal, but hopefully they'll chalk it up to nosy journalists with flexible ethics.

We truck the CPU down the fire stairs, Skye complaining in whispers all the way that this is stupid, that I don't have to take it, but he's a kid. What does he know? Some cop will come back at some point and if this is sitting there with its hard drive missing even the geniuses in the Burbank PD will realize I came back to get it because it's important. And I don't want anyone looking for my hard drive.

Because it's got my book on it.

B ack in Skye's car, I put the CPU in his back seat and peel off a hundred dollars.

"Here," I say. "An extra hundred to toss that in a dumpster at a McDonald's or a Jack in the Box. Any fast-food place. Their garbage gets picked up by private contractors later tonight or early in the morning so it'll be gone faster."

"Where are you going?" he asks.

I peel off another hundred.

"This is for giving me a ride out to Bel Air and not telling your mother."

"I don't know if I can do that," he says. "We keep a pretty honest house."

I peel off sixty more.

"Do you have a number where I can reach you?" he asks, taking the money.

"Why?"

"I'll keep you in the loop," he says. "Fill you in on whatever my mom knows."

"No," I say. "After you drop me off, your whole family should stay far away from us."

"Is it always so dramatic with you guys?" Skye asks.

"No," I say. "But it's never safe. The things that happened to us never end."

Standing outside makes me nervous, so I get on the floor. Skye slides behind the wheel and locks the doors. Good. He's learning.

"I feel sorry for you," he says as we pull out of the parking lot. "My mom talks about the six of you all the time. It doesn't sound like much of a life. Why don't they just execute the guys who did this to you? Then you could actually move on."

"It'd just be someone else," I say, putting Fine on the seat. "At least this way I know where the threat is coming from."

"Are those guys really that scary?" he asks.

"Scarier than you can ever imagine," I answer.

He stares down at me.

"You look like an idiot. Come on, it's totally dark."

For some reason looking like an idiot makes me feel self-conscious in front of this kid. Not a kid. He's twenty-six years old. By the time I was his age my life was pretty much over. I hoist myself up into the seat, careful not to hit the gearshift, and strap on the seat belt.

"Doesn't that feel better?" he asks. "It's almost like you're a normal person."

He throws me a smile. This kid's a charmer. I give him my best smile back, but even I know it's not worth much.

We drive for almost forty-five minutes. We get onto the 405 and head for the hills. I hate being outside this way, but at least moving seventy-five miles an hour on the freeway feels like the odds are more in my favor. We turn off into the boring little neighborhoods that cluster around Sunset, pass UCLA, and head through the West Gate, which feels like driving onto some old studio backlot, and then we're lifting off into the hills.

I haven't been around a stranger like this in sixteen years. It lulls me. It feels normal. I check the back seat to make sure no one's hiding there. Then I check it again. Layers of my skin peel off and flutter away behind me onto the shoulder of the road. I risk a look over at Skye. He's got Tommy's profile. It reminds me of how different things could have been, of what a different person I might have become, and it takes everything inside me not to reach out and lay my hand over his on the gearshift.

I feel nervous, twitchy, like I want to talk. My skin crackles, galvanized, and little prickles run up and down my forearms. I keep myself under control. I wait until we're a few blocks from my destination before speaking.

"Drop me at the corner," I say.

He pulls up and puts the car in park. We sit in the front seat like lovers at the end of a first date. The moment becomes loaded with meaning. It becomes uncomfortable. I see the peach fuzz on his cheek, backlit gold by the streetlight. He's looking at me, and my breathing is high and tight in my chest.

He has no armor. No protection. He looks like Tommy right before the doorbell rang that night. Suddenly, I want to give him something, something to keep him safe, something he can remember me by. Something that would be just his, that might make the difference if anything ever happened to him, that might keep him from turning into one of us.

I lean over and he gets very still. His chest stops moving. I press my mouth to his ear, and feel my warm, moist breath cupped by the coral-pink curl of his ear.

"Don't ever let your guard down."

It isn't much, but it's all I have.

Then I push myself out of his car and I'm gone.

Unless they're David Foster Wallace, no one wants the reporter to be part of his story, but the first step to understanding the crazy, mixed-up world of Heather DeLuca is to understand how she turned arranging this interview into a piece of performance art. Contacted via Facebook, her opening act was to unleash a mind-boggling 46 messages during which she (a) promised to reveal never-before-told details of her story, (b) assured this reporter she had physical evidence that would overturn the conviction of Rudolph Kring, the man currently serving six consecutive life sentences for the "Dream King" killings, (c) offered to be the subject of a photo shoot at the now-closed elementary school that served as Kring's home/torture dungeon, and (d) demanded $47,832 for all of the above.

The conversation continued via text message, fax machine, and telephone, and throughout that process Ms. DeLuca kept lowering her fee until we arrived at the following exclusive interview. Final price? $450.

So if you, the reader, find the ensuing kamikaze assault on common sense, spiked with squalid nonsense, demonstrably false claims, and tasteless conspiracy theories disturbing, upsetting, or just downright grotesque, please remember you're getting Ms. DeLuca at a $47,382 discount.

Even then, you might feel like the price is too high.

14

—"The American Dream Girl's Nightmare Life" by Rusty Squires III,
The Believer, August 2008

THE FINAL GIRL SUPPORT GROUP VIII:
Night of the Final Girls

I don't move until I hear Skye make a three-point turn, brake lights flaring against the trees, then he's heading back down the hill, and I step backward into the shrubbery and wait, scoping the street, making sure he doesn't come back, making sure no one is following me.

My go bag is heavy with the hard drive and it presses into the small of my back. It weighs a ton. Why shouldn't it? It's full of everyone's secrets.

I blame Russell Thorn. He was one of those bottom-feeders who viewed a talking-head slot on CNN as a career high. He'd interviewed almost all of us at some point, and along the way he'd figured out that I made extra money self-publishing romance ebooks under a couple of fake names. It's a bad joke, right? A woman who's never had a serious relationship writing about secret billionaires' second chances with their high school sweethearts, or rugged ranchers and the free-spirited animal rights activists who break their hearts. I don't disagree, but I'm good at it, and I need to make a living. Maybe I'm good at it because for me, all romance is a fantasy. I don't have any real-life experience to get in the way.

Russell got in touch and tried to blackmail me without blackmailing me.

"I don't know what to do, Lynnette," he said over the phone. "I could sell this article to a big outlet, maybe get a book deal."

"If you go public I can't write anymore," I said, nauseated at the thought of being stripped naked in public again, of every stalker and gutter-crawling media creep thinking Lynnette Tarkington is just a girl who wanted to find true love. I'd have to delete everything. Years of work. "I need to pay my rent."

"If you want me to spike it, you need to offer me something of comparable value," he said.

"Like what?" I asked.

"Why not bring about the demise of two birds with one stone?" Russell suggested, pretending this hadn't been his plan all along. "Why don't we co-author a little literary endeavor of our own?"

He promised he could get us a six-figure advance for a book giving the inside scoop on final girls with both our names on the cover, but it had to contain new material and it had to be about more than me. The title just popped into my head: *The Final Girl Support Group*. Dr. Carol had done well building a career based on her work with trauma survivors like us; maybe it was time I cashed in, too? I told him to go ahead and field offers, but to keep it quiet. I think he envisioned that I'd feed him information and he'd turn it into deathless prose, but after I hung up I realized: what did I need Russell Thorn for?

I decided to write the book myself and once he came up with an offer I'd do an end run around him and approach the publisher directly. It was a sleazy move, but Russell was a sleazy guy. Then I started writing and changed my mind.

Normally I write fantasies involving helicopter skiing and private islands, but writing about something that cut this close to the bone destroyed my defenses. Everything came out: Dani's guilt, Heather's addictions, Julia's intellectual pretensions, Marilyn's denial, Michelle's cancer, Dr. Carol's hunger for celebrity. I wrote it in a white-hot burst and immediately regretted every word. Sentence by sentence, it was nothing but betrayal. I couldn't publish it, no matter how badly I needed the money, so I cut off all contact with Russell and buried the document deep in my hard drive. I can't face throwing my writing away, and I foolishly thought it was safe, but I should have known that none of us is ever really safe.

Russell went berserk trying to get in touch, but I just blocked his number and put his email address into my spam filter. He must have been humiliated, having to go back to some editor empty-handed, and humiliation is a trigger for men. Did Russell stage the scene in my apartment? Was he wearing a bulletproof vest? Was he really dead when I ran away? Did he steal the book off my hard drive? It makes no sense for him to take it and then wait for Julia, though. But who else knew about the book? I never should have written that book.

Every few months, I reread the pages I wrote and sometimes add something new, but I know the only right thing to do is to drag the document into the trash. Somehow I never got around to it and now someone has gotten their hands on it and they know more about our lives than they should, and Dr. Carol wants to take me to the cops so I'm running to the only safe place I know anymore.

The street is clear, so I head uphill, going slow like I'm out for a casual stroll carrying a pepper plant in a soup pot, although the only people who walk in Bel Air either have a dog leash in their hands or a leaf blower strapped to their backs.

I stop at the corner and check out the entrance. Next to the front gate is a linebacker in a black Tom Ford suit and steel-toed combat boots wearing an earpiece. She's hired extra security. Smart. I decide to go over the wall. I hide Fine in some bushes, much to his irritation, and then I take a running start, jump up, catch a mass of creeper vines clinging to her enormous privacy wall, and haul myself up.

The leaves rustle too loudly and I pause at the top to make sure no one heard. I'm clear, but it's too high to jump, so I turn around and hang by my hands, dropping into the bushes on the other side.

I land on a bush and it sends me stumbling into another bush, and then I'm eating dirt. I stagger to my feet and get away from my landing zone as fast as possible. I figure with a guard at the gate I'll go in the front door, but as I get closer to the long private drive I realize she's running valet service.

Shit.

Marilyn's having a party.

You don't separate Heather from her drugs, or Dani from Michelle, or Julia from her feminist theory, and you don't separate Marilyn Torres from her social life. It's her religion. The week she got into that van to head out into the Middle of Nowhere, Texas, all she was dreaming about was being a debutante. She'd already spent months practicing the Texas Dip for her debut at the Women's Symphony League of Austin Jewel Ball.

But the rumor had been going around that someone was digging up graves and desecrating cadavers, and the thought that the mummified remains of the family patriarch might wind up wired to a headstone with his picture on the front page of the paper was enough to send Marilyn's mother to bed with Valium in one hand and vodka in the other. After all, they were some of the original Spanish land grantees in Texas. They had an image to uphold. So Marilyn, her brother, and three friends headed off into that broiling hot summer day to make sure that Granddaddy Torres's corpse was still reposing respectably underground.

That was when one old Austin family ran into another.

I try to avoid stereotypes, but in the case of the Hansen family they literally were inbred rednecks. Former slaughterhouse owners fallen on hard times a couple of generations back, their last women had died off earlier that year and the boys were feeling the need to breed. Here came this van full of firm young flesh and they fell on it like starving tourists at an all-you-can-eat buffet.

There are two lines you can't come back from once you cross them. Killing people is one. Eating people is the other. Marilyn's talked about what happened in group before, a long time ago, back at the beginning, and a lot of it had to do with straight razors, and being forced to wear a leather suit made out of human skin, and sledgehammers, and rendering vats. Most of us try not to remember the details.

Marilyn was the only one who survived. From July to August she stayed in her room, hiding from the press, then two weeks before the Jewel Ball she emerged and declared that she was going to the dance. Her parents warned her against it, her doctors warned her against it, the police warned her against it, but she went, and on the night of the ball she wore her big puffy white dress and while Johnny Mercer sang "Moon River" she folded like a rose and executed a perfect Texas Dip. A few folks called her shallow, but we know why she did it. Some people may have seen her do the Texas Dip that night, but us final girls all saw a raised middle finger aimed at the Hansens.

A year later, the surviving members of the Hansen family showed up at the radio station where Marilyn had gotten a job as a late-night DJ, hoping to anchor the local news one day. She made short work of Uncle Tex and the police took care of Viper, but Buddy chased her up the broadcast antenna. She Maced him in the face and sent him plunging eighty-five feet onto a squad car.

It's hard to hold your head up in society after something like that, so she moved to Dallas and then, after a failed first marriage, tried L.A., where she set her sights on the son of the founder of Rehabilitation America Partners, a private company that owns and operates forty-eight correctional facilities in thirty states, running something like eighty-five thousand beds. Now she's a committed vegan, an ardent social climber, and monstrously rich. And tonight, all three of those parts of her personality have converged at this party.

Another Escalade with tinted windows cruises to a stop, the driver comes around and opens the back door, and a fresh and dewy young woman in a peach gown gets out, led by an elderly mummy in a tuxedo who holds on to her arm like a leash. The driver gets back into his land yacht and cruises away and I get a wash of party sounds as the mummy and his shimmering pet pass into the house.

I really, really, really hate to break up Marilyn's big event, but more important things are happening. I decide that I'll slip around back, where there'll be less security, find her, and discreetly have a word. She might be angry with me at first, but once I've warned her about what's happening I'll ask her to let me stay. Just until I know where I'm going next. She can't say no.

"Excuse me," a man calls from behind. "May I help you?"

I don't even look. I know what security sounds like. I turn to my left and make my way down the shadowy side of the house, over the grass, toward the lights and laughter in the backyard. It feels like I'm backstage, getting ready to step into the spotlight.

"Excuse me," the man says, and his voice is closer this time.

Before I can break into a jog, a hand clamps down on my shoulder.

"Stop—"

I don't let him finish. I spin, brushing his arm off and stepping in close to deliver a knee to his balls. He twists and takes my knee on his thigh. He's a big guy in a dark suit and I panic. I reach for my fanny pack and my gun; I should have had it drawn in the first place. Before I can yank my zipper, he grabs my wrist and rotates my forearm so it's facing up, putting pressure on my elbow. I should have kept my distance because once a man gets his hands on you it's all over.

I try for my fanny pack with my left hand, but he gets my right arm in a wrist lock that commands my full attention, pushing my fingers back toward my chest like he's folding my palm flush with the inside of my wrist. My radius and ulna creak from the strain. He puts me on my knees, then folds me over onto my stomach, using my hyperextended wrist to control me.

Before I know it, his foot is on the small of my back, my fanny pack is unclipped and out of reach, and he's on his earpiece.

"We've got an intruder, armed," he says, low and urgent.

I stretch, reaching for the razor blade taped to my ankle, and he shifts his weight and brings his other foot down on my wrist.

One thing I have to say about Marilyn, she pays for top-shelf security.

Flashlight beams hit my face and someone zip-ties my wrists together. This has all gone wrong. What are they going to do to me? I try to struggle but they keep me in place with no effort.

"Call the police," one of them says. "We'll put her in the garage until they get here."

There's a pause and then scattered mutterings of "Ma'am," "Ma'am." One of them rocks me up off the ground so I'm seated, bound wrists behind me. In front of me stands Marilyn in a pale gray flowing thing that looks expensive. Constructed of well-bred bones, deeply moisturized skin, and a fabulous thick mane of dark hair, she's about the size of one of these security creeps' biceps.

"Oh, Lynne." She sighs. There's a glass of wine in one of her hands. "It is so sweet of you to drop by, but you can't be here tonight."

"We have to talk," I say.

"Okay, miss," one of the bruisers says to me. "You need to stop speaking right now."

I start to scream. That'll bring someone running.

The second my wail splits the air, Marilyn's face looks stricken, and one of the goons drops to a knee and clamps his hand over my mouth.

"Bring her around back," Marilyn says. "We'll put her in the guest cottage." She turns to me. "We'll talk later, sweetie?"

I bite the soft salty palm over my face, grinding my teeth down, really sawing through his flesh. He doesn't flinch.

"If I have him take his hand off, will you be quiet?" Marilyn asks.

I nod. He takes his hand off. I start to scream.

"Lynnette!" Marilyn snaps. I stop screaming. "I have guests! Whatever you've come for can wait. I am broken up about Adrienne and Julia, too, and we can talk later and that will be wonderful, but right now this is a benefit for retired circus animals. It is very important to me, do you understand? These lions have suffered enough."

"One hour," I say.

"Of course." She sighs again. "You are such a sweetheart to want to come and visit."

She leans forward and gives me a big "Mwah" on my cheek, leaving lipstick behind. Here behind her walls with her cameras and her security team she can be the flighty socialite she always wanted to be.

Security creeps lift me to my feet and lead me around the perimeter of the backyard.

"Unclip her hands," Marilyn says. "This isn't one of Jerry's prisons."

"One hour," I remind her as a goon snips my cuffs off.

We skirt the edge of the lights. The yard sprawls on my right, strung with Chinese lanterns and rich old men and trophy wives standing under tall metal outdoor heaters that loom like watchtowers. No one's watching their backs, or checking the exits, or showing any spatial awareness what-soever. On my left are the lights of Los Angeles, scattered across the blackness below the hills, looking cleaner and crisper than they have any right to be. The view from up here can trick you into thinking the world is a beautiful place.

"Keep going," one of the goons says, propelling me forward with a hand in the small of my back.

Up ahead, on the other side of the glowing blue pool, is a two-story Mediterranean cottage with a red tile roof. It's big enough for a small family. In the glow of paper lanterns hanging from the trees I see a goon standing at parade rest by its French doors, hands clasped behind his back.

They pop the door's hermetic seal and I get professionally propelled out of the cool night air and into the dry warmth of central heating. The guest house is lit up, full of Mission furniture, laid with heavy terra-cotta floor tiles, walls covered in tasteful Mexican art that's all colored dots and electric lines. There are cut metal sculptures peeled into the shape of rab-bits, and jaguars, and parrots, and snakes tucked into all the corners. It's a cottage full of things I could never afford, things I could never own. Nice things. Settled things. The kind of things you have when you don't need to be able to run out the door the second trouble comes looking for you. The kind of things you have when you can afford the security to protect them.

In the middle of all this jealousy-inducing luxury sits Heather, feet on the coffee table, watching TV, smoking a cigarette and ashing on the floor.

She looks up at me, all casual cool.

"What's up, Lynne?" she asks. "Shitty party, right?"

In this age of Glocks and AR-15s, of pipe bombs and high-capacity magazines, the arsenals of our movie monsters seem quaint. Teddy and his machete stalking campers in *Summer Slaughter*, the Babysitter Murderer with his butcher's blade, the masked killers of the *Stab* franchise and their hunting knives. Why do they chalk up such low body counts with these crude implements when they could mow down dozens of victims with a semiautomatic rifle? Why do their weapons become increasingly baroque in later installments: curling irons and ice skates, menorahs and outdoor grills?

The reason is simple: we need to believe death has meaning. Each murder must be unique, each victim must meet his killer one-on-one, each slaying must be given an appropriate amount of screen time. The real violence of a child entering a school cafeteria and spraying bullets at random is too cruel. It reduces human beings to a body count; it robs life of all individuality. It is the ultimate statement that we cannot abide: death is devoid of meaning, and it will swallow everything in the end. Against that nihilism, the violence in a slasher film is a comforting blanket drawn up against the chill of the infinite moral void of reality.

—"Slasher Movies in the Age of Mass Shootings" by David Thomas,
Film Violence & Film Art: A Manifesto, 2007

THE FINAL GIRL SUPPORT GROUP IX:
Final Girl vs. Final Girl

I'm so surprised that I can't say anything for a full minute, but that's okay. Heather does all the talking for me.

"Hi, Heather," she says, in a mocking voice that I think is meant to be me. "Nice to see you, too. So glad you're alive. You're so smart to come to Marilyn's. I've been running around the city all day like a dumb bitch."

There's a kitchen behind a pass-through counter on my right, a dark hallway on my left, the living room in front of me with French doors looking out into the dark woods. I step over Heather's legs and yank the curtains closed.

"I liked those open," Heather says.

There's no way to block the kitchen windows or the floor-to-ceiling windows wrapped around the dining nook. The fridge is empty except for a shriveled lemon, a box of Arm & Hammer, and a case of Perrier. I find steak knives in the third drawer I open. I take two.

"Is there a reason you're messing up my action?" Heather asks.

I go into the hallway and start checking the rest of the house.

"That's a waste of time because you're leaving," Heather calls after me.

Two rooms upstairs, both empty. I check the closets, under the beds, behind the shower curtain in the shared bathroom, underneath the sink.

Everywhere I go I leave the lights burning. I can't tolerate any shadows. I can't leave any hiding places. I go back downstairs.

"Does this door lock?" I ask, trying to find a deadbolt on the front door.

"I hope not," Heather says, lighting another cigarette off her first. "That'll just slow you down if I get shot and you have to run away real fast and leave me bleeding to death on the floor."

I guess she heard about Julia.

"It was a combat situation," I say, taking a step toward her, trying to disguise my shame with anger. "I had to make an instant decision." She makes eye contact, and I stop advancing and lamely add, "I made sure Julia was okay."

"I bet you did, Cowardly Lion," she says, dropping her butt in a Perrier bottle, where it sizzles. "Does Marilyn even know you're here?"

"She told me to wait," I say, dropping down to sit against the wall by the front door. It's the only place that's out of the sightlines of all those wide-open kitchen windows. "She said she'd talk to me in fifty minutes."

"Yeah, well," Heather says. "One person is a houseguest, two is a crowd, and I was here first."

"Why are you here?" I ask.

"My fucking house exploded and all my shit burned up?" she says. "I'm coming to Marilyn's. The bitch shits money. Where'd you go? Got Julia shot and ran away crying like a little baby? Well, there's no room at Casa Marilyn."

"I need to talk to Marilyn," I say. "This is serious."

"Fuck yeah, it's serious," Heather says. "Did you see upstairs? There's a fucking Jacuzzi. You're going to have to drag me out of this motherfucker, and I will fight you all the way."

"Do you have any idea what's going on?" I ask.

"I know exactly what's going on," Heather says. "Marilyn's got so much house she doesn't know what to do with it. I figure I'm doing her a favor staying here while Jerry's away. Camp out in this fly little guest house for the duration. She's got servants to do whatever the fuck I want.

She and me, we'll turtle down until all this blows over. I'd say you could stick around and watch my back but I don't have a death wish."

"The police are looking for you," I tell her.

"What's new?" she says. "I slept in the woods behind the halfway house. Okay, honesty time: I fucking passed out. After group? You bitches harshed my sobriety. Adrienne gone? That's the kind of shit that makes me need to drink. So I cadged some cash, bought a little Smirnoff Ice, and partied in the woods. I wake up with a killer headache and stroll home just in time to see everything I own on fire and cops crawling all over the place. I get in a cab and forty-five bucks later it's 'Yo homes, smell ya later, I'm the Fresh Prince of Bel-Air.'"

"Someone is gunning for all of us," I say.

"I'm going to start swimming laps," Heather says. "Get in shape. Lose some of this flab."

She pinches an invisible roll of fat around the top of her jeans and shakes it. Heather is a bundle of wire coat hangers squeezed into jeans that are more rip than jean, and covered in bruises, but in her head she still has all her baby fat from high school.

"We need to figure out a strategy," I say, ignoring her dysfunction.

"A strategy?" Heather laughs, and rummages in her purse. She pulls out a hand-rolled cigarette and lights it off her cigarette. From the smell, it's not tobacco. "What're you going to do? Fucking dress up like Batgirl and go swing around the city?"

"How did this person know where your halfway house was?" I ask. "How'd they know where Adrienne lived?"

But even as I say it I know where: my computer. I must have had their addresses in there somewhere.

"Halfway houses are full of chain smokers," Heather says. "They burn down all the time. Stop trying to be a hero. Everyone feels sorry for you because you're a paranoid with OCD. Obsessive-compulsive disorder."

"I know what OCD is," I say.

"I know what OCD is," she mimics. "Fucking Forrest Gump over here, you can barely walk through a door without having a nervous break-down and you're going to help anyone? You can hardly dress yourself. You look like a fucking twelve-year-old boy. The second the shit hits the fan you bolt like Bambi."

"We have to watch out for each other," I say.

"That's beautiful," she says. "But you're just sick enough to have ar-ranged this whole thing to keep group together. Out of everyone, you are the absolute fucking worst at letting go of the past."

Then, as if the universe is ganging up with Heather to prove her point, my past is on TV.

"Turn it up," I say.

"Turn it up yourself," Heather says, and then she turns to the plasma screen. "Holy shit, that's your boyfriend."

Garrett P. Cannon is on the screen and I'm frozen. Time has not been kind. He's wearing a cowboy hat and a bolo tie, everything in creams and dove grays, and he's grown a bushy white mustache, probably to give his withered old face some volume. His neck hangs slack and loose. He's still bleaching his teeth, but they look too white against his sunburned skin.

The slugline across the bottom of the screen reads *Shocking Revela-tions in Silent Night Slayings*. I stare, hypnotized by Garrett's wet, moving mouth, the way he's basking in the cameras like a reptile sunning itself on a rock. If there's one person I never wanted to see again, it's him.

His voice is the size of a mouse's. I can't help myself. I find the remote and turn it up.

". . . saying for years this case don't smell right," he drawls. "And after much tenacious investigation on my part I have uncovered explosive new information."

"At least someone's got a hard-on for you," Heather says.

"Without a doubt we will be seeking Lynnette Tarkington for further questioning," Garrett continues. "I am receiving unprecedented coopera-tion from the police in Los Angeles County and we are attempting to locate Miss Tarkington right this minute. In Utah, justice wears cowboy boots, and they're always ready to kick *BLEEP*."

The camera flashes back to an anchor gazing earnestly into the lens.

"Garrett P. Cannon, law enforcement hero, commenting on explosive new information in the Silent Night Slayings. Tune in tomorrow, when Nancy Grace gives her take."

"Have they said what it is?" I ask.

"Dude, didn't you hear?" Heather says, taking a deep pull on her joint. "There's explosive new information. Probably that you were the one killing people, you little psycho."

Whatever this is, I know they don't have anything. If they did, Garrett wouldn't have been able to keep his mouth shut. The fact that he's being coy means that he has a crummy hand and wants to keep the cameras on him for as long as possible. The last time Garrett had "explosive new information," it was that he'd written the script for the franchise reboot.

"This is so fucking boring," Heather says. "I need a drink. Nothing materialized in that fucking fridge in the last five minutes, did it?"

She stands up, checks the fridge, slams it, grabs her bag, opens the front door, and gets immediately swarmed by black-suited security.

"Miss, I'm going to have to ask you to go back inside," the short, wide, bald guy blocking the doorway says.

"Sir," Heather says. "I'm going to have to ask you to stick your dick up your ass."

"Miss . . ." he says. "I'm not going to ask you again."

"Let me tell you what I'm going to do," Heather says. "I'm going into that party to speak to my very good motherfucking friend, Mrs. Marilyn Blake, who pays your motherfucking salary. If you get in my way I'm going to jump in that pool, whip out my tits, and let this bunch of Charity Barbies get an eyeful of what natural Bs look like."

Short and Stocky wraps a hand around her biceps and squeezes.

"Ow, motherfucker," Heather hisses. "I'll scream."

"Can I get assistance at station twelve," Short and Stocky says into his earpiece.

I stay seated and out of trouble. I need a place to sleep tonight. Dani's safe in jail, Julia's probably under police protection in the hospital, and while I don't like the thought of Marilyn, Heather, and me bunched up in one location, at least this one's secure.

Behind Short and Stocky I see identical twin linebackers trotting toward us, Marilyn striding behind them, and then they're filling the door, pushing their way through, pushing Heather back.

"I'm sorry, Mrs. Blake," Short and Stocky says as Marilyn emerges from between the twins.

Marilyn's mouth smiles, her perfect teeth catch the light, her cheeks dimple.

"That's all right, Tom," she coos, and then she looks at me and her eyes are dead. "I told you to wait here."

"Lynne got hungry, dude," Heather says. "Have you ever tried to stop her? She's like the fucking Terminator."

"You will both stay here until I come for you," Marilyn says, her lips barely moving. "That is not up for discussion."

"You can't keep us locked up like one of your prisoners," Heather says.

"Like what?" she asks. "You arrive at my house and I have to pay your taxi fare and I give you a place to stay and you're a prisoner?"

"These dudes marched Lynnette in here like Nazis," Heather says, appealing to me.

"I'm not involved," I say. "I just need a place to stay."

"Is that all?" Marilyn tears a strip off me. "You sneak over my wall with a gun like a home invader because you want a sleepover? The only reason I haven't called the police is because there are some very sick, very old lions who need homes and the people who will pay for them do not like a scene."

"Marilyn," I say. "I need a place for one night. We'll be good."

She leans in.

"If I weren't having a party"—she smiles—"I would get Jerry's security detail to toss you out on your fannies while I sip white wine and laugh."

The security guards perk up.

"Screw you," Heather says, and starts pushing forward.

She hasn't taken two steps before all the security guys have her arms twisted up behind her back.

"I'm not going to repeat myself," Marilyn says as she turns to go. "Stay."

The security guys toss Heather onto the couch and are out the door before she even stops bouncing.

"You can't send us to our room, Mom!" Heather screams, running to the door as they slam it in her face.

It's locked. She rants for five full minutes and then the door opens and a stream of staff pour inside while the three security guys block the door. They lay out platters on the pass-through: ginger jelly sandwiches on gluten-free buns, mushroom rice balls, vegetable sushi rolls. Of course everything's vegan. Heather makes pointed personal comments about each and every person laying out food, and only stops when the last cater waiter puts three bottles of champagne in the fridge.

"Compliments of the lady of the house," he says, and then there's a puff of smoke and the room is empty and the door is locked and I'm stuffing my face. Before the first bite, I didn't realize how hungry I was.

Heather pours a water glass full of champagne and goes back to running me down.

"I had a good thing going until you showed up," Heather says. "You know what? You're an asshole, Lynne. I've always fucking thought that."

I keep eating. I need my calories in case I have to run.

"You're so quiet and everyone thinks you're all sad and fucked in the head," Heather says. "But I bet you know a lot more about what the fuck is going on than you're telling."

Heather and I used to be close, but when I realized how unstable she was I started keeping my distance. The things that happened to all of us are bad enough, but she's the only one who feels a need to embellish. Ever since I pulled away she's made me her target. It's not her fault, it's the drugs. Still, it makes me nervous that she thinks I know more about what's going on than I'm saying. Because I do.

As unpleasant as she is, I stay with Heather. Someone once told me that all you have to do to keep from being eaten by a bear is run faster than your friend. Same principle.

A lot of insults and two bottles of champagne later, the door breaks its seal and Marilyn storms through with a glass of ice water in one hand, wearing an enormous terry-cloth robe, wrapped and tucked and belted around her in big, loose, fluffy loops. Behind her is a maid carrying Fine in his pot.

"Does this belong to either of you?" Marilyn snaps. "Security found it outside."

I almost cheer, but instead I keep my mouth shut and take the pot in both hands.

"Thanks," I mumble.

"Did you get your fucking lion money?" Heather slurs, waving her glass at Marilyn.

Marilyn smacks it out of Heather's hand and it goes spinning into the wall. Champagne mists my face.

"What the hell?" Heather asks. She tries to stand, but she's too drunk and her ass pulls her right back down again.

"It's one a.m.," Marilyn spits. "And my house is empty. Do you know what kind of fund-raiser ends at one? A failed one. I spent an ungodly amount of money but my fund-raiser failed because about an hour after this one"—here she turns on me—"climbed over my wall with a gun and her stupid houseplant, the paparazzi showed up in my drive."

"I told you she's trouble," Heather slurs, pointing one wavering finger at me.

"They want to know why two final girls are hiding in my guest house,"

Marilyn snaps. "They know both your names, so I'm holding you both responsible."

"How'd they know we were here?" I ask.

"They followed you," she says. "Because you are sloppy and inconsiderate."

I didn't see anyone behind Skye and me, but maybe I missed them? Maybe one of those news vans picked us up at my house and followed us here? I've been missing too much lately. I feel old and slow and stupid.

"This is bad," I say. "That reporter, Russell Thorn, got shot in my apartment. Then they tried to shoot me. Then they shot Julia and burned down Heather's halfway house. Now they know we're here."

"They, they, they," Marilyn says. "Are you off your meds again?"

"I don't take meds," I say, jaw tight.

"Well, now we know your problem," Marilyn says.

"Someone's trying to kill us," I say. "That's what I came here to say. You can handle that however you want. I just need a safe place for one night."

A snore splits the room. Heather has passed out on the sofa. The two of us look at her for a minute, and then Marilyn takes a long pull on her glass. It's not ice water, I realize. It's vodka.

"Of course you can stay here tonight," Marilyn says, and for the first time she sounds tired. "I just really wanted to help those lions."

There's silence for a minute, except for Heather's snoring.

"Have you heard anything about Michelle?" she asks.

I know that Marilyn and Dani are close. The two of them were in touch by phone for years before group started. Dani has a place in her heart and that means Michelle does, too.

"She's in hospice," I say.

And then my arms and chest fill up with ice water because that means everyone's someplace safe except Michelle.

Marilyn massages the bridge of her nose with two fingers.

"I need to process this," she says. "I'll make some calls in the morning.

We will talk then. The house is alarmed, and security patrols all night, so please do not leave the guest house."

I feel bad leaving Heather in a room with so many windows, but she's too heavy for me to move. I turn out the lights and check the doors, then go upstairs. I hide the hard drive inside the box springs of the guest bedroom bed, and then I sleep in the bathtub with the door locked and the lights on.

I lie in the bathtub and decide to get out of here in the morning before anyone else is awake. I'll leave before the sun is up. I tell myself there's nothing I can do for Michelle. I can't be responsible for other people. I can barely be responsible for myself.

Fine sits on the counter in his pot, but he's so quiet I worry he's in shock. Too much change for one day. It's not healthy.

I wake up with Heather banging on the bathroom door.

"I gotta go, asshole," she yells as I scrabble awake, adrenaline pumping.

"Use the other one," I yell back, disoriented, voice shaking. The sun's already high on the tiles. I overslept.

"I want to use this one," she screams.

She won't stop pounding on the door until I drag myself out.

"Freak," she says, seeing my blankets and pillow in the tub.

I look out the window. It's quiet outside, just a few birds. The sunlight is liquid gold, steam rising off the surface of the heated pool. It's way too late to run.

I go downstairs and walk through the cool morning air to the house. Inside the sandstone kitchen the black marble island is loaded with a fruit platter, bagels, cream cheese. No matter what, Marilyn can't help it, she has to be a host.

"I do not have the capacity for rudeness," she says from the stairs. I didn't see her there. "Get a plate. There's tea outside by the coffee."

We sit outside at a wooden table under a rough-beamed pavilion attached to the side of her house. Plastic bubbles containing cameras hang from the corners of her roof; every window is alarmed. Two giants in sweat suits stand on the edge of the yard.

"Now," she says. "I've had my second cup of coffee. Tell me why you think everyone is trying to kill us."

"I have to get going, Marilyn," I say. "Is there a back way out of here?"

"Do you think I'm James Bond?" she asks. "Talk to me and I'll get you out the front way later."

I explain what's been going on, leaving out my book. In the middle, Heather drifts up, then floats away to the kitchen, then reappears smoking a cigarette. Marilyn makes her sit far away until she finishes, and winces when Heather flicks her butt in the pool.

"I need to go," I say. "You guys are safe, Dani's in custody, Julia's protected, but I need to go."

I pray she doesn't remember Michelle.

"Good riddance," Heather says. "Finders keepers."

"I made some calls this morning and spoke to my attorney," Marilyn says. "He's spoken with someone at the sheriff's office who says Dani is safe, and while she won't be arraigned for a few days, she and Michelle can go home as soon as the judge hears her plea. Julia is in the hospital and they have security posted on her room. You two are probably both getting warrants issued later this morning, so after breakfast you'll both need to pack up and I can call you cars. Do you have enough cash?"

"I knew you'd fuck up my deal!" Heather bawls at me.

Then I can't help myself. I feel the obligations pulling on me like chains.

"Make sure they post a cop on Michelle's room," I say.

Marilyn immediately knows what I'm getting at.

"She's dying," Marilyn says. "There's no point in someone killing her."

"There are better and worse ways to die," I say because, again, I can't help myself.

"Cancer *is* the worse way," Marilyn says. "I'm not trying to be callous,

Lynne, but I cannot afford to be pulled into whatever episode you're having. Adrienne was murdered by someone with a grudge, Dani fired a weapon at a police officer, Heather was smoking crack in her basement and set her building on fire—"

"I was passed out in the woods behind my house!" Heather protests.

"Bless your heart, you were too high to remember," Marilyn says, then turns back to me. "You and Julia, well, I only have your word for what happened. For all I know you shot her by accident. You do have a tendency to wave guns around and you've always had a flair for melodrama."

"We have to check on Michelle first," I say, trying to buy time, but also it's true. "You know I'm right. We owe it to Dani to make sure she's safe."

I mean it. I really do. But also if I can get Marilyn to take us to hospice in one of her big armored SUVs, then I can slip away. It gives me a chance to get out of L.A. before the cops bring me in and ask questions about Garrett P. Cannon's explosive new information.

Marilyn looks out over Los Angeles. The guys in sweat suits are joking around with each other, pretending to push each other into the pool. Marilyn feels safe here. Jerry's money has allowed her to build a fantasy land where she can enjoy the luxury of pretending that my problems aren't her problems. But she wouldn't have lived this long if she couldn't tell fantasy from reality sometimes.

"I will go and see Michelle," she finally says. "I owe Dani that much. You two can come if you'd like. But after that, we go our separate ways. We have nothing in common, Lynnette. We can't keep clinging to the past."

"How do we get out of here with paparazzi all over your driveway?" I ask. "We can't lead whoever it is to Michelle."

Marilyn smiles.

"Did you really think I only had one way out of my house?"

GNOMECOMING

They're small, they wear red pointy caps, and they stand in our gardens. But this gnome (Linda Davis, *Willow*, *Time Bandits*) is ready to party! Five hundred years ago, a diminutive demon cursed this small Canadian town to never play music or face her wrath. But now the local teens have decided to hold a homecoming dance . . . or should we say a *Gnome*coming Dance? When the rock and roll beat re-awakens this tiny terror, she'll prove that *small* means *scary* in a bloody rampage that can only be stopped by the one girl at Moosejaw High who's still a virgin. Packed with cutting-edge make-up effects and high tech computer wizardry, with a hit soundtrack featuring songs by Club Nouveau, Platinum Blonde, L.A. Guns, Fine Young Cannibals, and more, *Gnomecoming* will prove that when it comes to bloody mayhem, there's no place like GNOME!

CFDC AND CINÉPIX FILM PROPERTIES PRESENT
A GORD LARONDELLE PRODUCTION OF A FILM BY DEAN TREMBLAY
LINDA DAVIS GNOMECOMING
MUSIC BY HEATHER WANG
COPRODUCED BY GOLDIE VAN AND RALPH SCHAEFFER
EXECUTIVE IN CHARGE OF PRODUCTION LORNE MACDONALD
BASED ON CHARACTERS INSPIRED BY
THE LIFE OF CHRISTINE MERCER
WRITTEN BY DARCY MILLINER
EXECUTIVE PRODUCER GORD LARONDELLE
PRODUCED BY DEVLIN RUAN
DIRECTED BY DEAN TREMBLAY

CDFC CINÉPIX
FILM PROPERTIES

RATED R
COLOR · RUNNING TIME 87 MINUTES

—*Gnomecoming*, VHS box copy, 1989

TFGSG X

No one goes home from a hospice, but even so St. Claire's Hospice feels like a funeral home. There's no sunlight, no clocks, no direct lighting, no sound above a solemn whisper. Everything is beige or gray. Crosses hang in every room, faded hotel-quality paintings of meadows hang in every hall, and an abundance of nurses scurry around silently on crepe-soled shoes. Plastic holders stuffed with pamphlets about dealing with grief are affixed to every vertical surface.

"This is extremely depressing," Marilyn says when we step off the elevator.

"I'm going to watch TV," Heather says like a teenager, and slouches off to find the lounge.

We let her go and head down the neutral corridor full of open doors, following the numbers to Michelle's. Each door reveals its own tiny drama. Family members glance up at me from their deathbed vigils, nurses brush past us as they glide from deathwatch to deathwatch, strained respiration rattles from rooms.

I don't like it here. I can't see the exits, I don't know what's around the corners, and we keep going deeper. I wish I hadn't had this idea.

Finally, we get to 1211. I expected a cop to be sitting at the door, or a notice posted, or something letting people know that Michelle is in danger because of Dani, but her door's not even closed. We push it open and step inside.

A husk lies in the middle of the bed, swaddled in sheets. There are no IVs, no catheters, no heart monitors or machines. She's beyond that now. Even Marilyn wilts a little. This is the room where Michelle will die.

"Do you think that's bothering her?" a nurse whispers.

Marilyn and I give a start. We didn't even notice her follow us inside. She's giving the cross on the wall at the foot of Michelle's bed a meaningful look.

"I'm sure she doesn't mind," Marilyn whispers, and then the nurse is gone, leaving us with the love of Dani's life. We approach the bed.

". . . Dani?" Michelle whispers.

She's yellow, her lips are chapped, her eyes burn with an intensity that stands out against her waxy skin. Marilyn puts one hand on Michelle's forehead and smooths back her gray hair.

"Dani wants to be here," Marilyn tells her. "I know she'd give anything for that to be possible right this minute."

Michelle's lips try to form words.

"Lynnette," Marilyn says. "Go ask the nurse for a little sponge and a cup of water. Do you want some ice chips to suck on, honey?"

Michelle nods.

"And get us some ice chips, too."

I go out in the hall, unsure where to get all this stuff. I head to the nurses' station and they jump to it like they were just waiting for me to ask. I feel sweaty. There are no windows but too many doors, too many halls. Michelle's room has no alternate exits. I don't know my escape route.

When I get back to the room with my foam cup of ice chips, my yellow sponge in a crackling plastic wrapper, and my bottle of off-brand water, the nurse is coming out with the cross tucked beneath her arm.

"Do you think she wants to see a rabbi?" she whispers.

"Why?" I ask, genuinely confused.

"We'll be fine," Marilyn says from inside the room. "Thank you."

The nurse gives a brisk nod, and she's gone again. I go inside and hand off everything to Marilyn, then hang around the foot of the bed, as far away from Michelle as I can get while Marilyn raises the head of the bed and holds the cup of ice chips to Michelle's lips, and then, while Michelle sucks on the ice, Marilyn pats the damp sponge across her cracked lips. I marvel. Where did Marilyn learn to do all of this? Michelle rolls her eyes to her and looks grateful.

"You just rest," Marilyn says, stroking her hair. "I know you're tired."

"Thank you . . ." Michelle croaks. ". . . I know . . . I'm not pretty."

Marilyn smiles.

"Well, neither is Dani, so you two are a perfect pair."

Michelle grimaces and pants a little and I realize that she's laughing. One of her hands comes out from underneath the blanket and scrabbles desperately, clutching at the air. Marilyn takes her hand.

"I . . . love you . . ." Michelle says.

"We love you, too," Marilyn says. "And I know Dani loves you very much. You're the best thing that ever happened to her."

"She . . . promised . . . I could . . . be home," Michelle says. "When this . . . happens . . ."

"I know," Marilyn says.

"I wanted . . . to see . . ." Michelle says. ". . . she planted . . . new . . . we never got . . . enough . . ."

She yawns, a big jaw-cracker.

"I know," Marilyn says. "None of us get enough time."

"Be right back," I mumble.

All the deaths I've ever seen were fast and messy. Tommy. Gillian. Mom. Dad. I've never been around this slow fade before. Can't Michelle avoid it? Can't she yank a cord and have it over with? I'm angry at her for forcing me to watch her die. I'm scared. I know what I have to do.

I find Heather at the end of the hall in an alcove, sprawled over two chairs. CNN plays on a donated television set, turned down low.

"Your boyfriend just gave a press conference," Heather says.

"We're getting Michelle out of here," I say.

"Fuck yeah," Heather says. "This place is the pits."

She pushes herself to her feet, glad to have a goal, satisfied to screw the system. I give the TV one more glance as we go and see a photo of me at sixteen, all acne and bad perm. I feel a trap closing around me. I want to be outside.

"Marilyn's cool with this?" Heather asks as we walk.

"She's totally cool," I lie.

We go back into the death trap. Marilyn has pulled the only chair up to the head of the bed and she's holding one of Michelle's hands in both of hers, resting her elbows on the mattress. She looks up. Heather and I stand there, awkwardly.

"So, we took a vote," I say. "And we're taking Michelle home."

"We're what?" Marilyn says.

"Is Dani . . . coming?" Michelle pants.

"No," I say.

"Yes," Marilyn says to Michelle, then turns on me. "We're not going anywhere. We're going to sit with Michelle until Dani gets here. We are not going to move this lady."

"Michelle," I say, bending over her, surprised she doesn't smell bad. "Dani isn't coming. Not for another day or two. But we can take you back to the ranch right now, if you want us to."

"I don't . . . think . . . they'll let . . ." she gasps, her eyes reading my face from left to right.

"That's not something you need to worry about," I say. "Dani is in jail. They are not letting her out today."

"You don't know that," Marilyn says. "She might already be on her way."

"Really, Marilyn? You really think they already let her out?"

"Well . . ." She pauses, drops her eyes back to Michelle's hand.

"Exactly," I say. "Michelle, Dani won't be here. But we can take you to the ranch. Right now. You can be home. All you have to do is say the word."

Michelle stares at me the way only a dying person can, totally focused on my eyes, no bullshit, all attention.

She nods.

"Dani's flowers . . ." she says.

"You want to see Dani's flowers?" I ask.

She nods. Her lips quiver around the word for a moment before she can say it.

". . . yes . . ."

"This is fucked up," Heather says.

"Excuse me, but what are you discussing?" the nurse says in a normal tone of voice that sounds embarrassingly loud. We didn't even hear her come in.

We all turn. I imagine we all look guilty. The nurse looks confused.

"Nothing you need to worry about," I say. "Can we get a wheelchair?"

"Well, no," she says. "I'm afraid Miss Gateway cannot be moved. We're keeping her comfortable but she must remain here."

"Okay," I say. "I'll get the wheelchair."

"We don't even know who you people are," the nurse says, looking from Heather to Marilyn.

I brush past her and walk out into the hall. There's an empty wheelchair sitting halfway down with a big white stencil on the back that reads NO. 43. I roll it back to the room. Marilyn is in a conversation with the nurse. Michelle's feet are jiggling restlessly beneath her blanket. Heather is pressing herself into the corner, probably wondering how she can swipe some pain meds.

"I can't let you do this," the nurse says to Marilyn as I park the chair at the head of the bed.

"You don't get a vote," I say.

She sizes up the situation, looking from Marilyn, to me, to the chair, to Michelle, and scurries out.

"I resent you putting me in this position," Marilyn says.

"Okay," I say. "Help me get her into the chair."

Marilyn doesn't move. Instead it's Heather who whips back the sheets. I'm terrified to see what's beneath the covers, but compared to my imagination Michelle doesn't look so bad. There's not much of her left, but it's all tucked inside her hospital gown. It makes me feel brave enough to touch her. I scoop her up, one arm under her back, one under her knees. She's very cold and she doesn't resist. I lift, and she's lighter than I imagined. I goose her bony ass on one of the arms of the wheelchair. Michelle grimaces.

I settle Michelle in the chair, and immediately she starts shaking.

"Get her blankets," I tell Heather.

We tuck the baby-blue blanket around Michelle's legs, and Heather finds another one in the closet. I lean Michelle forward, drop it behind her back, and drape it over her shoulders. Michelle makes another pained face.

"Let me do that," Marilyn snaps, exasperated by my ineptitude, and she tucks the blanket around Michelle and settles her back.

Michelle pulls on Marilyn's arm with one quavering hand.

"Thank . . . you," Michelle says. ". . . thank you . . ."

Marilyn straightens and pinches the bridge of her nose.

"You will have a lot to answer for," she says to me.

"You take point," I say, feeling right, feeling on mission. "Heather, bring up the rear. Down to the second floor, over to the parking garage, and then to the car."

I glare at Marilyn until she gives me a nod.

We roll out of the room in formation, me pushing the chair, Marilyn walking in front of us, Heather following a few steps behind. I left Julia and Fine behind. I won't leave Michelle. There's a scrum of doctors and nurses and orderlies by the nurses' station. They step into our path.

"Excuse us, please," Marilyn says as we push through. "I'm so sorry. We're in a rush."

They scatter, then regroup and follow, and I hear a chorus of "Who are you?" and "Where are you taking her?" Then Heather does her thing.

"Back off!" she shouts. "Just back off!"

I hear the *clickety-click* of a box cutter blade sliding out of its plastic handle, and I don't need to look back to know she's taking wild swings, keeping them all back. We roll quickly, Marilyn setting a fast pace, passing doors full of red-eyed, crying families wrapped deep in their own private dramas.

"Excuse us," Marilyn chirps as she brushes past nurses. "Pardon me. So sorry. If you don't mind? Thank you."

The elevator bank is up ahead, and we're almost there when I see two security goons coming down the hall from the opposite direction. They have giant bellies, green baseball caps, green windbreakers, and they both look like they're on the wrong side of fifty. This might be the fastest they've ever walked in their lives.

One of them slows to a stop, blocking the hall, holding up his hand with casual arrogance as if of course we're going to stop because he's a man in a jacket that says *Security* on the back.

"Girls," he says. "Party's over."

Marilyn reaches him first, and my heart leaps to see her pushing the call button as she speaks, pouring all that warm Texas honey into her voice.

"Sir," she says. "We are her good friends, and we're zipping her home to pick up some things. We'll be right back. They told us it was fine at the desk and I do so hope we haven't done anything wrong."

"This is a hospice," the smaller security goon says. "People don't go home."

"Well, she just needs a few things," Marilyn says.

"I don't care about that," the one with his hand out says, stepping forward and covering the call buttons so Marilyn can't push them anymore. The two goons crowd their big bellies around her. "You need to let the doctors take this patient back to her room."

"How do you know her?" the other security goon asks.

"We all belong to the same book club." Marilyn smiles sweetly.

The elevator dings and the door rumbles open. There's a teenaged girl with black-rimmed eyes standing against the back, a pack of cigarettes and lighter in one hand. Marilyn places her body between the security men and the wheelchair and Heather joins her, standing shoulder-to-shoulder.

"What the fuck is your problem?" Heather asks. "She wants out. Is this a fucking prison?"

I push the wheelchair onto the elevator behind them.

"Miss!" one of the goons shouts, suddenly frantic as he sees me getting away. "You can't do that. Miss!"

I stop next to the teenager, Michelle facing the back wall.

"Marilyn?" I say. "We're in."

She and Heather step back into the elevator and Heather starts jamming on the 2 button and *Door Close* at the same time. One of the guards makes the mistake of grabbing Marilyn by her arm. The door tries to close but bounces off his beefy biceps.

"I can't let you girls do this," he says.

Marilyn reaches into her purse and pulls out a small black cylinder. She touches it to his crotch. There's a snapping crackle and the man leaps back like he's been kicked by a mule, then he's sitting on the ground, crying.

"I am so sorry," Marilyn says. "I feel just awful about this."

The doors close and after a gut-twisting second the elevator starts to drop. There's silence for a moment and then:

"You zapped him in the nuts," the teenaged girl says, incredulous.

"Fucking A," Heather says.

"I want you to know that I deeply, deeply resent the position you've put me in," Marilyn tells me.

The door dings and we get off on two.

"Have a nice day." Marilyn smiles at the girl as we leave.

We push through the double glass doors and enter the cool, dark garage. I listen for echoes of cop cars coming, for the squeal of tires turning corners, for squawking radio voices looking for four females, one in a wheelchair, but the garage is silent. I push the chair over the grease-stained concrete until we reach Marilyn's SUV.

"Let me back it out," she says.

"You'd better not fucking ditch us," Heather says.

"Sweetie," Marilyn says, "if I could figure out how to do that, I'd have done it long ago."

She pulls herself up into the driver's seat, then slams the door and her taillights flare red, then white, and she reverses out next to us. I lift Michelle into the back seat.

"I'm . . . sorry . . ." she says, short of breath, as I clip the seat belt around her. It's practically flat against the seat. There's not much of Michelle left.

"It's okay, sweetheart," Marilyn says, turning around in the front. "You just hang on and we'll have you at the ranch lickety-split."

"Shotgun!" Heather calls, hauling herself into the front seat. "What? I'm not sitting next to a dead woman. Nothing personal, Michelle."

Michelle tries to moisten her lips and speak, but she's too weak and her tongue is too dry. I sit next to her and we're out of there. There's no gate at the exit, probably because it'd be in bad taste to bring people here to die and then hit their families up for money on the way out. There are no cop cars waiting for us, not even a parking garage attendant to write down our tags.

With the wheelchair sliding and thumping around in the back, we crawl over the anti-tire devices at the exit and then pull out onto the street and head for the freeway. That's when we realize we have no idea where Michelle's ranch is.

"Julia's been," I say.

"Well, Julia's not here right now," Marilyn says. "Heather?"

"Don't you send her fucking Christmas cards every year?" she asks.

"To her PO box," Marilyn snaps.

"Michelle?" I ask. "Michelle?"

She's turned her face to the window and has her eyes closed, basking in the sunlight.

"Michelle, we need you to give us directions to the ranch," I say.

She nods, without opening her eyes, then says something. I lean in close.

"The 10," she whispers. "The 10 . . . the 10 . . ."

"Take the 10," I tell Marilyn.

We pass through downtown L.A., none of us talking much. Marilyn turns the radio to lite jazz. I listen for sirens. I know this isn't going to end well. I can already feel it starting to fall apart in my hands. Next to me, Michelle mumbles to herself.

"Sweetheart, what do we do once we're on the 10," Marilyn asks, flicking her eyes to the rearview mirror. "Do we get on the 101? Ask her if we get on the 101."

"Michelle," I say. "Do we take the 101? Do you have a street address I can put in my phone?"

"Did anyone bring her purse?" Marilyn asks.

"The 10," Michelle says. Then she says something else, and I lean in close. "I'm sorry . . ." she whispers. She looks like she's about to cry.

"It's okay," I say. "Really, it's okay."

I don't know if she heard me so I pat her hand. It's dry.

"She didn't have a purse," Heather says.

"I'm beginning to see some flaws in this plan," Marilyn says, looking at me in the rearview mirror.

"What exit do we take, Michelle?" I ask her again.

"Dani's flowers . . ." she says.

"That's right," I say. "We're going to see Dani's flowers. But we need to know how to get there. We're on the 10, so what exit do we take?"

"I'm going . . ." she gasps. "To see?"

"We just passed Venice Boulevard," Marilyn says. "I'm pretty sure the only exit we can take after this is the 405."

"Unless we're going up the PCH," I say.

"Oh, for Pete's sake," Marilyn says.

A ripe, rotten smell fills the car.

"Did she shit herself?" Heather asks, furiously fanning the air in front of her face and rolling her window down all the way. "Oh, fuck, it reeks. What's she been eating?"

Marilyn veers toward an exit.

"What are you doing?" I ask. We cannot stop. There are cops. There are monsters. We have to keep moving.

"I am not going to let this woman sit in her own mess," she says, curving down the exit ramp onto a surface street, heading toward a Ralphs supermarket. "She is Dani's special friend, and she deserves some dignity."

"Not much dignity when your pants are full of shit," Heather notes.

Marilyn parks, cuts off the engine, and rounds on Heather.

"This is a natural human process," she snaps. "We will accord her the respect that any of us would expect if we were in her situation. You two need to gently take her out of the car and get the mat I have for changing tires from the back. Lay her on it, and I'll be right back."

She snatches her purse and is gone.

"Lynne, make me a promise," Heather says. "If this ever happens to me, just throw me in a ditch and walk away."

She refuses to touch Michelle, so after I scan the parking lot I unbuckle her seat belt and pick her up. I don't want to touch her but I don't want to be like Heather either. What's wrong with us? I saw my family killed before my eyes and didn't make a sound, but confronted with my friend's wife's shit I'm squeamish? Why are we more comfortable with fast, dramatic deaths than the slow decay most people get? After all, isn't this why we fought so hard? To have the right to do what Michelle is doing right this minute?

"Of course Marilyn has a yoga mat for changing tires," Heather complains, spreading it on the parking lot next to the car. I lay Michelle down on it gently, but don't know what to do next. Her eyes track something across the sky. I look up but there's nothing there. We're too exposed. I can't see anyone coming through all these cars.

D id you two get her undressed?" Marilyn demands, returning loaded with bags.

"Hell, no," Heather says.

"You are such children," she says. "This was your idea, Lynnette. What are you waiting for?"

Marilyn insists that Heather hold up one of the blankets from the hospice as a privacy screen, and she bosses me into unwrapping the other one from around Michelle's waist and raising her hospital gown.

"I'm sorry," I tell Michelle.

I don't think she hears me.

She's wearing a diaper, and Marilyn briskly undoes it and I slide it off. It's full of a black, tarry mess. Marilyn folds it over and pops it into one of the empty shopping bags. Then she uses a gallon of water and some dish towels to wash Michelle's bottom. I keep an eye on our approaches. I listen for sirens. Marilyn blots Michelle dry, then makes me help pull another adult diaper up her legs.

Together we put the unprotesting woman into the back seat and buckle her up again. She doesn't seem to notice.

Marilyn rolls up the wet mat and tucks it into one of the shopping bags, still dripping water.

"Heather, go throw this away."

"I'm not touching that," Heather says. "Just leave it."

"We are not litterbugs," Marilyn snaps. "Throw this away or I'll smack you."

Heather heads off, lugging the bags and the wet mat. I keep an eye out for cops. She's back in a few minutes, then we're pulling out of the parking lot and heading down Olympic Boulevard.

Something scratches at me and I look down to see Michelle's hand, blindly scratching at my fingers. I don't know what to do, so I open my hand and she weaves her fingers into mine. They're strong. She never looks at me once, still staring out the window, eyes wide now, lips moving.

"Do you know where we're going?" I ask her again.

"To see . . . Dani . . ." she says. ". . . Dani's flowers . . ."

"This is useless," Heather says, putting her head in her hands.

"Get out your phone," Marilyn says. "We'll call Dr. Carol. She'll know where Dani's ranch is."

"She's going to freak the fuck out," Heather says, speaking for both of us.

"Yeah," I say. "I don't think that's such a good idea."

"Your last good idea landed us in this pickle," Marilyn says. "One of you is calling Dr. Carol or I will thump you."

"My battery's dead," Heather mumbles.

Marilyn thrusts her iPhone at her.

"Use mine," she says. "She's in the address book under Elliott."

Michelle takes a great, shuddering breath, then yawns. I count to five before she takes her next breath.

"I can't find it," Heather says, swatting away Marilyn's hands as they try to take back her phone.

They both feel very far away and quiet all of a sudden.

Michelle takes a sudden deep breath, then begins to pant.

"Um, she's not doing very well," I say.

Marilyn takes a quick look back.

"I found it," Heather says.

Marilyn overhands the wheel hard to the left. I slide into Michelle.

"We're not going to the ranch," Marilyn says, straightening the car.

"I thought that was the whole point?" Heather says.

Marilyn doesn't answer.

"How is she, Lynnette?" she asks.

"Not good," I say.

Marilyn parks and gets out of the car.

"You two, come," she commands.

I pull my hand out of Michelle's and slide out the door. She doesn't seem to notice. We're in a well-to-do suburban neighborhood, parked on the sidewalk near a city park. It's a big grassy square with two paths cutting it into quarters, dotted with trees and picnic tables. I don't see many people. We stand on the sidewalk, Heather slouched against the hood.

"Now what?" Heather demands.

"This woman doesn't have much time," Marilyn says. "Now I do not agree with your choices, but you might not have forced us to do the worst thing in the world. We need to be with her now. She is going to pass, and she is going to pass outdoors, and if she asks if Dani's here you are both going to say yes, and if she asks if she is at her ranch you are both going to say yes, also."

"But—" Heather begins.

"Especially you," Marilyn says. "This woman is not going to die in the back of a car."

Marilyn turns on me.

"Yes, ma'am," I say.

Michelle yawns and flexes her hands when I open the door, and the three of us, with Heather helping as little as possible, manage to get her into the wheelchair, then wrap her in the blankets. We push her into the little park. It's early and there are only a handful of old Chinese ladies doing tai chi, and an elderly man in pants up to his armpits jabbing at molehills with his cane.

"Over here," Marilyn says, and we roll Michelle to one of the picnic tables, and then I turn her around so she's facing in the direction of the sea. I can't see it but I can smell wet salt on the breeze from over that way.

The sun blasts down, turning the park preternaturally green.

"Dani?" Michelle asks.

"She's right here beside you," Marilyn says.

Heather mouths the word *liar* at me, but I see Michelle smile.

"Green," she says.

Marilyn rubs Michelle's bony shoulder through her hospital gown.

"Everyone's with you, Michelle," she says. "We're all right here."

Michelle's hand does a little leap from the arm of her wheelchair to my wrist, then slides down and finds my hand. I notice that she's clinging to Marilyn's fingers with her other hand.

"Good . . . friends . . ." Michelle says.

I almost don't hear her over the noise of the wind in the trees. She pants a little, squinting into the sun, then closes her eyes because it's so bright. She stops, then gives a gasp, stops again, then lets out a long, rattling sigh, and I'm holding hands with a dead woman.

I can feel Dani pacing in her holding cell on the other side of the city, frantic with fear, terrified that exactly what just happened has happened. The two of them were together forever, and whoever this is, whatever conspiracy they've woven, they've kept Dani from being in the one place in the world she promised to be. It's a cruelty so sharp it cuts me open. Whoever did this, whatever sick monster robbed Dani and Michelle of each other at the end of Michelle's life, I'm going to make them suffer.

It's a while before I can bring myself to pull my fingers out of Michelle's hand. It feels cruel.

"We should go," Heather says.

"We have to get her back in the car," Marilyn says. Now that her period of usefulness is over, she's at loose ends. "Take her back to the hospice, or something."

"We can't drive around with her," I say, and notice I'm whispering. "I think the police are looking for all of us now and your windows are not tinted."

"I vote we don't drive around with a corpse," Heather says.

"We are not leaving Michelle alone in a public park," Marilyn says.

"Okay," Heather says, and walks away.

"We are not leaving her here," Marilyn says. "It's illegal."

"Dani's not going to press charges," I say.

"The city will," Marilyn says.

"For what?" I ask.

"I don't know," Marilyn says. "Littering?"

I'm starting to get nervous again. We're out in the open with too many approaches. We've got a head start, but I need to convince them that we should use this opportunity to put some distance between us and all the people looking for us. The breeze moves wisps of Michelle's hair. I smooth them down.

"That beats it all," Marilyn says, digging through her purse. "Did you see my phone?"

"No," I say. "Look, we need to get moving. People are looking for us."

"I swear I just had it," Marilyn says, ignoring me.

"Marilyn?" I say.

"Lynnette," she says, stopping her search for the phone. "I just want to say—"

"Yes, I know," I say. "How unhappy you are with me."

"I was just going to say that we did a very good thing here today," she says. "Let's call Dr. Carol and take Michelle to the ranch. We can lay her out there."

"Good," I say. "It's a secure location. We need to get Julia first, then get Dani out of jail, hole up and ride this thing out."

The sound of Heather talking to a child gets closer. I look up and see her walking toward us, leading the old man with his pants up to his armpits by one arm. He stumps along beside her on his cane. His swollen, tender eyes stream water behind oversized medical sunglasses.

"Guys," Heather says. "This is Carl DeWolfe Jr."

"Pleased to meet you," he quavers, looking approximately in our direction.

"Oh, no," Marilyn says.

"He's going to sit with Michelle while she waits for her ride," Heather says.

"It's a dangerous park," Carl DeWolfe Jr. says. "A lady should not be unaccompanied."

"Exactly," Heather says, helping him sit down on the picnic bench next to Michelle's wheelchair. "That's why you're going to sit with Michelle and wait. It shouldn't be long."

"It is an honor," Carl DeWolfe Jr. says, inclining his head in Michelle's direction. "I enjoy a good conversation."

"She's more of a listener," Heather says.

She leads us away.

"This is low," Marilyn hisses at Heather. "Even for you, this is low."

"What's the big deal?" Heather asks.

"The big deal is that he might defile her," Marilyn says.

I stop walking and look back.

"I'm with Heather on this one," I say.

The two of them stop and see what I'm seeing. Carl DeWolfe Jr. pats Michelle's hand, chattering away at her, and then he leans over and adjusts the blanket around her shoulders, pulling it higher.

"Anyway," Heather says as we continue toward Marilyn's car, "I already called an ambulance. Here."

She hands Marilyn back her phone.

"You what?" I say, but Heather is already hanging back, separating herself from me.

"You can't just take things without permission," Marilyn says, scrolling through her call list. "Who have you been calling?"

Heather is grinning like she's ashamed of something, and I'm staring at her, and then I hear the voice that makes all the time disappear and I'm sixteen again.

"Well, hello there, pretty lady," it drawls. "Been looking all over for you."

Garrett P. Cannon comes up the sidewalk in his three-piece beige suit, cowboy hat pulled low to throw a slash of black shadow across his eyes. His white mustache squirms when he talks.

"You just try to run." He grins. "Because I am itching to take you down hard."

Cop cars pull up on either end of the street. Cops swarm up the sidewalk. Cops come across the bright green lawn. I stopped watching. I stopped checking my six. I stopped paying attention to my surroundings. I lowered my guard.

"What did you do, Heather?" I ask.

"It was you or me," she says. "You or me."

I look at the cops. I can go over the hood of the parked car next to me. There's a gap in their line, and I can make it to the street and run. I'm stupid, stupid, stupid. I can't believe I let my guard down.

"You did this?" Marilyn asks Heather like she can't believe what's happening either.

The police get between us, separating me from them.

"The rest of us are survivors," Heather calls at me, still backing away. "You were always just a victim."

She melts into the line of police and I know she's cut a deal, she traded me to save herself. It's what I did to Julia: abandoned her to save myself. It's unforgivable.

I tense, ready to fake left and run right, but Garrett knows me too well. The second my muscles bunch up he whistles between his teeth, and the cops are on me. I break the fingers and thumb of the first one who grabs my wrist, but there are more. There are always more. In the end, they take me down hard.

POLICE INCIDENT REPORT

Date of Incident: 12/23/90   Time of Incident: Appx. 9:30 p.m.

Location: Provo Behavioral Hospital

Details of Incident:

William Walker, an inpatient at Provo Behavioral Hospital, somehow obtained a Santa Claus costume on the night of December 23, 1990 from an unknown source. After the 9 p.m. lockdown, Walker put on the costume and strangled his roommate, HIRAM RANDOLPH, then pushed the attendant call button by the door. When attendants FRANK MCCRAE and SALLY NOLAND arrived, Walker stabbed MCCRAE in the eye with a sharp pencil, killing him instantly. He beat NOLAND unconscious and used her keys to let himself out.

As he attempted to exit Provo Behavioral, Walker entered the receiving room where two police officers were assisting with the intake of a disturbed individual. Surprising them, Walker managed to relieve Officer JACK W. FORREST of his service weapon, killing him in the process. Subsequent events are still being investigated but over the next two minutes, 26 rounds were fired in the receiving room, Officer SEAN MCKINNEY was wounded and Officer THERESA MALLORY was killed. Walker then escaped using Forrest's car. He proceeded to 212 North 1200 East Street, the residence of Lynnette Tarkington.

Reporting Officer: T. Larson   Date: 12/24/90

—incident report, American Fork, Utah, Police Department,
December 24, 1990

THE FINAL GIRL SUPPORT GROUP XI:
Better Watch Out!

The good thing about interview rooms is they always sit you facing the door. The bad thing about interview rooms is they're always full of cops. The bald hipster detective with a neck tattoo peeking over his collar sits across from me, bulging out of his Men's Wearhouse suit, hands clasped on top of an open manila file. A lady cop sits next to him in a navy polo shirt, arms folded, leaning back in her chair, radiating contempt. Everyone else is in the other room, watching on the camera that hangs from the ceiling. I assume Garrett's in there, probably eating popcorn.

"When did you first have sex with Santa Claus?" Men's Wearhouse asks.

I'm so surprised I almost open my mouth to answer. Are these Garrett's "shocking revelations"?

"Let me repeat for the hard of hearing," Men's Wearhouse says. "Can you tell us the date of your first sexual encounter with the Santa Claus Killer."

I need to know what the hell they're talking about, but no one ever regretted not talking to the cops.

"Lawyer," I say.

"Did you have sex with the Santa Claus Killer before or after he tried to kill you?" he says.

"Tried to kill you twice," Lady Cop amends.

"The second time wasn't him," Men's Wearhouse corrects her. "It was his brother."

The wall is a nice color. Sort of a pale yellow. I wish I could rest my eyes on it forever.

"Lawyer," I repeat.

"Do you recognize the man in this photograph?"

Men's Wearhouse slides an eight-by-ten glossy across the table. Ricky wanted to be an actor, and his headshots wound up in his file. There he is, three-quarters angle, giving me a sly smile from the tabletop. Casting directors probably thought he was charming, full of devil-may-care attitude, but all I can see is the crazy.

"Lawyer," I repeat.

I focus on Men's Wearhouse's neck tattoo. It looks like a woman's name. Lucille? Shanelle? Janelle?

Lady Cop makes an impatient sound, pushing air out between her teeth.

"What about this man?" Men's Wearhouse says, peeling up Ricky's eight-by-ten and putting down a mug shot of Billy.

Billy didn't take care of himself the way Ricky did. He lived rough, had his nose broken playing football, but he's got the same soap-opera-actor looks, although it's hard to tell from the picture. They beat him up before taking his mug shot. I'm not too sad about that.

"Lawyer," I repeat.

"The public defender's office is swamped," Lady Cop says. "We conveyed your request and they hope to have someone down here by the end of the day."

"Or tomorrow," Men's Wearhouse says.

"I'll wait," I say, trying to keep my lungs from cramping shut.

Men's Wearhouse and Lady Cop stand up and walk out of the room. They leave the photos of Ricky and Billy Walker looking up at me from the table.

The camera's still watching so I can't scream, or cry, or bang my head on the table, or do a single thing I want. It takes all my willpower. Is this what's getting spread everywhere about me? I had sex with Ricky Walker? I can't even think that sentence without my stomach feeling grease-slicked and slimy.

I focus on taking deep, full breaths. I don't look at the photos. I rest my eyes on the wall. After a long time the door opens and Garrett comes in alone, carrying a thin manila folder, wearing his parade float of a cowboy hat, and his shitty, patronizing smile.

"Nobody here but us chickens," he says, putting the manila folder on the table.

As usual, the room's not big enough for me, and him, and his cologne.

"I notice you didn't really have much in the way of conversation for Los Angeles's finest," he drawls. He pronounces it "Los Ang-guh-lees." "So I convinced those boys to give us some alone time. You and me are old friends, so let's bypass the pleasant banter, detour around the chitchat, wave a fond farewell to the 'how's the weather, preacher' part of the program, and get down to brass tacks. How's that sound to you?"

He looks into my eyes. It's like having a flashlight shine in my face, but I won't look away.

"I don't like liars, Lynney. But I'm giving you a chance to do the Christian thing and come clean."

He's so smug and arrogant that I forget myself.

"About what?" I ask.

"She speaks!" he says, making a big production of opening the folder so I can't see its contents. "Hallelujah."

The photos he pulls out don't bother me. I watched the real thing happen. But the way that one second I'm listening to him strut and preen, and the next the table is covered in glossy shots of my dead family, it draws a hot iron band around my chest. Now I know my lawyer isn't coming.

"Yeah, they always get me the same way, too," he says, smoothing down his mustache with his fingertips, watching me from beneath the brim of his hat. He pulls out the picture of my father's corpse and puts it on top. "I respected the hell out of that man."

He leans over the table, the brim of his hat bonking me in the forehead. He speaks low and slow.

"How long were you having carnal relations with Ricky Walker?" he asks.

The words don't make any sense.

"You know I didn't" comes out in a whisper.

"Billy says different." He smiles. "The boy has found Jesus and cannot tell a lie."

"My dad said you couldn't even direct traffic at a Bulldogs game without someone holding your hand," I say, making myself look him in the eyes. "Whose idea was this?"

He flashes me a thin smile that shows a slice of his teeth.

"So you're saying you didn't fuck Ricky Walker for six months before the killings? Your statement is that you didn't ask him to murder your parents? You're saying that you didn't tell him you hated your father? You didn't convince that poor psychotic boy to murder your folks? That's the problem with psychos, Lynney, you can lead 'em to water but you just can't make 'em kill the people you want. They tend to go hog-wild."

Suddenly I have an idea of what else is inside that folder and I can't hold on to the real world anymore, and I'm tumbling into this fucked-up, through-the-looking-glass horror show where everyone else is already waiting for me.

"That's not true," I say, but it sounds small.

"No one likes a cop killer, Lynnette." He smiles. "Especially cops."

"I didn't . . ." I begin.

"Aw, of course not," he says, cutting me off. He's trying to get me worked up. He's succeeding. "You're only an accessory. It's not just Billy's word, either. Because it doesn't matter how much Jesus a convicted serial killer has in his heart, most judges don't give that shit for credibility."

I see them all: Mom, Dad, Gillian, Tommy. I close my eyes.

"How did you think it was going to go?" he asks. "Was Ricky going to kill your boyfriend *and* your parents for you?"

I remember Tommy trying to protect me, Tommy not staying down, Tommy getting up over and over again no matter how bad Ricky hurt him.

I hear the manila folder open. A plastic evidence bag crinkles. He reads in a sickening falsetto.

"Dear Ricky, don't put your return address on your letter. My daddy is the chief of police and if he knew you were writing to me—"

That's when I go over the table.

They were waiting for me right outside the door. Men's Warehouse leads the charge and they pour into the room, forcing me down, crushing my rib cage against the table. They shackle me and drag me out of the room.

They haven't been wasting their time. One whole wall of the cell they throw me into is plexiglass. On the other side of the glass they've made a little display for me: an artificial Christmas tree, all set up with twinkling lights and everything.

Lady Cop taps on the window. She's wearing a Santa Claus hat and a big white beard.

I start screaming, and she just stands on the other side with all the other cops and laughs and laughs and laughs.

The cell where I'm going to die is smaller than Michelle's hospice room. It's brightly lit and they watch me through the plexiglass wall in case I try to kill myself before they can arrange to have me killed. The plexiglass is unbreakable. I know this because I already tried to break it. The walls are light pink cinder block, the floor is concrete. There is a slab sticking out from the wall where I can lie down. Behind the slab is a stainless-steel pedestal with a sink on top and a steel toilet on the other side. If I crouch over the toilet and bend down until my chest is on my knees I gain some small measure of privacy. They give me a roll of toilet paper but take away my shoelaces.

I don't hate Heather for calling Garrett anymore because I'm saving up all my hatred for myself. If all these cops weren't watching me, I'd have killed myself by now. I've got no shoelaces but I'm resourceful. I'd bite off my tongue and choke to death on my own blood if I knew they wouldn't be in here before I bled out.

It's cold. I fall asleep on the slab. There's no blanket. At one point, I wake up and a bunch of cops are watching me and singing Christmas carols. They've taped a Santa Claus decoration to the window so I can see his face, all red and jolly. They want me to give them a reaction. I can't help it. I give them one.

I wait for Marilyn to show up with a lawyer. I wait for Julia to arrive with the public defender. I wait for Dani, for Dr. Carol, for someone to save me from myself. Then I remember that Julia is in the hospital. Dani is in custody. And Marilyn and Heather and Dr. Carol probably hate me because they think I've committed the one sin we can't forgive: lying down with your monster. They all think I'm another Chrissy Mercer.

I can feel it out there. I'm on the news again. What they imagine I did. The slut who slept with the killer. My high school picture and Ricky's mug shot, our faces pasted next to each other like a couple at prom, bouncing all over cable news as a single image.

I look up and see Garrett standing next to the Christmas tree. When he sees me watching, he flips me the bird.

It's funny, but he's the only man I've ever loved.

Christmas Eve, 1988, American Fork, Utah. "Sweet Child O' Mine" by Guns N' Roses is everywhere, but I prefer "Never Gonna Give You Up" by Rick Astley because I'm a cheerleader, and I'm happy all the time, and I'm in love. Tommy Burkhardt looks just like Jordan Knight and my mom calls us Charles and Diana because she thinks he treats me like a princess. Even though we've only been dating for six weeks, it's six weeks that started in mid-November and takes me right through Christmas, and I know he's going to get me an awesome Christmas present.

My parents would probably have gotten a divorce if my dad didn't care so much about appearances. He's the chief of police of a small town and he's invested in that Norman Rockwell thing, so he hides at the office while Mom plays happy homemaker and makes everything as perfect as possible all the time. It drives us all crazy. They're doing the best they can, but Gillian and I both know something's got to give.

She's eleven, and we've talked about what's going to happen when Mom and Dad get divorced and we've decided weekends with Dad, weekdays with Mom, and we're not splitting up. Sisters stick together. Both of us hope it'll happen soon because right now we're walking on eggshells.

Christmas Eve comes, and Dad won dinner for two at that Italian place downtown, and he read in a magazine that they should try to have some together time, so he comes to Gillian and me all serious and asks for our blessing. The restaurant is where they had their first date, and he's so nervous his hands are sweating, and of course we say yes, and as he's leaving for their dinner he asks me to make sure his tie is straight and then he says, "Wish me luck," and suddenly he's not my dad at all, he's a guy going on a date, and I melt inside and actually pray they figure it out, kneeling beside my bed with my hands folded and everything.

I loved Christmas. I loved the nonstop Tabernacle Choir Christmas carols playing at the mall; I loved the animated movies about elf dentists and Rudolph the Red-Nosed Reindeer on TV; I loved Mom going into baking overdrive so the house always smelled like hot sugar and warm butter; I loved wrapping presents. It made me feel like peace on Earth was possible. It made me feel like a fancy dinner could solve Mom and Dad's marriage.

Tommy called to say he's bringing me my present, and I sent Gillian upstairs.

"Watch TV in Mom and Dad's room," I said. "Do not come downstairs."

"You've got a date," she said, and I hate her for being annoying and love her for being a kid.

I opened the door for Tommy and I'm totally blown away by how good-looking he is. I'm not bad, but I never thought I'd do this well, especially since Shasheena Grotepas had her eye on him. We made out for a while, and then he gave me my present: a Christmas tree pin with ruby and emerald decorations.

Twenty-two years later I know they're fake stones, but we were on the pool table in the rec room and I had my shirt off and he set it on the curve of my breast and I remember how the gold glowed against my skin and, like I said, I loved Christmas more than anything.

Mom and Dad weren't due back until eleven p.m., and it was only eight p.m., so even if they fought I figured we had at least two hours, and so I decided this would be the night we went all the way. Things got hot and heavy on that pool table, but I planned to move to the sofa upstairs. It was super-soft and had a ton of afghans so we could make a nest and take our time.

Then the doorbell rang.

"Is that your folks?" Tommy asked, sitting bolt upright.

"They have keys," I said.

I pulled his face back to mine. Sweat ran down my chest and pooled between my breasts. Dad always turned the heat up too high in the house. He hated the cold.

The doorbell rang again.

With a groan I rolled out from under Tommy, grabbed his hockey jersey, and pinned my Christmas brooch to the collar.

"Hurry back," he said as I pulled on my stirrup pants and started up the stairs.

Those were his last words to me.

I was sixteen, and kind of stupid, and we knew everyone in American Fork, so I just opened the door without looking out the window.

No one was there. It was freezing cold, but I stood for a minute, breathing in the woodsmoke from the neighbors' chimneys, with my boy-friend in the basement, his gift on my collarbone, thinking I was hot stuff, imagining I had the whole world on a string.

Then Santa Claus came around the corner carrying an axe.

At first, I didn't recognize Ricky Walker. All I saw was the Santa Claus suit and I thought it was someone on the hockey team playing a joke. I didn't think it was funny so I slammed the door in his face and turned the thumb lock.

It took him two swings to bust the door wide open and he came in with the cold. That was when I recognized him.

"Ricky?" I asked.

He came at me with his axe, and when I screamed Tommy came up-stairs. He tried to protect me, but every time he got in the way, Ricky hit him with his axe. Finally, Tommy's head was so misshapen that I begged him, "Tommy, stay down!"

Ricky embedded his axe in Tommy's neck, and then he came for me. I managed to scratch up his face, but he tore off my jersey, lifted me up, and carried me into the living room. My dad had been a big hunter before Gillian was born, and he'd bagged a white-tailed buck with a huge rack of antlers on a trip and mounted its head on the living room wall. That was what Ricky impaled me on.

At first I didn't understand what hurt so much, and then the antlers were pushing into me so hard I thought they'd tear me in half, and then they were inside me, and I watched them come out my front.

I was a little tiny thing back then, barely ninety-five pounds, and the antlers went in just above my kidneys and came out just below my rib cage. I hung there for ten hours in shock, and the antlers and the weight of my body kept me from bleeding out. I slipped in and out of conscious-ness as I watched Gillian come downstairs, as my mom and dad came home, as Ricky took care of them all.

When I was six I thought I was Gillian's mom. They let me make her Jell-O, and get her ready in the mornings, and even give her a bath until

I saw *No More Tears* on the side of her Johnson's Baby Shampoo. I always tried to be so careful when I washed her baby hair, but then I saw that label and it smelled so good, and the thick yellow shampoo looked like honey, and I poured half the bottle in her eyes because I thought "No More Tears" was a magic formula that meant she'd never cry again. She howled so loud my eardrums rattled, and Mom swooped in and scooped her up and pressed her to the side of her neck and got so angry.

"Lynnette," she said. "You have to protect your sister."

I'm sorry, Gilly.

He did things to her body, to their bodies, he performed scenarios, peeled the meat off their bones. At one point Mom and I locked eyes while Ricky was focused on Dad, and Mom saw the tears running down my face. She knew that if Ricky saw me crying he'd realize I was still alive, and so Mom attacked him. She took his attention. She got him to focus entirely on her for a long, long time. She was a good victim. I hope it didn't hurt. I hope she was drunk.

I'll never find out if Mom and Dad's date rekindled their romance. Ricky took the answer to that question away from me forever. And Mom never lived long enough to find out what happened to Charles and Diana.

When the sun came up, Ricky snored inside the bloody nest he'd built out of my family. I couldn't tell where Tommy's body ended and my dad's body began. Gillian was easy to keep track of, though. He'd put her head on the mantelpiece looking at me.

Ricky woke up, shuffled to the kitchen, and pissed in our sink. He was still in the kitchen when the first cop walked into the living room.

"Hello?" Mike Miller called from the broken front door. "Anyone home? Karl? Carol? I'm coming in."

I wanted to warn him, but I didn't want to give myself away. He got an axe through the chest. Garrett P. Cannon was the next cop through the door.

"Mike?" Garrett called, walking into the house. "Mike? You better not be stealing Christmas presents from the chief."

He saw Ricky splitting open Mike's rib cage with his axe. Ricky stood up and came at him. I heard Garrett drop his gun, cursing, and then he picked it up and fired five times. There was silence, and then Ricky came running back through the living room. I couldn't tell if he'd been hit because he was already covered in so much blood.

He smashed through the sliding glass doors at the far end of the living room as Garrett came after him, fumbling with his reloader. He seated it and emptied his gun into Ricky's back and I remember seeing Ricky flip over the railing on our deck, his feet going straight up in the air. They said he landed so hard it split his skull in two.

Garrett just stood there for a minute in all the gunsmoke, looking at the slick of skin and muscle and splintered bone that had been my family and the boy I loved. My brain felt far away, but I managed to wave my left hand in little circles at the wrist until Garrett turned around.

"Holy shit," he breathed, looking up at me. Then he went outside and emptied the rest of his ammo into Ricky's corpse. He got on the radio and called in all the backup he could find on Christmas morning.

They shot me up on painkillers before they sawed the antlers off and took me to the hospital. I was unconscious for almost two days. Garrett didn't leave my side the entire time.

I woke up unable to lie on my back, sore in a way I didn't think was possible. Even my toenails ached. Garrett brought me news and updates, he brought me flowers, he lied and said I'd been wearing a T-shirt when he found me. Topless unmarried girls making it with their boyfriends in Utah weren't going to earn much sympathy back then, and Garrett wanted to make sure everyone saw me as the pure and innocent victim in this story.

He sat next to me at my first press conference, the one where I leaned over and upchucked all over the table. He told my story for me, and on the interview circuit I sat next to him and smiled, and when they asked me questions I said he was "my hero," he was "my everything," he was "my knight in shining armor." It was true. At the time, the only thing standing between me and screaming insanity was Garrett P. Cannon.

Is it any surprise that I fell in love?

For two years I was a happy little idiot who did what she was told. I put it all behind me. I tried not to dwell.

"Why live in the past?" I chirped, smiling bravely.

My foster parents were everything I could have wanted. The next Christmas, they almost convinced me that things were normal. We rented movies, went ice skating, stayed in the house and played marathon games of Monopoly, cooked elaborate meals, anything to keep my mind off Ricky.

The following Christmas I gave Mike and Liz permission to try some Christmas decorations, and was secretly more thrilled than I expected when I saw wrapped presents with my name on them in the living room. I let myself think everything could be normal again. That Mike and Liz were going to help me have an actual life. I didn't count on Ricky's little brother, Billy. No one did.

Billy was serving time in a locked psych ward for attacking his next-door neighbor in a fight over what day they put out their garbage cans, and he blamed me for what happened to his big brother. When Christmas rolled around, he decided he just had to let me know how he felt. He got a Santa suit from somewhere and strangled his roommate, then started a shootout in the intake room that killed two people, both of them cops. Of course, when people realized whose brother he was, everyone went on high alert. I was desperate to speak with Garrett, but he was busy telling the press how he had to be careful about gazing into the abyss because it also gazed into him.

But he did take the time to post cops outside my foster family's house.

Four cops, actually, all outside the front door. Which meant that Billy came in the back. Carol was first. Then Mike.

I was too scared to move, too scared to run, and my scars throbbed like fresh wounds for the three hours he kept me in the kitchen. At first he beat me whenever I made a noise. Then he beat me for fun. He used a cast-iron kitty-cat doorstop that Carol loved. The back of my skull was so pulped they had to put a metal plate in. The few times I've flown after that I usually set off the metal detector.

I'm pretty sure he would have killed me if one of the cops hadn't rung the doorbell to use the bathroom. Billy shot him and went out the back. It took them twenty-four hours to find him hiding in a Nativity scene at a Lutheran church. Garrett shot him at exactly 3:14 a.m. on a rainy Christmas morning, then dragged him out bleeding and tossed him in the back seat of his squad car. No full-clip-in-the-back treatment this time. By now, Garrett knew that a live killer made all the difference when it came to book deals.

Once again, Garrett was waiting for me when I came out of surgery, ready to take credit for saving me a second time. Before, I'd worshipped the ground he walked on. It had been puppy love. This time I was eighteen and he wanted more than a puppy for his reward. The first time we had sex was in my hospital room. He was twenty-three years older than me. I didn't care.

He had a wife and kids, but when he wasn't at my apartment I'd call his house crying, begging him to come protect me. Garrett told his wife I had "imprinted" on him like a duckling. It was her second marriage. Her first husband had gone to prison for shooting her brother. She wasn't the kind of woman who asked too many questions.

For two years, Garrett was my everything. He handled all my media requests, looked over all my contracts, went to all my meetings, and I did whatever he wanted. I felt cared for and protected. I didn't see how much he was getting out of this, too.

Getting me out to L.A. and into the first *Slay Bells* movie was a big deal for him at the time. The producers needed a gimmick to make people notice their bargain-bin production, and I was dumb enough to believe Garrett when he said it'd be good for me. I never thought to ask how much they'd paid him. At the last minute I had a panic attack, bailed, and drove back to American Fork. He said he didn't mind that I'd screwed up his deal, but after that he stopped calling me as often, then he stopped coming by entirely, and after a while he forgot about me and I cried myself to sleep every night for a long, long time.

I thought Garrett had left me alone, but eventually I realized I had always been alone. I had done everything they'd told me to do, and it had happened again. No one had been able to keep me safe. No one had watched out for me. I was the only person who could keep me safe. And so I did.

Sometimes an entire year will go by when I believe that's the whole story. But in my heart I know I deserve to be in prison. In my heart, I know I deserve to be in Hell.

Of course, now that they have the letters, everyone else knows it, too.

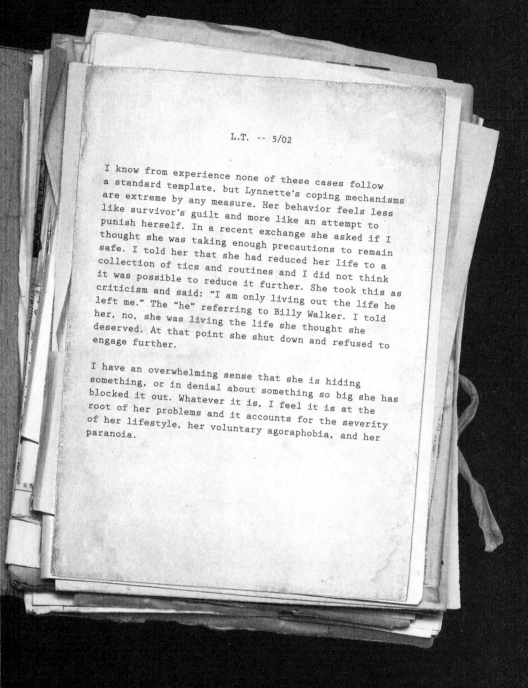

L.T. -- 5/02

I know from experience none of these cases follow
a standard template, but Lynnette's coping mechanisms
are extreme by any measure. Her behavior feels less
like survivor's guilt and more like an attempt to
punish herself. In a recent exchange she asked if I
thought she was taking enough precautions to remain
safe. I told her that she had reduced her life to a
collection of tics and routines and I did not think
it was possible to reduce it further. She took this as
criticism and said: "I am only living out the life he
left me." The "he" referring to Billy Walker. I told
her, no, she was living the life she thought she
deserved. At that point she shut down and refused to
engage further.

I have an overwhelming sense that she is hiding
something, or in denial about something so big she has
blocked it out. Whatever it is, I feel it is at the
root of her problems and it accounts for the severity
of her lifestyle, her voluntary agoraphobia, and her
paranoia.

—Dr. Carol Elliott, private notes on session with Lynnette Tarkington,
May 2002

THE FINAL GIRL SUPPORT GROUP XII:
Hellbound

It's cold in here. The central air clutches my bones. No one talks to me. No one tells me what's happening. Instead, they tape my letters to the glass wall so I can read every line. They're photocopies, but I can still see sentences I remember writing on my Holly Hobbie stationery with its roses twining around the borders.

Twice they take me out of my cell. Once to be photographed. Once for a cold shower. Both times when I come back, there are more copies of more letters taped to the glass wall. I do my best not to look.

Three times a day, the door opens and a cop brings a stack of high-sided brown trays into my cell and leaves one on the floor with all the ceremony of a dog dropping a turd. I count them to track time. One comes every five hours, starting at eight a.m.

Somewhere out there my paperwork is being pushed through the digestive tract of the legal system, and soon they will open my door and instead of taking me to the shower they will take me to a courtroom where they will set bail too high for me to pay. When that happens, I'll be sent into the general population to wait for my trial, where some no-hope lunatic will stab me to death with a sharpened toothbrush in her bid for fame. She'll probably be able to sell the shiv that killed a final girl for a couple of hundred bucks online. Even a shiv that killed a not-quite-final-girl like me.

And I deserve it.

That's what they always said about me: I'm not a real final girl. The other ones in group fought back and killed their monsters, but me? I just hung on those antlers like a piece of meat. I just lay there on the linoleum getting my skull pulped. I didn't save anyone. Garrett P. Cannon saved me.

Some cop drops a lunch tray: banana, apple, two slices of white bread, two slices of bologna, a packet of mayo, two sugar cookies, and a fruit punch. While I eat the apple, phrases from my letters jump out at me.

"*. . . wish you were here and we could escape . . .*"

"*. . . how is your acting career, are you in anything I've seen . . .*"

"*. . . did you hear the new Metallica album . . .*"

I remember being happy all the time in high school, but these letters tell a different story.

"*. . . Dad acts like we're suspects and he's just waiting for us to make a single mistake so he can send us to prison . . .*"

"*. . . he made Gillian scrub the shower with her toothbrush . . .*"

"*. . . wish someone stronger than him would show up and give him a taste of how . . .*"

"*. . . I hate him . . .*"

"*. . . this family is like being in Hell . . .*"

"*. . . wish he was dead . . .*"

"*. . . he'd be too scared to say anything to your face . . .*"

"*. . . please save me . . .*"

Dad had been in the army and had definite ideas about law and order. Maybe he was stricter than he needed to be, but I don't remember hating him this much. Every teenager thrives on conflict, however, and I can't imagine I was an exception. After Billy Walker I sanded down our rough times and polished up Dad's halo until it's bright enough to blind me to the past.

In fifth grade, Mrs. Margaret assigned pen pals. Most of them were in foster care, like Ricky. The other kids lost interest after a few months, but not me. Not Ricky. For six years we wrote back and forth and I never told him to kill my dad but I gave him my home address, I said we should run away together to L.A., I told him my dad yelled all the time and my mom was out to lunch. A few times I even told him I wished my parents were dead.

Teenagers talk like this, right? Even if it's ugly in retrospect. I didn't know there was a bloody engine inside his head just waiting for someone to turn it on. I never knew the key was shaped like a sixteen-year-old girl.

If I hadn't written to him, if I hadn't given him our address, if I hadn't asked him to rescue me, Ricky Walker would have gone to some other house. He wouldn't have killed the beloved police chief of a small town. He and his brother wouldn't have killed five cops.

In this freezing-cold police station, I'm surrounded by the only people on earth who hate me as much as I hate myself.

When I woke up in the hospital I thought they'd have the letters, but no one said anything. So I didn't say anything. I kept waiting for someone to say something, but they never did, so I never did, and after a while I began to forget I even wrote them. Sometimes I imagined them turning up because, after all, they had to be somewhere, and those were the bad nights. On those nights I'd make myself exercise until I dry-heaved, I'd force myself to clean my weapons until they were spotless, to scrub my entire apartment until sunup, to punish myself as hard as I could, but nothing I did hurt me as much as the thought of those letters coming out.

But they never did.

"Excuse me," a soft voice says. It's the cop, the one whose fingers I broke, the one who's wearing a green metal splint on his left hand. He's picking up my meal tray. "You finished?"

I haven't eaten anything except the apple. I can't eat with the wall of letters staring down at me. I see everything still on my tray. I nod. I'm finished.

How did the letters come to Garrett's possession? Invite Garrett to a mall opening in Alaska and he'd be there in a flash, as long as he thought it might boost his book and DVD sales. Taking the bait has never been a problem for him, but someone had to throw the bait out there in the first place.

When the young cop with the broken hand brings the lunch tray the next day, I stare at it for a long time. It's the same two slices of bread, the same mayo, the same sugar cookies, the same fruit punch, but there's turkey instead of bologna this time, and an orange instead of a banana. Who made that decision? There must be a kitchen somewhere in the station where there are people working to divide up loaves of white bread, counting slices of turkey, taking juice cartons out of the cooler. They're looking at their order forms, going over the inmate list, checking their inventory.

It's a miracle of logistics when you think about it. I bet if I were kosher there'd be a kosher option, if I were Muslim there'd be something halal. That takes a lot of people. That takes a team.

Heather got me arrested, but she got the idea when she saw Garrett on TV, and he was on TV because Billy Walker came forward with those letters. That's less than twenty-four hours after someone tried to burn down Heather's halfway house and Harry Peter Warden came forward and confessed to Dani's murders. And that was less than twenty-four hours after someone followed Julia and Russell Thorn to my apartment and shot them both. And that was the same day Christophe Volker sat in Adrienne's pantry waiting for her to come downstairs.

One person isn't doing this unless they're the most organized, highest-functioning sociopath in existence. This isn't a single monster. This is a convention of them.

The question: who has a vested interest in making me dead? I refuse to accept that this is all a coincidence, that a bunch of different psychopaths are pursuing their separate agendas, taking advantage of the situation as it unfolds. Not seeing a pattern is what got me in trouble with the Walker brothers. I'll never make that mistake again.

Someone got Christophe Volker onto Camp Red Lake. Someone convinced Harry Peter Warden to come forward. Someone got Russell Thorn to show up at exactly the right moment. Someone attacked us in my apartment. Someone found my letters. Who hates us this much? Who could coordinate people inside prison and outside prison? Who knows every single one of our weak points?

When the soft-voiced cop with the broken hand brings me my next tray he says, "You've got a visitor."

They take me to a warmer room with a long table running down the middle. There are partitions between plexiglass windows that look onto the other side of the room. There's a phone on either side of each window. Wordlessly, I'm taken to one of the booths and sat down. On the other side of the glass sits Dr. Carol.

She looks tired. She's not wearing makeup. There's a thick pile of papers on the counter in front of her. I drop the phone because my fingers are still numb and I'm so excited to see a human being who doesn't hate me.

"Dr. Carol," I ask. "What's going on? Did they tell you what's happening? No one's talking to me but I think I have this figured out."

"Stop," she says.

Even though we're only a couple of feet away, the phone is a bad long-distance connection. I lean forward and lower my voice.

"Someone is doing this," I say. "More than one person. It's the only way everything can be happening all at once. Someone is out to take down group."

I notice that she's looking over my right shoulder. I look behind me, but no one's there.

"We have to get somewhere defensible and start figuring this out," I say. "We need to get the visitor lists for Harry Peter Warden and Billy Walker. My guess is we'll see the same name on both lists. I'm probably safe in here for another day or two, so focus on getting everyone who's still at liberty together and to a defensible location. We're soft targets as long as we're scattered all over the place."

Dr. Carol looks at me with a complete lack of understanding. It's getting hard for me to stay calm, but I know I have to. I take two breaths before she speaks.

"Why did you do it, Lynnette?" she asks. "Why did you do this?"

At first I think she's talking about the letters, but then I read the top of the stack of paper in front of her. All I want to do is go back in time and undo everything, because I recognize the title page.

The Final Girl Support Group, it reads. *By Lynnette Tarkington.*

It takes all my strength not to hang up the phone.

"I didn't write that," I say automatically.

"It came in my email last night," she says. "Everyone got one."

As long as I keep looking down at where the plexiglass meets the desk I can pretend her face is as far away as her voice.

"Who?" my voice is very, very small.

"I have no idea how Marilyn and Heather feel," Dr. Carol says. "But I know that I am deeply hurt by your descriptions of me."

"This is what he wants," I say. "Don't you see? He wants us divided. He wants us confused so we don't focus on the important things."

"I have never regarded you as trophies," Dr. Carol says, ignoring me. "I don't collect you. You are my patients and I care about each of you deeply as individuals. I have devoted so much of my career to helping women like you. I have spent so much of my life trying to build a world where women like you don't have to exist."

"The important thing is to figure out who's doing this," I say. "That book's just a distraction. Someone stole it off my hard drive."

"You never should have written it!" she shouts, blowing out the tiny speaker in my ear. "To accuse me of neglecting my children by coming to group on Christmas Eve . . . how could you even think that? You're the one who fought loudest for us to have group that day. You think I treat you like pets?"

"I never said that," I try.

"It's in your book!" she says. "How can you sit in group thinking so little of me? Laughing at me behind my back? Why do you hate me?"

All my words keep coming back to hurt me. The letters. This book. Everything I ever wrote is a weapon turned against me. Everything I've ever thought comes back to make me bleed. Who's the one person who would know how to coordinate all this, who would know all our fears, who would know how to cripple us psychologically?

I look up and see Dr. Carol staring at me through the scratch-clouded plexiglass.

"Why?" she asks. "I just want to know why?"

"I don't know," I say.

"You should stay away," she says. "No one in group wants to hear from you right now. I don't want to hear from you right now."

And then I know. It's something about her reaction. It's too big, like a bad actor in a bad play trying to convince the audience of their grief by shouting. It's something about the fact that she's so upset yet she took the time to print out my entire book and bring it here like a prop. A bad prop. That stack of paper is too thick for the twenty-five thousand words I wrote.

"Why are *you* doing this?" I ask.

Suddenly there are so many reasons: maybe she needs a bump in her career, maybe she's a sociopath and thinks it's funny, maybe she thinks we're ingrates and wants revenge, maybe she just got tired of listening to us whine all the time.

"I hope you get the help you need," she says. She puts the phone down on the counter and there's a hard knock in my ear. She bends over for her purse.

"Dr. Carol?" I shout, trying to get her to hear me. "Dr. Carol!"

There's movement behind me. They're coming to take me away. She sits back up, rubbing her forehead, saying something I can't hear.

"Pick up the phone!" I shout, banging on the plexiglass. "Answer me!"

I shake the table and try to shout through the partition.

"Dr. Carol!" I shout, and I'm furious in a way I've only ever been furious with myself before. "I know you! We trusted you!"

Arms grab me at the elbows, hands press me facedown on the desk.

"I trusted you!" I scream. "I trusted you!"

They put cuffs on my wrists and grind the metal down into my bones and when they pull me up they twist my arms until it feels like my shoulders dislocate. I see Dr. Carol's back, running out of the visiting room, and she can't hear me no matter how loud I scream.

I need a phone, I need to warn everyone that it's her, but the harder I ask the less they listen. I smash the chocolate pudding from my dinner tray on the window of my cold cell and smear it across the glass. I clog my toilet with the green beans and the chicken patty. I bang the tray against my cell door for ten straight minutes.

Three deputies in riot gear come in and put me in shackles. I'm moved to an interview room and when they pick me up and carry me back my toilet is unclogged and my cell has been hosed down. It's still dripping wet. It's still bitterly cold. No one speaks to me no matter how much I explain what's happening.

I have to get to a phone. If I can get to a phone I can warn Marilyn and Heather.

I beg until my throat is raw and bleeding. I start to kick the glass and they send in the riot squad again. This time they take off my shackles and stuff me in a bright blue padded vinyl tube with armholes. It's an anti-suicide smock. They call it a Fergie. I try kicking the glass again but just fall backward and crack my head against the floor.

They leave me like that for a long time—on the floor, unable to move, facing my letters taped to the plexiglass wall.

I can't wait to see you again, the letter says in cursive girl handwriting.

I can't wait to make love with you again and you can tell me what you want to do to my dad.

I was a virgin when Ricky Walker came to our house on Christmas Eve. I never slept with him. How would that have even happened? I didn't write this letter. The handwriting is the same, and the stationery is Holly Hobbie, but she's baking muffins. In all the Holly Hobbie stationery I remember owning, she's gathering wildflowers. Conclusion: some of these aren't my letters. Some of these are forgeries.

When the cop comes in with my tray I try to tell him. I say I have to speak to someone. I beg him in my broken voice, pushing air through my shredded throat, but he doesn't listen. No one listens. I am not worth hearing anymore.

"I'm sorry," he says, dropping the tray on my floor without making eye contact, and scuttles away.

For breakfast he brings me a log of Nutraloaf and a small bottle of water. I beg him to please get me a phone, just one phone call, that's all I need. He doesn't look in my direction, he acts like this is an empty room and I wonder if I'm actually talking. Maybe I only think I'm talking? Maybe I'm going insane?

I talk out loud for a few minutes, listening to my sandpaper voice bounce off the walls, but that doesn't prove anything. I could be imagining that. I have no way of knowing if any sound is actually coming out of my throat.

The anti-suicide smock is hard to sit up in because it barely bends, so I lie on my back and stare at the ceiling and try not to think about the fake letters. I try not to think about the fact that we all trust Dr. Carol. We'll open our doors to her, we'll believe whatever she tells us, we'll go anywhere she asks.

I think about her files on all those baby final girls and I think about that file on her desk for Fugate, Stephanie, and I think about how long she's been collecting us and the cold creeps inside my suicide smock and pierces my flesh and cracks my bones.

But what if I'm wrong? What if Christophe Volker just finally snapped? What if some random stalker tried to kill Julia at my house? And Heather burned down her own halfway house and lied about it, and Harry Peter Warden made up a story to get out of prison, and Billy Walker finally decided to reveal the location of those letters, and I wrote that book, and I wrote those letters, and I'm trying to run from what I deserve.

When I put shampoo in Gilly's eyes, I saw that the label said *No More Tears* and I drew the wrong conclusions, then acted on them, and I hurt someone I loved. What if the only conspiracy exists inside my head?

No.

Dr. Carol is the only conclusion that makes any sense. It has to be Dr. Carol. It has to be.

Otherwise it's just me.

They give me another log of Nutraloaf for lunch but I don't eat it. When they come to drop the dinner tray it's the young cop with the broken hand, again.

"I brought you something," he says.

I struggle to sit up in the awkward fabric tube and manage to sort of prop the upper half of my body against the wall. My legs stick straight out in front of me. He checks over his shoulder, then quickly pulls a granola bar out of his pocket and drops it on my tray.

"You need to stay strong," he says, and gives me a smile.

They'll do whatever Dr. Carol Elliott says. They'll follow her to an isolated location where she can terminate their therapy, one by one. She'll take them to Sagefire, her wellness retreat in the mountains. That's what she'll do. Trap them there and stalk them, and they'll die, trusting her right up until the end.

"I need a phone," I croak.

"I'm sorry," the young cop says. "All I can do is the bar. That's all I can do."

I'm sorry, too.

The suicide tube keeps me immobilized and my muscles stiffen. My legs throb and ache with sluggish blood. I want to hug myself to stay warm but I can barely bend my arms. When the cop with the broken hand comes back, he looks at the uneaten granola bar and shakes his head.

He puts the fresh tray on my slab bed and squats, regarding me.

"Please," I say through cracked lips. "You have to get me a phone."

"Did you really love him?" he asks.

My brain is so numb I don't realize who he's talking about at first.

"Ricky Walker," he says. "Did you love him?"

"No," I croak, not sure where this is going.

"Too bad," he says, and reaches over and puts one big hand over my mouth.

He pinches my nostrils closed. I can't breathe. All I can taste is his salty palm. I can't get any air. I try to sit up but he holds me down easily with his broken hand. He looks over his shoulder, then turns back to me and he has all the expression on his face of a man filling up his car with gas. He's not angry. He's insane.

"Everyone's going to be so jealous," he says.

Who said the police couldn't be monsters, too? It's the end of the road, but my body reflexively keeps fighting. I scratch at his wrists but can't get any leverage in the Fergie. I try to kick but the fabric tube traps my legs. My skull throbs with black blood. Gray clouds rush in fast as I lose my peripheral vision and everything sounds so far away.

I didn't accomplish anything. I left Julia bleeding on my floor, I ran away, I got arrested, I wound up here, I died. All my plans were useless, all my strengths were weaknesses in disguise. I didn't save anyone. I wrote those letters. I wrote that book. That's all I ever did.

I make my lungs stop fighting. My visual field starts to turn black.

Garrett P. Cannon's voice floats down to me from the top of a well.

"About time," he says.

The cop turns. Garrett stands in the door of my cell.

The young cop lets go of my mouth and I hiccup in huge blasts of oxygen. I can't seem to get enough air to my brain. Still squatting, the cop goes for his sidearm. Garrett kicks him in the point of his chin with one cowboy boot and the cop drops on his ass, then sprawls backward, his skull smacking against the cinder-block wall.

"Asshole," Garrett says, and starts to stomp on him with his boots.

I black out.

```
 1    CARL HARTMAN: Okay. You and Sofia watched the boys go into the house?
 2
 3    MARILYN TORRES: Carlos and Tug, you know, they went in after that man. Then
 4    we didn't hear anything for a really long time. Luis wanted to go in after them.
 5
 6    CARL HARTMAN: Why didn't he?
 7
 8    MARILYN TORRES: Because he's 12. We wouldn't let him.
 9
10    CARL HARTMAN: Can you tell us what happened next?
11
12    MARILYN TORRES: This other man rides up on his motorcycle and he looked so
13    normal, he seemed like an okay guy. We didn't know who he was. He started
14    talking to us and made us feel better.
15
16    BOUDE ENRIGHT: What did he say?
17
18    MARILYN TORRES: Just, um, nice things, you know, like things you'd say if you
19    were a normal man.
20
21    CARL HARTMAN: And what happened next?
22
23    MARILYN TORRES: Then the other one came out on the porch with a shotgun.
24
25    BOUDE ENRIGHT: Hold on, can you, uh, which other one?
26
27    MARILYN TORRES: We hadn't seen him before. He was fat and short and had on a
28    Confederate flag T-shirt. And a shotgun that was, you know, also short and—
29
30    CARL HARTMAN: A sawed-off shotgun?
31
32    MARILYN TORRES: Yes, and the man on the bike who seemed so normal he took hold
33    of little Luis, and he, um, he . . .
34
35    CARL HARTMAN: Take your time.
36
37    CARL HARTMAN: Do you want to take a break? Do you need some water?
38
39    MARILYN TORRES: He took hold of little Luis and, uh, bent him, um . . .
40
41    CARL HARTMAN: Do you need a moment?
42
43    MARILYN TORRES: He bent him over the seat of his motorcycle.
44
45    BOUDE ENRIGHT: And?
46
47    MARILYN TORRES: He took a straight razor out of his boot and scalped him alive.
```

—transcript of Lt. Boude Enright and Deputy Carl Hartman interviewing
multiple homicide survivor Marilyn Torres, July 17, 1978

THE FINAL GIRL SUPPORT GROUP XIII:
The Final Sacrifice

When I wake up, I'm not in the Fergie. I'm in a different cell, one without the letters taped to the observation wall. There's a paramedic shining a flashlight in my eyes. He asks me how many fingers he's holding up. I take a chance.

"Three?"

They lead me to the shower. When I come out my street clothes are folded on a bench in front of an angry-looking female deputy. I dry myself with the washcloth-sized piece of sandpaper that passes for a towel, and pull my clothes on over cold wet skin, and the whole time I can still taste the young cop's hand on my tongue. The whole time I'm waiting for this cop to pull her riot stick and break my kneecaps, crush my windpipe, leave me choking on my own blood on the wet concrete floor.

Instead, she shackles me in an interview room for a very long time.

Finally, the door opens and Garrett P. Cannon comes in wearing one of his many tan suits and giant white hats.

"Ready to hit the road?" he asks. "You and me're headed back to Utah. The Los Angeles Pee Dee realizes they don't have the wherewithal to keep you safely incarcerated, so we're going to take a little trip back to American Fork, where you're going to stand trial as an accessory in the murder of your mother, your boyfriend, your poor little sister, Officer Miller, and your father. Trust me, Lynnette, we'll find a way to add on some years for your foster family and the three police officers killed in the line of duty there, too. We're going to have ourselves a fine old time."

He winks at me.

"Was it my doctor?" I ask.

"Who?" Garrett asks, grin fading.

"Was it Dr. Carol who got that cop to take a shot at me?"

"Officer Dean Foley was a superfan," he says. "Apparently he's been waiting his whole entire life to get his hands on you."

"He didn't do it alone," I say. "This is a conspiracy. Someone else will take a shot."

"Guess what, Oliver Stone?" he says. "I don't really give a shit. Let's go."

When the cop opens the door to the parking lot, the sun hammers into my eyes like nails. My ice-cold skin hungrily soaks up the warmth. This is why I moved to L.A. in the first place: no winters. My clothes haven't been washed in a week and they're limp and greasy, but the sun kisses me alive again and the air smells like something besides all-in-one cleaning product.

"Move your ass," a steroidal deputy says over my left shoulder.

I shuffle forward, following Garrett, chains singing on the concrete, trying to keep my head on a swivel because Dr. Carol could have her sniper here again, but I keep getting distracted by all the colors.

I'm overwhelmed by the minivans, and the SUVs, and the Trans Ams, and the bushes, and the blue sky without a single cloud. The breeze smells like California and I feel like a human sacrifice being led to the altar.

Just when my eyes are getting used to the sun bouncing off everyone's windshields, I have to squint again because the past twenty years disappear and there sits Garrett's 1976 cherry-red Cadillac Seville.

"That's a beauty," the deputy says, squatting to take the shackles off my feet.

"First car I ever owned," Garrett says. "It's gonna cost me $152 in gas to drive to Provo but she's worth every penny."

I don't want to get in his car. I remember being in it too many times before with his body on top of mine, his hands all over me, but when Garrett opens the back door and guides me inside with his hand on the back of my head, the way all cops do, from their first day of training till the day they die, I don't resist. What's the point? All I can do is go along.

He opens one cuff, then locks it around a restraint bar bolted to his car door.

"Comfy?" he asks, then slams the door without waiting for an answer.

I bask in the heat while he and the deputy shoot the shit. This car was Garrett's pride and joy, but now he's put in a restraint bar and heavy black metal mesh separating the front seats from the back. I try the door. It doesn't open from the inside.

"—but you come see me next and I'll be happy to take your money," Garrett says, getting in.

He slams his door and waves to the deputy, who's taking a picture of Garrett's ridiculous car with his phone. Garrett makes sure to hold his head at just the right angle to tighten up the loose skin on his neck.

"Seat belt, Lynnette," Garrett says, turning the ignition and sparking the engine to life. "Can't have you smashing your pretty little teeth out in an accident before I'm done with you."

We pull out onto the street. The Caddy sounds like a tank.

"We're going to hit the trail and it ain't gonna be no yellow brick road," Garrett says as he threads through late-afternoon traffic and the police station disappears behind us. "Unless getting a lethal injection needle stuck in your arm sounds like meeting the Wizard of Oz."

Cars pass on either side of us, riding high, looking down into the back seat where any of them could take a shot.

"You know," he says. "I bought this vehicle with the first check I ever got for that Walker brothers movie. Hell, they paid me for every day I was on set and all I ever did was make sure those actors playing peace officers didn't hold their weapons like a bunch of pricks."

I slink to the floor, my handcuffed arm sticking up. I'm still not protected from the sides, but at least no one can shoot me through the back window. How did it come to this? A week ago I was free; now my past has caught up with me and it's hungry. How did Dr. Carol do this alone? She needed help, someone we wouldn't see coming, someone like . . . Heather. Who called the cops, whose story never quite stays the same when she tells it twice, who could easily have burned down her halfway house, who was right inside Marilyn's perimeter when I got there, who called the cops and put me where Dean Foley could try to kill me.

"I never did think the fella playing me looked right," Garrett says. "But I guess it's hard to nail my aura. The way I carry myself and handle situations and suchlike. An actor can't learn that. You know what that director said when I told him I should play myself? 'Officer Cannon,' he told me, 'you would bring so much authenticity to the screen it'd make all the other actors look fake.' There's truth in that."

I press myself against the right-hand door to protect my torso and head from anyone coming by on the right, but I'm still wide open on the left. I slide to the floor. Why am I even trying? They've thought this through well in advance. They've been three steps ahead of me all along. I am weak and alone, and they are legion and strong.

"Goddammit, Lynne," Garrett calls through the black wire mesh. "Quit your damn crawling and sit straight, or I'm going to pull this car over and Mace you in the face."

Reluctantly I slide back up onto the seat, just as he pulls into a Carl's Jr. drive-through. Something Pavlovian goes off in my stomach and I start to drool. I'm so hungry it overrides my sense of self-preservation and I gawp at the pictures on the big menu board like a hick on his first trip into town.

"Howdy," Garrett says to the speaker. "I'll have a Guacamole Turkey

Burger, with extra cheese, small chili cheese fries, and a medium orange shake, and how about a small Diet Coke to go with that."

"That'll be $12.79," the robot voice says.

"Gotta watch my weight," Garrett, says pulling forward. "Oh, hellfire, Lynne, did you want something?"

He had to have heard my stomach.

"Yes," I say.

"You got any money?" he asks, looking in the rearview mirror.

"I'll pay you back."

"It's nine hours to Provo," he says. "Have some gum."

He pushes a twenty-five-cent pack of Big Red through the wire mesh and it falls on the floor. The hot buttery smell from his paper bag makes my stomach gnaw on itself. We pull back out on the highway and I promise that I won't beg him for a fry. I won't plead for a sip of his drink.

"Want to know a secret?" Garrett says between pulls on his straw. "I knew that Foley boy was sweet on you. I know about every single one of your stalkers. I made sure he was first up to bat when we took you down and I'll admit I was thrown that he didn't take a shot at you then. But all good things come to those who wait."

"You wanted him to kill me?" I ask, astonished that he still hates me so much. Maybe I'm wrong. Maybe it's not Dr. Carol who wants us dead.

"I wanted the LAPD to realize that they were singularly unsuited to your incarceration," he said. "I wanted to have some alone time together, just like the old days."

I feel weightless. We're heading up into the San Bernardino hills. Garrett unwraps his sandwich and takes a bite, then puts it back in the bag. Like he's saving it for later. I realize that he'd be exactly the person Dr. Carol would call.

"You and me got a bond, Lynne," Garrett says. We're past Rancho Cucamonga and traffic is thinning out as we head up 15 into the mountains. It's all rocks and dirt fields, mini-storage facilities with pictures of rats carrying trunks out front. I'm so hungry the smell of hot burger makes me light-headed. "We both know that sometimes you got to take things into your own hands."

Garrett talks too much when he's nervous, and he's only nervous when he's working up his courage to do something he doesn't want to do. I try the cuffs. They're clamped too tight. Even sweaty I don't think I can slip them. I look around for a weapon. Nothing but my teeth and nails and the pack of gum.

"You know, when I first heard that the Provo DA had those love letters I didn't believe him," Garrett says. He's not checking me in the rearview mirror anymore. "But when I went to the DA's office and read them, I swear I could feel everything that was settled opening right back up like a can of worms. Little squiggling wormies wriggling all over, messing everything up. I don't like worms, Lynne. I ever tell you that? It's why I don't fish."

My belt, maybe, I can wrap it around my hand and hit him with the buckle. I once planned to hide a razor blade in the lining of my jeans but I never got around to it. Over the years I have gotten soft, and weak, and lazy. And Dr. Carol has gotten smart, and organized, and strong. There is no option here that doesn't end with me dead. With all of us dead.

She got Adrienne killed and she's already broken Dani's heart by keeping her away from Michelle. She'll finish off Julia, then Marilyn, she'll take down Heather, and me, and . . .

Stephanie.

"DA got those love letters from Billy Walker himself," he says. "Had them buried near his brother's grave. Don't know why he never said anything before but who knows why a nutjob does anything? I loved your daddy, you know. He and me always saw eye to eye. I know he could be quick with his temper, but he understood I was a man who'd do what needed to be done. He could rely on me to make the hard decisions."

Stephanie Fugate. I think of her folder on Dr. Carol's desk. Her big, dumb, hopeful, brace-faced teenaged grin. Her wide eyes peeking out from underneath her bangs. The way she looks like Gillian.

She looks just like Gillian.

We pass a lonely wind farm where the big crosses turn slow, then we fly through a little speck of country living: a red-and-white sign for Tony's Diner, a yellow-and-black sign reading *Saloon* that looks like a first-grader painted it, a crumbling parking lot surrounded by a sagging chain-link fence. Then we're alone in the dry, brown hills again.

"I don't like anyone pissing all over my memories of the dearly departed," Garrett says. "I resent those letters showing off your daddy's shortcomings to the world."

I think about Stephanie and all those files of all those baby final girls in Dr. Carol's office. Why does she have them? She said it in the visiting room: "I have spent my life trying to build a world where women like you don't have to exist."

When is the cure worse than the disease?

Garrett slows the car, then takes a turn onto a narrow two-lane blacktop that squirms into the hills. We grind past some abandoned, half-built homes, and he pulls in behind one with busted-out windows, wires hanging from holes where the porch lights were supposed to go. Half the roof has been finished with red clay tiles; the other half is torn-up tar paper, ripped strips flapping in the wind.

Of course we're pulling over. Garrett would never mess up the interior of his Caddy. He puts it in park, kills the engine, and gets out. For a few silent seconds I scan my options. There aren't many. Maybe run for the half-finished house and try to get the drop on him?

Garrett opens my door, pulling my right arm along with it. He's got his gun in his left hand, held down by his side. I can't see the road from here. I don't think he's going to wait to get me inside the house. I've finally figured out the answer and it's too late. I'm too slow. Too dumb. Too useless.

"Come on out of the car, Lynnette," he says. "It's time we settled this."

"Garrett—" I begin.

"Nah," he says. "My mind's made up. Now turn around."

I step out, and my head spins, and I turn around, facing the trunk, my handcuffed right arm stretched behind me. I just wish I weren't letting Stephanie down. Once I'm in a shallow grave, who's going to save her? Who's going to warn her about Garrett P. Cannon and Dr. Carol? In the end, there were too many of them. In the end, I let down everyone I cared about.

There's a click by my wrist, and the handcuff opens. I close my eyes.

"What're you waiting for?" Garrett asks. His voice is far away. I open my eyes and he's heading for the house. "Come on."

Garrett vanishes inside and I could run, I could be gone in a second, but I need to know what he's playing at.

Curiosity was the faceless monster that stuck a pitchfork through the cat.

I pick my way across the rocky front yard, shaking with hunger and exhaustion, my wrist bruised. I pick up a dirty chunk of concrete. I feel better following Garrett into this dark house with something in my hand.

"What the hell is that for?" he asks, coming back outside and holstering his Colt. "You making paperweights?" He plucks it from my hand and tosses it back into the yard. "I figured we'd talk better in the sun. And let me be quite honest, I don't have a handle on this thing yet, and until I do I'm assuming my vehicle might be bugged. 'Cause someone knows an awful lot about everything before I do."

I eye him, waiting for his gun hand to come up fast.

"What the hell, Lynne?" he asks. "You thought I was going to jump you? Oh, hell, you think I'm going to shoot you?"

"Aren't you?" I ask.

"Are you kidding?" He smiles. "This whole thing smelled like ratshit from the word *go*."

Everything looks strange. The house, the yard, Garrett. He grins at me like we're old friends.

"What?"

I feel thick and stupid.

"Let me tell you something, Lynnette," Garrett says. "If there's one thing I've learned over the years, it's how to know when I'm being played.

Twenty years later, suddenly there's bold new information? That happens in the movies, not real life. Billy Walker told the DA about those letters because someone wanted you in custody and it wasn't a dumbass like Billy Walker. Why? You lost your looks a long time ago, and your ass is too skinny to fuck. I called my Hollywood contacts and your franchise is radioactive. No one wants to even think about it, much less reboot it. So who gives a shit about you? I figured they'd send someone out here to pick you up and bring you back to Provo and I figured at least you and me got history. So I volunteered."

"I don't believe you," I say.

"You don't believe me?" he says. Garrett licks his lips and gets angry. That's how I know he's not lying. "I stayed in that police station waiting for that cuckoo bird to make his move for three days! I brought you out here, I'm setting your ugly ass free; I want to deal with whatever bullshit is going on right now because I don't appreciate someone pissing all over the memory of the one man I ever truly respected and, hell, maybe we could even get a new book out of this, maybe write it together. My agent says that if you co-authored we'd get one hell of an advance, especially if there was some current event for a peg. I got a ghostwriter who will knock your socks off."

I can't look at Garrett anymore. I'm so grateful he's not executing me in the desert that I don't trust myself not to do something stupid. Like hug him. I picture him naked, gray snarl of belly hair, flat saggy ass, cowboy hat still on. That sobers me right up.

"So who's doing this?" I ask.

"I was hoping you'd tell me," he says. "Someone's gunning for you and your gal pals. Who'd you piss off?"

A plug opens in my belly and tension drains out in a cold flood. Someone is finally listening. It may just be Garrett P. Cannon, but I'll take it.

"It's more than one person," I say. "It has to be. Christophe Volker went after Adrienne and then everything happened too fast for it not to be organized. Someone called Russell and told him about my book—"

"You're writing a book?" He actually sounds hurt.

"Not like that," I say. "I never meant for it to get out."

"Then what's the point?" he asks.

"It was an exercise," I say. "For my peace of mind."

"Hippy-dippy bullshit," he grumbles.

"But someone got it," I say. "Off my computer."

"You ever heard of a password?" he asks.

I ignore him and keep going.

"They read it and they got Russell Thorn to go to Julia. She knew my address and so the two of them came to my place. Whoever shot them was waiting for us to be together. Then they burned down Heather's halfway house. Then Harry Peter Warden came forward about Dani. Then Billy Walker told the DA's office about those letters. It's all happening too fast."

"Someone who can organize communication from inside prison and outside," Garrett says. "That takes a lot of effort."

"Dr. Carol," I say. "Process of elimination. She's the only one who knows how to press all our buttons like this."

"Motive?"

"I think she's sick in the head," I say. "I think she believes that the only way to cure us is to kill us."

"A crazy headshrinker," he marvels, then he tries out a tagline. "The doctor is in . . . sane."

"Maybe there's more to it than that," I say. "Maybe she wants to write a new book and needs a peg."

"That'd be cold-blooded," he says, but I hear respect in his voice.

"It's a cold-blooded business," I say. "Right now I think if someone looked at the visitor list for Billy Walker and then for Harry Peter Warden they'd find her name on both."

"Someone would have to be a genius to check those visitor lists, wouldn't you say?" Garrett asks.

"Not really."

"Well, this genius already has," he beams. "I haven't paid Mr. Warden a visit quite yet, but there's one name that's all over Billy Walker's list like shit on a hog. And it ain't your lady doctor. She sent someone to run her errands. It's one of you girls."

I know who he's going to say before he says it.

"Chrissy Mercer," he says.

I was expecting Heather.

"Oh," I say, but I'm relieved for a moment that maybe Heather's back on my side again.

"Makes sense," he says. "Your lady doctor loves collecting final girls. She just didn't tell you she had the complete set."

My relief disappears and I feel sick again but that doesn't matter. It's possible, and if it's possible I have to see if it's true.

"Mr. Warden and I are going to have a little come-to-Jesus while you engage in some girl talk with Crazy Chrissy," he says. "I even brought some of your topless pictures to help flush her out."

Of course he still has those pictures.

"What about Provo?" I ask.

"Hell," he says. "I was never going to take you to Provo, Lynne. Your daddy would come back from his grave and kill me dead if I did that. Come on."

He crunches across the construction rubble and unlocks his trunk. Inside is my go bag and fanny pack. My pistol is still in it, my cash, my cell phone.

"I charged up your phone and helped myself to five hundred dollars," he says. "Finder's fee. I'll give you an invoice later. You can deduct it as a business expense. A 'thank you' would be the appropriate response. I know you got a hard time with social cues."

"What about you?" I ask, changing the subject.

"What about me?" he tosses back. "I figure I pulled over because you were complaining of cramps and then you had some associates jump me.

I'm thinking two, maybe three Black males, five-eleven to six-two, two hundred pounds apiece. One of them with a sawed-off shotgun. Maybe throw a skinhead in there, just to make it less racist."

"A skinhead and two Black guys?" I ask.

"All you got to do is pop me in the eye, scuff me up a little, handcuff me to my vehicle," he says. "Then you hike on back to that diner we passed. It's about a forty-minute walk. You can call yourself a cab from there. You're resourceful, Lynne. I'll keep in touch with you about Warden and keep an eye on your doctor and you go hunt down Crazy Chrissy. Right now you got a hunch. If our book is going to be a bestseller, we need proof."

"Why don't you punch yourself?" I ask.

"I can't bring myself to damage a work of art." He grins. "Now, come on. Enough fooling around." He secures his pistol in its holster with the snap. "I don't want my reflexes kicking in and shooting you. Aim for my right eye, and see if you can raise a bruise with those bitty little hands of yours."

And I realize that Garrett P. Cannon has saved my life for a third time.

"You think it's more believable if it was two Black guys and *two* skinheads?" he asks.

I knee him in the balls as hard as I can.

"Oofff!" he says, and goes down sideways, hands cupping his crotch too late.

"Just tell them it was one pissed-off girl," I say.

I pluck his keys out of his hand and get in the Caddy. I make a big loop around him as he struggles to his feet. I floor it and raise a brown dust cloud, and then I'm on the blacktop heading for the highway. I crank the air up high and punch the gas. I've got an emergency stop to make before I track down Crazy Chrissy.

Even though it's cold, that Carl's Jr. burger is the best thing I've eaten all week.

In 1991, my high school boyfriend and his best friend murdered eight of our classmates while attempting to groom me into being the "Final Girl" of their sick fantasies. Their warped dreams were fueled by horror movies, in particular those of the ultraviolent "slasher" genre.

With the help of several therapists, my family, and friends, as well as various antidepressants and anti-anxiety medications, I graduated from high school and entered Windsor College. I believed that I could leave the darkness behind and continue with my life. However, my first semester at Windsor I met Raymond Carlton. He appeared athletic, intelligent, curious, compassionate, funny, warm, and kind. He seemed almost too good to be true.

He was. Ray's good nature camouflaged a sociopathic desire for fame. In his quest to replicate the murders that had occurred in my high school, he slaughtered five members of my freshman class. He only stopped when I caught him assaulting my roommate and tackled him out the third-story window of our dorm room. As a result of my injuries from the fall, I am partially paralyzed to this day. Despite the best efforts of the paramedics, my roommate died.

Even today, Raymond Carlton continues to correspond with fans of his violent acts and I believe he encourages them to act out their darkest fantasies. No matter what the authorities try, they do not seem to be able to cut off all his lines of communication.

It is for this reason that I am writing once again to ask you to deny Raymond Carlton's latest petition for parole.

Julia Campbell

—Julia Campbell, letter to the Board of Parole Hearings,
California Department of Corrections, February 2009

THE FINAL GIRL SUPPORT GROUP XIV:
The New Blood

I decide to keep it simple. I'll just kidnap Stephanie Fugate.

The media spent a few days swarming all over the family, so it isn't hard to find her address: a nice neighborhood in Santa Monica. I drive as slow as I can make myself go and park across the street. Her house has two stories, three bedrooms, a two-car garage, and lots of landscaping. She's the older of two so she probably has the bigger bedroom over the garage. I'll go through the bushes, get on the garage roof, and convince her to come outside. I'm not sure how I'll do that exactly, but all I have to do is keep her safe for a few days. Our monsters get too worked up to drag things out for very long.

No muss, no fuss, my plan is foolproof because it's simple. I'm an arrow firing straight into the future. All my decisions feel right.

I shove open the driver's-side door, stand on the asphalt that's still radiating the day's heat, and before I can let the door swing shut a man says, "Tell me why you're watching my house or I'm calling the police."

He's standing in the shadow of a palm tree across the street, wearing shorts and a worn oxford shirt, and he's probably been watching me as long as I've been watching the house. He holds his phone in one hand and a leash in the other. At the end of the leash, a bow-legged Chihuahua glares at me.

I focused so hard on the house I forgot to check my immediate environment.

"The press has been ringing your doorbell all week," I say, improvising, eyes on his hand, making sure his thumb's not pressing connect. "Neighbors coming by, phone ringing nonstop. I bet you've already had a few people who lied to you about who they were. Those are her future stalkers and fanboys. I get why you're upset."

His fingers stab the phone three times, and then his thumb hovers over the screen again.

"I'm calling in three, two—"

I step forward, hand outstretched.

"Dr. Laura Newbury." I smile. "I'm a therapist who works with young people like Stephanie. You may know my partner in our practice, Dr. Carol Elliott."

His mouth drops open like a cartoon and he turns into another man, reaching for my hand with his phone hand, doing a doofy dad double take, sliding it into his pocket, grabbing my hand in his sweaty palm, and pumping my elbow up and down.

"You got our voicemails," he says, face full of relief.

"Dr. Elliott couldn't make it," I improvise. "So she sent me."

This will be harder, but better. I'll convince the Fugates to let me take Stephanie somewhere safe, and they won't send anyone looking for us because I'm Dr. Carol Elliott's partner. It'll let me drive a little slower, think a little clearer. I've just bought myself hours.

"You can't imagine what they've been doing to her," he says.

"Actually, I can."

"Ken Fugate," he says, still grinning at the surprise of it all. "My wife is going to be so relieved. I hope you don't mind, but can I see some ID? To be safe."

"Of course," I say, and step back to slam the Caddy door closed, which gives me the privacy to reach into my fanny pack without him seeing the gun. I've got five different identities in here; it takes me a second to find the right one.

Alternate IDs got intensely illegal after 9/11, so I paid extra to get these shipped all the way from China inside a book. Offset printed, die cut, a magnetic strip on the back, and a bar code make them identical to state-issued ID. The only difference is my picture laser engraved on the front next to Dr. Newbury's name.

"This license is expired," Ken says.

"I keep meaning to get it renewed."

"Two years ago."

"I've been busy."

The Chihuahua stares up at me, unblinking.

"You can call Dr. Elliott if you want," I say. "I'll give you her cell number. Tonight's parent/teacher night at Pax's school, though. That's her son. But I'm sure she wouldn't mind."

The Chihuahua just stares. What is wrong with this thing?

"Come on inside," Ken says, his celebrity crush overcoming his caution, turning toward his house. "I think all the media cleared out, but who knows. I'm sure the last thing you want is for anyone to know you're here."

"Absolutely," I say, following him across the dark street.

I control my breathing, I stay calm, I walk the way a famous trauma therapist's partner walks, confident and cool, like I have all the answers. I repeat my mantra over and over inside my head.

I am Dr. Newbury. I am Dr. Newbury. I am Dr. Newbury.

"Stephanie seems like herself," he says over his shoulder. "But this must be crushing. To have it happen twice before she's even sixteen? After the tennis thing she couldn't sleep; she stopped playing and that was her life; she lost weight. Then she starts going to Red Lake and bang! Total one-eighty. Now this? We don't know what to do for her."

Instead of going in the front door, he pushes open a white gate and we go around the side of the house. It's all windows. They don't know what to do for Stephanie? Start by boarding up all these entry points, that's what they should do. Harden their location. Act like there's an actual emergency happening here.

He unlocks the kitchen door while the Chihuahua keeps staring at me, and I'm glad they're at least locking doors. There's weather stripping around the edges and it makes a sucking sound when he pushes hard and I follow him into the cool, expensive kitchen that smells like fresh lemons.

A woman with gray roots in her blond hair leans against the sink, watching us. She probably saw us coming through all these windows. She looks like the kind of woman who demands a lot of explanations.

"Cheryl," Ken Fugate says. "You'll never believe it."

Cheryl scans my face as Ken unclips the leash from the Chihuahua's harness. The stove is huge, and its burners look like they could scorch a human face; the knife block next to Cheryl is full of German steel, and there's a meat tenderizer that could crack a skull on the butcher-block kitchen island. So many ways she could hurt me, all within her reach.

"Who's this?" she asks.

"It's Dr. Elliott's partner," Ken says as the Chihuahua clicks away into the house.

We all stare at each other for a moment, and then I put my hand out.

"Dr. Newbury," I say. "Carol and I are going to make sure Stephanie gets through this."

Cheryl launches herself at me, chin twisting to one side, forehead going up, eyes turning red, and she presses her body to mine, hands on my shoulder blades, hair blocking my sightlines. I try to hug her back, the way an award-winning therapist's partner would, as she presses herself to me, rendering my arms useless, holding me in place.

I am Dr. Newbury. I am Dr. Newbury. I am Dr. Newbury.

"Thank you," she whispers. "Thank you so much."

"Should we talk in the living room?" Ken suggests.

As we walk through the big white house with too many windows, I check out the locks on their front door (one deadbolt, one chain), see a recently installed alarm panel, and notice every single light is on, keeping out the dusk.

"I've got all Dr. Elliot's books," Cheryl says, going to a floor-to-ceiling bookshelf, and I see her hand floating over the shelves, and there they are. She even has the first one, before Dr. Carol learned about the marketability of a punchy title, *A Therapist's Guide to Trauma*. Cheryl's fingers stiffen, and she homes in on it.

"Time is of the essence for Stephanie," I say like I'm worth listening to, sitting on their white sofa with all the purpose of a doctor who cares about saving lives.

I have to put my back to the empty living room because they're standing by the other sofa. All that open space behind me makes my skin crawl.

Ken and Cheryl sit next to each other, Cheryl poker-up-the-ass straight, Ken resting his elbows on his knees. The low Scandinavian coffee table between us holds a silver crane with a beak sharp enough to stab out an eye and a series of glass orbs heavy enough to smash someone's teeth.

"I can't believe you came," Cheryl says. "I mean, you're not Dr. Elliott, but still, she wouldn't work with you if you weren't someone. Have you published any books? I assume when you're here it's like she's here, isn't it? Is she coming later? Not that I'm not sure you're a wonderful therapist in your own right."

"Honey," Ken says, putting a hand on her knee. "Let Dr. Newbury talk."

"Sorry," she says, flashing me a skull's hard smile. "It's been a difficult week."

We wait while she finds a Kleenex and touches it to the corners of her eyes, then blows her nose.

"We get hundreds of calls each week," I say, which sounds like something Dr. Carol, who treats so many patients with so much care, would say. "But Stephanie falls into a very special category of trauma victim, which is why I'm here."

"She'll be okay?" Cheryl asks in a very small voice.

"No," I tell her. I refuse to lie about this, even while pretending to be someone else. "That's not possible."

"What?" Cheryl's face collapses.

"Keeping her safe is the best we can do," I say, not sounding like Dr. Carol at all.

"Exactly," Ken says, rubbing Cheryl's hand. "Once she's safe, the hard work can begin."

"I need you to understand that Stephanie is what the media refer to as a final girl," I say.

Cheryl's eyebrows meet in the middle.

"No, she's not."

"Denial won't help Stephanie," I say.

"No," Cheryl says, standing up. "I'd like to hear Dr. Elliott's opinion. Can we speak to her? I want to know what she thinks. I'm sure you're a fine therapist, but she is who we called."

These two are really starting to frustrate me.

"Cheryl," I say, speaking loudly and assertively. "There are things happening you don't know, and they relate directly to Stephanie's safety."

"What?" Ken asks, reaching for Cheryl's hand without looking. She sits back down and unconsciously they lean into each other.

"A week ago, someone began targeting final girls in the Los Angeles area," I say.

"Some of them live here?" Cheryl interrupts.

"All of them," I say. "Obviously you're familiar with Adrienne Butler, but the day after she was killed, someone attacked Julia Campbell and Lynnette Tarkington."

"Who's Lynnette Tarkington?" Cheryl asks.

Is she kidding?

"A final girl."

"Do you remember that one?" Cheryl asks Ken.

"It's not important," I say, annoyed at their lack of focus. "What is important is that Stephanie is in danger."

"An officer drives by the house every three hours," Ken says. "We thought about hiring a private security outfit but our neighbors already hate us without strangers tromping through their yards. Do you think we should go ahead and pull the trigger?"

"The police, private security, they're useless," I say. "When one of these monsters comes after a final girl, nothing can stop him."

"But Christophe Volker is dead," Cheryl says.

"Volker is irrelevant," I say. "This goes beyond Volker. The danger is very real, and it's very immediate."

Something *click-click-clicks* on the hardwood floor and the Chihuahua prances into the room on its tiptoes.

"Come here, Gordon," Cheryl says, scooping him up. He sits on her lap and starts staring at me, again. Jesus Christ.

I really want to look over my shoulder. I don't like having this big empty room at my back, I don't like having this tiny dog's eyes boring into me, but a famous therapist's partner wouldn't look over her shoulder. Famous therapists and their partners aren't scared of tiny dogs.

"When's the last time you saw Steph?" Ken asks his wife, and before she can answer he's standing in the hall, calling up the stairs. "Stephanie, can you come down here a minute? Stephie?"

He turns to us, shrugging.

"I just feel more comfortable when I can see her," he says.

Cheryl and the Chihuahua stare at me while a door opens upstairs and Stephanie comes slouching down, holding onto the banister, then pads into the room.

She doesn't check her sightlines, she doesn't look behind the door, she's got no shoes on if she needs to run. Her face is soft with baby fat, her skin is so pale it hurts my eyes, and she's gotten her braces removed and dyed her hair as black as her lipstick. Black T-shirt, black jeans, she's a tiny dark star in the middle of this clean, white, contemporary living room.

"Hey," Stephanie says, and then her mouth opens in the same O of surprise her father's face made outside. "Oh my God, you're—"

I see her tongue hit the back of her top teeth to make an L and I stand up and launch myself at her, reaching around her back, slamming into her chest, dragging her against my body, pressing her to me, just like her mom.

"You're safe now, Stephanie," I say. "I'm Dr. Newbury. I work with Dr. Carol Elliott. I've come to talk to your parents about your safety."

She pulls back.

"Why?" she asks. "What happened?"

"Nothing, sweetie," Ken says, putting one big, calming dad hand on her shoulder. "You're absolutely one hundred percent safe here."

"Your father is trying to reassure you," I say, making eye contact, my hand on her other shoulder. "In reality, you could be murdered at any moment by a deranged lunatic who's killing final girls."

"I'm a final girl?" she says in a high voice.

"You're not a final girl," her mother says.

"Yes," I say. "You are a final girl."

Stephanie walks slowly to the sofa where I sat and sinks down.

"Someone else wants to kill me?" she asks, shrinking into herself. "Why? What did I do?"

Her mother and father start talking immediately, filling the room with reassuring noises, comforting sounds, saying things that aren't true to make her lower her guard. I sit next to her. I meet her eyes. I speak only to her.

"That's how your life is now," I say. "That's who you are. It didn't happen for a reason, you haven't earned it, you don't deserve it, but you need to handle it or you're going to die."

"Look," Ken says, cutting through Cheryl's noise. "I don't care for you traumatizing our daughter like this. It's not productive."

"You know what's not productive, Ken?" I ask, not taking my eyes off Stephanie. "Getting your daughter murdered because you didn't take this threat seriously enough even though one of the number one trauma therapists in the world is sitting right here warning you."

"What's Dr. Elliott's cell number?" Ken asks.

"We need to focus on Stephanie," I say. "I can keep her safe if you will let her go with me for the next three days. I can guarantee she will survive."

Cheryl hugs her Chihuahua to her with both hands.

"Where will you take her?" Ken asks.

"I can't tell you," I say confidently. "But—"

The doorbell rings.

"To be continued," Ken says, walking past me into the hall.

The front door opens and a voice says:

"I'm sorry to bother you so late, but I'm Dr. Carol Elliott, and I'm concerned your daughter might be in danger from one of my patients."

"Honey?" Ken calls from the hall, and she practically bolts past me, leaving the Chihuahua behind.

"Stephanie—" I start, looking into her eyes.

"You're Lynnette Tarkington," Stephanie says, and she almost cracks up.

"You need to trust me," I say, fast and urgent. "That woman out there wants you dead. I want to keep you safe."

"What?" she asks.

I hear urgent discussion in the hall. I can't make out the words, but any second they're going to come back into the living room.

"We're final girls," I say. "We understand each other. If you want to survive the next three days, come with me right now."

I get up and walk into the hall leading to the back of the house. My heart opens like a flower when I feel Stephanie fall into step behind me.

"Lynnette?!" I hear Dr. Carol shout behind us.

I think about reversing course, running at her fast, unzipping my fanny pack, pressing my gun to her forehead and squeezing the trigger three times, but then I'll go to prison and she can't be working alone and there will be no way to protect Stephanie from her partners.

"Hey!" Ken shouts.

"Stop!" Dr. Carol cries.

"Stephanie!" Cheryl yells, voice cracked with hysteria.

I reach back, grab Stephanie's wrist, and yank her after me. We crash through the kitchen, out the sucking side door, around the side of the house. Stupidly they follow us rather than cutting us off in the front yard. I hear Stephanie's bare feet meat-slapping the walkway behind me, quieter as we cross the grass, then louder again as we pound across the asphalt to Garrett's Caddy.

I open the driver's-side door, shove Stephanie across the bench seat, and then I'm sliding in, stabbing the key into the ignition, twisting. The big tank rumbles to life just as Dr. Carol runs across their front yard. She's wearing a white blouse. She stopped and did her hair and makeup. That's how confident she is. She didn't count on me getting to Stephanie first.

"Is that—?" Stephanie begins as I hit the gas and the big car surges forward.

I twist the wheel to swerve around Dr. Carol.

"It's the woman who's trying to kill us," I say. "One of them. There are more. A lot more. Sit on the floor and stay out of sight. I've got to do some tactical thinking. Once we're out of L.A., I'll tell you what's happening."

She slides to the floor without protest and shuts down. Good girl. Smart girl. Final girl.

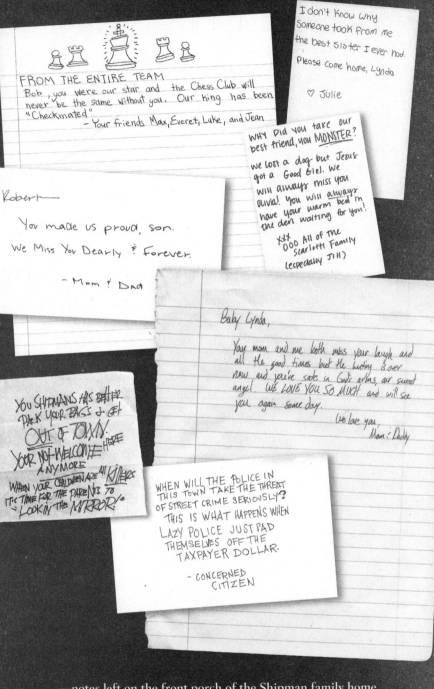

—notes left on the front porch of the Shipman family home,
November 1980

THE FINAL GIRL SUPPORT GROUP XV:
Dream Warriors

We get on the 10, heading for the 405. They're less likely to shut down a freeway than surface streets, but there are still so many ways they can stop us: Amber Alerts, highway patrol, traffic cameras, GPS tracking, outreach to radio stations. Garrett's Cadillac is the kind of car everyone remembers after it passes. I might as well be driving a neon sign.

Stephanie's phone starts playing a pop song.

"It's my mom," she says, showing me the screen from the passenger-side floor.

The car takes a lot of brute force to keep it in its lane at this speed. I keep my eyes on the road.

"Tell her you're okay," I say. "Tell her not to call the police. Tell her I'm not kidnapping you, I'm keeping you safe."

"They're going to think you're making me say that," she says as the pop song keeps drilling into my teeth. "They're going to think you have a gun."

"I do," I tell her, then reconsider. "Don't tell them that."

"Mom," she says, pressing the phone to the side of her face. "I'm—"

They don't let her speak until I'm getting on the 405 North.

"She *can* protect me," she finally says, then pauses to listen. "Yes, I—

I, yes, I know exactly who she is." Pause. "No, she's not crazy. I don't care what her doctor says. Mom?" Pause. "Mom?" Pause. "Mom!"

I reach over and already we have a rapport because she puts her phone right in my hand. Even over the Cadillac's roar I can hear Cheryl's voice squawking in panic. I press it to the side of my face.

"Cheryl," I say, then again louder. "Cheryl!"

"You'd better pull over right now and let my daughter out of that car!" she shouts.

"I will keep her safe for three days," I say. "She will not get hurt."

She's not listening. Between the engine rumble, keeping us in our lane, and the speaker distorting, I only catch the occasional word. I hear "lunatic," I hear "prison," I hear "psycho." That one hurts. Then quiet. The next voice cuts through all the static inside my head.

"Lynnette, it's not too late," Dr. Carol says. "Pull over and let the girl out of the car."

"She's staying with me until this is over," I say. "I'm going to protect her."

"From yourself?" she asks.

"We both know who I'm protecting her from," I say.

"Right now, what I know is that you're endangering a young girl's life," she says loudly, playing to Stephanie's parents, and I realize the mistake I've made.

I've left her behind to be the truth-teller, the explainer who puts all the blame on her unbalanced patient. I've given her all the leverage.

"Put me on speaker," I say.

"Lynnette, I'm not—"

"PUT ME ON SPEAKER OR THIS PHONE GOES DEAD!"

There's thumping. Then I hear echoes.

"Ken, Cheryl? Are you there?" I ask.

"My baby . . ." I hear Cheryl sob before she becomes incoherent.

"I want you all to hear me clearly," I shout into the phone. I want every word to be branded into their brains, directly from my lips, not filtered through Dr. Carol. "You know I'm armed. You put out a bulletin on a bright red Cadillac, you report Stephanie missing, you have this car pulled over by the police, you do anything to slow us down, and I'll kill her." I sense Stephanie go very still. "The minute a cop pulls this Caddy over, I'll put a bullet through her brain. She has an iPhone. We get the Amber Alerts. I'd better not see one."

I let it sink in for a second.

"Stephanie will call you every five hours so you know she's still alive. She'll turn her phone off in between, so don't try to track it. That's the deal. You shut up, sit tight, and you'll hear from your daughter every five hours until three days are up and you see her again."

Then I hang up and hold the phone out to Stephanie. She doesn't take it.

"They'll still call the police," I tell her. "But they'll argue about it for a couple of hours first. That's all I need."

She still doesn't take her phone.

"I'm not going to kill you," I say. "I'm trying to save your life. Text your mom and dad. Tell them you'll call in five hours. That'll buy us the time we need."

She takes the phone and gets busy while I get us to Westside Auto Recycling. They're in the middle of closing but I convince them to stay open. It takes a lot of money. Stephanie comes with me but she walks slow and drugged, like she's being forced at gunpoint. Like I'm holding her hostage.

We buy four used Chevy wheels and tires and I pay cash, then she helps me roll/bounce them back out to the Caddy. Two fit in the trunk, two fit in the back seat. We head toward Burbank, the car reeking of vulcanized rubber.

I can tell Stephanie wants to ask questions when I pull into the Burbank parking garage and drive up to level three, but she keeps quiet. Good girl. She checks the time when I ask. It's only been fifty minutes. I figure we have another forty left on our head start.

There's an empty space next to my Chevy Lumina with its four flats. I pull in and shut off the engine. The Caddy ticks to itself while I check my sightlines. Stephanie cranes around in her seat, trying to see what I'm looking at. No one's there. Whatever conspiracy this is, they're stretched to the limit. They can't spare the personnel to watch an escape route they thought they'd closed last week.

I get the jack out of the trunk and Stephanie watches while I jack up the Lumina and start loosening lugs.

"I don't like being out here," she says.

"The faster we change these tires the faster we're on the road," I tell her as I work. "Change the last two yourself. I have to make some calls."

"I've never changed a tire before," she says.

"You just saw me do two," I say. "Learn by doing."

She starts working on the next tire and I walk away and fish my burner out of my go bag and turn it on. None of these calls are going to be much fun.

"Leave me alone!" Marilyn screams so loud I have to hold the phone away from my ear.

I told her housekeeper I was Dr. Carol so she'd transfer my call to her bedroom. She's not happy it's me. There's a thump and a scuffle and I worry that someone's attacking her, and then her voice is ugly and close in my ear again.

"'A Texas debutante who never got told "no" by her father,'" she reads. "'When they rebooted her franchise, Marilyn Torres's descent into alcoholism was heartbreaking.' Alcoholism?!"

"No one was supposed to see that," I explain. "Someone stole it and sent it out to discredit me."

"It worked," she says.

I've thought hard about how to frame the next part.

"I know you hate me but you need to be careful," I say. "Don't leave the house. Don't let anyone visit. You're safe there."

"Don't tell me what to do," she says. "You, of all people, don't get to tell me what to do."

"Don't trust anyone," I say. "Not even Dr. Carol."

"Don't talk to me about who to trust," she says, and her speech is a little thicker, a little slurred. "I don't trust *you*."

"How're Julia and Heather?" I ask.

"I'm hanging up," Marilyn says. "I don't want you calling me back or coming around. I don't even want to look you in the eye because I think I'd spit."

"You have to listen to me," I say, and I explain why for a full minute before I realize she's hung up.

When I call back, her housekeeper won't put me through.

I call Dani knowing she won't answer but needing to leave a message just in case.

"What?" she asks.

"You got out," I say, genuinely surprised.

"Bail," she says. "Pending trial. I'm under house arrest."

"Stay home," I tell her. "Lock down. Don't let anyone on your property."

There's a long silence, and when she speaks her voice is measured and dead.

"They found my wife's corpse in the public park where you dumped her," she says.

"We wanted to take her home," I explain. "But she didn't know the way."

"What do you want, Lynnette?" she asks.

"You can't trust anyone," I tell her. "Not Dr. Carol. Not the police. No one."

"They told me you'd say that," she says. "Good-bye."

"Wait!" I shout. "Who told you?"

But she's hung up. When I call back, a recorded voice tells me that this customer hasn't set up her voicemail.

I try Julia, but get no answer. I try Heather but that AT&T customer's number is no longer in service. My skin feels too tight. I need them to listen but they won't even let me speak. When I get back to Stephanie she's taking off the Caddy's license plates and dropping them in the garbage. I'm glad to see her taking some initiative.

We pull out. After driving Garrett's tank, the Lumina handles like a soda can. We get on the freeway. It's a struggle to keep the speedometer under eighty miles an hour and the car drives rough with junkyard tires. I'm so focused on the road I'm genuinely surprised when I glance at Stephanie and see lights reflecting off her wet cheeks.

"I'm not actually going to shoot you," I say.

"I know," she says, dully.

"Then don't cry," I say. "Do you see me crying?"

"I don't even know what's going on," she says, and her voice hitches.

So I tell her. It takes us until the other side of Death Valley before I'm finished. I look at the clock. It's going on two in the morning. After I get to the part about kicking Garrett P. Cannon in the balls and stealing his car, I stop, and there's quiet for a long time.

Then Stephanie begins to choke, and shake, and I think she's crying again and all that was for nothing, and I feel my chest flash hot, and then I realize she's laughing. She laughs hard, and it quickly edges over into hysteria. She gasps out high-pitched peals of laughter, dissolves into hiccups, pounds on the dashboard with her heels. I let it run its course.

She just saw her friends murdered. Now someone's trying to kill her. She's bound to dissociate. I remember when this happened to me. Laughing when I should be crying, crying when I should be laughing, and at some point I got my emotions so mixed up I couldn't remember how I was supposed to be acting anymore.

"Is all that true?" she finally asks, breathless, trying to recover from her laughing jag.

"Why would I lie?" I say.

Before we go any further I need to ask a question of my own that's been tickling at the base of my brain.

"Why were you so quick to come?" I ask. "You don't know me."

Silent seconds slide by.

"I know who you are," she says, serious now. "I know that what's happened to me happened to you. I trust you."

"I'm not even a little bit convinced," I say.

Beyond the spill of our headlights, the desert is dark. A wire fence unscrolls on our right.

"You remind me of Alana," she says in the dark. "Like, exactly. She was my best friend at camp. If she got to grow up she'd be you. Whenever she said anything I knew she meant it. In my head, I'm pretending you're her."

I leave it there. Sometimes we have to follow our guts. That's why we survive.

"Can you get online with your phone?" I ask, letting her know the subject's closed.

"What do you need?" she asks.

"I need to meet someone, but they won't come if they know it's me."

"What do I do?"

"Go to ManCrafting.com," I say as a car passes, washing us with its headlights.

I hope the homepage isn't too intense for her.

"Oh." She sounds like she pricked her thumb on a needle, and then there's silence from her side of the car. "What is this?"

"It's a site run by the person I need to see," I say. "I don't want you looking around there; don't go on any of the other pages. I just want you to go to the contact page."

"This shit is creepy," she says. "What is it?"

"It's murderabilia," I tell her. "There's none of it on the contact page. Go there now."

"It's an email form," she says.

"I want you to type what I tell you."

We go back and forth for a while, and I have to spell out a lot of words ("No, P as in *Paul*," I repeat for the five hundredth time) but by the time we reach Tonopah we have this:

URGENT HELLO. I MUST SELL A LARGE QUANTITY OF ITEMS FOUND IN A MINI-STORAGE LOCKER THAT I PURCHASED. MY BOYFRIEND SAYS THAT YOUR SITE MIGHT BE INTERESTED IN THEM. THERE ARE SEVERAL PHOTOS AND SOME CLOTHES THAT BELONG TO THE KIND OF PEOPLE YOU ARE INTERESTED IN. PEACE OUT (that was Stephanie's touch), MARCIA

Stephanie presses send and now it's up to Chrissy.

In the rearview mirror, a cop noses out from around an eighteen-wheeler and draws up behind me.

"Before the guy came to camp," Stephanie says out of nowhere, "I was worried about what I wore, and whether I was skinny enough, and what to do with my hair, and what I ate, and trying to decide if I really wanted to learn coding, and maybe I should play tennis again."

The cop hovers behind me now, nose to my tail.

"Then all I cared about was staying alive," she says. "Everything got so clear. I wasn't thinking about the extra bullshit anymore."

If there's one thing I know how to do, it's listen to a final girl.

"Every time he hurt someone I knew it was like they were just water balloons to him," she says. "He was popping them, one after the other. But when I had to hurt him, I couldn't do it in time. He had his back to me in the loft and Alana was screaming for help and I just froze. I could have pushed him earlier but I wasn't strong enough. It wasn't until he came after me. I couldn't save anyone except myself."

"Sometimes that's all you can do," I say.

An exit is coming up. I put on my turn signal.

"I don't want to die like everyone else," she says.

I take the exit, and the cop car keeps going. I pull over on the side of the road and sit for a minute while black dots swim in my vision. Did he run my plates? Did he write them down? Is he going to remember a dark red Chevy Lumina when he gets back to the station house? Is he going to put the pieces together?

"He hit Alana in the head with a hammer," Stephanie says. "He just kept hitting her and hitting her. Why did he do that?"

No one's ever depended on me for anything before, except Fine. I imagine Marilyn, drunk in her master bedroom all alone, Heather sitting cross-legged on the floor, giving one of her monologues, box cutter hidden behind one leg. I imagine Dani, sitting at her kitchen table, crying, her guns locked up in their cabinet. I imagine Julia, unconscious in the hospital, her door unprotected. I think about Skye in his mother's house, typing on his computer, oblivious to anyone coming up behind him. I've never had so many other people to worry about before. I have to be safe. I have to be smart. That cop could have pulled me over, and if he had, everything would have been finished.

"You're not going to die," I tell Stephanie, and I'm saying it to myself, too. "No one else is going to die. I'll make sure of that."

```
 1   CHRISTINE MERCER: Then Matty tried to stop him but he hit him with that
 2   axe.
 3
 4   JOHN STRYCHER: Did you see what happened next?
 5
 6   CHRISTINE MERCER: I'm sorry, I'm so sorry, I was running, I don't know.
 7   I ran away. I'm so sorry.
 8
 9   DONALD THOMPSON: Take your time.
10
11   JOHN STRYCHER: Can you tell us what happened to Alexandra Cathcart?
12
13   CHRISTINE MERCER: Alex is hurt?
14
15   DONALD THOMPSON: We can't comment on her condition.
16
17   CHRISTINE MERCER: Is she dead? What happened? You have to tell me. What
18   happened?
19
20   DONALD THOMPSON: We don't know anything for sure right now.
21
22   JOHN STRYCHER: We need you to tell us what happened next, Miss Mercer?
23
24   DONALD THOMPSON: Miss Mercer? Do you need some time?
25
26   JOHN STRYCHER: Miss Mercer, did you hear me? Can you tell us what
27   happened next?
28
29   CHRISTINE MERCER: What was always going to happen next. The monster
30   came and gobbled them all up.
```

—transcript of RCMP officers John Strycher and Donald Thompson
interviewing multiple murder survivor Christine Mercer,
November 6, 1986

THE FINAL GIRL SUPPORT GROUP XVI:
Season of the Final Girls

Chrissy shows up half an hour early to scope out the Starbucks where we're supposed to meet. That's okay. We slept in the car last night and got up with the sun. By the time she rolls past the strip mall we've been watching it all day. Stephanie keeps playing with the radio. Every five hours she calls her parents but she's learning. She talks shorter and cries less each time. Otherwise, I insist she keep her phone off. It's making her testy.

"She needs to hurry her old self up," Stephanie grumbles.

"Patience will keep you alive," I tell her.

"Not if it bores me to death first."

I'd had an idea that Chrissy was sticking close to home, so we'd made for southern Alberta, near the location of her original crisis, emailing her from Stephanie's phone as I drove. It took a day and a half. We'd just crossed into Idaho when Chrissy let us know she'd moved away from Black Drum and lived south of the border now in eastern Montana. Stephanie would have thought I was an idiot if it'd turned out she'd moved to L.A.

Chrissy's more cautious than me, which earns her my grudging respect, something I never thought I'd feel. To the rest of us, Chrissy's a bottom-feeder and we try not to say her name. She's a traitor, a masochist, a turncoat, a liar. She's got Stockholm syndrome. We all feel sorry for her. We all despise her. But at least she's cautious. That makes her one of us, after all.

"Can I at least go in and see what she does?" Stephanie asks. "She hasn't seen my face before."

"Chrissy follows mass murder the way Canadians follow hockey," I say. "She's seen you. We're not blowing this now by underestimating her. This is how we survive. We look before we leap."

It's hot in the car but getting cooler as the afternoon shadows grow long. I only left the car for a little bit earlier today to use the bathroom in a Jamba Juice. No matter how often I wash my face, twenty-two hours in the car has covered it in a waterproof layer of grease. When this is over, the two of us will head back to Billings, maybe get a hotel room for a few hours where I can shower. My skin itches in anticipation.

"She's coming back around again," Stephanie says. Just a week ago, a maniac killed her friends in front of her and now she's on task. We're adaptable, if nothing else. "There, the maroon Chrysler."

The growling Made-in-America steel box rumbles past the Starbucks for a second time, crop-dusting a big blue cloud of exhaust over the street. Then it noses down the rows of parked cars, two over from where we sit. There was so much back-and-forth on email, so much flirting and deal making and confirming that I wanted to scream. I tried to avoid talking numbers, instead offering to show her the stash in person so she could make an informed offer. I tried to play dumb and straightforward, just a woman trying to make ends meet by picking through thrift stores and mini-storage units, trying to buy low and sell slightly less low.

I avoided talking about where I got the stash, I avoided mentioning any names, but I couldn't avoid telling her what I had. Hitting send on that email made me feel grimy:

THE ITEMS I HAVE ARE LABELED IN PLASTIC BAGS BY THE PREVIOUS OWNER. THEY ARE:

- SNEAKERS WORN BY RODDY TORRES (STAINED WITH DARK SUBSTANCE ON TOE OF LEFT SHOE)

- LIFE PRESERVER, BLOOD-STAINED, FROM CAMP RED LAKE (CAMP LOGO VISIBLE LEFT BREAST)

- COAT HANGER, TWISTED INTO BALL, WITH DARK STAIN ON END (WITH BILL OF SALE ATTESTING TO USE BY DANIELLE SHIPMAN)

- MASK WORN BY GHOST 1 (WITH BILL OF SALE ATTESTING TO ORIGINALITY)

- ONE FIRST EDITION "THE DREAM KING AND HIS KILLING KINGDOM" SIGNED BY HEATHER DELUCA, AUTOGRAPH READS "FUCK YOU VERY MUCH, HEATHER"

- FOUR HEADSHOTS, TOPLESS, OF ACTOR BARB COARD IN "SLAY BELLS" SIGNED BY LYNNETTE TARKINGTON

It was the last ones that pulled her out of hiding. I sent a photo of one of the headshots that Stephanie took on her phone. They're the rarest items in the lot. When we went to L.A. that first time, Garrett got me to sign a few topless headshots of the actress who would play me in the movie. I stopped signing memorabilia after I started group, so these are heavy collector's items. She could probably get close to five hundred dollars for each one. If I'd been an actual final girl they'd be worth more like eight hundred each.

"Are you actually going to give her those photos?" Stephanie asked.

"No," I said. "But she's going to want them. Bad."

We were already leaving Nevada when I noticed Stephanie's filthy bare feet. She hadn't complained once. I sent her into a Walmart with forty dollars. My face was definitely on an APB by then, and besides, I wanted to see if she'd run.

She came out forty sweaty-palmed minutes later wearing some knock-off black Chuck Taylors and carrying a family-sized bag of Sour Brite Crawlers.

"Breakfast?" she'd asked, offering me some.

"You need something more nutritious."

"Who's a grumpy girl?" she asked, dangling one in front of my face. "Does the grumpy girl need her nutrition?"

I snapped forward suddenly and sucked it out of her fingers. She laughed like a kid. Like Gillian.

She asks me questions; she wants to know about my life. I'm guarded at first, but she seems so genuinely impressed by my story and so upset when I show her my scars that I can't help myself. It turns out I like having someone riding shotgun.

When I slept, Steph drove, and when she slept, I drove. She did most of the sleeping because she's still wrung out, so by now I'm wired, eyeballs vibrating, smelling my own sleepy smell all the time. The inside of my mouth is coated with sugar from the Sour Brite Crawlers. I blindly reach into the bag and discover it's empty. When Steph sleeps she twitches and whimpers.

I got her side of the story in bits and pieces as we headed toward Montana. Apparently, Christophe waited in his car off the property until sundown, then he found a blind spot in the security cameras that surrounded the camp and crept through the perimeter. After that, it was all pitchforks through the chest, people impaled on pokers, arrows through the throat, and harpoon guns in the eye. He crushed her boyfriend's skull in a work clamp in the woodshop studio. They'd been dating for three weeks.

"We'd been dating for six weeks," I told her.

"Who?" she asked, chin resting on her knees, feet on the passenger seat.

"Tommy," I said. It was the first time I'd said his name outside group in over a decade. "I was a cheerleader. He was a football player."

"That's so Jack and Diane," she said. "Were you in love?"

I think about that sometimes, too.

"We weren't dating long enough to know," I told her. "I feel like I was, but if I'm going to be honest we never got a chance to find out. I was planning to go all the way with him when Ricky Walker rang the doorbell."

"I was a virgin when I met Paul," Steph said. "I didn't love him, but I think he loved me. Did you date anyone after?"

"Not really," I said.

Realization flickered in her eyes.

"So wait a minute? If you were a virgin when you were dating Tommy and you didn't date anyone afterward, are you . . . ?"

Her eyes and mouth yawn wide with horror.

"I had a boyfriend," I said. "Kind of. Afterward."

"Kind of?" she asked.

"Garrett P. Cannon," I said. "And no, I'm not a virgin."

I think about how Tommy and I never had sex. I think about how I'd never know if my parents' Christmas Eve date saved their marriage. I think about how much Gillian loved horses and never got to ride one. I think about how I didn't protect my sister. I think about protecting Stephanie.

Here comes Chrissy now, strutting across the parking lot, heading for the Starbucks. I haven't seen her in more than ten years, but I'd recognize that cocky stroll anywhere. Chrissy struts like she has all the time in the world. Not like me, racing from one safe place to another, scanning the angles of approach, trying to make sure I spot any potential predators before they spot me.

"That's her?" Steph asks.

"Stay low," I tell her.

Chrissy wears mom jeans and a denim jacket. Big heavy purse over one shoulder, fifteen minutes early. She pushes her way into the Starbucks and disappears.

"Now we wait," I say.

"She looks young," Steph says.

She picks up the empty Sour Brite Crawlers bag and uses her wet fingertip to chase sugar from its corners, knees on the dashboard, watching the Starbucks door. Her phone sits in her lap. I hear it vibrate.

"It's her," she says.

I reach over and touch her wrist. I find myself doing this a lot, finding excuses to touch her.

"Don't answer," I say.

We sit in the hot car, the bag rattling as Stephanie extracts every single grain of sugar like some kind of methodical ant while her phone keeps vibrating. She shows me the emails as they come in, each one another stage in the process of being stood up. There's the question (*Am I at the right Starbucks?*), there's the begging (*PLEASE let me know when u r coming!*), then anger (*Do NOT contact me again and I will make sure all buyers know u r a liar!*), and then Chrissy comes storming out of Starbucks, heading for her car.

"That took almost forty-five minutes," I say.

"So?" Stephanie asks.

"That means those pictures I signed are worth way more than I thought they were."

Chrissy's maroon beater sails past us, floating on a big cloud of pale blue exhaust. I wait until she's way down the road before I twist the ignition and pull out after her. Earlier Steph and I had a long argument over who got to drive but I won. I'm the big sister, after all.

At first we're driving through a sprawl of planned communities and retail outlets, but soon the name-brand stores are replaced by dollar stores and churches. We pass carpet stores that are eternally going out of business, judging by the sun-faded yellow banners in their front windows. We pass strip malls that are nothing more than a row of *For Lease* signs. I ride Chrissy's exhaust, hanging back, making sure Stephanie has an eye on her phone's map, always trying to keep at least four car lengths between us.

"She's getting on Route 2," Stephanie says, and I follow.

We merge and take off-ramps and on-ramps and construction detours, and as the sun sinks lower we get off the highway onto two-lane blacktop. I pray she doesn't go over the border. I'm not sure my Dr. Newbury ID could handle the Department of Homeland Security. We pass something called the Troy Group, dozens of parking lots and warehouses spread out over acres of raw dirt. Then we pass houses with vinyl siding pressed right up to the street, limp, sun-bleached American flags staked to their porches, claw-footed bathtubs full of dead plants in their side yards.

The road winds back and forth, switchbacking as it rises into the hills, and we turn a corner and suddenly Chrissy's not there. Then I see her car parked in front of a boxy brick church. We zoom past before I can stop, and wind up lurking in a side street about a quarter of a mile up ahead.

"Keep your head down," Stephanie says.

"I know what I'm doing," I say.

Even though I don't have a valid driver's license, and I'm making this all up as I go along, and I'm functioning on nothing but confidence, I want to project authority. Steph needs to think that I have this situation under control. I need to make her feel safe.

Chrissy's car blows past us ten stressed-out minutes later and we pull out and keep following, blasting past thick runs of trees that give way to buildings clinging to rural intersections, and then we're turning off the new blacktop onto old asphalt, and it's nothing but trees lining the mountain road on either side. We're in a deep trench of foliage, the orange sun blocked out by leaves, and it feels like the dark is coming fast.

The road winds and dips and climbs and dips again, and I figure we have to be getting close to where we're going. I focus on keeping Chrissy in sight up ahead, and Steph focuses on not distracting me. We both know that if we lose her now the last two days will have been for nothing. Stephanie chews her nails. It's healthier than candy.

There are no other cars on the road, so I hang back. There are occasional trailers set deep on overgrown lots, and plywood signs nailed to two-by-fours offering *Bunny Meat—$10!* and *HairCuts for Man and Woman.* I get the feeling anyone who could has long since moved away. I play Chrissy out in front of us, letting her take the lead, then reel her in closer, then let her run again. We drive deeper into the hills.

We come around a curve almost right on top of her as she slowly pulls onto a dirt track branching off one side of the road, and I scream past in the other lane and keep going until it feels safe enough to pull over. I make a three-point turn and idle next to a piece of rotten plywood leaning against a telephone pole that says *Firewood* in orange spray paint. From here we can see the head of the dirt road. Chrissy's car is already deep in the woods. Five seconds later and we would have missed her entirely.

"What are we waiting for?" Stephanie demands.

"I don't want to roll down that driveway like this," I say. "She might be waiting for us to pass and in a few minutes she'll pull out again. For all we know, that driveway's a trap. We need to wait until dark."

"More waiting?" she asks, throwing herself back against the seat.

"More waiting," I confirm.

The woods are silent and their dimness shades into blue, then gray, then the road loses the last of the light. Darkness presses against the car windows from all sides. Chrissy doesn't emerge from the dirt driveway and I can only hope it's not a shortcut that leads to another stretch of blacktop running parallel through these hills. I have to hope this is where she's gone to ground.

Stephanie folds the Sour Brite Crawlers bag over, then over again, folding it into increasingly smaller rectangles before unfolding it, pressing it flat, and starting all over again. I watch our blind spots, I watch the end of the dirt driveway, I watch the woods, and finally I can't put it off any longer.

Opening up my fanny pack, I pull out my little .22 and make sure it's loaded.

"I need something, too," Steph says.

"I'm going in alone to talk to Chrissy," I say. "I should be back in an hour. If not, I want you to come after me."

"Unarmed?" she says.

"If I'm not back in an hour, or if I don't call your cell phone by then, sneak in through the woods and find me."

"Great," she says. "So I'll use harsh language, or what?"

I hand her a can of pepper spray from my fanny pack and zip it back up tight. I open the car door and the door buzzer screams in the night.

"This shit doesn't work!" Steph calls after me.

I close the door fast to turn out the light and get my night vision back. The trees are full of shrieking crickets. I jog along the shoulder of the road and cut through the woods to where the dirt driveway turns off. My feet crunch loud through the dead leaves as I enter the darkness to find Chrissy, the fallen final girl.

As excited as I am to have Something
alive in my house, I don't know if
I'm ready for the responsibility.
BUT— I've already named him:
Final Plant. So it's too late now.
I can even hear his voice in my head.
I crack the black-out drapes for 1 hour
a day so he can sun bathe. He likes
America's Funniest Home Videos like I
do, and romantic comedies. I don't think
he understands Friends though, the way
no one locks their doors and are always
walking in and out of each other's
homes. I keep sitting and staring at him
and sometimes in the middle of the
night my chest hitches and I wake up
having a panic attack. Because what
if he dies? What if I have to
evacuate and leave him behind? I can't
have another life on my hands, I can't be
responsible for someone else. I can't, I
can't, I can't. But the thought of putting
him out with the trash makes me feel physically ill.
+LATER*

Fine said something really interesting ➔

—Lynnette Tarkington, personal diary, January 3, 2001

THE FINAL GIRL SUPPORT GROUP XVII:
Bride of the Final Girls

I keep my pistol in my hand as I slip deeper into the woods. Who knows what's out here, who knows what Chrissy's going to think when she sees me, who knows how bad this could get. The trees bunch together, sucking the moonlight from the air as I crunch deeper into darkness. Then I see a dead body hanging from a tree limb. I drop to one knee, stomach fluttering with moths.

It spins slowly, and it's a child, maybe a baby, and then I walk up and touch its foot—wet, moldering, plush. It's a Pink Panther hung from a noose. On the other side of the tree is another noose, and in this one it's a baby doll, stripped naked to reveal its hard plastic head and soggy pillow body, hanging by the neck. I see more of them suspended overhead, an orchard of rotten fruit: Barbies hung by their hair, six to a branch, stuffed animals rotten with rain, a dead tree with Disney characters nailed all the way to the top. There's Pluto with a nail through his throat, Minnie with both gloved hands crucified to the trunk, Mickey with a spike through his forehead, still smiling. The trees are covered in cartoon tumors.

I keep moving through this toy cemetery, slower now. These are woods that someone uses, that someone is familiar with. I come to a washer, glowing white in the dimness. My head bumps a wind chime made of screwdrivers. They clack against each other crazily. I see abandoned appliances half-buried around me, rusty painted metal sprouting from the ground.

I am knee-deep in someone's crazy. Chrissy's crazy.

Up ahead the tree trunks thin and in the clearing I see a sagging ranch house, the spine of its roof broken and bent. There are lights on inside. It's surrounded by mossy outbuildings. A shed leans against one side; on the other is a doghouse stuffed with scrap lumber. There's a carport getting absorbed into the trees farther back with a bunch of oblong lumps wrapped in blue tarps stashed underneath. Behind the house rises a massive, hulking black shadow: an enormous prefab barn, looming over the roofline to menace the fifties home slumped in the foreground.

I step back and bump into a warm tree trunk. It moves. It's a man. Huge, solid, he towers over me. My first instinct is to run, but I have training. I throw an elbow into his midsection, then drop into a squat and sweep his feet. My elbow feels broken, my shin hits his boots, and pain rockets up my leg. I drive my knee into his crotch and it's like cracking my kneecap against a wall.

His eyes are tiny; his head is a lumpy tennis ball. He's wearing a black sweatshirt and military pants tucked into his boots. He grabs my wrists and grinds the bones together and I drop my gun. I bite his hand. He doesn't even flinch. He keeps bearing down as I kick his shins, stomp his toes, grind my teeth into his filthy skin. He stinks. His BO suffocates me.

He grabs me by the hair and pushes my head down between my knees. I lose my balance and stumble and feel fire in my forehead as he hauls me up by my scalp. He lifts me, and I have to grab his wrist with both hands so my hair doesn't rip out at the roots. The pain nauseates me. My weight doesn't bother him at all.

If Stephanie could see this she would lose all her confidence in me.

Then we're out of the woods and walking across the yard, into the light, and up three brick steps and he's kicking open the screen door. The pain in my scalp flares and I pull my box cutter out of my front pocket and in one swipe I slice off my hair, taking off some of my skin along the way. He lets go and I drop three inches and stagger sideways on shattered glass ankles, touching one knee to the floor.

The house is too warm and it smells like yesterday's cooking. When I look up, he's walking into the kitchen. I bang out of the storm door and run for where he took me, finding my gun in the rotten leaves, then I'm barreling through the door as he comes back out of the kitchen with a knife. My arms go up automatically into a Weaver stance, finger on the trigger, both hands cradling my gun.

"Stop!" a woman shouts.

I'm already squeezing the trigger and then Chrissy is standing between us. I shift my aim at the last minute and the air snaps and there's a hole in their drywall and gunsmoke hanging in the air.

"Both of you stop," she shouts, holding a palm flat out to each of us.

I don't move and neither does Pain Freak. He keeps staring at me, still holding his knife, not even breathing hard.

"I should have known it was you, Lynnette," Chrissy says. "You don't actually have those photos, do you?"

"Tell him to put the knife down," I say, not lowering my gun.

"You broke into our home," Chrissy says.

I keep my .22 right in the middle of his deflated head. There are nicks all over his skull from where he shaves himself bald. I keep my front sight rested on the black scab covering his right temple.

"She's an old friend, Keith," Chrissy says to him. She caresses his biceps. He stinks like a horse. How can she bear to touch him? "Why don't you go out to your workroom while we catch up?"

He turns and walks back into the kitchen. I hear a knife drawer open and metal clatter as it slams shut. The back door swings open, then slaps closed. There's silence in the house.

"You wasted my entire afternoon," Chrissy says. "How do you propose you make it up to me?"

"I wanted to warn you," I lie. "Someone's trying to kill all of us."

Chrissy evaluates me for a minute, then smiles.

"I know what you can do," she says. "You have to sign a few books before you go. Come into the kitchen."

She leaves the room like I don't matter and I hear the fridge door open. I lower my pistol.

I always knew Chrissy was dangerous. While the rest of us pasted our shattered lives back together and tried to put these monsters behind us, Chrissy embraced them. She became their loudest advocate and their most vocal defender. She pursued every conspiracy theory and used the settlement from her homecoming night massacre to fund legal challenges to their convictions.

Dr. Carol had a theory. She thought that because the prosecution relied on Chrissy's eyewitness testimony, and because her monster was her godfather, maybe she had a deep-seated sense of guilt and needed the monsters to forgive her. I had a simpler theory: she was batshit crazy. And crazy people are dangerous people.

But I didn't come all this way to stand around a living room by myself, so I muster my courage, lower my weapon, and follow her to the kitchen.

The house either never got finished or it's being taken apart. There's unpainted drywall nailed up in the living room, the doorframe to the kitchen is an unfinished two-by-four, and the kitchen has orange extension cords strung everywhere. There's a coffeepot on the table, next to a blender. The counters are crammed with shopping bags, cookie jars, pie plates.

"Why don't I make us a nice cup of tea?" Chrissy says.

She's standing at a dishwasher that's been pulled out from under the counter, filling a kettle from a gallon jug.

"Just sit anywhere," she says.

I move a stack of mail off a wooden dining room chair with loose joints and sit, back to the wall, where I can cover the door and the window. I put the .22 on the table in front of me. Its grip shines with sweat. I wipe my palm on the leg of my jeans. Pill bottles cover the table, advertising mailers, plastic shopping bags stuffed with yellow rubber gloves and dish towels with their price tags still on.

"This was my parents' first house," Chrissy says, putting the gallon jug down by the overflowing sink. "It's actually worth less now than what they paid for it in the sixties, isn't that crazy? You'd think the land would be worth something at least."

"Sorry about that," I say.

She plugs in the kettle and hunts through cupboards for tea. None of her kitchen cabinets have doors.

"This is coal country but there's no more coal," she says. "The chemical they use to wash the coal impurities contaminated the groundwater. They say it's safe to drink, but babies get boils inside their mouths, and people's gums bleed. They've been suing that chemical company for almost eight years."

She goes elbow deep in a cabinet by the fridge and comes out with a single Lipton tea bag. She finds another dried tea bag in the sink, peels it off the top of a pile of dirty dishes, and rinses two mugs.

"Why'd you come back?" I ask.

"Keith likes it here," she says.

The crazy comes off Chrissy like perfume.

"Someone killed Adrienne," I say. "Did you hear about that?"

Chrissy smiles. It infuriates me. The kettle screams. She pours the tea.

"Here you go," she says, putting the cup down in front of me, not making a grab for my gun. I take a sip. It's too hot and tastes bitter. Chrissy dumps two shopping bags off a chair and sits. "We've always disagreed on the meaning of our experiences."

"A psycho and his brother tried to kill me," I say. "Same thing happened to all of us, essentially. What's to disagree on?"

"You say tomato and I say shamanistic vision quest that uses an ordeal to lead us inward on a journey of spiritual discovery and eventual synthesis and peace."

"You're right," I say. "We do disagree. But at the end of the day, someone's targeting final girls. They've killed Adrienne and they've done their best to kill me, they've put Julia in the hospital and burned down Heather's halfway house. We need to work together. You think they're not coming after you?"

"That's always been your biggest flaw," she says. "You've always had this the wrong way around, and as long as you do you'll live in fear."

"So you won't help?" I ask.

"With what?" She laughs. "I'm not going to join some kind of final girl superteam."

"You keep up with Billy Walker and Harry Peter Warden," I say. "You communicate with them regularly, right?"

"Those men don't deserve what's been done to them," she says.

"And you sell their . . ." I have a hard time with the word. "Art."

"No comment," she says.

"Don't be coy, Chrissy," I say. "We found your name all over Billy's visitor sheet. We'll probably see it all over Warden's. You're being used. Someone's turned you into their private messaging system."

Then I realize Chrissy hasn't blinked once since she sat down. I've assumed she's the middleman, but what if she's the full thing? What if Dr. Carol never asked Chrissy for help at all? I thought we were running away from danger, putting distance between Stephanie and me and Dr. Carol, but what if I've steered us right into its heart?

"Do you ever hear from Dr. Carol?" I ask, wanting to pick up my gun so badly my hand cramps.

"Does she still run your little sewing circle?" Chrissy smiles. She still hasn't blinked.

"Has anyone asked you to contact Warden or Walker for them?" I ask. "I don't care, but I need to know."

"Of course you care." She laughs. "You wouldn't have spent so long suing me if you didn't."

"That was Marilyn," I say. "And she finally dropped it. Right now, no one cares that you sell this crap for these guys and drop money into their commissary accounts. I mean, it's sick, and it's morally objectionable, but right now we've got bigger issues. We think whoever's behind this might be using you to communicate."

She studies me for a minute.

"Whoever's behind what?" she asks. "You think I'm a stooge for some mysterious consortium of shadowy men who want you dead? And you want me to violate the trust of these artists so you can take revenge on a conspiracy you're not even sure exists?"

"It's not revenge," I say. "It's self-defense."

"It's a perversion of nature," she says.

I reach into my fanny pack and take out the folded-up glossy eight-by-ten and spread it on the table. It's one of the Barb Coard shots. Chrissy sits up straight.

"That's a rare piece," she hisses between her teeth. "You're devaluing it."

"I've got three others," I lie. "I'll sign them again and date them. There are only four others on the market. It'll be worth your while."

She gives me a patronizing smile.

"I have all the money I need. Right now, it's more about curating my collection than acquiring new items."

"Then why were you so eager to buy what I was selling online?" I ask. "Before you knew it was me?"

"Oh, Lynnette," she says, all smug self-satisfaction. "You really think I didn't know it was you all along?"

I want to slap that smug smile off her smug face. I could pick up the gun and shoot her, not anywhere vital, just in the kneecap. Somewhere that would hurt. She didn't play me. She wasn't playing me. I'm not that stupid. I didn't just walk into a trap.

"I've been following the news out of Los Angeles with a lot of interest," she says. "I knew this was coming before any of you. I've always loved you, Lynnette. I always thought that if anyone was going to come here and ask me the right questions it would be you."

The kitchen window is a shiny square of darkness. I don't hear any movement in the rest of the house.

"Do you know who it is?" I ask.

"I noticed the numbers almost two years ago," she says. "I wondered what they were. Don't you wish you knew what I know?"

"What numbers?" I ask.

"The numbers in the emails," she says.

"What numbers? What emails? Who's been in touch with you?"

"You were always more of an unfinished victim than a real final girl," Chrissy says. "But it's a sign that you're here now. I think this is your crisis come at last."

Her eyes shine and I realize we're very, very far from civilization.

"You're so lucky," she breathes. "I think you're about to become a real final girl."

There's a long silence and I check the doors, convinced she's giving someone a chance to sneak up, but the kitchen is empty.

"I just put it all together," she says. "Oh, it's so beautiful. It's finally your time, and I'm the next step on your path."

She presses her hands to her breastbone and closes her eyes in bliss.

"Glory," she says. "Come. My computer is in the museum."

She pushes her chair back and stands and I do the same. I follow her down a short hall to the back of the house, past her laundry machine and dryer.

"Whenever I get online I have to walk through my museum," she says, hand on a utility room doorknob. "It reminds me daily of the journey each of us has taken. And now you'll be taking that journey, too. Prepare yourself, Lynnette. I'm so happy you'll finally know what it's like."

She opens the door and cold air pours out like she's opened a fridge. She reaches around the doorframe and turns on the lights. I hear fluorescents flicker to life up and down the enormous prefab barn latched onto the back of her house. But in front of us there's only a small closet with black curtains at the other end. Above them hangs a 10" knife, its blade smeared with something dark and tarry. It's crossed by a tire iron clotted with hair.

"Those are Dani's," she says. "They were very difficult to obtain, but they've always made me feel closer to her. It's the weapon her brother used to transform her friends, and it's the tire iron Dani used to kill her brother. The yin and the yang. Passing beneath them inspires reflection."

I feel slightly sickened. Then she's walking forward, taking a flashlight off a shelf next to the curtains and pushing them open with both hands. Beyond them it's dim, and this feels like a very bad idea.

"Come, Lynne," she says. "Let me show you so many wonders."

"And the emails," I say, trying to keep her anchored in reality.

"Those, too," she says. "If you're still interested in them after I show you my museum."

I wipe my hand on my jeans and then make sure the safety is off my .22. Then I follow Chrissy into her murderabilia museum.

ALL OUR MONSTERS ARE THE SAME MONSTER, the male monster. The Bzou wolf, the vampire, the troll, the ogre. Bannik, the Russian demon who travels by night and flays disrespectful children. Bluebeard, who kills his child bride.

What is the story of the Minotaur but the story of Teddy Volker at Camp Blood: youths sent to a faraway place where they cannot escape, stalked and murdered by a monster in a ritual sacrifice?

Our monsters are the night visitors, the child stealers, the boo-baggers, the baby guzzlers. They are the men who eat children. It is the oldest and only story, our attempt to imitate the two divine acts of God: creation and destruction. Birth and death. Women get birth, so men must settle for death. And they've become experts on the subject.

—"The Monsters, Our Makers: From the First Flood to the Final Girls" by Christine Mercer, first published in the *Journal of Comparative Folklore,* November–December 2009

THE FINAL GIRL SUPPORT GROUP XVIII:
Curse of the Final Girls

Her house is a disordered wreck, the product of a disordered mind, but in Chrissy's museum everything is filed away, lined up on a shelf, bagged and tagged, cataloged and classified. The second we enter the dim, quiet first room her breathing slows and her movements become liquid smooth.

This room is lit by a few grandmother's lamps, with a fussy carpet on the floor fresh out of some matron aunt's parlor, stitched with ruby-red roses that bulge like bloody organs, festooned with looping vines and flowering garlands that look like intestines.

"I apologize for amateur hour," Chrissy says. "But you'd be surprised at how much demand there still is."

Shelves line the room. They run all the way up to the top of the temporary walls that Chrissy has capped with wire mesh. Above them I can see darkness, then the metal girders holding up the prefab roof high above. On the shelves, most people would see nothing special: nails, glass bottles of dirt, an old caulk gun, curled leather shoes, a child's clown doll, rows of ring binders and scrapbooks, an orderly progression of brand-new plastic bags containing nail files and hairbrushes clotted with wisps of hair, a pair of barber's scissors tarnished with age, an antique iron with white fingerprint powder still on the handle, a brick standing alone.

But I know what I'm looking at.

Nails from H. H. Holmes's Chicago murder house, gravel from where Bonnie and Clyde were shot, the caulk gun Robert Berdella used to seal his victim's ears, shoes worn by Albert Fish, a lock of Charles Manson's hair, John Wayne Gacy's clown toy, a Christmas card from Ted Bundy, a brick from Sharon Tate's home.

For a certain segment of the population these are status symbols more powerful than an S-Class Mercedes or a house in the Hamptons. It smells like a thrift store from Hell in here, heavy with the scent of old blood and dried sweat. Sour fear sweat from the people who ran for their lives, musky hunger sweat from the men who brought down the hammer.

"These wannabes had no vision," Chrissy says. "Come on, we don't want to hang around here for too long. Their lack of ambition might rub off."

I don't want to follow her through the black-curtained doorway on the other side of the room, but I will see this through to the end. I check my phone: one bar, and it's been thirty minutes. I want to text Steph and update her, but she's my ace in the hole. I can't give her away.

"Coming?" Chrissy asks from the darkness.

I know what's in the rest of her fun house: rare bottles of wine for the high-end collectors. The men for whom price is no object. If you are what you buy, what does it say when you just spent $6,143 on the harpoon that pinned a pregnant cheerleader to the wall of a boathouse in 1978?

But I will not quit. I will see this through. I cross the threshold and enter the dark. Chrissy has dragged in temporary walls and built a maze that winds through her barn. We're standing in a long hall lined with closed doors and dark doorways.

"Do you know how long it took me to get this right?" Chrissy asks. "Six years. That's an artist's timetable. Who spends six years building something that's not art?"

"It smells," I tell her.

"That's their musk," she says. "And the perfume of our sisters. You know, I've always felt for you, Lynne."

"Thanks?"

"No, I'm serious," she says. "I always felt like it must be so hard to be you. I knew my calling from the beginning, but for you it must have been so confusing. You were lumped in with the final girls but you were never blooded, you never experienced your initiation."

"How much of your weirdness do I have to put up with, Chrissy?" I ask. "Because if we can just fast-forward through some of it that'd be great."

"You're so funny," she says. "You stand on the threshold of something magnificent, and you don't even comprehend."

She walks forward, leading me into the dark. Something brushes against my face, light as a spiderweb, and I flinch, trying to keep it away from my lips. It's a dirty crocheted shawl. It was a mistake to come here. I'm betraying everyone I know by listening to Chrissy's sickness. It's clear that she's been festering out here in the woods too long, waiting for someone to show up so she could vomit her crazy all over them. I bite the inside of my cheek hard, the pain giving me something to focus on. I need to know about her emails.

"What happened to all of us?" Chrissy asks. "Do you ever stop and wonder?"

"Like, why me?" I ask.

"No," she says. "Like why this? Why all these murders?"

We keep walking deeper into her museum, past dark display cases, past rows of Styrofoam heads wearing what I think are wigs, then realize are human scalps. She stops outside a dark doorway and waits for me to catch up.

"Murder is man's attempt to steal birth from women," she says. "We make children, they kill them. We create life, they create death. It's the way it's always been."

"What does that have to do with our monsters?" I ask. Monsters. Sometimes the word sticks in my throat because it sounds too big, too mystical, too dramatic. But here it sounds right.

"Don't you see?" Chrissy asks. "It's a vision quest. An act of self-creation. For the monster, they aren't murdering people. They're murdering parts of themselves. They murder the slut, the nerd, the stoner, the jock, the cheerleader. Those are all different facets of their own personalities."

"Dani will be excited to hear that you consider her friends aspects of her brother's personality," I say.

"Not literally," Chrissy says. "You're resisting what I'm saying by clinging to semantics. I'm trying to tell you why they do what they do."

"Because they're psychopaths," I say.

"That's such a small word," she says. "Does it make you feel superior to give them a diagnosis, to file them away in a little drawer? You know they're bigger than that. If it were just a psychological problem we could find a cure. This is a metaphysical problem."

"It's a criminal justice problem," I say.

"These parts of their personalities are problematic because they are weak," she says, ignoring me. "The monster wants to be tough, he wants to be dangerous, he wants to be hard, so he kills the soft parts of himself. But the journey always ends at the same destination: no one is left except the monster and the final girl. No matter how much he destroys those other parts of his personality, he can't destroy the essential feminine side of himself. Even destruction can't unmake creation. That primal feminine impulse, that procreative urge cannot be undone. When you boil everything down, when it's reduced as far as it will go, that's what's left. Creation and destruction, female and male, life and death, birth and murder."

She leads me into the room. It's pitch-dark. Chrissy leans to her right and flips a switch and dozens of low-wattage gallery lamps glow and we're at Camp Red Lake circa 1978. A stained counselor's sweatshirt is crucified to the wall above me, and camp pennants run along the top of the walls. Shaved logs sliced in half hang from lanyards with *Camp Red Lake Cougars* wood-burned into their white meat. Camp Red Lake Frisbees are lined up like display plates from the Franklin Mint next to footballs and a canoe paddle signed by all the girls in Cabin 21.

"The guy who ran their camp store was cleaning out his surplus on eBay. I went a little overboard," Chrissy says.

There are nine framed photographs in a row over the sweatshirt, each one a different smiling teenager. I recognize Valerie Bates, Adrienne's best friend. She talked about her a lot when she gave her lectures. Then I notice the grimmer souvenirs scattered in between the summer fun. A bow and arrow, the head of the arrow dented and bent. A spear gun with a cracked rubber band. A machete.

The room smells slightly of pine. Chrissy must have an air freshener in here to give it that woodsy scent.

"Camp Red Lake," she says. "Did you know it was built where the Mono Indians lived? They believed in the Ninitikati, a walking skeleton that had eaten all its own flesh but remained eternally hungry. It pursued women and ate them and their children. Once it started hunting them, it never gave up and their only choice was to kill it. But it never died. No matter what they did, Ninitikati could put itself back together. It's an idea that haunts those woods, a spirit looking for a vessel. Bruce Volker had no history of mental illness before what happened. According to everyone who knew him, he couldn't even stand the sight of blood."

"You're getting very mystical with people's lives," I say. "These aren't abstract ideas, they were actual human beings."

"But who cares?" Chrissy asks. "Who cares that they died? Nine little girls and Bruce Volker died at Camp Red Lake and so what? You add up all of our friends and family who have ever died and you've got less than fifty people. Fifty million people die every year. So why do people care about us? What happened that made us all so famous? How did we become the idea that stuck? Down the road here, Simmons White realized he'd get steady disability payments if he didn't have an arm, so he went out and borrowed a chain saw from his neighbor and tried to slice it off. When his daughter went to stop him, he chopped her into pieces, and decided to do the same thing to his wife. You know how much I could buy that chain saw for? About eighty dollars. The sledgehammer that belonged to the Hansen family? The one that killed Marilyn's boyfriend? It sold five years ago for fourteen thousand. What's the difference?"

"I'm getting tired of this, Chrissy," I say.

"No," she says. "You have to understand. Our deaths mean more. They're bigger. More symbolic. They have resonance. Don't you ever stop and ask yourself why?"

She slips back through the doorway and leads me across the gloomy hall. Empty black openings gape from the walls, and hallways curl around corners. From overhead comes the tick of cooling metal as the day's heat leaches out of the sheet-metal roof.

I step into another dark alcove with Chrissy and hear a snap, and a woman materializes in front of me, floating in midair. My guts jump six inches backward and I'm about to follow when I see it's an enormous puffy white dress suspended in midair.

"It belonged to Marilyn," Chrissy says. "Her Jewel Ball dress. The one she wore in '78."

It hangs from dozens of monofilament fishing lines, pulling it into shape, giving it body and form. It looks like an invisible Marilyn is inside.

"It was stored in her parents' vacation place on the Gulf," Chrissy says. "I saw it on a TV special and had to have it. I paid their housekeeper almost eight hundred dollars to get it for me. Sometimes I come in here and just commune with her."

The walls are thick with corsages, champagne glasses with flaking lipstick on the rims. There's a framed photograph of all the debutantes from that year, and there's Marilyn in the middle, beaming, trying so hard to look like she didn't just watch her friends die two months before. Above it all, high up on the wall, in the place of honor, is a grimy sledgehammer.

"Is that—" I begin.

"I don't intend to sell anything in this room," Chrissy says, cutting me off. "So I don't want to comment on the provenance."

"You're really creepy, Chrissy," I say.

"Creepy Chrissy," she says. "That's what they called me in high school.

Well, before homecoming. After homecoming I was a hero, a survivor, a victim. After homecoming I was everything they needed me to be, and everything they were scared of me being, all rolled up into one."

"Chrissy," I say. "I want to see those emails."

"And you will," she says. "But, Lynnette, when all that's left is the final girl and the monster, what happens? She pacifies him, like the virgin and the unicorn. The unicorn is wild and ferocious, but when it sees the virgin maid it lays its head on her lap and grows calm. The final girl and the monster are two sides of one person. Think about it. One runs fast, and screams, and is resourceful, and fights for her friends. The other is slow, and implacable, and silent, and he kills, and is alone."

"And then, fuck him," I say. "He goes to prison. Or gets killed. So women rule. Awesome."

"No," she says. "That's never what happens. Don't you know your own story? He comes back. And eventually, she kills him. And that's the moment when he's complete. She sets him free and in doing so she frees herself. She's the yin to his yang. Don't you see?"

She flips off the light and I follow her back into the hall because I don't want to be alone with that floating white dress. We wind deeper into the dark maze, and she clicks on her flashlight so neither of us walks into any walls.

"I just want to show you this one real fast," she says. "I think it might be too hard for you to stay inside for very long, but it's so striking."

She pushes open a chain-link door and turns on the light. The two of us stand in the doorway, and I am staring into horror. I want to cry.

"It's Heather's," she beams. "I invited the Dream King here and he built it himself. I had to sell all of my own memorabilia to pay for his services, but I think it was worth it."

My brain can't wrap itself around what I'm seeing.

"How . . . ?" I start.

"The Dream King goes where he wants," she says. "They'll find eventually that the man they have in prison serving his time had nothing to do with what actually happened. But he's a servant of the King and he would never tell. The Dream King is very careful about how he feeds now. It's shocking, isn't it."

My mind tries to pick apart the howling insanity in that room, and if Heather were here right now I would forgive her for betraying me. I would forgive her for betraying everyone. It's so much worse than she ever said.

"Don't get sucked in," Chrissy tells me. "We've still got a long way to go."

She turns out the light and closes the gate, and I pull myself away from that room.

"Be strong, Lynne," she says.

Putting one hand on my elbow she steers me around a corner into another room, and the harsh fluorescent lighting assaults my eyes.

"This is your room," she enthuses. "I think about you all the time."

It's totally empty, just prefabricated walls and a black curtain over the door. The floor is bare concrete, and the slightly flickering fluorescent fixture hanging in the center of the ceiling makes my pupils ache.

"You haven't gone on your journey yet," she says. "But there's so much potential. I'm excited we'll be filling this one together."

She snaps the light off and then she's guiding me into another room. When the lights come on again the room walls are very far away and I'm surrounded by people. I turn and stare at them, and they turn and stare at me, backing away, raising their .22.

"This is Julia's special place," Chrissy says. "It's all done with mirrors."

I calm my breathing and examine the walls. They're covered in mirrors, their frames wrapped in aluminum foil or painted silver so they're barely visible. There's waist-high glass shelving along one of the walls and on top of it are the heads of the Ghost, two of them, yawning at each other.

"The older one's actually a replica," Chrissy says. "The second one cost me quite a bit of money. One of the guys who invented Facebook owns the original."

"How much have you spent on all this, Chrissy?"

There are X-rays of Julia's spinal column mounted in a lightbox, photocopies of reports from her physical therapist, a display case containing three stained and corroded hunting knives. My reflections and I stare at it all in sadness and wonder.

"It was worth it," she says.

"Was it?" I ask. "I mean, I know you're on this mystical kick, but what's the point?"

"Come on," she says. "I'll show you the emails."

She leads me into the hall and down another dim corridor.

"I'm so proud of you," she says over her shoulder. "See, Dani is the jock. Heather is the stoner, Julia is the nerd, Marilyn is the whore—sorry, but she's been married twice—Adrienne was the cheerleader because she was always rooting for you guys. He's coming for everyone one by one, and he's going to come for you last. You're going to become the final girl of final girls."

"What about you?" I ask.

"I'm a humble servant who shows you the way." She smiles.

We come to a large, open office space against the back wall of the barn. A desk lamp burns on a computer table next to an iMac surrounded by packing supplies. Chrissy leans over and boots it up.

"Don't you realize what purpose monsters serve?" she asks. "Monsters always guard treasure, but it doesn't have to be literal. It can be knowledge, transcendence. In the center of the Minotaur's labyrinth lies something precious: monstrous knowledge. Each of us has a monster we must confront, a monster designed to test our personal weaknesses. And in the end, they bring about our deaths. Not literal death, but death as the conclusion of this phase and the beginning of another. Death is the harbinger of transformation, that which precedes a new life. No, dammit. I don't want to upgrade to OS 10.6."

She jabs at her keyboard.

"Fearing death is just resistance to change," Chrissy says. "There we go."

Windows fill the screen. She sits in her ergonomic chair and starts scrolling through email.

"When I realized what was happening I put them all in their own folder," she says, clicking through. "Here."

The email is from orchomenus@hotmail.com. I didn't know anyone still used Hotmail.

HELLO,

I AM A COLLECTOR OF UNUSUAL ITEMS AND OF UNUSUAL PERSONS. I WISH TO OBTAIN A SMALL PIECE OF ART—PREFERABLY CHRISTMAS THEMED—FROM BILLY WALKER OF THE SILENT NIGHT SLAYINGS. DO YOU THINK THIS IS POSSIBLE AND WILL YOU QUOTE ME A PRICE. I WOULD ALSO LIKE YOU TO PASS TO BILLY THIS FOLLOWING REQUEST IN FULL

"DEAR BILLY,

I AM A ADMIRER OF YOUR WORK AND FEEL YOU ARE FALSELY ACCUSED OF THOSE CRIMES. I THINK YOUR BROTHER IS A GREAT HERO AND A MAN WHO SHALL LIVE FOREVER. I WANT TO COMMISSION A ARTOWRK FROM YOU OF SOME SIZE. IT SHOULD BE A SCENE OF THE NORTH POLE WITH COLORS AND ON THE LARGEST PAPER YOU HAVE. I LIKE ELVES AND SANTA TYPE SCENARIOS AND WOULD APPRECIATE YOUR IDEAS.

80-4 38-18 121-24 163-22 28-13 215-15 247-6 247-14 63-1.

AVID FAN"

"Did you send this on?" I ask.

"Of course," she says. "I visit Billy every three months and I always have commissions for him, information to assist in his defense. I like to bring him books. If you got to know him, I think you'd like him."

A nail presses into the center of my forehead, right between my eyes. I didn't think this would be so hard.

"That sounds beautiful," I say.

She rumbles open a filing cabinet and pulls out a folder stuffed with paper.

"So I printed this out and took it to him," she says. "And two weeks later he called and asked me to write down exactly what he said. Here."

COMMISSION ACCEPTED. $325, TB TRANSFERRED INTO COMMISSARY
$25/TRANSFER x 13 TRANSFERS

SANTA ELVES RIDING REINDEER BESIDE HOLE IN ICE.

MRS. CLAUS WATCHING. BIG BREASTS

134-29 35-3 190-3 190-9 254-2 36-22

"He made me repeat the numbers back to him three times," she says. "And that was just the beginning."

She pulls more paper out of the folder, printouts of the emails, notes she jotted down during phone calls or visits, and every single one of them ends with a string of numbers. Sometimes they repeat, sometimes they don't, but there's clearly a pattern.

"How many artworks did he commission from Billy?" I ask. It hurts me to talk about Billy like he's a normal artist, exhibiting in galleries and negotiating with buyers.

"Six over eight months," she says. "Although he never did a three-hundred-twenty-five-dollar one again. It's too bad. I think Billy's best works are his larger pieces."

"How many communications?" I ask, thumbing through the overflowing folder.

"Almost a hundred," she says.

"They're a code."

"Of course," she says.

I put the papers down. The barn feels very big, and very dark, and the two of us feel very small huddled together in this tiny pool of light.

"You already figured it out, didn't you," I say.

It's not a question.

"I cracked it by the second commission." She smiles. "It's a book code, like they do in *Red Dragon*, you know, the first Hannibal Lecter book? The letters refer to page and line numbers. It's the first letter or word on every line."

"What book?" I ask. "It'd have to be one that Orchomenus knows Billy has in his cell."

"*The Diary of Anne Frank*," she says. "Every prison has a copy."

I imagine these two perverts, thumbing through their battered library copies of *Diary*, flipping past *Despite everything, I believe that people are really good at heart*, coordinating their sickness.

"What did it say?" I ask.

"Orchomenus told Billy about the letters you wrote to his big brother." She smiles. "And he paid him to tell the police about them and to lie and say he'd buried them where Orchomenus had them hidden. When the time was right, that is. Orchomenus knows you very well, well enough to forge your handwriting on some extra letters they threw in to make your complicity clearer."

Elevator in my guts, going down. My legs don't feel strong enough to hold me up, but there's no chair and I'll be damned if she's going to see me faint.

"Who is it?" I ask.

"Don't you know?" she asks. "After all, you're not Billy's final girl."

"Whose am I?"

"You probably would have figured it out eventually," she says. "You might not be the smartest one of us, but you've always been the most stubborn. You're Orchomenus's final girl."

She smiles at me, all smug and secure, and I'm suddenly aware that there are too many woods around this house and not enough people.

"Who is he?" I ask. "Orchomenus at hotmail. I know you know."

"Do you know what Orchomenus was?" she asks, putting the folder back in her filing cabinet. "It was a city in ancient Greece. Once a year it held a Feast of Dionysus where the priest would wield a naked blade and pursue fleeing women into the night. If he caught any of them he had the right to slay them with impunity. This has been going on for so much longer than you think."

"I can make you tell me," I say, gesturing with my pistol.

"I thought it would be obvious," she says. "Orchomenus is Dr. Carol."

I thought I was prepared for the evidence when it appeared, but nothing can prepare me for this betrayal. I am validated and destroyed simultaneously. The monstrous knowledge crushes me, slow and heavy, and I couldn't point my gun at her right now if my life depended on it. And I think it does.

"I bought those letters in a mini-storage auction a long time ago," she says. "I'd had my eye on it because I knew the unit belonged to the head of the foster home where the Walkers grew up. I took them right to the public defender. They returned them six months later. Said that an 'expert' had reviewed them and deemed them not relevant. Just the typical product of an adolescent girl. Not even worth a mention. I held on to them until Orchomenus contacted me to buy. I asked for an email from their real account. Something I could verify. Plus twelve hundred dollars. People only value what costs them money. It's sad, really."

I breathe deep to calm the panic attack I feel starting to cramp my lungs, but they spasm instead and I hiccup. I lower myself onto my haunches. How many of our secrets does Dr. Carol know? Why didn't she kill me in her house? What game is she playing with our lives?

I hear Chrissy rummaging through her drawers and my chest aches. Someone. Please help me. But Dr. Carol is my monster and there's no one who can help.

Except Stephanie.

She'll come. She'll come with her pepper spray, and Keith will be in the woods waiting for her. And he'll have a pickaxe, or a drill, or a butcher's knife, and she'll only have my pepper spray and she's right: that shit doesn't work.

"I found out later that the public defender's 'expert' was Dr. Carol. She told him those letters had no value in 2004, and then she bought them from me in 2009," Chrissy says. "Her understanding must have matured in those five years. Your little support group is just the killing ground she's created for the ultimate series of sacrifices in which she, the last monster, and you, the final final girl, will transcend together. You needed me to lead you to the heart of the Minotaur's labyrinth because you can't face the truth, so you came to Crazy Chrissy. Did you know that all the best oracles in classical mythology were crazy?"

She knew about the letters. For six years she knew about the letters and she never said anything to me. How long has she been planning this? She even wrote new ones, and I see her in her study, door locked, bent over Holly Hobbie stationery, fabricating sex between me and Ricky Walker, and if I needed to know how much she hates us, it's this much.

The floor tips dangerously. The walls revolve around me. There's a soft digital ding from the iMac and a pop-up window appears on the screen.

"Oh, look," Chrissy says. "Keith just texted. He's found something in the woods."

I am stupid and I am dumb and I underestimated just how crazy Dr. Carol really is. I see Chrissy's feet standing in front of me and I try to look up, I try to raise the gun, but my entire body is a cramp.

Something bites my right shoulder and it goes dead, and my legs stop working and I'm looking at the ceiling and I feel pressure on my waist, and the fanny pack is coming off and I see Chrissy and she's holding my pistol in her right hand and there's a stun gun in her left. My right arm feels broken.

"Let's go into the living room and see what Keith thinks we should do with your little friend." She smiles. "Sometimes he needs to be let off his leash."

Stephanie, I'm so sorry.

You were never safe with me.

continued from page 37

Think of how many creation myths start with murder. Kronos castrated and killed his father, Ouranos, and then Kronos cannibalized his own children until Zeus castrated and killed Kronos. In Norse mythology, Odin, Vili, and Ve killed their grandfather, the giant Ymir. So much blood flowed from his body that it flooded the universe and formed the oceans. His flesh became the land; they shaped the mountains from his bones and raised his skull up on four pillars to become the vault of Heaven. Man formed from the maggots that feasted on his corpse.

From the beginning, this world has been built by cannibals out of the corpses of their forefathers. *Mors janua vitae*: death is the gate of life.

—"The Monsters, Our Makers: From the First Flood to the Final Girls" by Christine Mercer, first published in the *Journal of Comparative Folklore,* November–December 2009

THE FINAL GIRL SUPPORT GROUP XIX:
Final Girl's Revenge

What have you found, Keith?" Chrissy calls when we reach her living room. "What do you have there?"

Keith swings open the storm door with his hip and lugs in a bag of bones. He's holding her underneath her arms and she's limp. His eyes are red and raw. My heart sinks because Steph must have sprayed him and it didn't do shit.

"She's dead," I say.

"Assuming makes an ass out of you and me," Chrissy says, putting a hand on my arm. "Keith will let us know if he decides to go in that direction."

The storm door swings shut on the back of Stephanie's calves and makes a scraping sound as Keith yanks her inside, shucking off one of her fake Chuck Taylors. He half throws, half dumps her onto a sagging armchair in the corner that's covered in dirty clothes.

"You found someone nosing around, didn't you?" Chrissy asks, like she's talking to her dog.

He casually tosses the Mace on top of the layer of McDonald's bags on the coffee table.

"Girl," Keith mumbles.

I think he has an erection. He presses the back of his forearm against the crotch of his jeans.

"Stephanie," I say, starting to walk toward her.

Her face is pale and blood drools from a black dent in her forehead. Leaves stick to her hoodie. Her eyes are open but I'm not sure she's seeing me.

"Don't," Chrissy says, grabbing my belt and pulling me backward. "Crowding Keith is a bad idea."

She looks me dead in the eyes and holds my gaze until I nod, and then we both consider Keith. He's squatting on his heels, elbows resting on his knees, hands on Stephanie's leg, looking like a giant squirrel staring up into her face.

"What are we going to do with her, Keith?" Chrissy asks in a kindergarten teacher's voice.

"It's Stephanie," I say. Repeating a potential victim's name creates empathy. I don't think it'll have any effect on Keith, but if it can even get him to hesitate for a second it might make all the difference. "From Red Lake."

"We know who she is," Chrissy says.

Chrissy stares down at Keith, and Keith stares up at Stephanie, and Stephanie's eyes roll around the room until they stop on me.

"Lynnette?" she says, thick-tongued. "I came."

I need to keep her thinking I can protect her. Right up until the end. Even if I can't. She won't die scared.

"We should go," I tell Chrissy, remembering her in the museum: *Sometimes he needs to be let off his leash.* "We should go and not bother you anymore."

"You're so cute," Chrissy giggles.

Keith hunches his neck down and practically wriggles with pleasure. The room is charged and at any second someone is going to commit to the next step and none of us will be able to go back.

"I want to go now," Steph says. "Okay? Can we please go?"

Gillian got that same hitch in her voice on Christmas Eve. I heard it when she walked into the living room, not understanding what was going on even when Ricky Walker turned around and saw her.

"Lynnette," she'd said as he'd started toward her. "I want to go back to bed now. I won't tell anyone I saw Santa. Tell him that I won't tell. Please, Lynnette?"

And I hung there, pretending to be dead because I was so scared that when Ricky ran out of victims he would take a closer look at me and I didn't want to die.

"Lynnette?" Gillian said right before he picked her up and she started screaming, and it's Stephanie saying it now and we're in Chrissy's junky living room and I need to get out of here.

Keith stares hard at Chrissy.

"What is it?" she asks.

"Want," Keith demands.

And Chrissy looks at me, then at Stephanie, then at me again, performing some kind of mental arithmetic, adding up the pros and cons, and then she smiles. It's a smile that I'm growing to associate with nothing good.

"An artist needs to practice or his tools lose their edge," she says. "I don't want Keith getting dull."

"My head hurts," Stephanie says.

"You don't understand," I say, and inspiration makes me brave. "She's a final girl. Keith can't do anything to her; he has to save himself for you. She has her own monster."

Chrissy shakes her head and smiles.

"This isn't a religion," she says. "It's not like Keith's going to Hell if he goes off his diet." She turns to Keith and gets his attention. "You need to make her last, lover."

Keith nods and holds up two fingers.

"Two days," he says.

"It's a good thing all the neighbors moved away," Chrissy says. "She looks like a screamer."

"You can't do this," I say. "She's a final girl."

"You need to get going, Lynnette," Chrissy says. "Once Keith starts it's hard for him to stop. I'm not in any danger, but you've got a destiny to fulfill."

I'm playing all my cards and they're not making any difference.

"With her," I say. "She needs to go with me. I promise you, Chrissy, just let her go with me. She's a final girl."

Keith stands and begins to search through the piles of garbage on the floor, then puts his chest on the carpet, his butt in the air, and he reaches underneath the couch.

Chrissy goes and sits in Stephanie's lap and plays with her bangs. Steph jerks her head away, and Chrissy grabs her chin with her fingers and holds it in place.

"This one's no final girl," she says. "She's a little monster. Keith loves to work with this kind of material."

Keith stands up from the couch, a dented and stained aluminum baseball bat in one hand.

"Lynnette?" Stephanie says because now she sees the bat and she sees me edging toward the front door, and her eyes are big and wet over Chrissy's shoulder.

"'He is the tender butcher who showed me how the price of flesh is love,'" Chrissy recites, holding Stephanie's chin and looking into her eyes. "'Skin the rabbit,' he says! 'Off come all my clothes.'"

Keith takes a practice swing with his baseball bat. It makes a sound that goes *schwoop*.

Chrissy turns around and raises her eyebrows at me.

"You'd better run," she says.

Keith takes another swing with his bat. This time, it scoops a dent out of the wall.

I run.

I close the distance to the door in two long strides, and out of the corner of my eye I see Keith notice my movement and take a step toward me, and I crash through the screen door, not even opening it first, and I hear the clear plastic panel in the center split, and the back of it bang off the side of their crappy house. It almost drowns out Stephanie's screams.

"Lynne!" she shrieks, over and over again.

Even out here, I can hear Chrissy laughing.

I'm down the steps in a second and my feet slip on the gravel driveway, but I pump my arms and drive my feet down into the dirt and I run as fast as I can, putting distance between myself and the house and Stephanie's screams. I only have a few seconds.

I tried to take Keith down before and I might as well have punched a tree. I race down the dark driveway, shadows on either side, panting and crunching gravel, forcing myself to run faster. I need to be faster.

You need to protect your sister.

I reach the Chevy and slide inside. The ignition turns and the engine hums to life and I'm wrenching the wheel to the left and plowing down the dirt driveway toward Chrissy's house. I keep pressing down on the accelerator, passing twenty-five, passing thirty, passing thirty-five. The car's tires barely cling to the dirt. I'm hitting potholes and ruts so hard the top of my head slams into the ceiling. The tires leave the road and come down hard again and again. If they land wrong I'll slide into a tree and die. Passing forty, passing forty-five. I switch on my headlights, and Chrissy's white house springs into view dead ahead. The house is made of sheet metal and vinyl siding, probably cost twenty-four thousand dollars in the sixties when her parents bought it, and as structurally sound as a wet cardboard box.

I left Julia behind. I left Fine behind. I won't leave Steph.

The world jogs crazily up and down in my windshield. I'm clinging to the steering wheel. Passing fifty, passing fifty-five. The sound of the tires goes quiet when I leave the gravel driveway.

I'm going sixty miles an hour when I slam into the front of Chrissy's house.

The wall fills my headlights, then it fills my windshield, then it's exploding and the house is collapsing onto the car and the world sounds like it's splitting in half. The airbags explode into my face and my sinuses are full of white powder and I feel like someone just broke my nose.

It takes me a minute to notice that the car isn't moving anymore. The only sound is the engine revving while I dumbly mash down on the accelerator. I'm trapped in a world of rubble. I put it in reverse and the tires spin, then catch, then there's drywall sliding off the roof and down the windshield and falling off the hood as the Lumina drags itself backward out of the house. There are sick, wheezing sounds coming from beneath the hood and one of the headlights is dead. I see the damage. The entire side of the house is caved in, and shattered sheets of drywall avalanche out of the entry wound. As I watch, the roof slowly sags sideways, and the kitchen ceiling collapses in an explosion of white dust.

I leave the car running and get out but it instantly stalls. It's shocking how quiet the night is. The only thing I can hear are crickets. I pick my way through the rubble the house vomited across the dirt. I tried to aim the car at the front door, away from the corner where Stephanie sat, but by the time I made contact I was barely in control. I grab the edge of the hole I tore with the Lumina and haul myself inside. Big slabs of drywall slide beneath my feet. Thick white dust hangs in the air. A wave of wreckage smashed into the opposite wall, but to my left, the room looks pristine. Stephanie sits in her chair, frozen in shock, hands wrapped around her head, knees pulled up to her chest. The car kicked up the TV and it took Chrissy square in the chest, smashing her backward through the Sheetrock. Her jeans-clad legs stick out from underneath. I don't see Keith anywhere.

I turn away. I don't want to look at Chrissy's body. I make a blind spot in my mind and swear not to look in that corner of the room again.

"Steph, I'm here," I say, wrenching my hips out of joint as I pick my way over the rubble to her. "Are you okay?"

"You drove the car into the house," she says, numb.

"I came back," I say. "I came back."

I help her up out of the chair and jump when something grabs my ankle. I'm so keyed up I scream even before I look down and see Keith's bloody white arm sticking out from under a pile of drywall, hand clamped around my leg.

"No, no, no, no," Steph says, seeing it and backpedaling out of my arms, shaking her head.

"Steph," I say. "Don't panic."

The hand bears down, pressing my bones together, and I bring my other foot up and stomp on his fingers, hard. I hurt myself more than I hurt Keith. The pile of rubble shifts as Keith starts to haul himself out. I kneel, pick up a long wooden splinter, and punch holes in his hand again and again, the splinter getting slick with his blood. His hand finally spasms open and I yank my foot away.

The rubble erupts as Keith stands, silent and unstoppable. His spine has been twisted out of shape and he's bending over too far to one side. I'm frozen, just a few feet away, Steph in my arms. Keith takes a step forward and his legs give out. He goes down on his hands and knees, then turns his red-rimmed puppy-dog eyes to me.

"Hurts," he says.

I hear vertebrae popping as he stands back up and the spell is broken. Limping, hobbling, slipping, falling, I drag Stephanie through the hole and out of the house. I get her to the car and shove her into the passenger seat. Her eyes fix on something over my shoulder and I turn. Behind us, Keith has dragged himself out of the shattered side of the house, hunched over but moving, his baseball bat held in one hand like a cane. I slam the door and run to the driver's side, going around the back of the car, not wanting to pass too close to Keith.

I get in and lock the doors. Keith keeps coming. I turn the key and nothing happens. Keith takes another lurching step. I turn the key again and the starter grinds but the engine doesn't catch. Final girls learned a long time ago not to rely on things other people take for granted. We all know that elevators and telephones never work when we need them. And cars. Especially cars.

Keith lets go of the side of the house and takes three fast steps toward the headlight, and then he sees me through the windshield and focuses, and comes for me.

I turn the key again. The starter grinds and I sob as the spark catches and it roars to life. For a second, I contemplate stomping on the accelerator and crushing Keith between the front bumper and the house so that black blood fountains out of his mouth, and then I think of Chrissy's legs sticking out from beneath the television set and stomach acid scorches my throat.

I throw it into reverse and get the hell out of there.

The Chevy screams at me all the way, and its engine keeps racing for no good reason, but I get us to a doc in a box out on the highway and for five hundred fifty dollars they throw six stitches in Stephanie's scalp and give her some Demerol. Back on the highway I get us eighty miles away, then find a Motel 6, and I drag Stephanie to bed. I get her shoes off, make sure she has water, because waking up with dry mouth from Demerol can be horrible, and then I put the chain on, push the chair up against the door, and slump down in the bathtub and cry.

I'm a murderer. I killed Chrissy. I stopped the life of a human being. Chrissy was terrorized like me. Stalked like me. Saw her friends die like me. And I killed her. I bite a towel while I scream because I don't want Steph to hear. The other final girls were all blooded, they all had to kill their monsters to stay alive, but not me. I possummed my way out. Killing was what the Walker brothers did to me, not what I did to anyone else. Like Chrissy said, I create, I don't destroy.

Of course, what have I ever created except an empty fortress that I locked myself inside, a life with no friends except for a plant that was only alive inside my head? And my book? And those letters?

All I ever created was shit.

My thoughts feel heavy and absolute, irrevocable and final. I have murdered someone. Whenever I watched a movie and some hero refused to kill the villain because "then I'll be as bad as he is," I dismissed it as a bunch of moralistic hand-wringing by balding Hollywood scriptwriters who had only ever killed the last roll of toilet paper. But they tapped into a universal truth. I'm living in a new world now, and in this world I am a murderer.

I can't take it back, I can't fix it, I can't make it better, but I can do one thing about it.

I can never do it again. I swear harder than I've ever sworn anything since I was a little girl: I will not kill again. No matter how many lives it will save. No matter how much it puts my own life at risk. No matter what. No more killing.

At some point I fall asleep because when I open my eyes I'm cold and I have a headache and my neck is sore. I stand up and stretch, feeling the vertebrae in my back pop one by one. A slit of sunlight pours through the windows where I didn't get the curtains quite closed. Stephanie lies in the exact same position I left her in, but after a nervous moment I see her chest softly rise and fall. I relax. No one else is dead.

I lost my fanny pack in Chrissy's house, so it won't be long before the cops find my Dr. Newbury ID and then they'll contact Dr. Carol and she'll tell them about me, and they'll have my name and last known location. While the cops hunt me down, she'll isolate everyone someplace. Sagefire, probably, her yuppie wellness retreat outside L.A. I need to warn them.

I lift Stephanie's phone off the bedside table and step outside. I've seen her tap in her PIN enough times to memorize it (1223) and I unlock her home screen and don't read any of the eighteen unread texts because I respect her privacy. I try Dani but the phone just rings, same with Marilyn, Heather's number is still not back in service, and that's it. Julia's still unconscious in the hospital, and then I realize: Skye. He wrote down his number, and I dig out that piece of paper, and I call.

"What happened?" he asks, picking up on the first ring.

"Skye?" I say. There's a long pause. "It's Lynnette Tarkington."

"I figured," he whispers. "Who else would call me at six forty-five in the morning from a number I don't know. Dude, what did you do?"

"Nothing they say about me is true," I warn him.

"They say you abducted that girl," he whispers. "They say you stole some retired cop's car and beat him up and left him on the side of the road. They say you escaped custody and are a fugitive who's wanted for questioning."

"Yeah, well, okay," I admit. "Those things are true but everything else is a lie."

"My mom's super pissed," he says.

"You need to go stay at a friend's," I say. "Get your little brother and go someplace. Get out of your house."

"Can't," he says. "Mom's taking everyone on a road trip."

"No," I tell him. "That's a bad idea."

"She's pretty passionate about it," he tells me. "She's taking Pax and me and a bunch of people up to Sagefire. Pax loves it up there."

"What people?" I ask. "Who's going?"

"Look," he says. "I've got to go. She's going to kill me if she finds out you called."

He hangs up and when I call back I get voicemail.

It's too far back to L.A. Sagefire is only an hour and a half outside the city. We can't get there in time. I imagine her loading up Marilyn and Dani and Heather, going to the hospital to pick up Julia. Getting them all alone at her retreat. I can't think about it.

I call Julia, because even though I'm going to get her voicemail I want to hear someone's voice.

"Who is this?"

Her voice is strong and clear.

"Julia?" I say.

"Oh, Jesus," she says. "Lynnette?"

"Are you okay?" I ask.

"No," she says. "I'm not okay. I got shot three times in the legs. Did you abduct a kid? Are you insane?"

I need to assess her condition.

"Does it hurt?" I ask.

"Getting shot in the legs?" she asks. "What, because I'm paralyzed? You think it doesn't hurt? Here's an idea, Lynnette. Why don't you go get shot in something you don't use, like your head, and report back, okay? Jesus Christ. Dr. Carol told me you'd had a breakdown."

"Have you seen her?" I ask.

"She's picking me up later," Julia says. "They're discharging me this morning. You were right about one thing—we are all in danger. From you. Dr. Carol's taking us somewhere safe until you're in custody."

"Sagefire," I say.

"Well, there goes that plan," Julia says. "I can't believe I came to you thinking Heather had written that book and it was you. And now you've kidnapped a child. I thought I knew you."

"It's Stephanie Fugate," I tell her. "The girl from the Camp Red Lake massacre. I'm keeping her safe. Listen, I saw Chrissy—"

"You're keeping a kid safe and you took her to see Crazy Chrissy?" Julia shouts. "You really are out of your mind."

"Julia," I say. "You know me, so please, listen for one minute. How did Christophe Volker get Adrienne's home address? How did he know how to sneak into Camp Red Lake? Why did Harry Peter Warden and Billy Walker both implicate Dani and me at the same time? Someone shot you. Someone tried to kill me in jail. Someone's coordinating all this and Chrissy knew who."

"And?" she says.

"It's Dr. Carol," I say. "I've seen proof."

"Proof from Crazy Chrissy?" Julia says.

"Trust me," I tell her.

"You've made that an impossibility," she says.

"Then be safe," I say. "Don't trust anyone. I'm begging you. Call Marilyn and get her security guys to pick you up, and get her and Dani and Heather and just go anywhere for forty-eight hours. That's all I'm asking. Don't tell me where you're going. Don't tell Dr. Carol where you're going.

Just go. We're alive because we were the smart ones. We're the ones who didn't go in that basement. We didn't open that door. Please."

There's a long silence.

"Are you still there?" I ask.

"Well, I'm not going to tell you if I'm doing it or not," she says.

"Right, of course, great," I say, and then I think about Pax and Skye. "Wait, before you go, Dr. Carol has two kids. See if they'll come with you. I mean, they're her kids but I don't think she should be around anyone right now. Not until I've . . ." Fact is, I don't know what I'm going to do. "Not until I've talked to her."

"Good-bye, Lynnette," Julia says. "I hated your book."

I feel drained. I go back into the room, put the phone back by Stephanie's head, and I'm drinking a cup of terrible in-room tea when I notice her looking at me. She touches her stitches.

"Am I okay?" she asks.

The shaft of sunlight coming through the curtains is strong and bright and dust motes dance where it bisects her stomach.

"They said you didn't have a concussion," I tell her. "Drink some water."

Steph sits up in bed, grabs the bottle, and gulps it down.

"You saved me," Steph says, unable to believe it. "You saved my ass. He was going to beat me to death with that bat and all of a sudden everything exploded and that TV knocked her block off."

"I don't want to talk about it," I say.

"She deserved it," she says.

"I'm not a killer," I say, which is going to make it very hard to deal with Dr. Carol.

"That's not a good survival instinct," Steph says.

I'm irrationally angry with her for making it sound so easy, but I don't want to fight. I open up my go bag and focus on lining up what I have left on the table. Leatherman, small Maglite, lockblade, GPS, twenty-five feet of nylon rope, four pairs of flexi-cuffs, $830 in cash.

"Ugh, I stink," Steph says. She gets out of bed and paddles to the bathroom on stiff feet and drinks from the tap, then fills her bottle again and gulps it down.

"If it's me or them," she says, wiping her chin, "it's going to be them, every time. That's all there is to it. You better get used to that."

"I don't want to get used to murder," I say.

"I didn't realize you were such a bleeding heart," she says, flopping back on the bed and adjusting the pillows behind her.

My .22 is the last thing I take out of my bag. I put it on the desk.

"We'll throw that off the first bridge we find," I say.

"Hell, no," Stephanie says, getting up and crossing the room. "No one's making me their punk again. You may have gone all kumbaya but I still want some stopping power."

She picks it up and aims it at the door, holding it to one side like she's seen in the movies.

"I don't want to kill anyone else," I say.

"Then leave it to me," she says in a voice that's too tough, too confident.

She doesn't know what murder really is. But I let her have the gun. Eventually, she'll learn how useless it is.

At the bottom of my go bag is *War Ghost*, Pax Elliott's homemade comic book. It feels like he hustled me out of a hundred dollars for it two months ago, not seven days ago. I hope Julia does what I asked. I don't want to have to deal with those boys when I go see Dr. Carol up at Sagefire.

"We'll head for L.A.," I tell her. "We can refill your prescription on the way."

I flip through the comic book. The drawings are about what you'd expect: amateurish and horrible. I can barely tell what I'm looking at.

"I don't think the car can make it," Steph says. "We may have to rent one. Do you have a credit card?"

I'm looking at a page in the comic, and I can't answer. An oversized figure with his mouth wide open, full of jagged teeth, and Xs for eyes, has sunk his talons into a lion and is ripping its head off. Red scribbles are everywhere. A wide-open mouth is a sign of sexual abuse; claws for hands represent possible violence, as does the oversized body in relation to the small child he looms over. Overuse of one color may be a sign of emotional imbalance. So are the Xs for eyes, and the fangs. But it's what's written on the monster's chest that takes my breath away.

Sky.

"If you have a credit card we'll just rent a car, right?" Stephanie repeats.

Sky Man is so evul he tears the head off cats, the caption reads. *Big cats, little cats, our cats, neighborhood cats. Sky Man hates cats.*

My hands go numb.

"Are you listening to me?" Steph asks. "You say this is so urgent, so let's get back to L.A. But we have to rent a car."

I page back with trembling fingers and read from the beginning. Page after page features a monstrous Sky Man looming over PX-1, a tiny robot who cowers from his rage.

Sky Man can shoot a gun real fast, the caption reads.

"I can shoot through a building from across the street," Sky Man brags in a word balloon, holding a rifle with a scope. *"I kill all the Last Ladies!"*

Sky Man is burning down a building.

"Take that, Dream King!" he shouts.

Sky Man will kill the Mean Girls, the caption reads over a picture of Sky Man chopping off the heads of six women. One is in a wheelchair. Crayon blood fountains from their necks. Six necks. There are six of them. Six final girls.

"Are you totally spaced out?" Stephanie asks. "Hello?"

Sky Man says that when he is finished, the caption reads, *we will be the only people left in the world and all the enemies will be deaded. Sky Man will kill them all the enemies! Then mommy will come home again!*

Sky Man. Skye Elliott.

I think about Chrissy getting an email from Dr. Carol's account.

I remember standing in Skye's room and him saying, *I set up all the email servers for my mom's business.*

Dr. Carol's son. Her home office. Her computer. How he got my book. How he saw her notes. How he knew all about us. How he got us to do his work for him. The monster is coming from inside the house.

I drop the comic into my bag.

"We need to go," I tell Stephanie. "Grab your phone, get your stuff, we need to get to L.A. We'll call Julia on the way."

We call her fourteen times before we reach the state line. She doesn't pick up once.

JUDY HICKS: If you start to hurt let us know and we'll take a break.

2

3   JULIA CAMPBELL: Are you sure you got him?

4

5   DWIGHT RILEY: You got him, ma'am. When you tackled him out that window.

6

7   JULIA CAMPBELL: Sure, yeah, go me. Last time there were two.

8

9   JUDY HICKS: If we can return to the night of the murders?

10

11   JULIA CAMPBELL: Well, I came in the door of our room and there he was and I

12   didn't think. I just did it.

13

14   DWIGHT RILEY: Ma'am, um, are you in pain?

15

16   JULIA CAMPBELL: Sorry, winded.

17

18   DWIGHT RILEY: Want us to call the doctor?

19

20   JULIA CAMPBELL: I'm not in pain. I can't feel any pain. If my legs are broken

21   they should hurt like hell.

22

23   JUDY HICKS: Let's return to the night you encountered Raymond Carlton.

24

25   JULIA CAMPBELL: How many painkillers do they have me on?

26

27   DWIGHT RILEY: Should we get the doctor?

28

29   JUDY HICKS: We should get——

30

31   JULIA CAMPBELL: Why can't I feel it when I pinch my legs like that?

32

33   DWIGHT RILEY: Just one moment, ma'am——

34

35   JULIA CAMPBELL: Please. Please. Don't pretend you can't hear me. Why can't I

36   feel anything?

——transcript of San Diego PD officers Dwight Riley and Judy Hicks
interviewing multiple homicide survivor Julia Campbell

THE FINAL GIRL SUPPORT GROUP XX:
The Final Chapter

We fly through the prairie.

We took the Chevy to a body shop and paid the guy my last eight hundred dollars for new bumpers and a windshield. I make him give me a loaner for the day it'll take to do the work.

"Keep her under sixty-five and don't go on the highway," he tells me.

"Absolutely," I tell him.

We hit the highway and I keep it at eighty-five all the way.

Julia won't pick up. Neither will Dani, and Heather's phone remains out of service. Marilyn has blocked Stephanie's number. They've all turned their backs on me because they think I slept with my monster, because they read my book, because they think I'm crazy. My only proof comes from Chrissy and a messed-up child's comic book. They'll never believe me.

I press the gas pedal down. The car's frame shakes ominously. Stephanie rambles for the entire drive.

"Everyone thinks the wolves in the park are dangerous," Steph says as we pass a sign for Yellowstone. "But it's the bison that attack people all the time."

Stephanie talks like she needs to remind herself she's alive. What happened in Chrissy's house must have shaken her more than I thought. She reads billboards out loud. She states her opinion on the drivers of other cars. I don't answer. I need to get to California.

We take route 30 to circle wide around Salt Lake City, heading toward Wells on 80. There's no way I'm going anywhere near American Fork, even if it is faster.

We don't stop in cities. There are too many people in cities. We drive through an America made of four-lane highways and lined with rest stops. Cities are billboard clusters bisected by off-ramps and merge lanes.

Bruises and scratches cover Stephanie's arms and face. I wonder when I can cut the stitches out of her head. She stops calling her parents. I don't notice until ten hours have passed.

"You gave up?" I ask.

"What do they have to say?" she asks. "The police are already after us. I mean, we're probably both going to jail. Where are we even headed?"

My body vibrates inside my skin. Are they with Dr. Carol or did Julia listen and get them somewhere safe? Did she get Skye to go with her? Are they at Sagefire? I don't even know where we're going.

Sometimes you don't know why you're doing anything anymore so you just keep moving even though you're out of options.

"We need to stop," Stephanie says.

"No stopping," I say.

"I have to pee," she says.

"Go in a cup," I say. The back is full of empty coffee cups. I'm so caffeinated my eyeballs vibrate inside their sockets.

"I'm not peeing in a cup," Steph says. "*You* pee in a cup."

"I will when I have to," I say. "You'll hold the wheel."

"Gross," she says, crossing her arms and looking out the passenger-side window.

The loaner's heater is stuck and hot air blasts us both in the face the entire way.

"I'm broiling," Stephanie says, and I don't disagree. My feet feel hot and sweaty. "I'm actually cooking alive."

We drive through a night so black that if we turned off the headlights the planet would disappear.

We fill the back seat with fast-food wrappers. A couple hundred miles ago we had a trash bag, but at a certain point the entire back seat of the car became a trash bag.

I tell her about Skye. I tell her that he's the one doing the killing. I tell her we need to stop him, but I don't know how. I can't hurt him, but no one will believe me no matter what I say. I'm out of ideas. My plans have reached their limits. I'm just motion now.

"Call him," she says.

"We can't," I say. "We'll lose our advantage."

"What advantage?" she asks. "If you think he's going to kill everyone, call him."

We're past Reno on 80 now; all that remains is a straight shot out to the coast, then south. I call him on Steph's phone. I have a hard time hitting the right keys. I hesitate before putting it up to my ear, and then I commit.

It's ringing, then goes to voicemail.

"Skye," I say. "It's Lynnette. I . . . we . . . where are . . . will you call me back?"

I hang up.

"That was a good message," Steph says. "I'd definitely call you back. It sounds like you're asking him out on a date."

I'm crashing hard and the engine keeps lulling me to sleep, my head snapping back and then forward.

"You know how this has to end," Steph says from the passenger seat. "If that guy's the one doing it, we kill him."

"There has to be another way," I say. "Maybe I can talk to him. We can all just go our separate ways and, and, and just leave each other alone. No one has to die. We can have a happy ending here."

I know I'm babbling. Every word out of my mouth sounds less convincing than the one before. She's a guided missile locked onto her target, and I'm a philosophy student failing her oral exam.

"Figure out where we're going," she says as Taco Time franchises give way to Tender Greens. "That's all we need to do."

"How?" I ask, and I realize I can't let her know I'm lost. I can't let her know I'm panicking. "No one's talking to me! I don't know who to call!"

The glow of Sacramento is staining the horizon orange by the time I make the call I've been dreading.

"Who're you dialing?" Steph asks from the passenger seat.

"Garrett," I say.

"What the fuck are you doing that for?" she asks. I look down to hit send. The tires veer. Steph yelps. "Jesus FUCK!"

I drop the phone and keep the car on the road. The heater keeps blasting me in the face. I've sweated through this T-shirt so many times it's gray. The car smells like the load of garbage we're carrying in back. I dig Stephanie's phone out of my crotch.

"Think about it," Steph says. "Why're you calling him?"

"He'll help me," I say.

Quick as a snake, she snatches her phone away. Not thinking, I grab for it. She has the advantage because morning traffic is picking up and I can't take my eyes off the road.

"Stop hitting me," she snarls. "I'm doing you a favor. He's going to get you arrested the second you call from this phone."

"Garrett is straight with me," I say.

"You stole his car," she says. "You abandoned him on the side of the road. All the other cops think you escaped custody. You kidnapped me."

"I'll chance it," I say.

"Not with me in the car," she says. "He takes me home and my parents will lock me in the house and then I'm a sitting duck. If this kid's coming for you, he's coming for me now, too. He'll . . . have to go through my family."

Her voice hitches. She can't bring herself to say "kill her family" because it's too ugly. I take deep breaths. Someone else relies on me now. I have to think about her.

"Okay," I say. "I won't call him."

"What's he even going to say?" Steph asks. "You saw some kid's comic book and are convinced your therapist's son is a serial killer? Do you know what that sounds like?"

Signs for San Francisco try to lure us west, away from our path.

"I know how to spot that kind of thing," I say. "The violent imagery, the triangular teeth. The dialogue wasn't anything a kid could come up with. It was too specific. You saw the book."

"I saw a bunch of little-kid drawings," she says.

"It has to be him," I say, and I sound like I did when I thought it was Dr. Carol.

Does this ever end? Will there always be someone out there turning little boys into monsters? Will we always be final girls? Will there always be monsters killing us? How do we stop the snake from eating its own tail?

Steph looks out the window.

"There's a rest stop coming up," she says.

"We're four hours from L.A.," I say.

"So what?" she practically screams. We're starting to work each other's nerves. We haven't had any sleep. We've been fifteen hours in the car without a break. I want to tear my face off. "No one will even talk to you. They won't take your calls. Where are we even going?"

"I don't know!" I say. It's the first time I've admitted it, and now that it's out I double down. "I don't know! But we have to do something! We have to go somewhere! We can't let him kill us! Not again! Not like this! Not while I can actually save everyone this time."

Steph kicks the dashboard with both feet.

"I want out of this car," she says. "Pull over at the rest stop."

"Why?" I ask, suddenly scared I've pushed her too far.

"Because I have to pee and I'm not going in a fucking cup!" she yells.

I find a parking space and we both get out of the car and walk away from each other. I stand on a median of yellowed grass carpeted in cigarette butts. How many of these were smoked by men on the prowl for hitchhikers? How many were butted out by runaway kids before they hitched their final ride with the wrong driver? I breathe in the exhaust and stale oil stink until I'm calm again, then go back to the car and begin cleaning out the back seat.

I glance up and see Steph talking on her cell phone, walking toward me. The back seat is full of paper cups sloshing with melted ice, congealed fries, greasy sandwich wrappers, triangular cardboard boxes for the Sbarro slices that Steph loves.

"Okay," she says. "I love you too."

She hangs up and stands looking down at me for a second before she smiles and says in a soft voice:

"Here, let me dump those cups."

Working together we unearth the back seat and reveal the carpet. It's stained and stinks of cold grease, but at least it's not a rolling garbage dump anymore.

"I talked to my parents," she says. "Told them that I was coming home. That I'd see them soon. They seemed calmer. I guess?"

"Do you want to go home?" I ask.

She shakes her head.

"When do I feel like myself again?" she blurts out. "How long does it take?"

I think about Garrett and all the women in group and how they all treat me like I'm crazy. Maybe they're right.

How did I wind up trapped inside this life? Where did I go wrong? The Walkers punched my ticket at sixteen, and ever since then everything has been leading me here. Abandoned, broken, useless at everything except being scared and staying alive.

"I don't know," I say. "But if I ever feel that way, I'll let you know."

"Oh," she says.

Suddenly Steph looks very small and cold and vulnerable. I stand up, take a deep breath, and give her a hug. It has all the warmth of rubbing two bricks together. Her hair smells filthy. There's no give, no yield, no softness in either of us. I end the hug and am filled with a sense of having done the right thing. Maybe this is what makes a life? Responsibilities, obligations, who we tie ourselves to? Maybe that's what I've been missing?

"We're going to be in L.A. soon," Steph says. "What's the plan?"

I am insane and stupid, but this girl relies on me. She's just a kid. I should send her home. I should go my own way, keep driving, maybe up to Canada, never come back, break up the band. But I can't. Even if they hate me, I can't walk away from my obligations. This movie that is my life has to end. It can't keep going on like this forever. I won't let Skye die. I won't let this keep chewing up more and more people. I won't let messed-up parents keep making monsters, and I won't let these boys keep making more final girls. It's not some profound and ancient ritual. It's just a waste of a life.

"I don't know," I say. "I don't know where anyone is. I don't know if they're with Julia, or Dr. Carol, or at Sagefire, or with Skye. I don't know anything, Stephanie."

"Why don't we go to Dani's?" she says.

"Dani?" I ask.

"Wherever everyone is, she'll know," she says. "And no matter where they are, Dani'll be at her ranch, almost definitely. You said she's stubborn and suicidal, right? We find her, talk to her, find out where everyone is, maybe convince her to come with us to at least check Skye out, and the others will listen. Everyone respects Dani."

She's talking like she knows us, and then I realize that she does. We're all final girls now.

"Yeah," I say, and then I have to admit, "I'm not really sure where her ranch is."

"I'll find it," she says. "She runs a horse rescue place for abused ponies? I can look it up on my phone. Big Sky Haven Ranch."

"You know the name?" I ask.

She checks out the toes of her sneakers.

"I was kind of a superfan," she says. "Of Dani, not you. I'm sorry."

Of course. It all makes perfect sense. Dani always knows what to do. We get her on our side and everything will be all right.

"You navigate," I say. "I'll drive."

"You're the boss," she says.

It's time for this to end. After Stephanie, there will be no more final girls.

THE DREAM KING CONSPIRACY

No one had ever heard about Heather DeLuca until producer Avi Poolos made her crimes the center of New Line's big-budget *Deadly Dreams* in 1989. With effects by Screaming Mad George and Rick Baker, this big-budget (by New Line standards) movie had a Hollywood gloss and made buckets of money. But for fans, the faux-romantic goth atmosphere and the glossy, shallow glitz felt heartless. *Deadly Dreams* is the Las Vegas of slasher movies.

As reporters began to investigate the original crimes, what they turned up was what appeared to be the sad case of a school custodian accused of pedophilia, an unrelated series of suicides, and three accidental deaths that all happened to be linked by nothing more than simple geographic proximity. And as for Heather DeLuca? She seemed to be less of a Final Girl and more someone who had avoided an assault charge with a self-defense plea. It all looked like a publicity department fabrication created out of whole cloth, and fans felt betrayed.

—"The Dream King Conspiracy" by Blaze Sullivan,
Fangoria, March 2003

THE FINAL GIRL SUPPORT GROUP XXI:
The Final Chapter II

The first sign of trouble is the sign.

Dani's ranch is near Elizabeth Lake, twenty miles outside L.A. in those flat little hills that always look like they need a bath. Grubby humps with dust-coated trees clogging their folds. It's a light brown world covered with scrub.

It takes us an hour to find the right road, and half an hour to find the little dirt track that leads from the road onto Dani's ranch. Out here in the country no one thinks to put up street signs or house numbers. If you have to ask, you don't belong. I hate the country.

I'm doing fifteen miles an hour when we see the gate.

"Do we just open it?" Steph asks, looking up from the map on her phone.

There's a ditch on either side.

"I can't drive around it," I say.

The engine idles. I scrutinize the gate. The chain is wrapped loosely around the post five or six times to hold it shut. This is where you get out of your car and the monster rises up out of the ditch, where his hand shoots up out of the sand and grabs your ankle.

Nervously, Steph gets out. I lock the doors after her. I watch the ditch, I watch the sand, I check my mirrors. She reaches the post, stops, and turns back to the car. She points to the ground. I pantomime-shrug at her through the windshield. She bends down and lifts one end of an un-painted board. It's old and someone has carved letters into it and filled them with white paint:

BIG SKY HAVEN RESCUE RANCH

Now that I see it, I also see the post it was nailed to. There's raw yellow wood snagged on the nails like it was recently ripped down. Dani would never do that. Dani throws out Heather's coffee cups. Dani uses a lint brush on her flannel shirts. Dani picks up leaves from the parking lot and tosses them back into the bushes when she walks to her truck.

Steph drops the board, unwraps the chain, pushes open the gate.

"Get in," I call out my window. "We need to get to her house."

I can't take the car over fifteen without feeling like I'm about to crack the suspension, so we creep up the road too slow, leaving the gate yawning open behind us. Then we see the smoke.

"People burning leaves?" Steph asks.

A column of black smoke rises up through the stand of eucalyptus trees ahead of us. The car crawls, and sweat pours down my sides, stroking its ghost fingers over my clammy skin.

We drive into the trees and come to the house. It's a neat little farm-house in a clearing surrounded by a split rail fence with a big circular parking area out front and a water pump in the middle. Dunes of wild-flowers sway around the pump. The soil beneath them is dark black, moist and new. The flowers Michelle wanted to see before she died. Against all this brown dust they stand out like fireworks.

The house is tucked back in the eleven o'clock position on the circular drive. To the right, at about three o'clock, a path leads to a stable. Dani's truck sits in the drive and the front door to the ranch house stands open.

Neither of us can take our eyes off the bonfire that's burning in the middle of the parking area. Wooden dining room chairs are piled up, and weak orange flames lick their legs in the sun. A heap of blackened books smolders beneath them, and a few charred magazines blow around in the dirt.

We got here too late.

"Do you see Skye's car?" I ask.

"I don't know what Skye's car looks like," Steph says, pulling out the .22. She checks the chamber like a pro. I should have re-armed myself.

"I doubt he's still here," I say. "But let's check."

We step out into the hot breeze. I look inside the trunk. There's a cut-rate jack made of pressed aluminum in a greasy cardboard box. It's barely better than nothing. I let it dangle in my right hand, and the two of us approach the house, instinctively circling from opposite sides.

There's movement inside, and I plant my legs and tense. Steph snaps her attention to the front door and raises the .22 in both hands. Good girl. A figure comes out hauling an enormous rolled-up carpet. It stomps across the yard, carpet dragging behind it like a dinosaur tail, and I recognize the square shoulders, the solid shape, the lack of curves. Dani looks up to make sure she's still heading toward the bonfire and sees us, wipes the sweat from her face, then puts her head down and keeps storming toward the flames.

"Dani?" I call.

She drops the rolled-up carpet on the ground next to the bonfire and catches her breath. Even from thirty feet away I can feel the heat chapping my face.

"Dani?" I try again.

She bends over and picks up the carpet by the middle, then hauls it up and shoves it forward in one lunge. It topples the stack of burning chairs and they hit the ground in front of me, giving off great big tumbleweeds of pale sparks in the sunlight. One bites the back of my hand.

"Dani," I say. "What happened?"

She stops, halfway through the turn to go back to her house. Her hand drops to the Glock holstered on her thigh when she sees Steph coming from the other direction.

"That's Stephanie," I say to her. "Camp Red Lake. She's the one who met Christophe Volker."

Dani steps back so she can keep both of us in her field of vision.

"What do you want?" she asks.

"Someone knocked down your sign," I say.

"It's all gotta go," she says.

Then she slumps, takes her hand off her pistol, and trudges back to her front door. Stephanie gives me a questioning look, gun lowering, and I shrug. Halfway to her front door, Dani reverses course and steams back at me, fists balled at her sides.

"What's—" is as far as I get before she punches me in the stomach.

I double over, hands on my knees, and throw up on my shoes, the jack clanking into the dust. Dani stands in front of me, not moving as I cough up bile, and then I force myself upright and she slaps me across the face. My head comes off my neck. She gives me another shot to the stomach and I fall on my knees in my own mess.

"No, Steph!" I say, holding up one hand to stop her from coming at Dani.

It doesn't help; she's feeling protective.

"Hey," Stephanie squeaks. "Hands off."

Dani doesn't even turn her head, just straight-arms Stephanie in the chest, sending her backward, arms windmilling, flinging the .22 away in a big arc, before going down hard on her butt.

I try to get to my feet and Dani winds up one leg and plants the toe of her boot deep in my stomach. I stay down.

"You wrote that book," she says, standing over me. "That goddamn book. What the hell was going through your head to write trash like that? You think I'm in a codependent relationship with my Michelle? My every-thing? I use her to isolate myself from group? You think that?"

She kicks me again. I'm not fighting back. I rest my swollen cheek in the dirt. I deserve this. Her hands grab my collar and she yanks me to my feet. I hear my shirt rip. I can see her gray eyes. Her pupils are pinpricks.

"You think my guilt over killing my brother has eaten me alive?" she demands, and slaps me. "It's made me 'politically deranged'?" She slaps me again. "You think I keep Michelle in my shadow?"

Another slap. I can taste blood in my mouth.

"I'm sorry," I say through swelling lips, wetness trickling down my chin. "I never meant for anyone to see it. I did everything I could to get Michelle back here to die."

"Don't say her name," she snarls, pushing her leathery face into mine. "You don't get to say her name."

She slaps me again, and then there's movement at her side. Steph has the .22 and is coming back, holding it at the end of one outstretched arm. Dani drops me on the ground like a bag of garbage and grabs Steph's wrist, twists it, then kicks her feet out from under her. She draws her Glock and aims at the back of Stephanie's neck. I need to stop this. Now. From the ground I show Dani my hands.

"It was my journal, it was private, the guy stole it off my computer," I say. "The same guy who's been manipulating all of us. He got Volker to attack Stephanie and kill Adrienne. He burned down Heather's halfway house. He shot Julia. He paid Harry Peter Warden to tell the cops he committed Nick's killings. He's the one who tried to make you think you killed your brother for no reason, Dani. I saw Chrissy. She told me all of it. He communicated with Walker in code. He's trying to discredit us in public, and then he's going to pick us off one by one."

Dani cocks her head like she's considering my theory. Steph starts pushing herself up from the ground, ready to come at her again. The two of them lock eyes. Dani adjusts the grip on her Glock.

"Ah, who cares?" Dani says, breaking her gaze, spinning on one heel, stomping back into her house, holstering her pistol, and leaving Steph and me in the dirt.

"I thought you were mentally ill," Steph says. "But she's seriously crazy."

The carpet smokes on the pile, sending out greasy black billows of soot. It smells like chemicals.

"Viking funeral," I say, sitting up.

I spit out a mouthful of blood. Aside from bruises, I don't think she did any permanent damage.

"She needs to get her shit together," Steph grumbles. "This is more serious than her girlfriend."

"Not for her," I say.

Dani staggers out the front door of her house, dragging a mattress. It's huge and floppy and gets stuck in the doorway. She punches and kicks it, hauls it out, then drags it through the dust to us. When she reaches the smoking bonfire she lets it drop. Ashes blast out in a cloud and instantly suffocate the flames. Cold smoke unrolls into the blue sky.

"Shit," she says, wiping a tie-dyed bandana across her grimy forehead.

"Will you talk to me, Dani?" I ask, standing. I can't unbend all the way. "I don't know if you know what's going on, but things are really bad. We need to know where Julia took everyone."

She looks at me like it doesn't matter who I am.

"Her glass of water's gone," she says. "The one by her side of the bed. It was the last thing her lips touched. She drank half and every day since she's been gone the water level's been getting lower and lower, and I knew what was going to happen but as long as there was even a bit left it wasn't happening. Then yesterday I looked and it was dry. It used to be her glass of water and now it's just an empty glass. There's nothing left, Lynne. It's all gone."

Her face goes slack. Her eyes are lifeless. I've never felt the way she does about anyone.

"I don't want to be here anymore without her," she says. "I can't be alone again. I can't."

She turns and heads to the barn, leaving Steph and me stranded in her wake.

"Can't you get her to listen to you?" Steph asks.

Dani comes out of the barn with a yellow and red gas can banging against one thigh. She stands on the edge of the dead bonfire, unscrews the cap, douses the mattress, shakes out the last few drops, tosses the can, then pulls a pack of matches from her breast pocket, lights them all and flicks the pack onto the mattress.

FWOOMP!

It goes up in a fireball, and the reek of hot gasoline blasts my face. I feel my nose hairs crisp. Steph and I limp backward a few steps but Dani doesn't move. Her face shines beet red in the blast-furnace heat.

I motion for Steph to stay where she is and I circle around to Dani, who's basking in her destruction.

"I never wanted to hurt you," I say. "I don't want to hurt anybody."

"When they found Michelle's body, some old wino was trying to kiss her," Dani says.

"That was probably Carl DeWolfe Jr."

"Huh," she says, and there's a long silence. "At least she was outside. She wouldn't want to die indoors. But when she needed me most, I wasn't there."

"Because of Skye," I say. "Dr. Carol's son. He's organized this entire thing. He's insane. He's playing us all."

"I only wanted to be there for Michelle," Dani says, desolate. "That's all I ever wanted."

She's not hearing me. We both stand there, watching her furniture burn. Steph stares at us through the heat shimmer from the other side of the bonfire.

"Dr. Carol's son is dangerous," I say. "You have to believe me. And now he's with Julia and Marilyn and Heather, and I don't know where they are. We have to find them."

"They're at Red Lake," Dani says.

Of course.

Adrienne bought Camp Red Lake because she knew the problem with survivors. They detach from other people, they withdraw, they rely on routines rather than actual healing to give the appearance of stability. They go numb.

The irony is not lost on me.

We tend to die, women who've been through the fire. Sometimes we choose obvious ways, suicide and overdoses; sometimes we're more subtle, marrying someone who likes to use his fists, or we drink too much and keep getting behind the wheel until we run out of luck.

Adrienne saw the problem and so she created a solution. She reopened Camp Red Lake with her movie money and tried to save us all. Therapists split campers into teams, and they stick with each other for their entire stay, they do their therapies together, they are held accountable to each other, take responsibility for each other. No one finishes a race or wins a game until the entire team crosses the finish line. The official literature calls them teams and teammates. They call themselves family. They call themselves Sisters.

Adrienne's follow-up shows that more than sixty percent of these families last, that Sisters stay in touch with each other for years, that they move to be closer to each other, that they stay in each other's lives. That they rescue each other. The first families left Red Lake in 1991. The women in them are around thirty-six years old today. Two of them are married. Six of them work at Red Lake. All of them made it. None of them died. Adrienne saved their lives.

"Come with me?" I ask Dani. "Please?"

I know what'll happen if I take Steph and leave. When Dani runs out of things to burn she'll kneel next to this bonfire, face the hills, take her Glock, and go be with Michelle. I have to save someone.

She keeps staring into the fire.

"Marilyn and Heather and Julia are in danger," I say. "You've always kept us safe. We need you now. One last time."

When she talks again, her voice is very small.

"I'm done," she says.

Her back slouches, her shoulders slump, her eyelids droop, the corners of her mouth sag. I can't tell if she's sweating or crying or both.

"Please, Dani," I say.

If we leave, she'll put that gun in her mouth. Everywhere I go there are final girls dying. I'm sick of it.

Dani shakes her head.

"I can't do this alone," I say. "I've been trying it that way all my life and it hasn't worked out so good. I need you, Dani. One is none and two is one, isn't that what you taught me?"

After a minute she stops swaying and looks at me.

"Let me take care of something," she says.

She walks toward her barn and I return to Stephanie.

"She's coming," I say. "She just has to lock up."

"Great," Stephanie says. "Um, what's she doing?"

Dani is walking into the barn, unholstering her Glock as she disappears into shadows. A few minutes later six horses trot out, riderless and unsaddled, glossy in the afternoon sun. They smell the fire and shy away, milling in a nervous circle, trying to duck back inside. Dani blocks their way, raising her Glock, and there's a dry slap as she fires into the dirt between their hooves.

My stomach jumps; each gunshot punches me in the heart as she empties her clip into the ground, into the air, sending the horses breaking into motion, galloping away, eyes wide with terror, foaming at the mouths.

"They stand a better chance on their own," she says, and that's when I realize she doesn't plan on coming back.

The loaner is almost out of gas, so we pile into Dani's truck. It's got four seats. I take shotgun. Steph sits in the back behind Dani.

"You know how to get to Red Lake?" I ask.

"Since 1991," she says.

The engine roars, she drops her truck into gear, and we bounce down the road away from the ranch. I turn back in my seat and see Steph looking worried. Behind her I see a dust cloud from the horses as they disappear into the hills and the smoke from the bonfire rising up into the clear blue sky.

P. DECKER: I understand that you'll speak when you're ready, but your parents have already lost one child. It'd make them feel a lot better.

D. SHIPMAN: It won't.

P. DECKER: Why do you think that?

D. SHIPMAN: I'm a monster.

P. DECKER: I see a young lady who did something very brave.

D. SHIPMAN: I killed my brother.

P. DECKER: To save the lives of two children.

D. SHIPMAN: No one will ever look at me the same again.

—Dr. Philip Decker interview with multiple homicide survivor
Danielle Shipman, November 8, 1980

THE FINAL GIRL SUPPORT GROUP XXII:
The Final Nightmare

Dani barely talks on the three-hour drive, but I manage to pry the story out of her. Julia called yesterday, told her that she and Heather were heading to Red Lake in one of Marilyn's big armored SUVs. They could pick her up or meet her there. She told them not to wait.

"What about Skye?" I ask.

"They had a big fight with his mom," Dani says, shifting lanes to pass a slow-moving Subaru. "Told her they had a safe location but couldn't tell her where it was. Told her the kids could come but she couldn't. Made up a story about keeping people spread out. She told them her kids weren't going anywhere without her. She couldn't stop the older one from leaving, though. Her little one stayed behind."

"That's something," I say.

Other cars are passing us. If I were in the driver's seat I'd have it floored, we'd be flying, we'd be screaming forth to rescue our people, but Dani drives like she's on her way to pick up some hay. I wrote down Julia's, Marilyn's, and Heather's numbers and gave them to Stephanie. She's been calling since we left the ranch.

"Any luck?" I ask, looking in the back.

She's hunched over her cell phone, texting away.

"Keeps going to voicemail," she says. "I've tried texting but none of them show as being read. I requested a delivery report but it doesn't look like they're going through."

"Is there a landline at the camp?" I ask.

"Googled it, called, got voicemail," Steph says.

I really want Dani to step on it. He may have already started, although it's still light out. Most monsters wait until dark.

"We need a plan," I say. "So we don't fall all over each other like the Three Stooges. You want to try to put something together?"

"Nope," Dani says.

And that's pretty much that. I want to press my foot down over hers on the gas pedal but I have to get on Dani's wavelength if this is going to work. So I wait.

Twenty miles later she asks me the big question.

"What're you proposing to do with Dr. Carol's boy?"

"I don't know," I say. "I don't want to hurt him. I don't want anyone else to get hurt. I'm sick of people dying."

"Before sunrise tomorrow, people are going to die," Dani says. "Pretty sure of that."

It's so cowboy I almost laugh, but I don't because in my gut I know she's right. She always is.

We hit traffic outside Bakersfield, and by the time we're headed up into the mountains it's late afternoon. We've all been lulled into a stupor by the long drive, and as the truck starts to wind up the switchbacks I feel the adrenaline draining out of my veins. I'm feeling wrung out.

"There," Steph says. "Is that it?"

Up ahead we see the sign for Camp Red Lake, and Dani slows. It's small and discreet on the side of the road, the way Adrienne wanted, just yellow paint on dark red boards spelling out *Camp Red Lake*. Dani rotates the wheel and the truck splits off the road and glides onto the blacktop leading up the hill where Red Lake lies. The county isn't responsible for this road, Red Lake is, and it's paved with seamless black asphalt so new it sparkles.

Halfway up the mountain, shadows getting long, Red Lake up above us, Dani takes a turnoff.

"What are you doing?" Steph asks.

"Gotta piss," Dani says. "Better get it over with before we get there. Gotta get the guns out of the back, too."

She parks in a pull-over that looks out over the valley. There's a picnic table with an empty Diet Coke can on it, a scenic view sign, a running path heading off into the brush. It's paved with chalky white rocks.

"Wait here," Dani says.

She gets out of the car, detours to take the Diet Coke can and throw it away, then walks into a row of scrub about thirty feet in front of us. I notice that Steph is rustling through her backpack in the seat behind me.

"We really do need to come up with a plan," I say, starting to turn around.

A sledgehammer hits me in the back of my head and my eyeballs compress, then go black. When my vision returns, my head is halfway outside the car, sunlight stabbing my eyes, and it feels like my skull's the size of a beach ball. I want to lift my head to look back into the truck and a sheet of shattered safety glass rains down on my neck, falling down into my shirt. Steph crawls over the seat and settles behind the wheel. There's my little .22 in one of her hands. I can't smell anything. My face won't move. My body doesn't work.

She looks at me and reaches over my shoulder. I try to lift my arms but they have pins and needles running up and down them. Steph yanks the door handle and it swings open, dumping me out on the rocks. I'm tangled in my seat belt and then it comes free and I sprawl on the ground.

In my peripheral vision I see Dani coming out of the bushes, button-ing up her jeans. I want to scream and warn her but I can't even do that. The car door slams far above me, and an engine starts. The truck rolls over both my legs but it doesn't feel like anything compared to my head. The tires roar over the gravel and there's a metal crack and the sound of broken glass as it slams into Dani and then she's sailing backward. I see her smash into a tree, midway up the trunk, and her body bends in a way it shouldn't, and then she bounces forward and lands facedown on the edge of the parking lot.

Stephanie reverses back to where I lie and turns off the truck. She gets out. I want to see where she's going but I can't turn my head. I hear car doors opening and closing and then I space out for a little while and when I come to I'm hearing footsteps crunch through the gravel toward me.

"You stupid statistic," she says, squatting down next to me.

Did she think Dani was going to hurt us? Or was too suicidal to be trusted? Was she confused? Did I do something to make her think I would hurt her? But I know what the real answer is. She's not one of us. She's never been a final girl. Chrissy was right. She's a Monster.

"It's a pussy pistol but it's the thought that counts," she says, holding up my dainty little pistol. "You idiots with your machetes and your martial arts. If you want to rack up an adult-sized body count you need some Smith & Wesson."

I feel limp, squeezed out, empty. All I can do is lie on the ground and die. I look up along her long arm and see that her face is a black sun radiating waves of hatred and contempt.

"You think you're such a badass," Stephanie says. "Do you know how pathetic you are? I've watched one person after another take you down, and when it was my turn it was even easier than I thought. You've had other people holding your hand for your entire life. You're not even a real final girl."

She leans down and holds her finger under my nose.

"Fuck," she says. "You're still breathing. Okay, I guess I need something a little heavier. Don't go anywhere."

She crunches over to the truck, and I hear the door chime going *bong, bong, bong,* as the back opens. I hear the zippers of gun cases. There's a shotgun being pumped. Then her sneakers crunch back over the rocks and reenter my field of vision.

I've been played. I've been a moron. I brought her right up here into the heart of Red Lake. I was wrong about Skye. I was wrong about everything. And now I'm going to die.

Death actually is a moment of clarity, and in this instant I know Steph's right—I've needed other people's help my entire life. I keep thinking I've cut myself off, but there've always been other people. The only thing I'm going to do on my own is die.

My head is enormous and numb and even blinking gives me a headache so I stop and stare up at Stephanie standing over me. She's very, very tall and I see that she has one of Dani's shotguns hovering over my face. She steadies the barrel. The big empty circle rests right over my forehead. My brain sends my body signals to run, to move, to get out of the way, but my muscles have all gone on strike.

"I really freaked when you showed up at my front door," Steph says. "I thought you'd actually figured something out, but then you took me on a super-bonding soul sisters road trip? You've wanted someone to put you out of your misery for years, so relax, you Suicidal Tendency. I'm the final final girl, and you're just last year's—what've you got to smile about?"

She snarls that last bit because my eyes have shifted to the right and I can't help it, I've twitched my mouth up just a little. Steph follows my gaze and her face falls.

"Shit." She sighs.

Dani is gone.

I hope she's running right now, I hope she's on her way up to Red Lake to warn everyone, to get help, to get ready for this Monster. Let me be the sacrifice that buys them time, let Dani get to them and then they'll come down on Stephanie like the wrath of God.

Steph walks to the bushes, holding the single-barreled shotgun to her shoulder, barrel down at a forty-five-degree angle, ready to bring it up and punch a hole through Dani the second she spots her. She pauses and looks back at me, debating which way to go.

I want to shout *Run, Dani! Go!* but my head is mush and I think I can make my right cheek twitch if I concentrate hard enough, but that's about it. I wonder how I look with half my skull missing.

Maybe I moved, because Steph cocks her head at me, then gives up and turns back to the bushes, but she's too late. She may have been ready for me, but she's not ready for Dani. Six feet of ranch-hard muscle rises up out of the bushes and grabs the barrel of the shotgun and deftly turns it away from herself and then Dani punches Stephanie in the throat.

The blow snaps Stephanie's chin to her chest, and the gun goes off. Dani stands crooked, hunched over, in pain, something broken inside her, but she controls the barrel of the shotgun and keeps it pointed away while punching the side of Stephanie's head with her fist over and over again. Then she twists the gun, and it comes out of Stephanie's grasp, and Dani brings the stock down on the small of Stephanie's hunched back.

Stephanie hits the ground face-first, and Dani limps away from her, coming toward me. Her face looks pale, her lips move soundlessly, her teeth are caked with blood. She drops heavily to her knees, sets the shotgun down, and I realize she's crying. I'm pretty sure it's from the pain.

"Lynne," she chokes, reaching a cut-up hand to the side of my face.

That's when Steph rises up behind her.

Dani senses something is wrong and she turns, right into the butt of the shotgun smashing down onto her forehead. I want to shout something, I want to warn her, but my face isn't working. I think my brains might have seeped out into the gravel. The butt of the shotgun takes her dead center in the face. Something thick crunches. Stephanie is grinning, and then Dani grabs Stephanie's ankle and pulls, dumping her on the ground, and then she's up and running, hobbling fast, limping away from me, leaving big fat droplets of blood in her wake, disappearing back into the bushes. Steph scrambles to her feet, aims the shotgun, pulls the trigger. It explodes fire.

Steph runs to where Dani disappeared, pumping shell after shell into the shotgun and firing again and again, then stopping and scanning to see if she can detect Dani, then firing again. I don't think this thunder will ever stop. Finally, there's silence. A bird starts to sing.

Stephanie stands over me again. I realize that I have to play the oldest trick in the book, the one I used before with Ricky Walker. I play possum. Stephanie bends over and feels for my breath, but I've stopped breathing. I dimly feel her tug on my right earlobe and I think she's pinching it, but my head is made of wood. I don't move. She spits on one of my wide, staring eyes. I lie still. Then she laughs.

"This one doesn't even count," she says. "She basically killed herself."

She walks over to the truck and throws the shotgun in the passenger seat. Shotgun riding shotgun, I think stupidly to myself. She starts the engine. The truck idles for a minute and I think she's changing her mind, but I can't allow myself to turn my head to look because I know she's watching me.

Relief floods my veins like a drug when she roars out of there, leaving a cloud of white dust hanging in the air. I lie still for a minute, brains spilling out in the dirt, and I wonder who's going to go warn Red Lake. I wonder if Dani made it up there to tell everyone what's happening. I wonder if Steph is going to get there first and cut through them like a bullet. I lie there, and I wonder who's going to save the day, and blood pools around my head, and I die.

Now, I understand that fear can be fun. I myself love roller coasters. That little flutter of anticipation when they lower the safety bar. That thrill when you fly around the big curve and you feel like this time it might really be out of control. That whole all-over-your-body sense of relief when it brings you safely home. But what does it say about us that so much of the entertainment we consume is about killing women? I want you to think about that.

How is the murder of women fun?

[PAUSE]

You go to the big new thriller, you finish your popcorn, go out for dinner, talk about the plot twists with your friends, it's just another part of your evening out. But no one brings that woman safely home. Her body is left back there on the screen while everyone goes on with their lives. Let's think about what that means. Let's think about what's wrong with us.

—speech by Adrienne Butler, Cincinnati, Ohio, January 2010

THE FINAL GIRL SUPPORT GROUP XXIII:
Resurrection

Bushes fall before my wrath. I hurl myself into trees. I keep pushing up the mountain with the balls of my feet until my calves ache the way my swollen, broken head aches.

"Stupid," I say to myself.

But I don't say it out loud because every sound hurts my shattered skull. My entire world is getting up this hill, one foot after the other, and no matter how much my muscles scream, no matter how much my chest burns, I don't stop. I'll only stop when I'm dead. Which might be sooner than I think.

"Stupid girl," I say to myself.

I take another step.

The world spins around me.

"Stupid fucking girl."

I take another step.

"Stupid dumb fucking girl."

Standing up in that parking lot was the hardest thing I'd ever done. Pain nailed me to the dirt. Even getting spiked on those antlers didn't hurt like this. The only person who could make me stand up was Adrienne.

"What are you lying there for, Lynnette?" she asked, looking down at me.

"Can't . . ." I told her.

"You can," she said. "You know why? Because if you don't get up, then all that time I invested in you was a waste. It'll mean I've failed. And I don't fail. I grew up in a high-pressure household, Lynnette, so failure is hard on me. So if you give up, then little perfect Miss Adrienne has screwed up, too, and that's going to be hard for me to reconcile."

She knelt by my head, and I felt her hands slip beneath my armpits, and I felt my body bending in all the wrong ways, tendons screaming, muscles shaking, and then I stood, swaying in the middle of the parking lot, standing over a puddle of my own blood. Alone.

Now I'm getting up this mountain if it kills me and it just might because everything hurts so much and then I fall to my knees because the woods are gone and I'm kneeling in pine cones on the edge of Camp Red Lake. On the other side, a big pinewood sign shouts *Welcome*, and behind it a vast green lawn leads to the Main Lodge, its raw logs glowing orange in the pink twilight.

"Didn't count on Billy Walker getting there first, did you?" I ask Stephanie inside my tormented, pulsating brain. "Goddamn titanium plate in my head, you moron."

I never thought that one day a Walker brother would save my life, but after Ricky left me with half my skull caved in they had to insert a plate to hold my head together. Stephanie plinked me right in the middle of it with her little .22. Scalp wounds bleed like stuck pigs, and I'm scared to look in a mirror, but for now I'm alive.

But it hurts. Oh God, it hurts so bad. I push myself up onto my feet and stagger forward on what feel like broken ankles, eyes locked on the Main Lodge, and then I'm stumbling over hard asphalt and I look down and I'm in the circular drive that runs in front of Camp Red Lake and I look up again and I start to cry.

"No fair," I whisper. "No fair."

Ahead of me sits Dani's enormous red F-150. The driver's-side door stands open going *bong bong bong* and all my willpower drains out through my feet because Stephanie is already here. I haven't heard any shooting but my head is a ringing, roaring waterfall of pain.

That climb up the hill, wanting to die every step of the way, it was all for nothing because Stephanie is already here and everyone I know is dead.

I lean against a parked SUV, probably one of Marilyn's armored monsters, and I avoid looking at my reflection in its shiny sides. Even with the titanium plate, Steph's bullet hurt me. My brain aches with damage.

Even if everyone else is dead, I'm going to stop her. I start limping toward the Main Lodge. I don't want to hurt anyone, but I have to stop her before she hurts more people. My stride lengthens, my feet sink into soft grass, the lodge sways from side to side, and my head is a pulsating pain bulb at the end of my neck.

I push myself up the steps, walk between the massive cedar columns still wrapped in yellow crime scene tape, and drag my legs over the pine-planked porch, push open the front door, and step inside.

Everything smells like wood. Enormous age-lacquered beams support the roof two stories overhead, its rafters and ridge piece lost in the late-afternoon gloom. A towering fieldstone fireplace anchors one end of the vast lobby and a mezzanine circles the rest. Someone's stapled Polaroids of grinning Sisters and their families to every surface, encrusting the posts with women baring white teeth, arms slung around each other's shoulders, while sign-up sheets, bulletin boards, Xeroxed schedules, and safety posters spin in and out of the shadows around my throbbing head.

In front of me sits the circular welcome desk and over it aged iron letters spiked to the wall spell out *Sisters, all.*

Except Stephanie. She's the piece that sticks out. The one that doesn't belong.

Where is everyone? Where are my Sisters? Are they hiding? And what about the staff? They'd closed down after Christophe Volker came, but a skeleton crew still has to be here. Eight people? Ten? A whispering voice inside my skull tells me it only ever gets this quiet when everyone is dead.

Two arrow-shaped signs hang on either side of the front desk, rope letters on the one pointing to the right reading *Tuck Shop* and rope letters on the one pointing left reading *Dining Porch*. That's what I want. It's almost five. People are going to want to dine.

Defenseless, I enter the Minotaur's maze, limping left, pushing through two swinging doors made of rough wood still covered in bark, and I walk into the mess hall. Big slabs of pale pine march away from me in orderly rows like autopsy tables with empty benches on either side. An abandoned canoe hangs upside down from the ceiling, and the entire far wall consists of glass doors leading out onto the dining porch. A bloody handprint smack in the middle of one is the only sign of life.

A sign reading *Salad/Sundae Bar* sways gently over a pile of laundry on the floor. I lower myself, knees popping, and realize this boneless sack of clothes is the body of a woman. I turn her over. Not much of her skull is left. Her face is smeared across the floor. I wonder if she was pretty. I wonder if she was happy. I wonder who her Sisters were. She wears a Red Lake T-shirt and the nametag on her right breast is obscured by biological matter. I wipe it away with my thumb.

"I'm so sorry, Marcie," I say, and mean it more than I've ever meant anything.

I look into the kitchen where another person lies facedown, their T-shirt saturated dark red. This one looks like a man.

Stephanie was here.

How many people have died because I trusted her?

Something bumps politely against a wall and I whip my head around, sending pain spiking through my temples. I see a storage closet door closed tight and make my way over and stand to one side because it has a porthole window in the middle and I don't want whatever's in there to see me. I give the door a push. It doesn't move, but maybe it's just heavy. I brace myself and push again and it rattles against its deadbolt lock. I hear something creak inside. Why would Stephanie lock herself in a storage closet? She wants to be out here killing people. I press my face to the glass.

It's dark so I cup my hands and look. Something moves in the dimness.

"Hey?" I whisper-call.

I pray my voice hasn't traveled too far into the building. I tap one knuckle against the glass. Whatever it is moves again.

"I see you," I say.

Whoever it is rolls backward, deeper into the dark.

"Are you hurt?" I ask.

"Lynnette?" A muffled voice wafts out through the door, down around my belly button.

"Julia?"

The deadbolt snaps. Something flashes on the edge of my vision and I duck down and spin, catching a flock of birds lifting off from the wide lawn outside. Silver sparks from their wings. Julia comes out of the closet in her chair, a low sturdy model with big rugged wheels that slant in at the top. Behind her stand two numb teenaged boys and a nervous woman who looks like she goes camping a lot.

"Lock it behind me," Julia tells them. "We'll get you when it's safe."

They obey and I feel so tired that it's only Julia, that there are still more people left to find, that Stephanie is still out there killing.

"What the hell is going on?" Julia asks.

"It's Stephanie," I say. "Stephanie Fugate."

Julia's forehead knits in the middle for a minute and then goes smooth.

"The Red Lake girl?" she asks. "The one you kidnapped? Jesus Christ, Lynnette, your people skills are shit. She's walking around here with a machine gun."

"I don't think she has a machine gun," I say, remembering the shotguns in the back of Dani's truck.

"Let's stand here and argue about the caliber of weapon the girl you thought was your new best friend is using to murder everyone," Julia says.

My brain gives a dark throb that makes me want to throw up.

"You look like shit, so I forgive you," she says. "Cell phone service is down but there's a landline in the nurse's station we can try for."

"What about Heather and Marilyn?" I mumble through numb lips as we start to move.

"Down by the lake with everyone else," she tells me. "I came up here to get sunscreen. About twenty of the staff are having a memorial service for Adrienne."

I'm not listening. I'm standing still. From this angle I can see past the bloody handprint on the glass doors, around the lone tree that blocked my view of the middle of the wide green lawn before. A person sprawls on the grass. I recognize the flannel shirt. Julia looks where I'm looking.

"Is that—?" Julia begins.

"You get the phone," I say. "I'll get Dani."

I start outside but Julia cuts me off at the French doors.

"You think I can't do stairs?" she snaps, and zips around me.

Julia's already at the lip of the dining porch when I get outside. She leans back in her wheelchair, puts one hand on the banister, and practically flings herself down the three steps to the ground, her wheels absorbing the impact. I try to keep up.

"Shag your ass," she calls back at me as her wheelchair chews up the lawn.

Running makes my head sick, so I walk fast, looking behind us, checking the approaches, left, right, ahead, behind. A scattering of trees rise from the lawn but otherwise it's totally exposed. Clear sightlines from every direction. Far to the right sits the campfire amphitheater and stage. Ahead of us is the treeline, the air between the trunks already dark purple. Back in those trees are the cabins, and beyond them lies the lake where twenty more victims wait for Stephanie.

Dani doesn't look good. Her legs point in two different directions, neither of them natural. She's facedown in the dirt, mouth open. I notice with relief her shoulder blades moving up and down. She's breathing.

"Put her legs across my chair to help with the weight," Julia says. "We need to get back inside and get to the phone."

I can't.

"I'm going to rest for a minute," I mumble to Julia, waving one hand.

I'm too tired. The ground pulls on my hips. I need to sit. I crouch, not sure how to make it down safely.

"What are you doing, Lynnette?" Julia shouts from far away.

I need to rest.

"What are you doing, Lynnette?" Adrienne asks.

She's walking with me across the lawn. My clothes stink of cordite. She's wearing a white sweater and jeans.

"Trying not to get killed?" I tell her/told her.

"That's enough for you?" she asks. "Continued respiration? That's all you have to offer the world?"

"It's a good place to start," I say, wishing she would stop making me feel so guilty all the time.

You have to protect your sister, my mom says, standing over me while Gilly wails into the side of her neck.

"I'm no Yoda," Adrienne tells me. "But you think your sister died so you could quit? You think Tommy died so you could stop when things got too scary? There's more to life than staying alive."

"Shut up, Adrienne," I groan.

"You wouldn't feel so guilty if you didn't know I'm right," she says.

Gravity wins. My butt thuds onto the grass. A hard jolt goes up my spine. My head floods with hot blood. The lawn turns into a merry-go-round and spins me past the lodge.

Far away, back by the lodge, a black insect runs at us. I watch it get bigger and come into focus. It's a man in black tactical gear, wearing a gas mask. There's some kind of automatic rifle bouncing on his back, but in his hands he's carrying an axe, just like Ricky Walker. His legs are moving, eating up the grass between us.

"Oh shit, oh shit, oh shit," Julia says, bending from the waist, pawing at Dani.

He's seen us, and I don't know who he is but he picks up his pace, and I feel so tired but I swing my head to the treeline and it's not so far away.

You can, Adrienne says.

I push myself to my feet and the world gives another lazy revolution, my head swimming in a sea of pain, and I pray that not everything around here has changed too much over the past ten years.

You have to protect your sister, Mom says.

I grab Dani's belt and try not to listen to the popping sounds as I haul her up, then sling her around and her legs hit Julia in the chest, and I let her take some of Dani's weight and I stagger forward.

"Cabins!" I think I shout.

My stomach heaves, my brain throbs, and I stumble fast for the treeline. Julia keeps up, both hands shoving her wheels down hard, her chair flying along beside me, my head exploding with every jolting step as the treeline rocks wildly in my vision, and the back of the first cabin emerges from the trunks and I correct our course.

Something chatters behind me and the air flutters overhead. He's stopped to shoot. I hope he's stopped to shoot. Every foot we put between him and us is safety.

Up ahead, Heather slouches out of the trees, carrying a green beer bottle, and Marilyn emerges beside her in some kind of summer dress and big straw hat situation, a giant handbag over one shoulder, and I say to Julia, "Get that cabin open!"

"The cabin made of wood? The cabin full of windows?" she shouts back.

I scream a sharp, angry sound and then she's tearing across the grass in her chair, tires chewing it up like a lawn mower, trusting me at last, and I'm staggering under Dani's full weight, and Marilyn's there, ducking under Dani's other arm, knocking off her straw hat, and something chatters behind us again, and Dani gets shoved forward and I feel the impact travel all the way down to the aching soles of my feet.

"Haul, Lynnette!" Marilyn shouts in my ear, and we drag Dani between us, the world bouncing painfully, and then the dark trees close around us, and I see Julia make some kind of daredevil turn in her chair, the whole thing almost tipping over, spraying up big plumes of dirt, and she throws herself up the three steps into the cabin, hitting the door with her body, pushing it open, leaving her chair toppled on its side, one wheel spinning.

Heather's in next and then I find the strength to shove myself up the stairs and through the door, hauling Dani, and Marilyn gets it closed just as Death slams into it from the other side.

"It's made of fucking wood!" Julia screams from the floor.

Marilyn makes an animal moan deep inside her throat as she takes in the six big windows marching down the wooden walls, three on each side, glowing with afternoon light. They see the wooden walls, the splintery floor, the planks on the door, but none of them spent the time here with Adrienne that I did.

I drop Dani's weight onto Marilyn and lunge at the bed on my right, stretching, reaching, praying. A booted foot hits the door, shaking it in its frame.

My finger slams into a knothole in the wall at the head of the bed, wood scraping the skin off my knuckle, and I rip it out, and wear the wooden square like a ring as I punch the red button it hid with my other hand.

The cabin tears itself in two. Marilyn shrieks. Heather drops her beer. Julia covers her ears as motors and gears and bolts blast machine screams into our ears. Six deadbolts shoot home in the door. Wooden boards drop from the top of the frame of each window and I run to them, dizzy, catching my hip on the edge of beds, grabbing the double handles they expose with both hands, yanking them down, slamming metal shutters over the windows.

"Help me!" I scream.

Marilyn gets two, I get four. At the end, I vomit thin gruel.

"It's still wood!" Julia says from the floor and we hear the machine gun rip and I recognize the sound; even without the L.A. street canyon making it echo, it's the same kind of gun that turned my apartment into a shooting gallery last week.

The cabin is dim now. The door vibrates in its frame, but no splintered holes appear, it doesn't fall apart. Another burst. Glass shatters but the steel shutters only do a spastic shimmy as bullets tap-dance across their surface. They hold.

"Panic cabins," I pant. "Adrienne had them built so I'd feel safe. Steel shutters. The door and walls have steel sandwiched between the wood. The floor's poured concrete underneath the planks."

"Cool," Heather says, and walks to the door and screams, "Fuck you, gimp!"

Whoever it is puts another half clip in the door. We hear the bullets stitch over steel.

"Now we're stuck," Heather says. "Good plan, Lynne."

"We call for help," I say. "Whose phone works?"

"No one's," Heather says. "We're essentially fucked."

"Dani's bleeding too much," Julia says, applying pressure to Dani's back. There's fresh wet blood all over her clothes, her arms, her face.

"So we're stuck in a cabin, there's a killer outside with a machine gun, Dani's going to die, and we have no way to call for help," Heather says. "I guess I'll have to save us all with my fucking superpowers."

She lies down on one of the cots and flips a blanket over herself, nuzzling into the pillow.

"You're going to sleep?" Julia asks.

"I've got a condition," Heather snaps from behind closed eyes.

"I'll call 911," Marilyn says, reaching into her straw handbag and pulling out a phone that looks slightly thicker and chunkier than average.

"No reception," Heather says.

"Haven't any of y'all heard of a satellite phone?" Marilyn asks.

I can't hear anything outside. I don't know if the Monster is waiting by the door or if he's gone to the lake. I don't know where Stephanie is or what she's doing. I don't even know if this is Stephanie. Where did she get all this gear? But it doesn't matter. I shove the counselor's bed aside.

"Quit making so much noise," Heather says, eyes still closed.

"Hello," I hear Marilyn enunciate. "I'd like to report an active shooter situation."

I put two fingers in another knothole, this time in the floor, and lift a larger panel to reveal a bolted trapdoor.

"What the hell?" Julia asks.

"There are twenty of Adrienne's people by the lake," I say.

"You can't—" Julia begins, but I don't listen, just release the hatch and drop through into the soft cool sand underneath the cabin. I stand up.

"Bolt it behind me," I say.

Then I duck down and reconnoiter. The slit of light between the bottom of the cabin and the ground looks clear: no legs in black combat pants, no tactical boots. I scramble through the sand toward the front of the cabin. Behind me, I hear the trapdoor bolts slam into place. Good.

I scramble out on my hands as my knees give out and stand, swaying. The trees and cabins rock dangerously and shadows rush in around the edges of my vision, but I see a brighter light in front of me through the trees and I know that way lies the lake. The shooter can't be there yet. They'll have to pass three more rows of cabins, the chill-out yurt, the nature observatory, and the sweat lodge.

Behind me, the splintered façade of the cabin shows scorched galvanized steel peppered with charred pockmarks. I stumble-run to my left, heading parallel to the lake, and when I reach the end of the row of cabins, I put my hands around my mouth, pull a deep breath into my bruised lungs, and turn my body into a single shout.

"Stephanie!" I roar, and I hear my voice echo up into the tree canopy high above. "I'm still alive. You want me. Come and get me."

I'm winded. Black spots flicker and strobe in my vision and then one of them swarms at me with a purpose, and I realize it's dropping to one knee and I see fire flicker from its shoulder and bees scream past my face, tugging my hair in their wake.

I turn and run.

The Wellness Barn looms up ahead of me in the gloom, a big red wall of wood with peaks on either end facing me like raised eyebrows. It's the biggest building at Red Lake after the Main Lodge, built back in the early nineties when Adrienne took over. It's full of EMDR rooms, narrative medicine offices, art therapy studios. Lots of rooms, lots of doors, a labyrinth where I can get whoever this is lost, keep them angry, make them waste their time, stay focused on me, not the twenty soft targets down by the lake. I'll lead them in one side, then up through the studios to the far end of the second floor where there's a secret crawl space in the walls. It's a game of hide-and-seek and by the time they give up the police will be here.

The French doors come up and I put out my hands to stiff-arm them open, and as I crash through them in a shower of wood and glass I remember too late they don't push, they pull, and then I'm tripping over their shattered bottom rail, sliding across the floor of the entrance atrium on the heels of my hands.

I hurt. My head swims in a sea of pain. Everything smells like lemongrass and cinnamon, and the cool tinkling of a feng shui water feature in the corner would ease the pain in my skull if I hadn't just gotten shot in the head. Suspended stairs float up one wall to the second floor and skylights let pink light stream in from high above. On the wall someone's painted in flowing script:

Sometimes all we have left is a wish and a hope.

Then the air explodes behind me and bullets stitch across wishes and hopes. I force myself to my feet and there's no time, they're on my heels, the stairs are too exposed, and I lurch to the right and crash through the first studio door.

I barely have the door closed before a body hits it high and hard. It almost comes off its hinges, but I manage to hold it shut, pressing it into the frame. There's silence from the other side for a moment, then the blade of the axe slaps through the wood, almost splitting my left hand. I yank it back and snap the deadbolt into place as Death hacks the door into pieces. I hear myself sob.

The door comes apart too fast. I think I might have made a serious miscalculation. The Wellness Barn is made of hopes and dreams, not galvanized steel and reinforced concrete.

The door explodes out of its frame, pancaking to the ground, almost taking me with it, and I'm running, my head a throbbing bag of blood, then something sweeps my legs out from under me and in the wall of mirrors to my right I see a bloody scarecrow going ass over heels as I trip over a yoga ball.

I turn, shove myself up, give it a kick, and the pink ball lifts off the floor, launching itself straight at the ruined door and into the shooter, knocking their knees out from under them. They fall down, letting go with their gun, and the mirrored wall explodes into silver triangles and shattered circles that rain to the floor.

Every studio in the Wellness Barn has two doors, and I fly through the next one and stumble into a wall of world music, crash through a display of healing crystals, take a massage table in the hip. The spectral sounds of the universe swirl around me, harps glissando, chimes vibrate, crystal keys plink out the mysteries of life. I stumble across tatami mats while the aching music of oneness picks me up and tries to carry me away, and I make it out the next door as the shooter comes in, crunching crystals beneath their boots.

The next studio is L-shaped and it's music therapy and the shooter is too close for me to do anything but run. They fire and xylophones explode, cymbals roar in a frenzy as bullets shred a drum kit, and guitars explode with hollow pops, filling the air with raw spruce splinters.

I turn the corner of the L and my feet shoot out from under me and my brain splits down the middle as I hit the floor hard with one shoulder and I scramble to my feet and keep moving, but I realize my plan has failed. I can't lose them. They're too close. My feet dig into the carpet and I launch myself at the door ahead because I don't have a plan anymore, and then I have a plan.

You have to protect your Sisters, Mom says as Gilly howls.

I'm the decoy, I'm the distraction, I'm the sitting duck. I just need to keep them here while everyone else gets away. I just need to run out my string.

Adrienne was right: there's more to life than staying alive.

The door flies open under my hands but not fast enough and I hit it with my forehead, and I'm in a long room full of pink and white streamers and helium balloons in Adrienne's favorite colors and there are cupcakes and soft drinks and I've gone back in time, I'm in first grade and part of my brain knows it's a reception for after Adrienne's memorial but part of me is a child, screaming, running, *I'm quick as a bunny, Mom.*

The shooter comes in behind me too fast, too close, and they squeeze off rounds that evaporate balloons and chop streamers to confetti and dig into the far wall painted with tribal designs and I'm every girl who's ever run from a man with a weapon, every girl who ever ran for her life across spaces where she was supposed to be safe. I crash into the next studio and I'm Julia running through her dorm, I'm Heather running down her high school halls, I'm Marilyn running through the Texas afternoon, I'm Dani running through a hospital, I'm Adrienne running through this camp, this camp where there will always be a girl running and screaming and screaming, and I'm Lynnette, running at last, and he can't catch me, I'm as fast as all of us put together, I'm faster than Billy Walker, I'm faster than the Ghost, I'm faster than the entire Volker family, I'm the fastest girl in the world.

I push myself, sprinting, legs pumping, head bouncing on the end of my neck, and this is it, this is my last race, and I slam the wooden door open and run into the humid chlorine cloud of the aquatherapy studio. I can trick the shooter into one of these pools in the concrete floor, force them down, use their heavy gear against them, but they're already in the doorway and I don't even have time to slam it in their face. They shove it open with their elbows, gun raised, and I fall forward, the steel tubes of a pool ladder chipping my pelvis, and one foot goes in warm water and I pull it out and slosh-limp-slosh across the room as fast as I can to the three doors in a row that are the only place left to run.

The pain in my head is so bad I'm almost blind. The door on the far right is in front of me and I'll get inside, I won't stop; I'll crash through the window on the opposite wall and make it outside, and hide in the woods. I crash inside and there is no window. There is no other door.

It's an individual hydrotherapy room, all sandstone tile and a big white tub and a toilet and a sink and a massage table and the door flies open behind me and knocks me forward and I'm tumbling, stumbling, feet flying, and I take the lip of the tub high in my thighs, and my feet go over my head and I'm sprawled across the bottom of the tub staring up at my mom as Gilly screams into the side of her neck.

I squeeze my eyes shut and black blood pulses behind my lids because I don't want to die. I open them and my head is full of broken glass shredding my soft brain, and Death stands over the tub and it is the biggest thing in the world.

Death points its gun at me, a TEC-9, one of those video game guns that boys think are so cool. It's a terrible gun, but not at this range. Death wears black tactical gear, covered in belts and straps and pouches and all those things little boys think will make them strong. The gas mask hides Its face. Tactical gloves cover Its hands. It's wearing a black helmet and this is all overcompensating for how small Death feels inside. On instinct, I look at Its shoes.

Under Armour zipper tactical boots, and fire sparks inside my head.

"Skye?" I say.

Where's Stephanie? Is she helping him? Is he helping her? Is she dead? Was I wrong and she's one more final girl notched into his belt?

His breath rasps through his gas mask. Then he says something, and the mask muffles it, but all my strength leaves my body because I still hear the words.

"You'll die alone and no one cares," he says.

My mom presses a screaming Gilly to the side of her neck. *You have to protect your Sisters.* And I couldn't even do that. *I'm sorry, Gilly. I'm sorry, Dr. Carol. I'm sorry, Mom and Dad. I'm sorry, Mike and Liz. I'm sorry, Fine. I'm sorry, everyone.*

I'm sorry I can't fight anymore.

Skye adjusts his grip on his weapon.

I'm sorry, Adrienne.

He points his gun at my face and its muzzle is a yawning black hole big enough to swallow the world.

And Heather is on him, streaking in from out of nowhere, the heavy white porcelain lid of the toilet tank in her hands, and she brings it down on the back of his neck and follows through on her swing. The porcelain lid explodes on impact into a thousand razor shards that pepper my face. Skye's body bends in one direction, his head bends in another, and he falls forward, catching his face on the edge of the tub as he goes down. He doesn't get up.

For a moment, there's no sound but the two of us breathing.

"Where's everyone else?" I finally manage.

"Back in the cabin," Heather says. "Locked in."

It doesn't make any sense.

"But how did you get here?" I ask.

Heather's panting but manages something close to a grin.

"Like I said, I'm into some higher-level shit that you could never understand."

After what I saw in her room at Chrissy's museum, I don't doubt it for a minute.

I start picking myself up out of the Jacuzzi, and Heather leans down and starts unbuckling Skye's helmet and gas mask.

"Is he alive?" I ask.

"Mostly," Heather says, working at his chin strap, finally getting it free.

"Don't move him," I say. "His neck might be broken."

She pushes back his helmet and peels off the gas mask and I see his face, dark circles painted around his eyes, hair soaked with sweat, eyelids fluttering. It really is Skye.

He must have hated us all so much.

Heather stands and delivers a hard kick to his balls. Her kick moves his body like a heavy sack of laundry.

"We shouldn't move him," Heather says, punctuating her words with more kicks to his crotch. "Definitely not. Don't want. To have. A spinal cord. Injury."

I take a step toward her and my head spins dangerously fast, feeling like it might float away. I put one hand on her shoulder to steady myself.

"Stop," I tell Heather. "Get his gun."

She bends over and picks it up, then centers it on his chest, looking down through its sights at the Monster sprawled on the floor in the wreckage of the eco-friendly bathroom.

"Heather," I say. "He's her son."

She doesn't acknowledge me. We stand like that for what feels like a very long time. Finally she lowers the gun, then tosses it into the tub with a loud clatter.

"Fuck it, right?" she says.

"Fuck it," I say. "No one else dies today."

"Well, isn't that a big ball of sunshine," Stephanie says from the door.

Heather starts to turn, but Stephanie has the shotgun against the back of her neck. Through Heather's throat it's pointed right at my face. Stephanie stands in the square stance, motionless, butt of the gun against her shoulder, cheek welded to the stock, ready to let her body take the recoil, her nonfiring hand directing the barrel. Heather's back is to her, I'm on the other side of Heather, Skye's body takes up half the bathroom, and there's nowhere left to run.

"That's the second time you've saved yourself by playing possum," Steph says. "How'd you do it?"

"Plate in my head," I say.

"Goddamn," she says softly. "To be honest, I barely skimmed your Wikipedia page. I'm not interested in roadkill. This skunky junkie, on the other hand, she's big game."

"Fucking superfans," Heather says.

"Whatever, grandma," Stephanie says. "My man and I have been running you for weeks like rats in a maze, and now we're gunning you down like fish in a barrel. You stupid old bags don't have a lot to be proud of. This was about as challenging as a wet fart."

What sticks with me is "my man."

"Skye . . ." I begin.

"We met online," she says. "No one's going to remember you losers after this. Skye and I will be heroes. People will be talking about the statement we made here for years to come. You're just pointless nostalgia and we're here to sweep you into the trash. Everyone needs to stop clinging to the past."

"Pull the trigger or shut the fuck up," Heather says, but I can see her face and it's only her voice that's brave. "You're as boring as my last boyfriend."

Stephanie smiles.

"Okay," she says.

I have to keep her talking.

"You did all this to be famous?" I say. "You killed all these people to be on TV?"

"What else is there?" Stephanie asks.

I remember the file in Dr. Carol's house, the one with Stephanie's picture on it. I realize how Skye found her.

"He reached out to you first, didn't he?" I ask.

"You don't have time for our dating history," Stephanie says.

"He groomed you," I say. "He told you how evil we are because he hates his mom and then he groomed you."

"Not even close," she says, but I can tell she doesn't like being an object rather than the subject.

"This isn't girl power," I say, panic-talking now. "You're Skye's puppet. In court your lawyer's going to claim emotional coercion. You weren't responsible for your actions. The man was in charge all the way. You'll be just another victim of a powerful, manipulative male."

"Don't try to run a game on me, Lynnette," Stephanie says. "We're equals. That how love works these days."

"You think it's about you and Skye?" I ask. "This is about him and his mommy. You're the sad daughter-in-law to his psycho obsession, a footnote in his case file. We'll get the memorials, we'll be the heroes, he'll be embraced by a bunch of sad little boys on the Internet, but you don't fit in anywhere. You'll be forgotten because all you ever did was say 'yes, sir,' 'no, sir,' and pulled the trigger when Daddy said."

"Fuck you," she says.

"You know I'm right," I say. "Unless you kill him, too." I give it a brief pause. "He's still alive."

Heather is darting her eyes from left to right, shaking them "no," and her mouth is mouthing *no* and she knows what I'm doing and I ignore her.

"He's pretty banged up," I say, looking down and to my right. "I bet you could finish him by hand. That would make a statement."

I'm committed now. For the first time in years, I'm not scared.

Stephanie's eyes narrow and they flick down to Skye and that's all I'm going to get. I pray for speed.

Everything happens at once. I drop low and shoulder past Heather, leaping up and forward, ignoring the iron bands clamped around my skull, and one arm is going up and out and thrusting the barrel of the shotgun away like I saw Dani do earlier. The air in the bathroom explodes and my hand is on fire, palm searing, sticking to the barrel, and my shoulder breaks and the room fills with gritty gray gunsmoke. Somewhere beside me, Heather is falling into the tub.

My feet don't touch the ground and I'm tackling Stephanie. My head clips the doorframe as I take her down and it throbs so hard I almost black out, but not enough to make me forget to land on her body. I hear all the air whoosh out of her lungs when we hit the concrete floor with my full weight on top, the burning-hot shotgun trapped between our chests.

We're lying half-in and half-out of the hydrotherapy door and I'm too weak to hit her, or cut her, or shoot her, so I just wrap my arms and legs around her and hold on tight.

She bucks and squirms and screams and fights, trying to worm her finger into the trigger guard, but she's just a kid after all, and I keep her on the ground, pressed to the tile; my arms keep her from getting any leverage, my legs wrap around her calves to keep them from pushing up. I use my battered chin to force her skull down until I'm pinning her head to the ground, and our faces are close enough to kiss.

She spits and screams and howls, but she's not going anywhere, and after a while she knows it. She starts to scream in my ear, so loud my brain goes white.

Eventually I make out what she's saying.

"Kill me!" she's screaming, over and over again. "Kill me! Kill me! Kill me!"

They pull me off eventually, and by then they have flexi-cuffs on Skye, and Marilyn and Heather put a pair on Stephanie. As they drag her to the other side of the room she keeps her eyes on me.

"You should have killed me, you fucking skank," she spits.

I'm tired. I hurt everywhere. Fresh pain creeps into every inch of my body.

"You'll go to trial," I say, exhausted. "You'll go to prison."

"Fuck you!" she screeches. "I'll fucking escape!"

I'm so tired of all this hurting and killing and these threats and this endless litany of fear that has been my life.

"No, you won't," I say. "You're not that smart."

Let her live. Let her and Skye live. Let them live and see just how small and meaningless their murders were. She's killed so many people and you know what? The world, just as uncooperative and stubborn as always, keeps spinning along.

Dying isn't the important thing. It's nothing more than the punctuation mark on the end of your life. It's everything that came before that matters. Punctuation marks, most people skip right over them. They don't even have a sound.

Date: 2/13/09
From: Stephanie Fugate <StephSlays@live.com>
To: Skye Elliott <SkEllraiser@hotmail.com>
Subject: SYN-ER-GY

O NO—I'm being stalked by an unusually slow killer armed with a ridiculously impractical weapon. Eek! It's a boat hook! A machete! A shish kebab skewer! An AR-15 makes all that bullshit irrelevant. These bitches only think they're tough until they go up against some serious firepower. All that old fashioned shit is for grandmas and babies. We can bring modern day tactics and weapons to what's always been an old fashioned knife fight.

SCHOOL SHOOTING + SLASHER SCENARIO = SYNERGY!

I don't care what their reputations are—they're just a bunch of crying coozes once we get them in our sights and start pulling the trigger. Final girls? They're bags of meat with overblown reputations who've only ever gone up against slow-moving morons who don't know how to rack up a modern day body count.

137-A

—email from Stephanie Fugate to Skye Elliott,
Prosecution Exhibit 137-A

THE FINAL GIRL SUPPORT GROUP XXIV:
A New Beginning

A chrome dolphin leaps from ultraviolet waves.

Three lumpy pink elephants link arms and form a kickline, shouting, *Happy Visiting Day!*

Sometimes the biggest journeys begin with the smallest steps, proclaim a pair of legs in scuffed sneakers.

That one's for me. Right now, all I can take are small steps.

When they processed me through the metal detector, the new plate in my skull didn't beep because it's surgical-quality polymer, but they spent a long time x-raying my cane and confiscated my Tylenol 3, which is bad because I feel a headache coming on. They patted me down and felt me up. By the time they allowed me into the Central California Correctional Facility, I felt ninety years old.

Getting shot in the head turned out to be the miracle cure for panic attacks. When I woke up in the hospital, Julia told me I'd been unconscious for three days while they let the swelling in my brain subside. I waited for my lungs to cramp or my throat to close but all that happened was a slight elevation in my heart rate. I guess my body figured if there was anyone else in Stephanie and Skye's conspiracy they would have taken their shot already. I still don't feel safe, but for the first time since I was sixteen I'm not scared all the time either.

"Is everyone okay?" I asked Julia the next time I woke up, and she started saying something with too many words and I passed out again.

The TV was always on in my room and people drifted in and out telling me things I couldn't understand as I slipped into unconsciousness and back out again, floating on big waves of painkillers.

In my lucid moments I watched Skye's lawyer. He held daily press conferences where he read extensively from his client's manifestos. Turns out he's a big men's rights activist and their plan is to claim that Skye was the victim of an out-of-control feminist conspiracy. Skye's venom is getting amplified and re-amplified all over the Internet. It would have been easier for Dr. Carol if I'd let Heather shoot him.

We all got famous again. So famous, in fact, that when I finally got out of the hospital Marilyn sent a car and two security goons to pick me up. We had a very nice conversation in their car about the hold one of them had used to take me down in Marilyn's backyard. When I'm able to walk unassisted again he's going to teach it to me.

My apartment was still evidence, and my landlord was suing me for tens of thousands in damages. I had nowhere to go, no life to get back to, I had nothing except an endless parade of people who wanted to put me on the news to "tell my story." They all want to know how I "feel."

No one's asking me how I feel as I sit in the visitor's area of the CCCF looking at the stock-art inspirational posters and the amateur-hour murals on the walls. If they did I'd tell them that my jaw aches, the scalp around my new plate itches, and an ugly brown headache throbs behind my eyes. And I'm beginning to think I've made a mistake coming here.

Marilyn arrives before I can change my mind and leave. Allowable jewelry is limited to a single necklace and one ring, strapless dresses are forbidden, and you can't wear orange, beige, blue denim, or forest green, but they do allow sun hats and she's carrying an enormous white one in her hand.

I get a kiss on each cheek.

"Have you heard from Dr. Carol?" I ask, wiping her lipstick away.

"I wrote her a note," Marilyn says. "I think we're going to have to accept that she'll be out of circulation for some time."

I spent the first two days after I got out of the hospital trying to reach Dr. Carol, but I could never get through. She read one public statement and that footage got aired over and over again. Dr. Carol looking down at a piece of paper shaking so hard in her hands she had to place it on the table. She recited a series of short, stiff sentences asking for everyone to please respect her privacy in this difficult time. It didn't do any good. They hounded her until she disappeared. None of us could get her on the phone, none of us could reach her by email. I wanted to help her. I wanted to tell her it's okay. She'd done so much for me. But I didn't get the chance.

"Dani's not with you?" Marilyn asks.

After I got out of the hospital, Marilyn offered me her guest house but I wanted to be somewhere quiet. I asked Dani if I could stay on her ranch. She didn't say no, so I took that as a yes. I like it out there. I can see anyone who's coming from a long way away. All her horses came back, and I like spending time with them. I like the way they smell, how they move, the wary way they check out the world. I think again that Gillian loved horses, and she never got to ride. I'm building up to it. Maybe.

"She's at PT," I tell Marilyn. "She's getting a ride with Julia."

They're going to have to rebuild Dani's left leg, her left hip, and both knees. For the first two days, she refused to get out of her hospital bed. On the third day, Julia rolled into her room and clapped briskly.

"This pity party is hereby canceled," she said as a nurse rolled in an empty wheelchair. "It's time you got out of that comfy coffin and started living again."

Julia loves knowing more about something than someone else, and she definitely knows more about wheelchairs than Dani. She came out to the ranch and the three of us spent a week making it accessible, the two of them in chairs, me with my cane, just three broken-down final girls and a couple of contractors from town. Dani's gotten so good that she bought one of those Freedom Chairs and disappears into the desert for days at a time.

The first time she vanished overnight I freaked out. When I saw her returning through the scrub in back of the house the next day around dusk, sawing away at her push levers, bumping hard over the dirt, I ran out and gave her hell. She waited until I ran out of steam.

"I like sleeping under the stars," she said. "I watched the hawks, I watched coyotes. Michelle came and sat with me for a while. She didn't say much but she listened. I'll probably go out and see her pretty regular now."

She levered past me toward the house, then stopped and said:

"I liked you better when you didn't talk so much."

"Do you hate me?" I ask Marilyn, as we wait together in the empty CCCF visiting room.

Plastic tables are bolted to the linoleum floor, there are no windows, there's a play space in the corner with dancing cartoon animals painted on the walls. It looks like the saddest grade-school cafeteria in the world.

"Do I hate you?" Marilyn asks.

I nod. I'm thinking about my letters, thinking about the book, thinking about how I called her a spoiled alcoholic, thinking about all the mistakes I made.

"Let me show you something," she says, putting her big straw purse on her lap and pulling out her enormous phone. She swipes her thumb down and down and down and then taps her screen and holds it out.

At first I don't understand what I'm looking at and then I don't know how I missed him.

"Fine!" I say out loud.

She's transferred him from his pot into one of the soft, loamy flower beds surrounding the guest cottage. He's grown since I abandoned him, unfolding new leaves, tiny green peppers blooming from his buds, spreading his roots wide, unfurling new fronds.

It feels like a touch of mercy I don't deserve.

"I hope it's okay," Marilyn says.

"Fine," I say, and it's embarrassing that I'm talking to not even a plant but a picture of a plant on someone else's phone, but I can't help myself. "Look at you. You're growing up. And you're surrounded by so many sexy ferns."

Huge, primordial ferns rise from the ground around him.

"He was all cooped up in that pot," Marilyn says. "There was no room for him to grow. I mean, his poor little roots were traumatized. I hope I did all right."

Fine won't be coming with me anymore. He won't sit on his perch and watch TV with me ever again. He isn't mine anymore.

"It's great," I tell Marilyn. "It's perfect. I think I was holding him back."

"There's a lovely pepper bush in there waiting to come out," Marilyn says. "He's going to just grow and grow. Next time you see him, I bet you won't even recognize the little guy."

You see, I tell Fine inside my head. *You're going to be better than ever.*

"And now you've got an excuse," Marilyn says.

"For what?"

"To come visit," she says.

She tucks her phone back in her bag and I sit on the hard plastic chair and stare at the humming vending machines on the other side of the room and try to figure out why I feel so lonely.

"I miss Adrienne," I finally say.

"Me too," Marilyn says.

"She was the best of us," I say, and my chest aches.

I turn my head to study a mural on the far wall. It's of a sunset on a tropical beach that looks like it was painted with several different shades of mud.

"No," Marilyn says, and she takes my chin and turns my head to face her. "You're the best of us, Lynnette. You never quit. You never stopped. You saved everyone."

Faint lines radiate from the corners of her eyes, and tiny indentations mark her upper lip. I can see her roots. A single hair sprouts from her chin. I've never seen anyone this closely before. I've never been seen this closely before.

She leans back and rummages in her purse, looking for gum.

"I'm in suspense about Dani," she says, finding a pack of Big Red. "The visitation rules said no denim, no camouflage, and no fabrics that resemble state issued-inmate clothing. What's she going to wear?"

After Dani disappeared inside that day, I stood out back by myself for a while and looked across the desert. Hordes of cicadas sawed their legs together in the eucalyptus trees as cliff swallows swooped and darted, chasing bugs. Something stirred into motion far to my right, and I watched the sandy tail of a snake disappear beneath a creosote bush.

White moths fluttered between dusty scrub underneath a pale crescent moon in the early-evening sky. Away in the hills, cars glittered and flashed like tiny jewels, and I thought about how many people were out there. There were so many people.

Something tapped my foot and I jumped, then realized it was just a cricket. It sat there on my shoe, pulsing for a split second, and then, with a snap, it was gone. In the distance, I heard one of the horses snort.

There's so much life and it just keeps going. Maybe not everyone's life, but Life. It doesn't stop for anyone. Chrissy said there were only two forces in the world and they balance each other: life and death. Creation and destruction. But she's wrong. There's only one. Because no matter how hard we try, we can't stop life. No matter how much we fight, no matter how many we kill, things keep changing, and growing, and living, and people get lost, and fall away, and come back, and get born, and move on, and no matter what it's all so much, it's all so hard, the way life just keeps going and going.

"Hey, y'all!" Marilyn hollers beside me, waving one arm. "Over here."

Julia and Dani roll toward us in their wheelchairs from the far end of the room, Julia talking and talking at Dani, who's totally focused on steering her way through the plastic tables to where Marilyn and I sit in a small circle of folding chairs.

"They tried to make us use prison wheelchairs," Julia says. "I asked them how they'd feel about an ADA lawsuit and I practically had to draft one before they let us through."

I look at us with our wheelchairs, and stitches, and gauze pads, and aluminum canes. We look like models at a surgical supply convention.

"Your man's waiting outside," Dani says as she rolls to a stop.

When my taxi pulled up outside the CCCF earlier, I didn't see Garrett P. Cannon at first. He had on an obnoxious new dove-gray hat and matching suit with one of his bolo ties so I don't know how I missed him. He caught me as I limped across the sidewalk to the entrance.

"Gratitude comes hard for you, I know," he said, dropping his Dutch Masters cigarillo and grinding it out with the heel of his cowboy boot. "But even so, I'm thinking you should spare some thank-you-kindlys for the law enforcement hero who made this all possible."

"Hello, Garrett," I said.

"I hollered your name three times," he said. "At least."

"Yeah, I'm sorry. The pain from my injuries make it hard for me to walk so I really have to focus. That must be inconvenient for you."

Once I get started walking, I can't stop for too long or I start to stiffen up, so I kept going but I moved so slow it was easy for Garrett to keep pace.

"Don't get your panties in a twist, Lynney," he said. "I'm just saying, I had to bend a lot of rules and call in a lot of favors to get y'all some alone time in there. Not many men would do that for a woman who treated them the way you treated me."

"I'm very grateful, Garrett," I said.

"So this afternoon I'm going to call my agent about our book," Garrett said. "You said we'd write it if I set this up, and I think you'll agree that I've done a hero's duty. Obviously my name will go first on the cover."

I stopped and faced him.

"Garrett," I told him. "When I said I'd write a book with you? I lied."

I started limping forward again to the sound of him cursing me up one side and down the other.

Inside the visiting room, Marilyn asks, "When does this start? We're all here."

No one knows where Heather is, but we assume she's okay. I would have liked to tell her that I don't blame her **for calling** the cops but, as always, Heather isn't going to give anyone **an ounce** of satisfaction. Marilyn set up a small bank account for **her and** told us there were regular ATM withdrawals. Maybe someone killed Heather and took her card. Maybe she's looking for the Dream King. Maybe she's just out there somewhere, being Heather.

We all turn when we hear the door open at the far end of the room, but it's only a tall corrections officer with a big belly striding between the tables. He's wearing a beige shirt and dark green pants and for some reason people in this field still think it's okay to have a mustache.

"I'm Captain Winslow," he says, and none of us get up.

He goes around our circle, introducing himself to each of us in turn. I'm surprised at how soft his hand is when we shake.

"I want you ladies to know that I need to be in here with you the entire time," he says, looking sad about it. "But I will respect your confidences. Just pretend I'm part of the wall."

We all nod, and then he's gone, and no one says anything. Sitting hurts, and my joints ache. The air in the room gets too thick to breathe. Right now, we're all having second thoughts, but before anyone can change their minds, the door opens, and Captain Winslow leads Stephanie into the room.

She's not wearing makeup, but her hair is thick and glossy, and it looks like she's got polish on her nails. She's wearing a light blue shirt and jeans, with shackles on her wrists locked to a chain around her waist. There's a look of terror in her eyes that she carefully replaces with bored nonchalance as Captain Winslow brings her closer.

This was my idea. Everything I'd predicted back in that Camp Red Lake hydrotherapy room had come true. Stephanie hadn't actually killed anyone, just put Dani in a wheelchair and me on a cane. She'd shot one of the food service workers and they'd lost an eye, but all the rest of the murders were Skye.

The two of them had put a lot of effort into the whole thing but where Skye was all cold calculation, Stephanie drove him crazy by improvising. She'd done the first part according to plan—befriending Christophe Volker, letting him into Red Lake, telling him where Adrienne lived, and then she pushed him out the hayloft because she thought it looked more real. When I showed up at her house, she decided to come with me on a whim. That was Skye she'd been talking to at the rest stop on the way back to L.A., reassuring him everything was still on track.

His master plan had been to murder everyone his mother ever cared about, to leave her all-important career broken into pieces that could never be repaired, to humiliate her in front of the whole world, but he teamed up with an erratic partner who got her rush from near misses and close calls. He probably would have shot Stephanie at the end out of sheer frustration if Heather hadn't stopped him first.

Stephanie would have been victim number nine.

A long time ago I tried to watch one of Adrienne's *Summer Slaughter* movies, but I turned it off after twenty minutes when I realized they weren't going to tell us about any of the victims. I remember how sick I felt as human beings with families and dreams were reduced to splatter effects who only got first names. It's important to remember their names.

There was Russell Thorn.

The woman at Red Lake who lost an eye was named Eva Watanabe.

Jack Burrell.

Brenda Jones.

Marcie Stanler.

Edna Hockett.

Julius Gaw.

Amanda Shepard.

Remember their names but let the world forget Skye Elliott. Let them forget Stephanie Fugate.

Stephanie's parents got a lawyer who claimed her PTSD from the Tennis Coach Killings made her an aggressive hybristophile. She lost herself in the love of a Monster in a version of the "if you can't protect yourself from being killed by them, join them" philosophy. I don't think her lawyer was wrong. Skye spent two years seducing her, grooming her, transforming her into his perfect playmate. Another girl to add to his list of victims. She got twenty-five years for each of the three charges of assault with a deadly weapon, and three of battery causing serious bodily injury. She'll be in here for the rest of her life.

I thought about it for a long time, but I couldn't see it any other way. Technically, she might not fit the description, but no matter how you look at it, she's been victimized by a Monster and I have a responsibility. I'm not leaving anyone behind. It's what Adrienne said to me once when I told her I thought I didn't deserve to survive.

"That's your vanity talking," she told me. "You just want to be special. Let me tell you something: no one is too far gone to be brought back. No one is too lost to be found. No one."

This probably won't work. Stephanie will resist everything we do, she'll mock my efforts, she'll fight us all the way, but if there's one thing I learned from Adrienne it's that it doesn't matter. We can't help ourselves. This is what we do. You never stop trying to save your Sisters.

It still surprises me that everyone agreed. Then again, maybe we all need a reason to keep seeing each other. Maybe we all need a reason to live.

Captain Winslow sits Stephanie down in a folding chair, then disappears to the other side of the room. Stephanie's made her face bored and blank, radiating contempt, already determined to ignore our appeals to her better nature, already opening her mouth to say something shocking.

I beat her to the punch.

"Stephanie," I say. "Welcome to the Final Girl Support Group."

Ever wonder what happens to those final girls? After all their plans go belly up and all their weapons fail? After their defenses crumble and they've been shot in the head? After they've trusted the wrong people, made the wrong choices, and opened themselves up at the worst possible moments? After their lives are ruined and they're left at thirty-eight years old with nothing in the bank, no kids, no lover, and nothing to their name but a couple of ghosts and a handful of broken-down friends?

I know what happens to those girls.

They turn into women.

And they live.

ACKNOWLEDGMENTS

The author wishes to thank certain individuals who made big impressions in the movies, without which this book would not exist.

Summer Slaughter
Adam Goldworm (R.I.P.), Teddy, *Summer Slaughter II*, *Summer Slaughter Part III in 3-D*, *Summer Slaughter IV*
Stephen Graham Jones, Bisected Counselor, *Summer Slaughter V*
Harold Brown, "Machete Head" Reporter, *Summer Slaughter VII*
Daniel Passman, Evil Lawyer, *Summer Slaughter VIII: Teddy Goes to Washington*
Patrick Chu, director, *Summer Slaughter IX: Teddy Zero G*

Panhandle Meathook
Joshua Bilmes, producer, *Panhandle Meathook 2, 3, 4*
Eddie Schneider, Man in Freezer, *Panhandle Meathook*
Brady McReynolds, Sunbaked Cadaver, *Panhandle Meathook*
Valentina Sainto, "Suzy", *Panhandle Meathook*
Susan Velazquez, "Marilyn", *Panhandle Meathook*
David Litman, Deputy in Bear Trap, *Panhandle Meathook 2*

Gnomecoming
Jessica Wade, producer, *Gnomecoming*
Alexis Nixon (French Horn), Danielle Keir (Tuba), Fareeda Bullert (Mellophone), Daniela Riedlova (Piccolo), Jin Yu (Timp Toms), Marching Band, *Gnomecoming*
Claire Zion, Screaming Girl, *Gnomecoming*
Jeanne-Marie Hudson, Vice-Principal Hunt, *Gnomecoming*
Emily Osbourne, Wallflower, *Gnomecoming*
Megha Jain, Coroner, *Gnomecoming*
Laura Corless, Stabbed by Paintbrush, *Gnomecoming*

Slay Bells

Cat Camacho, producer, *Slay Bells 2: Hell for the Holidays*, *Slay Bells 3: Evil Elves*

Julia Lloyd, Caroler, *Slay Bells*

Luke Dunlavey, Lawn Dart Victim, *Slay Bells 2: Hell for the Holidays*

Laura Price, Scary Elf #1, *Slay Bells 3: Evil Elves*

Lydia Gittins, Cantor, *Slay Bells 4: Festival of Frights*

Deadly Dreams

Doogie Horner, Dead-Eyed Pizza Monster with Beard, *Deadly Dreams II: Sweet Screams Are Made of This*

Nicholas Rucka, director, *Deadly Dreams 3: Dream Queens*

Roxanne Benjamin, Baby Doll Monster, *Deadly Dreams IV: The Final Frightmare*

Ted Geoghegan, "Gorpus", *Deadly Dreams IV: The Final Frightmare*

The Babysitter Murders

Hannah King, Psych Ward Nurse, *The Babysitter Murders*

Kristin Johnston, Candy-Eating Girlfriend, *The Babysitter Murders*

Nicholas Scott Sanburg, Furious Neighbor, *The Babysitter Murders*

Mike Hickey, Dead Vending Machine Repairman, *The Babysitter Murders II*

Diana Romanova, Dr. Strumpf, *The Babysitter Murders II*

Cat Scully, Mainframe Technician, *The Babysitter Murders III: Samhain*

Kris Gilbreth, Human Sacrifice, *The Babysitter Murders III: Samhain*

Eric Mueller, Druid, *The Babysitter Murders III: Samhain*

The roots of the slasher movie stretch back to Alfred Hitchcock's *Psycho* (1960), based on Robert Bloch's book of the same name. While Bloch stated many times that his book was based on the real-life crimes of Ed Gein, far more clippings were found in his files regarding Wisconsin's infamous children's entertainer and serial poisoner, Floyd Scriltch. When Hitchcock purchased the rights to Bloch's book, he also optioned the life rights from the sole survivor of Scriltch's infamous "Easter Bunny Massacre," Amanda Cohen. Cohen was instrumental in the detection and capture of Scriltch and paid a heavy price for her bravery. This book is dedicated to her memory.